A COLLAR FOR CERBERUS

A COLLAR FOR CERBERUS

MATT STANLEY

THISTLE
PUBLISHING

*A Alicia Renales Toboso por Semana
Santa y todo lo que pasó después*

No pleasure is in itself evil, but the things which produce certain pleasures entail annoyances many times greater than the pleasures themselves.

Epicurus

ONE

Never meet your heroes. It makes sense. Artists are not what they create – they're just conduits for something purer and less real. Meet them face-to-face and you encounter questionable politics, poor personal hygiene, messy relationships and – worst of all – the banality of normal. They're just people. Perhaps even more so.

I knew this before I set out for Dimitsana. I'd read enough author biographies. And anyway, had I *really* expected to meet him? Was there any reason he'd actually be in his ancestral village? The implausibility of it was sufficient reason to go anyway and call it a pilgrimage. I'd have a coffee in an old square beneath a bell tower (probably) and perhaps notice some minor detail from one of his books. A rusty weather-cock. The bow of a foot-polished step. The wheeze of the wind around a weathered gable. Something. Something that would bring me closer to his writing and be my little secret. If I ever met him, I'd be able to say, 'That description of the fog in chapter thirteen of *Gods and Satyrs*...' Then maybe just say 'Dimitsana' and wink.

To which, he'd probably look at me like I was a moron and sign my book with a perfunctory smile that reinforced the dictum never to meet your heroes.

But he wasn't going to be there. The article I'd read had been printed the previous year. He could be anywhere now.

And besides, I wasn't in Greece to meet him. I was travelling and this was just a side trip. The same I'd be making to Delphi, Mycenae, Olympia and the rest.

When I stepped down from the bus – the only passenger so late in the season – and watched it pull away with a crunch of gravel and a cloud of diesel exhaust, I felt I'd made a mistake. I was in the heart of rural Arcadia. Beside me was a vast and steaming gorge. The creak of a single cricket was the only noise. Then it stopped – perhaps aware of my presence – and the silence became so sudden, so profound, that the landscape seemed to expand around me.

The bus wouldn't return until the following day.

I was fumbling unnecessarily with the straps of my backpack when a figure appeared on the road from the village. I squinted and put on my sunglasses to observe an old, bow-legged woman approaching.

Up close, she was wretched: matted yellow-grey hair, dried spittle flaking at the corners of her mouth and one eye revolving erratically in its socket. Her faded dress was stained and dusty. Evidently she was one of those village widows who live out loveless lives of poverty and disrespect long after their husbands have gone, eventually going mad with loneliness and derision as the rest of the village waits for her heirless property. I'd read Nikos Kazantzakis.

She held out her hand for alms and muttered at me. I had only notes. She started to tug on my shirtsleeve with twig-like fingers. Her pleadings turned into a cracked incantation that might have been a prayer. I could either walk out of Dimitsana or into it.

I hoisted the bag on a shoulder and stepped past her, striding towards the village with the energy of embarrassment and guilt. She didn't follow. She just stood there waiting, watching me. Would she wait all night until the next day's bus?

Houses appeared: one-storey stone places with sagging terracotta roofs and sun-blasted shutters hanging askew. Then larger buildings with concrete upper balconies, their reinforcing rods weeping ferrously down the whitewash. Cars were covered in dust and had leaves caught around their tyres from some distant downpour. A dog in the shade raised his head briefly to watch me pass.

Following the road round the left, I came upon a kind of square on the corner where a concrete terrace had been built out over the void of the gorge. Here, the houses were more handsome with wrought iron balconies. A couple of cafés with faded promotional umbrellas straddled the road and at each sat a handful of old men: whiskery and becapped, their walking sticks hooked over seats and their marble table tops archipelagos of coffee cups and ashtrays.

I paused in the middle of the street: tall, pale, back-packed – as foreign to this place as a Maasai warrior in an inner-city mall. Every old man looked at me.

'*Ya sas!*' I said, having diligently read the back of my guidebook.

They returned the greeting in an uneven chorus and the tableau stayed the same, as if they were expecting a show. I *was* a show: the only interesting thing to happen so far that day. A talking point. The moment stretched.

I nodded and walked stiffly to the nearest café, where I dropped my bag beside a table and sat, now part of the audience. A young man emerged from the café interior and I ordered the iced coffee that seemed to be *de rigeur*.

So this was Dimitsana. There *was* a clock tower. I'd also glimpsed some cobbled streets that might justify an hour or so of exploratory wandering. I'd need to find a room at some point. If pushed, I could take a long siesta. Then an evening meal at one of the *tavernas* and an early night. Only twenty-fours to go.

Sipping, I thought again of Irakles Bastounis: novelist, Nobel laureate, playboy and *enfant terrible* of literature's last great era. The photo accompanying that *New York Times* article had been an archive image of his 1990s face: a little jowly and with long grey hair pulled into a ponytail. He must have refused a newer photo.

I looked around at the other customers in my café and at the one opposite. No ponytails. It probably wasn't the kind of village where an old man could have a ponytail and stay credible. In fact, it surely wasn't the kind of village a man like Bastounis would choose to live, even if he had been born here. Still, the article had hinted that the author might have little choice if his fifth divorce had followed the pattern of the previous four. There had been that ironic aside in his Nobel acceptance speech – delivered while half drunk – about him getting the medal but his ex-wife the prize money.

I looked from face to face, trying to make chronological adjustments and wondering how well we really know an author's face. I'm sure I could pick out Edgar Allan Poe's tortured forehead in a crowd, or Henry Miller's lanky baldness. But would I know Steinbeck in a supermarket? Nabokov in a bank queue? There was nothing especially distinctive about Bastounis – at least, no longer. He'd once been a matinee idol – his powerful chin lit just-so, his hair slicked in a perfect static wave. Or a Homeric hero: grizzled with a Papa Hemingway beard and a sailor's cap. Now he was just old like the other villagers.

Could I ask the waiter and make it sound nonchalant? 'Somebody said a famous writer lives here. Hercules someone…?' Then what? Knock on his door and say something inane? It would be better to see him in action, doing something that would work well in an anecdote. A fistfight. Wrestling an escaped bull. Entrusting me with his final unpublished manuscript.

I became aware of a man at a nearby table watching me. I turned and he switched his gaze into a quest for the waiter, calling out an order before returning to his Greek newspaper. Had he been looking? His dark Ray Bans made it difficult to tell. He was an old man dressed much like the rest – trousers, shirt, cap – but, unlike the others, sitting alone. A walking stick hung from the edge of the table. His head was closely shorn under the brown cap and his chin was white with a few days' stubble.

Was that the chin of Irakles Bastounis, once caressed by beauty queens and struck by Norman Mailer? Was that the fleshy, famously broken nose, more used to fine wines and cocaine than this mountain air? There *was* something … some flicker of vague recognition. He'd lost some weight since the ponytail picture if it was Bastounis, though he still had the physical presence of an ex-boxer. The jowls were gone, replaced by tan-riven folds. How does one recognise a Nobel prize-winner in a café? How does one engage them naturally in conversation? The full impotence of my pilgrimage became clear. Even if it was him …

He turned and stared over the frame of his sunglasses with titanium eyes. 'Yes?'

'I … Sorry. I was just … I thought you might be Irakles Bastounis. He lives here … might live here.'

'Who?'

'A writer. *The* writer. An author from this village. Very famous. Do you know—?'

'No.'

He went back to his paper. Something about those eyes – like Robert Shaw in *Jaws*. I nonchalantly took my phone and searched for pictures of Bastounis. The nose looked right. He was definitely thinner if it was him ...

'What are you doing?' he said

'Er, just looking at my phone.'

'I told you I don't know him.'

'Sorry. It's just that ... well, you do look a bit like him.'

'I'm not him.'

'Yes. Sorry. I'll ... Sorry.'

It was almost certainly him. If I could just tilt the camera to get a photo ...

'Are you taking a picture of me?'

'No?'

He dropped his paper and turned towards me. 'If I *was* him, this famous writer, what would you say?'

'Well ... I'd say, er, thank-you. You're a really great ... I mean, I'd say your books have really inspired me.'

'Inspired you how? To do what?'

'You know, in the sense of ... wait. Are you saying you're him?'

He gave a brief, almost non-existent nod and turned back to his newspaper. 'You have your anecdote. Embellish it by all means. Now leave me alone.'

I sat as if slapped.

Expressionless, oblivious, he turned a page and continued reading.

I opened my mouth but nothing would come. Should I tell him how rude he was, this man who'd experienced and achieved more than I probably ever would? I was an ant next to his elephantine talent. And yet ...

'Okay. I'll ... I'll tell people you were charming company.'

He stopped reading. He may have smiled – just a flicker. He closed the newspaper, leaned back in his seat and took off the sunglasses. Those eyes again.

'What did you expect? Paragraphs to flow mellifluously and fully formed from my tongue? A welcome into my home and the secrets of my soul? A conversation, perhaps – cigars, fine liqueurs, *bonhomie* – between two fellow humanists. Great pals! Or were you looking for truth: the *answer.* Look at you! I can almost see the amniotic sheen on you, embryo that you are. And in your wake comes tumbling the roiling placenta of your meagre sustenance – the cannibalistic reading list that would bring you to me. Rabelais, Henry Miller, Celine, Cendrars, Camus. Sartre, maybe – the old hypocrite. And don't forget your prescribed holiday reading. Fowles' *Magus,* Miller's *Colossus… Zorba,* naturally. Perhaps some of that terrible crap by Lawrence Durrell. Have I missed any? Well, now you have my attention. That's what you wanted, no? I've acknowledged your existence and our fates are now inextricably entwined for eternity. Apotheosis achieved. So… entertain me.'

His stare was radiographic. Caustic humiliation throbbed in my face. There was indeed a copy of John Fowles' *The Magus* in my backpack.

He smiled – pristine teeth no village dentist had ever polished. 'No? Is our colloquy over so soon? I'm disappointed. I thought perhaps you'd come to me with a bulletin from the world of culture. Urgent intelligence: a new aesthetic nihilism out of Romania! Read Negoitescu now and embrace the void. Ha!'

How I hated him then, and frequently afterwards, for seeing through me so clearly, so easily. How I hated my naiveté for having expected anything other than this. I, with my good degree in literature from a respectable British university, and he, the novelistic Gargantua (I *had* read Rabelais) famous for his intellectual irascibility. I was a gnat on the pediment apex of his Parthenon.

My voice emerged a broken thing. 'I'm … sorry. I just wanted to … you know …'

'Touch the hem? Kiss the ring? Bask in some kind of aura in the hope that you'd be transformed? What blasphemous atheism is that? If you'd understood anything from my books, you'd know not to think so. If you'd understood anything … But, you haven't. You've misread them. I don't consider you a reader.'

'You don't know me …' A pathetic offering. And dangerous.

'Really? With your backpack and your bus ticket and your "quest". You're an "adventurer", aren't you? Is this a gap year? Have a few "experiences" and then back home for the steady job, the loveless marriage and the life of numbing sterility, nostalgically nursing those formative travel anecdotes as a grief-deranged mother nurses her still-born child – making a shrine of your experiences in journals and scrapbooks, photographs, sketches and inept watercolours. All of it preserved as your premature epitaph: "I met Bastounis in Dimitsana. I had a coffee with Bastounis. I bonded with Bastounis in the sepia perfection of the fabricated past …"'

He sipped water and I saw him looking at the phone I'd put on the table. I almost knew what was coming.

He pointed at it. 'And here we have the talisman of the modern adventurer. Not the staff of Hermes, or Heracles's club, but the electronic umbilical to the world. Always safe. Always connected to Mom and Pop. Update your blog. Check the headlines back home. Make a selfie of the experience and upload it to the site where fifty-thousand others have posted the same picture. A condom to protect the questing phallus from the hot uterine horrors of life.'

He turned back to his table, unfolded his paper and opened it at the article he'd been reading. He spoke without looking at me:

'There are rooms available above the café opposite. Ask at the counter.'

I stood and lifted my bag, feeling as if I'd been in the ring with him for five minutes. Something had to be said.

'Thank-you.'

It's only later you think of the things you should have said: the arguments and zinging ripostes. Always too late.

'Hm-mm,' he said, not looking up.

I walked across the gulf of sunshine into the other café and up to the counter.

'A room?' said the middle-aged man as he dried a glass.

'Yes, please.' The politeness caught in my throat.

Key and money changed hands.

'I saw you talking to Bastounis,' said my landlord. The slight American accent hinted at extended exile before returning here. The Greek homing instinct.

'Well, he did most of the talking.'

'He's a miserable bastard. Nobody likes him. Nobody here has read his books. He's not special. I think that makes him angry.'

'I've read his books and he was angry with me.'

'Me, I like John Grisham.'

'Right. Why is he even living here? Why not in Los Angeles or Mauritius?'

The landlord rubbed his thumb and forefingers together. 'Wives cost money. Someone said his lawyer told him to live here for a year to make it seem like he's broke. Or perhaps he's broke. His family's got a house up the road ...' A shrug. 'I dunno.'

'Do other people come here looking for him?'

'Eh, sometimes. Journalists. Americans. He beat up on one guy last year.'

'A *fight?*'

'In the café there. Tables flipped, fists flying. One thing about Bastounis: he might be old but you don't wanna rile him. He's dirty. They took the other guy away with tubes in his face.'

'Jesus.'

'Yeah. Maybe you got off easy, eh?'

'It doesn't feel like that.'

He didn't hear me. He'd set a trio of fresh coffees on his tray and was taking them outside. I went up to my room.

I must have lain there for a couple of hours, balcony doors open, listening to the sounds of the street and being mildly depressed by the utilitarian décor. I'd expected characterful wooden furniture and exposed brickwork, but it was all whitewash and bulk-purchase bucolic paintings. The brand-new electric mini-hob with single, unused aluminium pan seemed especially taunting.

My copy of *The Magus*, a folded corner splitting it midway, mocked me on the bed. Could I possibly finish it now, its every word reinforcing the hollow aspirant Bastounis had read in me? His words felt like evisceration, and not because they were unjust or false. Was I truly that predictable?

I was enough of a would-be intellectual, even then, to accept the criticism. The stuff about the phone was true enough. I'd thought it myself. And hadn't I known even before the meeting that I really had nothing to say to the man, nothing to offer him but embarrassing obeisance? I'd been badly prepared. I recalled a story about Nabokov meeting a young butterfly collector while out doing the same and initially cutting him dead. Then the lad showed that he knew his lepidoptery and was deemed worthy of conversation with the great man. I wasn't worthy. I'd left my net at home.

What hurt most was the thing he'd said about me not being a reader, as if he, the author, could decide whether I was capable of understanding his work. Of being worthy enough. As if, with that comment, he'd taken back the pages I'd read. I loved his work. He was one of my favourite authors – an artist I could only dream of being. He – yes, and those others he'd listed – were the reasons for my solitary travel in search of experience: an experience he evidently disdained because … why? Because it was merely emulation or homage?

The outrage didn't last. As I lay there listing to the putter of ancient mopeds, the hourly chime of the church bell, old men coughing and the wind-whimsical susurration of some unseen cataract within the gorge, I began to appreciate the glamour. However horrible the experience had been, I'd met Irakles Bastounis and been crushed by the force of his rancour. He hadn't just dismissed me; he'd taken the time and attention to comprehensively take me apart. Surely there was some kind of privilege in that? I'd been worthy of more than violent unconsciousness and tubes in my face.

I wanted desperately to tell someone about it. I scrolled through my contacts list and formulated messages couched in the most blasé tones. *Just had coffee with Irakles Bastounis*, or, *Guess who just accused me of being an embryo? None other than…* But I sent nothing. That's what he expected me to do. It was the obvious thing. The predictable thing. Maybe he'd see it later on Twitter and think even less of me than he already did. Could I possibly keep it to myself? The idea was novel: an experience that remained wholly secret, burnished in private until it glowed with exclusivity.

His words started to come back to me then and I raced to jot them in my travel journal: original prose from a Nobel laureate – the first the world had heard from him in more than a decade. What had he said? The amniotic sheen? Something about a placenta and the umbilical phone. Questing phallus. Uterine horrors. Something about the mother and her still-born child – that devastating image plucked effortlessly from the free-form flow. The man extemporised in consistent metaphors!

The rest came back to me only in flashes. Something about sepia. Something about Romanian nihilism. Where had that come from? Was the name he'd given genuine? If only I'd recorded the rant on my umbilical phone. I could have uploaded that and got a million hits. Bastounis speaks! Bastounis destroys feckless English graduate. My future anecdote, as he'd immediately intuited, was already being embellished for performance.

That's when I began to understand his anger. He'd become another Greek ruin on the tourist trail – his glories in the past now visible only in the element-ravaged majesty of tumbled pillars and fractured blocks. Evidence of unmatchable greatness, to be sure, but ultimately a subject for postcards. His books were still in print, but books weren't life. Not to a man like Bastounis.

For a while, I worked on a monologue of my own: a sort of sophisticated apology that would show him that I understood and that I was a worthy reader. I honed it so I could say it in a single breath, not giving him chance to cut me down. I needed to show him that I wasn't hurt by what he'd said – that I was in some sense grateful for the encounter.

But I didn't see him when I went out later. The terrace over the gorge had acquired tables and I ate an excellent *moussaka* with a Greek salad, scanning the street constantly to see if he'd pass. I walked up and down the village a few times, peering into windows and gazing up at balconies without success. I could have asked someone where he lived, but I wanted any meeting to seem coincidental – as if I hadn't spent hours brooding over it.

The night ended with me sitting among the old men at the café, drinking retsina and pretending to understand their discussions. There was much apparent derision of Bastounis, albeit in *sotto voce* tones in case the man himself should leap from the night and incapacitate defamers.

I seemed to be the only tourist in town and there was undeniable glamour in it. I was a pioneer – off the beaten track in Arcadia: mythical paradise, home to Pan, the bacchanals and dryads. It *was* an adventure, albeit one soured with the bile of Bastounis, who, I half-imagined, was watching disdainfully from an upper balcony, observing my callow youth. Turned out he'd been doing exactly that.

TWO

Aggressive knocking woke me the next morning. I grasped for my phone and squinted at the screen. 6.30am.

'Who is it?'

The knocking continued. I untangled my legs from the sheet and sat on the edge of the bed rubbing my eyes. Should I put on my shorts?

'*Who is it?*'

'Open the fucking door.' A gruff, masculine voice. Weary rather than angry.

'Wait a minute!'

I unlatched the door and opened it a crack, ready to ram it closed with my shoulder.

Irakles Bastounis stood in the hallway. He was dressed exactly as he'd been the previous day and was leaning on his walking stick.

'Drive me to Nafplio,' he said.

'What?'

'Are you deaf? I want you to drive me to Nafplio. In a car. Today.'

Could he see through the crack that I was wearing only underwear?

'Do you know what time it is?'

'Yes, I know.'

'But yesterday at the café…I don't understand.'

He looked away and tapped the walking stick irritably against the floor. 'You're in a daze. Meet me in the café opposite in ten minutes. I'll buy you breakfast. We can talk about it there.'

He limped off down the corridor.

I went to the balcony and peered down to see him cross the road. He sat at the same table and ordered. He looked up at my room. Could he see me between the flaking louvered doors? I stepped back into the dimness and sat again on the bed.

Had he forgotten the insults of the previous day? Perhaps he was suffering from dementia. Why would I drive him anywhere? I'd barely driven a car since I'd passed my test, and I'd never owned one. Besides, I had plans. I was travelling.

He had me cornered. I couldn't leave the building without walking right past him. The bus wasn't due for another six hours. Could I just hide out in the room and make a break for it at the last minute? Why didn't *he* get the bus to Nafplio if he couldn't drive himself?

I bundled my stuff into the backpack and sat on the bed. I brushed my teeth and sat on the bed. I looked down at the café and saw him staring up at the balcony. He had all the time in the world.

He looked at his watch and the irony was palpable. I come here to meet him and now I was avoiding him. Worth a second go?

He slid the menu towards me as I sat at his table.

'I recommend the *spanakopita*,' he said, nodding towards at the vestigial flakes on his plate. He poured water from a chilled carafe into his glass.

'What's this about?' I said.

15

'I want you to drive me down to Nafplio. I have a car. It shouldn't take more than three or four hours.'

'But why? Why me? There's a bus. There must be loads of people here who could take you. I mean … How do you know I can drive?'

He adjusted his cap and smiled fractionally. 'I went into your room last night and saw your driving licence with your passport.'

'*What*? You broke into my *room*!'

'I broke nothing. Dimitris is a cheapskate. He has the same lock on every door. One key is all you need. You were eating. No harm done. Calm down. Here, drink something – you look like you're about to have a stroke. Besides, it wouldn't make any difference whether you had a licence. You could drive to Nafplio a hundred times and never get stopped. I have no licence myself.'

'Then why don't you drive yourself there?'

'Ah, the bloody English: always overreacting – so rule-obsessed and propriety-driven. It's not like you were molested in your sleep. You think cleaners don't root around people's rooms in hotels? Is your passport a secret document?'

'Did you … did you look at my travel journal?'

He failed to conceal a smirk. 'The Romanian name I quoted yesterday was "Negoitescu." I jotted it in the margin. But don't bother looking him up. There's no such philosopher. It's the name of a barber I once knew in Hollywood. Are you choking? Drink, drink – I need you alive. And to answer your question: I can't drive anymore because of my leg.'

He tapped the curved top of his walking stick where it hooked on to the table. 'An etymological irony – though I suppose you don't get the joke.'

I glared.

'The Greek word for walking stick is "Bastounis". I'm now defined by my infirmity. The idiot villagers here find it very amusing. Fucking yokels.'

'It seems they hate you.'

That seemed to please him. He got the waiter's attention and ordered the spinach pie with an iced coffee before turning back to me.

'So ...'

'I'm not driving you anywhere, Mister Bastounis. I've got my own plans. It's not as if we've, you know, established a great *rapport* in the last twenty-four hours. I mean, you've insulted me and broken into my room and—'

'Why are you here?'

'Are you kidding? You just woke me up and asked—'

'No. Why are you here in Dimitsana? Not for the culture, to be sure. Not for the architecture. I've seen no walking boots. You came here for two things: for a "travel experience" and, potentially, to meet the Famous Writer.'

'You're speaking in scare quotes.'

'Ha! That's good. But my point is this: what have you to lose? Wouldn't driving me down to Nafplio be a better and more interesting use of your time than travelling to another tawdry ancient site or overpriced campground with all of the other experience-seekers? Get yourself a proper anecdote – go on a road trip with me. Nafplio is worth a visit in its own right. It's a beautiful place with castles and Venetian architecture. I'm sure it's in your guidebook.'

Had he flicked through that as well? I'd circled Nafplio in the contents and folded down its page.

'Why do you need to go to Nafplio so urgently?'

'That's my concern. Look – you said you'd read my books. Perhaps I was a little hasty yesterday in denying you as a reader. If you've understood even the most basic

principle from them, it's that you have to be spontaneous. You have to take the risk and say "Why not?" Even
if it takes you down a wrong path. Maybe that's the idea
that's brought you here, I don't know. Now I'm making that
challenge personally. What have you got to lose? Drive me
to Nafplio and see what happens. Call it an adventure –
maybe the first in your life. Maybe the last. What did Twain
say? You regret the things you didn't do rather than the
things you did.'

The spinach pie arrived. He leaned back in his chair
as I cut into the flaky pastry and ate, half hating him for
everything he'd said and done, half luxuriating in the fact
that I was having breakfast with Irakles Bastounis. If any
other man had given me this speech, I'd have smelled the
sophistry. But Bastounis had lived it. He'd fled this village
aged fifteen with a band of gypsy performers, learning
their prestidigitations, dancing to their music, defending
his honour by knife and being initiated into a world of feral
passions … or so he'd told it in the first volume of his autobiography *The Stables of Augeas*.

'Of course, I'm not able to pay you,' he said. 'If you do it,
you do it for the ride. For the thrill alone. After Nafplio, it's
up to you. Go where you like.'

'How will you get back here?'

'It's not your problem. I'll find a way.'

He smiled and I knew what he meant: that he'd find
another gullible young traveller to insult and beguile.
The thought made me inexplicably jealous. I was interchangeable.

'Why me? I thought you held me in utter contempt. I'm
just an embryo, right?'

'Listen – I'm not going to flatter or apologise. I'm going
to walk up the road. If you decide you want to do it, just

go towards the end of the village until you come to a dusty Peugeot parked outside a three-storey stone house. That's me. Before lunchtime would be good. It gets too hot later.'

He put his money on the table, levered himself standing with the arm of his seat and limped along the street without looking back. If you hadn't known, you'd have thought him just another old man.

The waiter came to take the plates and glasses, lingering as if he wanted to say something. Then:

'Are you going to do it?'

'What?'

A shrug. 'I was listening. Will you go with Bastounis?'

'Would *you* do it?'

'With Bastounis? No way. I didn't read his books. And he's an angry man. Nobody here would do it, not even for money. But if Metallica came and asked me to go on tour... Different story. I could write a blog about that. My friends would shit!'

'Yeah, I guess.'

I ordered another spinach pie (they *were* excellent) and observed the town waking up. Battered 4x4s passed through on their way down to the markets of Megalopoli and Tripoli. Old men ambled and smoked. The sun crept further into the street, warming the stone. The gorge breathed a cool scent of earth and dewy pastures. Not much had changed here in a hundred years. We were beyond the world.

Do it? Don't do it? My usual problem: indecision. Fear. Overthinking. He was right about that. Would it be three hours of more abuse – the kind of sustained demolition that would leave me in need of counselling? And there was the bigger worry: driving. I'd not driven for, what, three years? Even then, I'd driven in constant anticipation of death or maiming. Imagine Bastounis as a back-seat driver...

My landlord from the café opposite wandered over the road, drying his hands on his apron.

'Bad news, *filë*,' he said. 'I just had a call from KTEL in Tripoli.'

'Yes...?'

'No bus today. Next one's tomorrow. You wanna stay another night? I'll give you a good price.'

'Why? What happened?'

'Something mechanical. I wasn't really listening.'

'And they've only got one bus?'

'Eh, this ain't Athens. It's happened before. You wanna stay?'

'Let me think about it...'

He gave a *moue* of indifference and wandered back across the road.

'You could hitch!' called my eavesdropping waiter from behind his counter. 'But do it now. People go to town now.'

I slurped the last dregs of coffee from the ice. Decision time.

The old Peugeot was so covered in dust that it was difficult to discern the colour. Someone had recently used a finger to write *malakas* in the dust on the boot and I saw that it was a dark blue Peugeot 504. 1970s? It looked like trouble – difficult to drive. Recalcitrant. Would hitching be easier?

The three-story house looked grand but was poorly maintained. Peeling shutters hung askew and the iron-studded door seemed a century old. The balcony on the second floor was open. I raised the heavy ring of the verdigris-mottled lion's-head knocker and held it aloft for a moment. Still time to change my mind.

I let it fall.

'It's open!' came his voice from the open window. 'Come up!'

The narrow hallway was dim and smelled of cold stone and mildew. A bevelled oval mirror glaucously reflected my apprehension. A flight of uncarpeted wooden stairs warped away from the wall up into darkness. It was a house conceived by Poe. A crypt. My footsteps thumped hollowly.

Bastounis was in an upper room with few signs of permanent habitation. The floor was dusty with shining pathways of most frequent use. A straight-backed sofa was heaped with boxes. A handful of large shipping trunks seemed scattered at random. Against the wall opposite the balcony was a single fold-out bed, its sheets coiled and creased.

He was leaning over one of the trunks, supported on his stick, apparently searching one-handed for something.

'Take a seat,' he said, waving vaguely at the room. "I'll be just a minute.'

I could see nowhere to sit so I stood and looked into the nearest trunk. It was full of books: hardbacks, curling paperbacks, notebooks, large volumes that could have been encyclopaedias or dictionaries. I saw *A Short History of Decay* by EM Cioran, *Ecce Homo* by Nietzsche and volume two of Diogenes Laertius' *Lives of the Eminent Philosophers*. There were the *Confessions* of both Rousseau and St Augustine. On the floor just in front of the box was a single piece of paper folded three times. I picked it up and unfolded it to see the letterhead of a hotel in Montreux in Switzerland.

The addressee was "Alcaeus" and the typed text began, "I so enjoyed your review of my last, which managed to transcend the myopia of..." The signatory was Vladimir Nabokov. It weighed suddenly heavier in my hand. Nabokov: my all-time literary hero. The master.

MATT STANLEY

'I think... I think you might have dropped this,' I said.

He looked round. 'Uh? Oh. Just throw it in the trunk. Or keep it. Whatever. Most of this stuff is going to Chapel Hill when I die. I don't even know what's in some of these trunks, but neither do they. Manuscript drafts, notebooks, letters – all trash. The detritus of a life.'

He read my expression and smirked. 'Ah, but you're one of them, aren't you. They collect the flotsam and jetsam and enshrine it in their libraries as if it has inherent worth. Bits of the True Cross – enough fragments to build a galleon of their own imagining. Who wrote that letter?'

'Nabokov.'

'A perfect example. All you need to know is in his books. The rest is just old-world privilege, uxoriousness and butter-flies. An awkward guy. A dull life. He would have admitted as much.'

'Did you ever meet him?'

'No. He was never part of the game. He was a reluctant player, at least. I respected him for that.'

He turned back to the trunk and continued his excavation.

'Are you looking for something? Can I help?'

'No. But tell me why you decided to come.'

'The bus was cancelled. And I'm not really a hitcher.'

'Is that so? Do you believe in fate?'

'No.'

'Good.' He pulled a slim sheaf of papers from the trunk, scanned the top page and rolled them into a tube, which he tucked inside his jacket pocket. He dropped the trunk lid with a billow of dust.

'Okay, I'm ready. Grab my bag there.'

A small leather holdall sat beside the door. I lifted it. Not too heavy – probably just clothes.

He limped down the stairs ahead of me, leaning heavily against the bannister rail. In the street, he locked the ancient door and passed me the keys.

'The car's open. Just reverse it out into the road.'

I jerked the driver's door open, hoping he couldn't read my apprehension. The interior smelled like hot vinyl and must. Dead flies littered the dashboard. The rear seat was covered in a litter of yellowed newspaper, food wrappers and sundry junk. His shape loomed darkly imprecise through the opaque filth of the side window. I adjusted the seat backwards, then forwards a bit. I set the rearview mirror and caught a flash of my pale, perspiring forehead. The procrastination had to end at some point.

I turned the key, covered the pedals, released the handbrake ... and jerked the car into a stall. It was my first driving test (fail) revisited. Deep breath. Handbrake on. Turn the key again. Stall again. Fuel sloshed back and forth in the tank.

'Are we going to have a problem?' he said, his voice muffled by the glass.

'I'm not used to ... The clutch is just ...'

But I was talking to myself, palms wet on the wheel. Was this adventure? Was this experience? When he'd first fled the village, he hadn't driven himself away with the gypsies. There had probably been gaily-painted caravans, or a truck. Literature so seldom reveals the minutiae of engineering issues.

I managed to reverse it on the fourth attempt, whereupon he threw his stick and bag into the back and dropped heavily into the passenger seat beside me.

'You drive like a woman.'

'It's this car. It—'

'There's nothing wrong with the car. This car won rallies. It's rear-wheel drive like a Porsche and it has magnificent suspension. Go to Cairo or Kinshasa and you'll see taxi drivers with this car and a million miles on the clock.'

'Right.'

'Well, you know the way. Down through the village and follow the bus route. I'll tell you where to go when we get to Tripoli.'

And as we rolled slowly past the two cafés, I couldn't have said what was foremost in my thoughts – the terrifying mountain road before us, or the fact that Irakles Bastounis was my passenger.

THREE

He barely spoke between Dimitsana and utilitarian Tripoli. Just the occasional comment on how to handle the car, its vagaries, its advantages. A chauffer now, I didn't know whether to be affronted or relieved at his lack of attention. Also, there was the road to consider, with its nauseating sinuousness and blind bends that lured us to the void. I gripped the thin, hard wheel and leaned forward, peering through a half-moon of semi-clear windscreen, too nervous to attempt cleaning it lest I veer off the verge into cartwheeling death. The brakes – it was true – were very good.

I observed him when I could, attempting to drink in as much of the experience as I could. He sat with his hands in his lap watching the road ahead and nodding when particularly satisfied with a gear change. Was he actively trying to ignore me? Or was I just a figment to the man: a civilian unworthy of his time, his voice or thoughts?

I'd read both volumes of his autobiography, *The Stables of Augeas* and *Dionysus in Rehab*. I'd read his three major novels, *Gods and Satyrs*, *Lapidary Rain*, and *Cassandra*. Huge books – monumental in the sense of Roth's *American Pastoral* or Heller's *Catch-22* (he'd known them both). Era-defining books, though perhaps currently out of favour in the same way that Mailer's books of the sixties and seventies seemed now to reek too strongly of testosterone and a specific cultural moment. Then there was the style – nobody else like him. There'd been comparisons with Nabokov, McCarthy, Joyce and others, but nobody is truly alike at that level. All are unique and immeasurable. He was one of those whose prose gives you vertigo, halts your breath and forces you immediately to re-read and discern the hidden power of its silences and syllables. If only he'd belittled me in writing: a consummation devoutly to be wished.

I rehearsed conversational gambits as we drove, but each seemed more trite and naïve than the last. As if I, a mere graduate, could engage him on his own subject. I recalled seeing an audience with Susan Sontag in which someone had asked her if she used a pen or a typewriter to write. She ignored the question with such absolute disdain that it seemed one hadn't even been asked. The audience-member turned an apoplectic shade of purple.

So many things I wanted to ask him. How was it being married to Miss Venezuela (for six months)? Is it true you fought a duel with Kerouac towards the end when he was a stumbling drunk? What did Hemingway tell you in Idaho that made you write *Cassandra*? Marilyn Monroe – really? And why haven't you published anything for twenty years? Is it true there's an unseen novel that you refuse to release – your masterwork, like that epic poem of Cendrars' that nobody has ever seen but which was supposed to mark the birth of Modernism?

My heart rate was calming after the no-rules traffic of Tripoli when he turned to me.

'Did you tell anyone about meeting me, or driving me today?'

'The waiter at the café heard you say it and—'

'No. I mean anyone outside Dimitsana. The world beyond. The Internet.'

'Nobody. I didn't know it was a secr... *hey*!'

He'd plucked the phone from my breast pocket and was squinting at its blank face.

'Give me that!'

The car swerved across the centre line as I grabbed for the phone. He held it away from me, trying to make it work.

'Look. I'll show you. Just... *what the fuck*!'

He'd tossed it out of his open window just as another car was approaching. Its horn blasted but it didn't stop.

I stamped on the brakes. Bastounis braced against the dash. Litter vomited from the back seat. I got out and walked to where it lay.

Its screen was a crystal spider web impregnated with gravel. The other car had gone right over it.

Bastounis remained seated. We were in the middle of a mountain pass, the Argolic Gulf a cobalt plate far below us, dry grasses quivering, the road emanating heat. Airy silence.

I brandished it at him through my open door. 'You owe me a new phone.'

'You should thank me.'

'*Thank* you?'

'You're welcome.'

'You're insane! You've lost it.'

'What are you going to do?'

'Do?'

'Look – I can't drive the car. We're on a remote road. Your phone is broken and nothing will fix it. We can stay here until somebody comes, or you can get back in the car and drive us to Nafplio. If a new phone will placate your infantile need to be perpetually connected, then we can organise it.'

'More insults.'

'An insult? No – an observation. Consider the glamour of our situation: two strangers sharing a journey in a distinguished old car. The scenery has a raw and elemental beauty. Our destination is new to both of us, I having not visited the place for decades. One day – maybe in only a year from now – you'll look back on this very moment and your damaged phone will be of no significance: just a facet of the story. Nothing you could have sent or received on it would have been as interesting as the experience of having it destroyed. I've never owned such a device. But then I can't remember more than a handful of specific phone calls in my entire life. Perhaps they meant something at the time, but now they're utter voids. Your generation should know this. You're living in a cloud, in a bubble. Now – why don't you get in before a bus or truck comes sweeping round the bend and destroys *you*.'

I tossed the phone to the roadside, sat and slammed the door. I started the engine ... and stalled it.

Bastounis released the handbrake. He nodded: try again.

My anger seethed. I took the next corner too fast and had to fight the wheel for control. He sat serene, unruffled.

'What phone calls?' I said.

'Excuse me?'

'You said you remembered only a handful of phone calls. Name one.'

He looked out of his window and I understood. He didn't want to tell me. It was none of my business. But he'd used it in his little monologue just now and he'd made me angry. Now, perhaps, he realised he owed me some placation. It was just a matter of how little he could give me.

'Or was that just more rhetoric?' I said.

He smirked, whether at me or at some memory retrieved. 'Okay. I'll tell you one. It was Valeria – you know about Valeria, right?'

I nodded. The Venezuelan beauty queen. Miss World, 1970-something.

'It was just after the divorce had gone through. A bad time. Very bitter. A lot of anger on both sides. Anyway, she called me to tell me she'd found a new lover – a better lover. In fact, she was in bed with him at that very moment. He was inside her. I could hear him panting as she gave me a detailed description of their position, his prowess, his endowments. She talked right up until the point she couldn't talk anymore. Then she left the receiver on the bed beside her – on the pillow is how I imagine it – and let me hear their copulation to the end. Maybe you think it was just a ruse to make me jealous – a woman's vindictiveness. But I knew those sounds. I knew it was real. And yet I listened to the whole thing. I didn't hang up. That's a phone call I remember. I think about it sometimes. Maybe it was the best sex we ever had.'

The buzz of the tyres and the engine's drone seemed louder after that.

He said nothing more and I didn't ask any of the dozen questions I wanted to. It occurred to me only later that he must have chosen that story just to shock and silence me. Perhaps he thought me a virgin. I wasn't a virgin, but I'd known only two girls. One, practically speaking. No Latina beauty queens.

It wasn't until we'd descended from the peaks to the gulf shoreline that he spoke again.

'Do you know where we are?'

'Near Nafplio?'

'This is Lerna, where Heracles killed the nine-headed Hydra. His second labour.'

'It's an actual place?'

'Of course it is. We're also close to Nemea, where he killed the monstrous lion, and to Tiryns where his tormentor

King Eurystheus reigned. But the Hydra is an interesting one. Our hero used its poison on an arrow to kill Nessus, who had his revenge when Heracles's wife, Deianira, gave Nessus's blood-stained shirt to Heracles. The poison tore flesh from his bones and sent him mad. Triumph and tragedy in one labour.'

'You know your mythology.'

'So should *you*. These are our roots.' He turned to me. 'I'm serious about that.'

'Okay.'

The sea appeared between buildings on our right until the buildings disappeared and we were driving virtually on the beach. Up in front, across the flat expanse of the sea, the fortress of Nafplio sat pale atop a huge rock. A carpet of terracotta rooftops spread at its base – the old town. It looked impressive. There was an earthy, foetid smell in the air. I sniffed at the open window.

'The olive processing plant,' said Bastounis. 'Once smelled, never forgotten. When I lived in America, I'd sometimes buy a jar of olives in brine and open it just to remind me. Turn left just up here – see the turn?'

'But Nafplio is straight ahead.'

'We're going to Tyrintha first. Tiryns, where the labours of Heracles were given.'

'Is it far?'

'What do you care? It's close to Nafplio. Your ordeal will soon be over.'

I took the turn. It barely looked like a road – more like a driveway that would end at a vacant lot or a dilapidated concrete structure. The coast road had been littered with defunct nightclubs, empty dealerships and failed go-cart circuits. Anonymous scrubland stretched out either side of us. Arid brown hills rose ahead.

My "ordeal," he called it. True, he was lacking in charm. And he'd destroyed my phone. But the idea of leaving him in Nafplio and just walking away was beginning to seem odd. Not the way I'd imagined it would end. The time had passed so quickly and we'd barely spoken.

We passed through an avenue of plane trees and over a disused railway track before arriving at a junction in front of a cream-coloured official building. A school? A town hall?

'Left,' said Bastounis.

And there it was, right in front of us, next to the official building: a great wall of impossibly ancient polygonal blocks that looked like it had sighed under the weight of four millennia of weather, war and earthquake. In the afternoon light, it had a golden hue against the brilliant blue of the sky. Warriors had set sail from here to fight the Trojan War. King Eurystheus had reigned here even before that, when lions roamed these plains and monsters inhabited the caves and valleys. The gigantic Erymanthian boar, the plague of Stymfalian birds, the many-headed Hydra – children's stories that became suddenly credible in this place, this mound of worked masonry that had stood forty centuries as civilisations passed, mere dust on the wind.

'Take the right turn. There's a car park at the visitors centre.'

His voice was tight with some emotion. Anticipation? Nostalgia?

'Is it a book? Are you writing a book about Heracles?'

He looked sharply at me. 'Go inside and get two tickets. Here... take this.'

I took the money and walked towards the large whitewashed building. There were no other tourists inside and a bored young woman sold me the tickets without speaking.

When I emerged into the light again, Bastounis was closing the car boot. He walked towards me with his walking stick and held out his hand for the ticket.

'Go. Entertain yourself. Don't wait around for me. I'll see you back at the car in, what, an hour?'

I looked at the stick. 'Are you going to be—'

'Don't patronise me.'

He started towards the entrance. I watched him go, wondering if perhaps this was some kind of trap. Was he going to abandon me here? Maybe he could drive after all. Based on our short acquaintance, it seemed entirely possible. On the other hand, it wasn't as if he could out-sprint me back to the car park. I just had to keep him in sight.

I followed, passing him without comment, and ascended to the top of the citadel. Dry grasses quivered in the wind among colossal stones. History and archaeology could barely conceive what it must have been like to live here as the people watched ships leave for Troy. A different religion, a different cosmogony, a different understanding of past, future and time itself. An existence of fear, perhaps – of always-impending invasion, or divine wrath, or the vagaries of the elements bringing famine or destruction. And yet their stories were our stories: gods and heroes, challenges and prizes, sacrifices and triumphs. Nemea still existed, as did Lerna and Stymfalia of the troublesome avians.

I walked around in a daze of ignorant yearning, examining fallen lintels or vast jambs, pressing my fingers against implausibly perfect joins between blocks, and standing within the famous stone-built tunnels: geological intestines that smelled of urine and swirled empty drinks cans in their vortices. The surrounding plain was dark with orange groves, an occasional cypress rising like a lone mast in the verdant sea. Only one other visitor seemed to be there: an energetic older lady striding about in a large sunhat.

The world was still a mystery when this place first grew. Lands beyond the horizon were tales and rumours. Nations beyond the sea were myths and legends. The sky was populated with deities. In place of knowledge they had wonder and imagination. What did I have but a few megabytes of memory in which to summarise eternity? My phone had given me access to more than they could ever have conceived, but it meant nothing to me. It simply magnified the ocean on which I was adrift.

I was on the way back to the car when I saw Bastounis. Or rather, I heard grunting and the chink of metal against rock. Following the sounds, I came upon him lying face down in the scrub, his stick beside him and his arm wedged beneath a vast tumbled block.

'What happened? Did you fall?'

'Shh! Get down. Use the cover of the rocks there.'

His arm withdrew. He was holding a trowel. A pile of fresh earth showed that he was digging under the rock.

'What are you doing? Isn't this a protected historical site? You can't just—'

'I'm not taking anything of theirs. Duck down!'

I crouched, looking around for the sun-hat woman. Bastounis jabbed at the earth under his boulder, his cheek awkwardly against it as he grasped around the cavity.

'Ah.'

His hand emerged, brown with earth and clutching something wrapped in a piece of soiled canvas. He put it inside his jacket's breast pocket and held out his grubby hand.

'Help me up.'

I hoisted him to his feet. 'What's that?'

'It's mine. I'm stealing nothing.'

He pocketed the trowel and started walking back towards the car.

I remained. 'Are you not going to, I don't know, hide the evidence?'

The small pile of earth showed unambiguously that someone had been digging.

He stopped and turned. 'Why? An animal could have done that. You think CSI are going to examine tool marks? Besides, everybody does it. There are more Mycenaean artefacts in the houses around here than in any museum, trust me. Let's go.'

'Still … It's an impressive place, isn't it.'

He stopped. 'You really think so?' His look had that same intensity as when he'd spoken about Heracles at Lerna.

'Yes. I mean, it's amazing. The history.'

He set his cap straight. 'History … History is just numbers and names. Tiryns is more than that. I wonder – can you feel it? In the rocks? In the soil? We're standing on a conduit here. People have built on this site for all of human existence. Why? Just because it was raised above the plain? Historians will tell you as much. But it's nothing so prosaic. They knew, the people who built these walls. They felt it. They worshipped it. They lived greatness. That was a time before civilisation numbed us to who we really are.'

'Are you talking about ley lines – Stonehenge and all that? Mystical forces.'

'Don't mock it. Tell me – have you felt it here? An important question. Have you felt the amorphous, ineffable sense of something beneath – of some attraction not magnetic or gravitational. A power. Faded now, but still emanating and accreting simultaneously. A sense of invisible mass. Do you feel drawn or affected?'

'I…guess. It's something I can't explain. I don't know anything about the place but I suppose I feel *something* – some kind of, I don't know…?'

His expression said nothing. 'Back to the car. I'm getting hungry.'

The fortress at Nafplio was visible for most of the way, its walls and towers seeming to grow out of the rock. The town announced itself with an increasing volume of concrete buildings and shops, petrol stations and plate glass: an ugly approach that seemed born of crass utility, as Tripoli had been. No appreciation of the area's history or heritage – just throw up a building as cheaply as possible within the local regulations and deck it with gaudy, artless signs. Wasn't this supposed to be one of Greece's most beautiful towns?

Bastounis said little apart from giving occasional directions. The final approach took us ever closer to the citadel until we were directly below it, the rock peak now too high to see out of the car's windows. It was only as we headed into the old town that I began to see the charm. The narrow streets almost seemed to touch our sides. The buildings were palpably old, some ruined. I noticed at least two domed roofs, presumably of ex-Ottoman mosques. It was like driving in Venice, the road our canal.

'Here. Turn right,' said Bastounis.

The road was narrower still, and made dark by abundant flowering bushes that burst over the peeling wall on one side. We stopped at a large, rusting gate and Bastounis reached over to jab the horn a couple of times.

'Where are we?' I said.

'This is the home of Greece's greatest living poet: Kostas Konstantinopoulos. You don't know him. He hasn't been translated. Our journey is over. We'll organise some money for your phone and you can go.'

'Oh...'

The gate clanged and slid to the side on a squealing rail. A man of about Bastounis's age, but wispily thin like a hermit, appeared and beckoned us into the courtyard, where a burst of plum-coloured bougainvillea erupted across the masonry. I saw lemon and orange trees growing in a swatch of garden to the rear.

A thought rushed into coalescence: I didn't want to be alone again with guidebook Greece. There was another, better, more interesting one and I wanted more of it. More of *him*.

FOUR

The two men embraced, evidently with wry comments and comparisons on their respective ageing. The walking stick was assessed and the joke made about Bastounis's surname. I stood by the open boot, bag in hand – the anonymous driver picked up along the way.

It was Konstantinopoulos who acknowledged me, nodding in my direction and presumably asking who I was. Bastounis answered with a laconic summary that seemed to displease the poet. He looked at me with an expression that reminded me of Byzantine icons I'd seen: the sunken face, the gossamer beards, the sharp noses and huge eyes that had glimpsed beyond the mortal veil to the other side. He approached, his hand out.

'You must forgive my friend. He has lived away from his country long enough to forget the meaning of *philoxenia*: hospitality.'

Bastounis grunted a retort.

'You will be my guest while you are in Nafplio,' said Konstantinopoulos. 'My house has many rooms. Come – let me show you.'

He walked ahead, vigorous in his asceticism, and we ascended a dark wooden staircase past yellowed wallpaper that looked a hundred years old. The landing was bright with daylight and dominated by a mahogany or ebony grandfather clock of fantastical detail.

'Forgive the obvious metaphor,' he said of the clock. 'It's German. You can have this room. It has the best view. Make yourself comfortable and join us on the roof when you're ready. There is a bathroom at the end of the corridor. Don't be alarmed if Odysseus comes to see you.'

'Thank-you. I...'

But he'd already gone. The room was an antique parlour: an ornate steel-framed double bed, a clutter of mismatched wooden furniture, dusty ornaments and an old leather armchair whose shining seat had bowed with weight and age. As I stood there, bag over my shoulder, a black cat entered the room and paused at my intrusion. Perceiving no threat, he trotted towards the armchair and jumped into its polished basin. Odysseus, I presumed.

The view from the window was so astounding that the house itself might have been built around its frame. Before me was the tiny island fortress known as the Bourtzi, its harmony of turrets, towers and crenellations seemingly designed by a cubist rather than a general. It glowed in the afternoon sun: a sculpture fashioned from the yellow vanilla ice-cream of old adverts. In the foreground, small fishing boats were tethered along a palm-lined promenade. In the far distance rose the barren, stony mountains of Arcadia. The saline breeze was a kiss. The light seemed to magnify the colours and to have its own volume, as if all was seen through a lens of pure spring water.

Odysseus began to purr.

A fugitive thought: if only I had my phone. I could take a picture of this and send it back to the dank and miserable world of England as proof that I wasn't just wasting my time on whimsical adventures. Let them see this room and this view and then talk to me about responsibility and the job market and the tyranny of the CV.

But no photo could capture the sense of balmy air on skin, of excited contentment and the privilege of access to this walled sanctuary. Why would I *want* to share this with anybody and cheapen it by absorption into social media's ceaseless effluvia – just another ping or tinkle on another device, deserving only of a nanosecond of somebody's fractured attention. Was this Bastounis working in my thoughts already?

I laid my bag at the foot of the bed and went in search of the roof up another rickety stairwell whose top was a rectangle of limitless blue. They were sitting at a cast-iron table amid a view of even greater majesty. The fortress walls of Palamidi towered over the town to the north, imposing on a lesser fortification atop a rocky escarpment. The old town to the south was an angular abstract of terracotta roofs and domes beyond which lay the port and the bow of coastline topping the Argolic Gulf.

The two stopped talking at my arrival. Bastounis looked away.

'Welcome!' said Konstantinopoulos, pushing out a chair with his foot.

'This place is fantastic,' I said.

'Yes. Yes it is. And wait for the sunset. What will you drink? We are having ouzo.'

I had an ouzo, watching the spirit turn milky as it mixed with the ice. Could there be a better drink to enjoy in the sunshine below an Aegean sky? I should have felt awkward here in the company of these two old Greeks, but the situation was dreamlike. I was caught in a current more powerful and compelling than my volition. The easiest option was surely just to flow. Maybe tomorrow I'd be out on my own again: a passenger again. A tourist.

'Irakles tells me you need a new phone.'

'Yes. There was … an accident.'

'I'm sure. I will give you the name of a friend in town. You'll pay nothing.'

'Thank-you.'

'I hope you don't mind, but Irakles and I have not seen each other for many years. We'd like to talk this evening. I suggest you spend some time exploring Nafplio. If you can give us until midnight.'

'Of course. I'm very grateful for …'

'It's nothing. Irakles tells me you are a student of literature.'

'Yes, well, I've just finished a literature degree. I'm afraid I didn't do much poetry, though. Mostly novels and drama. Of course, there was Milton and Shakespeare. Chaucer. But nothing, you know …'

'Greek. Why would there be? The Greeks don't read their own poetry. They are proud to be of Homer's kin, but prefer the Hollywood versions of his work.'

'The *real* Philistines!' said Bastounis, who had been brooding.

'Thank God you have delivered him from his Dimitsana exile,' said Konstantinopoulos with a smile. 'Another winter there and he might have enacted a massacre.'

'Mister Bastounis told me that your work isn't translated.'

'Why would it be if even the Greeks won't read it? Much of it isn't published at all, though I have printed at my own expense. Do you write, or have you any ambitions that way?'

'I've thought about it. It's a dream of mine. I mean, I've tried …'

I was aware that both of them were looking at me with something like pity. It was like telling Marco Polo I'd been on a package holiday, or Casanova that I'd had a girlfriend.

'At some point,' said Konstantinopoulos, 'if you are fortunate, you learn that your only true audience is yourself. If you can't write for yourself alone, you are finished. The world does not care. Write not for the money or the acclaim, but because it is in your human nature to do so. That is the route to sanity and salvation.'

'He's right,' said Bastounis, staring out to sea. 'God help us.'

I sipped my ouzo and realised that I hadn't eaten anything since those *spanakopites* in the village. The alcohol was making me lightheaded. The colours around us seemed to be saturating in the liquid light: tourmaline trees, tanzanite sky, citrine-tinged clouds and garnet rooftops. I was inside an expressionist painting. I took a black olive from the bowl on the table and smelled that same tang we'd experienced on the coast road.

Bastounis saw it and smiled to himself. Bastounis saw everything.

'Ah, here we go,' said Konstantinopulos, nodding up at Palamedi's walls. 'The show begins.'

The light was indeed changing. What had been a luminous yellow-gold crown atop the massive monolith was now mellowing into burnished brass, then copper. The rock of the hill transformed from undistinguished earth into burned sienna and then an incandescent purple as if lit from within. The sky behind cast auric edges on bloodied clouds. Cooling and receding into darkness, the rock glowed otherworldly violet – a mirage – before taking a silhouette's cloak. The whole transition took just minutes. Precipitous night.

'Wow,' I said.

The old men said nothing.

Would I remember this in all of its vividness? The colours, the sensations? The air so still and benign. The sense of privilege. Could one willingly select an experience and log it in an impermeable vault of memory for future use? Surely there was too much data. I could write it in my journal, but it would be mere words – a wretched, impotent grasping after the truth of it. A greetings-card version riddled with cliché and classroom stylistics. How I despised my journal then – traitor to my purpose.

Bastounis could have written it. He could probably do it in a sentence or a phrase: some delicate impressionistic equilibrium of onomatopoeia and assonance that transcended ink and paper. What must it be like to live this scene as him, with his lifetime of experience colouring it all? Was I alone in wanting to skip the implacable chronology of coming decades in favour of faster enlightenment? Bastounis had been so painfully right about my naivety.

Konstantinopoulos turned to me.

'Would you mind…?'

'Of course, of course. I'll go into town and… walk around.'

'Many thanks. I will leave the gate open for you.'

Bastounis seemed not to register that some agreement had been made, or that I was leaving. Perhaps, in his mind, I'd already gone. I'd served my purpose.

Nafplio was even more attractive on foot. I walked past ornamental orange trees to follow a crooked street lined with light and tavernas. It was still too early for the Greeks to be eating, but a breaking wave of empty chairs had spread across the pavement in welcome. As I passed, smiling waiters tried to lure me with incantatory lists of dishes: *mousaka, ktopodia, soutzoukaikia, salates, horta, loukanika, pastitsio…*

I was starving, and the smells made it worse, but I wanted to eat among people. I also wanted to find an Internet café if such a thing existed here. Too inhibited to actually ask someone, I wandered aimlessly with the rationale that I was seeing the sights.

Eventually, as I appeared to be leaving the old town, I found a grubby-looking Lotto shop that seemed to have a few screens inside. All but one of them was occupied by a teenage boy staring intently into the aether of some online game, his face illuminated by the unnatural play of colours. I went in and was shown to a keyboard of hideous uncleanliness and a sheen of some sticky residue that might have been spilled cola or just the sebaceous accumulation of a million adolescent keystrokes.

I opened my email account (waiting minutes for a connection) and looked at the inbox. Just a handful of messages, three quarters of them spam. A couple of university friends had written to tell me about how they hated their jobs but loved the money, how they missed the intellectual stimulation but also saw it as an indulgent irrelevance in the real world. These were bulletins from the real world to me in my fantasy realm: my Neverland.

I shouldn't have come to Greece, they thought, just like I shouldn't have spent those lost months working in shameful retail saving up for it. The message from my mother would say the same: are you enjoying yourself? When are you coming back so your soul can be slowly sucked from your body by the exquisite despair of dutiful employment? Forget art and literature, son. Pay off your loans. Get a mortgage. Get married. There is no higher plane of being and experience. There's only this numb acquiescence, this anaesthesia of supply and demand, spending and saving and living for the tiny pinhole of light up ahead that's a holiday or retirement or death.

There was nothing from Clara.

My fingers hovered over the diseased keys: molars of some yawning beast. Nobody in the Real World cared about the Nafpliot sunset I'd just seen. Nobody cared that I'd met and driven Irakles Bastounis, least of all my mother. *Who? Oh, that's exciting! What did he write? Can he offer you a job?* Even my friends would find it less immediately interesting than their new TV. It's not as if I'd met a genuine celebrity: that singer with the thirty-second career; that chef with the tattoos; that personal trainer who does the diet books.

I typed a message – "Phone broken. Everything fine here. Will be out of contact for a while." – and sent it to everyone. Neverland was waiting outside.

I found all the people in the square: a marble-paved rectangle that drew me through buildings and set me in the heart of the town. A great Venetian warehouse occupied one end of the square and a squat ex-mosque the other. In between were grand old buildings with ornate balconies, painted shutters and fancy mouldings. Half a dozen cafés spilled their chairs and tables out over the shining marble tiles and almost every seat was occupied with people talking, drinking, laughing. A storm of children boiled about the square, chasing balls, squealing and riding bikes or scooters. Above it all, the spot-lit fortress reared as a false constellation.

I took a seat and ordered an ouzo, knowing they'd bring olives or crisps or pickled fish with it. And I let myself slide into the life of the town – part of something vibrant and colourful. People were smiling and relaxed rather than drunk and desperately pretending. No whooping and raucous haranguing here. No extravagant vomiting and pavement-rolling histrionics. In an hour or so, I might wander back along that road of tavernas and choose the one where most Greeks seemed to be eating. Then maybe I'd waddle, over-satiated, in search of the small beach I'd seen on the map in my guidebook. I had to stay out until midnight.

As I sipped my drink, I saw a blonde-haired girl enter the square near the old mosque. An obvious tourist, she wore baggy linen trousers and a loose shirt. I saw red-painted toenails in strappy sandals but she wore no make-up that I could discern. She was pretty, but aware she was walking on to a stage where she'd be observed by women and men in different ways. She seemed to be alone. My impression was that she was looking for a place to settle, as I had, and to watch the evening unfold from the anonymity of the auditorium.

I sat up straighter and willed her to look in my direction. If she did, I'd wave her over. *Hey – sit with me. We're both strangers here. Let's share the evening. Tell me about yourself. Me? Oh, I'm staying here in a private house with the Nobel Prize-winning author Irakles Bastounis. Have you read him? Great man. Perhaps you'd like to meet him…?* But she walked on, oblivious to my existence, and disappeared around the side of the big Venetian warehouse that was now the town's museum.

I wondered if the two old men were still up there on the roof: the poet and the novelist. What would they be discussing? Hadn't I read somewhere that writers seldom discuss their craft when together – no more than they'd discuss their bowel movements. Such things were organic processes beneath discussion. Creative peristalsis. The endocrinology of ideas. No, they'd probably be discussing money or women or food. Or death. There must come an age when you know death is the next room you'll walk into, when what lies behind is inescapably and oppressively more than what there is to come. The thought frightened me, distant as such things were. It was an alarm bell heard faintly but persistently.

'How do you like the ouzo?'

The man on the next table was leaning over to me. Greek? The accent was vague.

'Oh, I like it.'

'Where are you from?'

'England.'

'Enjoying Greece? Where have you been so far?'

'Er, I've not really been here long. Just Athens really...'

'You like the history, eh?'

'I suppose so. I mean, I'm no expert. I'm just travelling.'

'You should also visit some of the villages if you want to see the real Greece. There are some very pretty ones in Arcadia. Stemnitsa, Karitaina, Dimitsana...'

'Yes, I've been there.'

'To Dimitsana?'

He turned his chair towards me.

'Yes... Just yesterday, in fact.'

'An interesting place. Nice architecture. A few notable people have come from there: bishops, archbishops. A patriarch. I think there's also a famous writer who lives there...'

He was staring at me now.

'Really?' I said.

'You're not interested in literature?'

'Well, I did a degree in it, but, you know, we don't read *everything.*'

'Of course. How did you come to Nafplio from there? By bus?'

'I... I'm sorry... I don't want to seem rude, but—.'

'Hey, just being friendly! We're in Greece now, not on the Tube in London. Eyes down! Say nothing! Should I...?'

He scraped his chair back into position and made a sort of apologetic bow.

I smiled stiffly, guilt and embarrassment warming my face. The guy continued to sit there, watching the activity of the square as if no conversation had taken place.

Had I been too defensive? Too English? Was I being paranoid? Should I apologise? I was oppressively aware of his presence and of his assiduously ignoring me. The setting had suddenly lost its glow. Ruined.

I paid and walked back to the street of tavernas, looking behind me to see if the guy was watching. He seemed not to be. That stuff about being interested in literature was certainly weird. I couldn't recall if he'd already been sitting at the café when I'd arrived, or whether he'd sat shortly after I had. I wondered if I should mention the encounter to Bastounis and Konstantinopoulos, or whether it would make me appear even stiffer and more British that I must already seem to them.

I chose a busy place and ate an excellent octopus in red-wine sauce, a plate of puréed fava beans and a few too many pork *souvlakia*. But the guy at the café had unnerved me and I watched the tides of people warily in case he passed.

The entire evening was surreal – a junction or hiatus beyond which everything would go back to normal but also be forever slightly changed. The day I'd travelled with Bastounis. Maybe he'd make an oblique reference to me in some future, possibly posthumous, *meisterstück*: some word or phrase I'd uttered that had stayed in his memory. That might be my sole claim to immortality. My secret.

After eating, I wandered up and down the stepped alleys of the old town, exploring apparent *culs de sac* that revealed passages between buildings. Almost every turn held some novelty: a Turkish drinking fountain inscribed in Arabic, a tiny chapel, a line of Mycenaean wall, a fortified Frankish gate, a mosque absorbed into the structure of a neighbouring building. The place was a collage of historical elements: a pawn of empires. I wanted to live there.

I walked a path that followed the base of the headland, past noisy cafés and restaurants, past the Bourtzi and a small park with children playing, to an unilluminated stretch, where I sat on a stone bench and stared out into the blackness of sky and sea. The stars were clear and the coast on the other side of the gulf was a discarded necklace of lights. The pines exhaled scented resin. The shushing rocks wafted salt and iodine. Voluptuous night.

I worked on a daydream of that blonde girl emerging from the darkness to find me alone here. Her initial surprise and fear. My placations and explanations. My obvious status as a sensitive romantic. Her thigh soft against mine on the stone bench. A shooting star, perhaps... No. Too incredible, even by my standards.

The thought occurred that nobody knew where I was. Nobody could even guess. Nobody could locate or contact me. It was the absolute opposite of fame. I'd effaced myself from the world, if only for a moment, and discovered a pocket of purest solitude where my self could emerge: a malformed and undernourished thing in search of some sustenance beyond the meagre fare I'd so far fed it. Worthy literature. Philosophy. Epigrams, apothegms, and reverently-jotted quotations. The self could starve on such a diet. It needed experience. It needed life.

The following day, I'd need to find somewhere else to sleep – unless I could persuade Konstinopoulos to let me stay at his place a little longer. My eyes unfocused on the night, I wove a daydream of him offering to employ me as his amanuensis. I'd spend mornings out in the town doing errands and evenings on the roof watching sunsets. Maybe I'd just never write or call home again.

The house was silent when I let myself in after midnight. Konstantinopoulos had left a light on for me and I cursed every creak of the stairs as I went up to bed. The view from the window was no less perfect, and now there was a jasmine-like perfume rising through it from the garden.

I lay in bed listening to the sounds of people on the promenade and trying to place this day in my top five of best days ever. The competition was mild. Getting my degree result. Losing my virginity. That time when I was fourteen and Uncle Geoff had taken me to a car show where I was able to sit inside a Ferrari. Not exactly Byronic.

I worked some more on my daydream of staying in this room, learning Greek and perhaps becoming a poet. The slide from imagination into dreams was imperceptible.

FIVE

I woke at dawn, having forgotten to close the shutters. The sea was mirror-flat, reflecting a perfect replica of the Bourtzi. The Arcadian mountains were mist-breathing gills. I lay listening to birdsong and smelling pine resin on the breeze until I heard kitchen sounds and footsteps going slowly up to the roof.

Konstantinopoulos was sitting alone at breakfast. Figs, orange juice, bread, honey. He looked older and frailer in this light, his skin loose and spotted, his body almost skeletal inside an oatmeal-coloured cardigan – a spirit caught between realms.

'Good morning,' he said. 'Did you enjoy Nafplio?'

'It's beautiful. I think I could live here. I'll definitely stay on a few more days. I don't know if you rent rooms here, but...'

He was smiling. Had he anticipated my suggestion?

'I was hoping Irakles would be awake to discuss it but... Well, there's been a change of plan. He wants to continue his journey and we, or rather I, was hoping you would agree to drive him.'

'*Me?*'

'I appreciate you may have your own plans and perhaps limited time, but—'

'No. It's not that. It's … well, I thought he didn't like me at all. I mean, I think he's a great, great artist but he's not shown me much … affection.'

'That is Irakles. But he can no longer drive and there are things he needs to do. It's not seemly for him to travel by bus and train, though he's by no means famous enough in his own country to be bothered. Still, he's a private man and there are people who might pursue him.'

'Who?'

'Oh, journalists. Fans, possibly. Perhaps you've heard the rumour that he is has some manuscript that he refuses to publish – his greatest work yet. Or that he is about to embark on such a work. Certain people would be interested. There is profit to be made out of an old writer. Maybe even more so after his death.'

'*Is* he holding an unpublished book?'

'I could not say. The important thing is whether you would be willing to indulge an old man. *Two* old men, actually – I would be grateful if somebody could be with him. I cannot.'

'Where does he want to go?'

'He'll tell you when he awakes. I am afraid neither he nor I can pay you. I hope you would do this thing out of curiosity or benevolence alone. You brought him this far … But you look doubtful. I can assure you there's nothing illicit involved.'

'It's just that … Did he tell you anything about Tiryns.'

'Indeed.'

'Well, you know, it looked kind of suspicious: digging around under a rock at a protected archaeological site. He said it wasn't illegal, but …'

'Do you want to know what it was? The thing he excavated?'

'I know it's not my business…'

Konstantinopoulos took something from his cardigan pocket. It was the same dirty rag Bastounis had pulled out from the rock.

'Here. Open it.'

He put it in my hand – an object about the size of a small saucer but flatter and heavier. I unfolded the corners of rough hessian and saw gold. A man's head and shoulders in profile. Roman numerals I couldn't decipher. A name: Alfr Nobel.

'Is this…?'

'Indeed. The Nobel Prize for Literature. Irakles' prize – the medal part of it, at least.'

'Why… Why did he bury it? Why he dig it up?'

'Ask *him*.'

I looked at it. The Nobel Prize. In *my* hand. One of the many things I could never dream of owning or deserving. One of those things that denoted the apogee of a human span. A platinum disc. An Olympic gold medal.

The poet smiled.

The sound of retching echoed up to us from inside the house: Bastounis suffering from too much retsina, perhaps. Coughing and muttering followed.

I handed the medal back reluctantly. It was a talisman.

He rewrapped it and returned it to his pocket.

I poured orange juice and spread honey on the soft bread. The town was still eerily silent, as if the wider landscape was holding its breath.

'Mister Bastounis called you Greece's greatest living poet,' I said.

'There is not so much competition, and the dead ones were far greater.'

I conjured a question and weighed it for naivety. Bastounis would have scoffed at it – but the poet?

'I wonder...How does one become a writer? A *good* writer, I mean – like you and Mister Bastounis. An artist. People say it's all about practice and wide reading.'

He looked down and pursed his lips. His knobbly fingers played with the marble edge of the table. I saw again that Byzantine face: all eyes and spirit.

'The greater art is living. When the experiences of life are copious, writing is a by-product – you might say an excretion or overspill. In older days, they might have called it bloodletting. Writing itself is not the thing. For its own sake, it is only an exercise, a game. It must have energy behind it. It must be a distillation. First comes life. Then – if we are fortunate, if we practise, if we read – the writing will come. Not to everyone, and perhaps not even in the way we want or expect. Perhaps you know that Irakles wanted to be a poet. But his soul is that of a storyteller. Prose is his art.'

The orange juice lay bitter on my tongue. What hope for me: the cipher? The graduate embryo.

Bastounis emerged squinting into the light, dressed exactly as I'd first seen him: pale shirt, dark trousers, cap, walking stick, white stubble on his chin. He moved carefully, as if his brain were a raw egg yolk sloshing in his skull.

'Have you told him?' he said to Konstantinopoulos.

'Only the basics. The detail comes from you, Irakles.'

Bastounis sat and watched me. He didn't seem entirely convinced. Or perhaps he just resented needing anybody's help.

'Drive me to the south,' he said. 'We take the Monemvasia ferry this morning and from there to ... other places. Pretty places. I'll pay the accommodation and food, but there's no fee for you. Do it – if you do it – for the same reason you came looking for me in Dimitsana: the same reason you brought me here.'

53

'For the camaraderie?'

Again, that sliver of a smile. Konstantinopoulos stifled a laugh.

'Very well,' said Bastounis, adjusting his cap. 'Do it because it's living and because you don't know what's going to happen next. Do it because you're dead for much longer than you're alive. Do it because… Okay. Okay. Let's make it interesting. Let's make it a mythicosophical journey. I, Irakles Bastounis, agree to set you twelve labours: twelve challenges in payment for your assistance. Twelve challenges on how to live life fully. You may not like some of them, but Heracles didn't choose his labours. There may be monsters to slay. There'll be shit to shovel from the blocked stables of your soul. How about it? I'll be your King Eurystheus and you'll be the young hero: demigod of your own conception.'

'Mythicosophical?'

'A new word. Greek, naturally: a mixture of myth and wisdom. The first labour has already been issued and remains in progress: be spontaneous. Take the risk. Rise to the challenge. Eleven more will follow, each drawn from my own experience.'

I looked to Konstantinopoulos for advice, but he offered only a sphinx-like grin. He'd already told me everything I needed to know.

Had the two writers conspired on this last night while I'd been in town? How to persuade the malleable young Englishman to play chauffer a little longer? It was a scheme designed so perfectly for what I thought I wanted most in life. It was the kind of thing I might have anticipated in a dream.

'The ferry leaves at ten,' said Bastounis, reaching for the figs.

❧ ❧ ❧

Ten o'clock saw us still in Konstaninopoulos's yard, the car engine running and the two men embracing with many warm valedictions. Bastounis had assured me that ferries were always late and that there was no need to fret so neurotically. The poet offered a brief wave and a 'Look after him!' as we reversed. It wasn't clear who he'd been addressing.

The oil-stained tarmac of the quay held a handful of cars and around fifteen people intending to travel. No ferry was visible beyond the Bourtzi.

'I told you,' said Bastounis. 'Late. We could have stayed with Konstantinopoulos and watched the ferry coming.'

He leaned back in his chair and tipped the cap over his eyes.

I was looking at the blonde girl – the one I'd seen in the square the previous night. She was now wearing white shorts and a T-shirt. Her tall backpack leaned against her leg and she was looking down the gulf. Great legs. We'd be together in the confined space of the ferry. Maybe I could offer her a lift at the other end. *Hello! Me and my Nobel Prize-winning friend were wondering…*

'She's your type is she?' said Bastounis, an eavesdropping eye peering sidelong at me from under the cap.

'Well… I wouldn't say I had a type.'

'Of course you do. Sexuality is formed even before we're aware of it. Maternal influence, TV, advertising. Even the toys you play with. You like the virginal type: the ones you can impress. The ones, you suppose, who are impressed by intelligence and sensitivity rather than the crass masculinity you reject because you can't emulate it. That's your type. The grateful kind.'

'Thank-you, Doctor Freud.'

'Ha! But it looks like you have a rival.'

A couple of local lads had wandered along the quay, probably drawn to the girl as to some molecule of blood in a million parts of seawater. The taller of them was wearing a transparent shirt fashioned from black gossamer stuff (manmade) and his black hair was sculpted into a sort of pompadour. His words were indistinct, but the dumbshow told its own story. I could have written the script.

'Hi. Waiting for the Monemvasia ferry?'

'Er, yes.'

'You have beautiful eyes and body.'

'Mm. Thank you.'

'My friend has a very nice bar near here. Come for a drink with us?'

'I'm waiting for the ferry...?'

'Ah, it's always late. I like your shorts.'

'Right.'

She was beginning to look uncomfortable. As usual, these guys didn't know when to stop – or that they shouldn't even start. She was looking to the other passengers now, perhaps hoping one would help her out.

'Now is your chance to be the hero,' said Bastounis. 'This moment.'

I sat. I tried to think of the words I might use. *Hey, buddy!...* Buddy? What was this – a 1950s biker movie? What did guys like this call each other? Dude? Bro?

Bastounis took his walking stick from between our seats and opened the door.

'What are you doing?' I said.

'What you patently can't.'

He walked over to them and stood beside the girl. He said something. The pompadoured buffoon set his shoulders and fired something back. *Who are you, old man? What's it you? You've had your day – now get lost.*

Bastounis spoke – no indication of anger or aggression in his demeanour. He spoke at some length: one of his withering monologues, evidently, because the youth seemed to diminish under its onslaught, visibly passing through the stages of belligerent, affronted, challenged, embarrassed, humiliated and finally emasculated. He and his friend walked back into town muttering to each other and without even a safe-distance comeback.

The girl thanked Bastounis while I hoped and dreamed that he'd gesture to me in the car as if to say, "No – thank *him.*" But he limped back and fell heavily into his seat.

'What do you say to them?'

'It's not what I said. It's how I said it. With young men, it's the same approach as with dogs.'

'You might have mentioned me to the girl.'

'You had your chance.'

'Is this one of my twelve challenges failed?'

'Not yet.'

A plaintive note echoed up the channel: the ferry's horn. A tiny, rusting hulk soon emerged: the kind of thing I'd expect to see crossing a lake or river rather than the open ocean. It couldn't have held more than twenty vehicles.

'I wonder if your reversing has improved?' said Bastounis.

It turned out my reversing was an occasion for irritation (crew), amusement (passengers), and perspiring frustration (me) as I stalled multiple times and failed repeatedly to back the Peugeot into its allotted space. When finally I eased myself out between the door and the van next to me, Bastounis was waiting.

'Now you know why the ferries are always late.'

We ascended to the upper rear deck on a clanging mesh staircase and took seats to watch Nafplio recede. What kind of a pair did we make: the infirm old man and the gangling neophyte? Could we have been mistaken for grandfather and grandson? Despite Bastounis's obvious Greekness and my obvious Englishness, he looked frailer and more etiolated this morning. I toyed with the idea of calling him *papou*, as I'd heard the local children say to their grandfathers, but sensed this might end with his walking stick in my teeth.

The engines rumbled and the wake churned. A hot cloud of acrid smoke washed over us from the funnel. The land slid sideways and began to recede. It was only then that I noticed the man standing on the quay – the same guy who'd tried to engage me in conversation in the square the previous evening. Had he come to see someone off? He wasn't waving. I watched as he took a phone from his pocket and called someone, his eyes on the departing ferry all the while.

I looked sidelong at Bastounis, but he hadn't noticed the man. I was being paranoid. An overdeveloped fictive urge, perhaps. Too many spy novels as a kid. Dead-letter drops. Covert surveillance. Bugging.

I watched the terracotta tapestry unfurl before us as the magnitude of Palamedes's peak became fully evident. A tiny town, really: a pocket of history caught in the folds of its geography. Konstantinopoulos's house was visible out on its own but the roof terrace looked empty. He could so easily have gone up and watched us go by.

Bastounis sat serenely beside me, his hands folded in his lap. It was the first time I'd seen him not visibly tense. Perhaps it was the ferry – leaving the land, making his escape from the Dimitsana exile and setting off on a journey as he had with the gypsies half a century earlier. That particular adventure had ended badly as I recalled. An unexplained death, a scattering of the troupe, Bastounis torn from his first love and arriving fugitive in Piraeus to sign up as lackey on the cargo ships. Hence his current peace? The memory of the sea, the smell of industrial lubricant and hemp. The seismic thunder of the diesels.

'Mister Konstantinopulos showed me the medal.'

'Did he?'

'He didn't tell me why you'd unearthed it, or why he had it in his pocket. He said I should ask you.'

'But not that I'd answer, eh?'

'You've got to admit … It seems a bit of a mystery.'

'It's no mystery. You know enough to figure it out. Think about it.'

'Well—'

'In your head.'

Nafplio was soon just a shape on a distant horizon. We cruised south past the out-jutting headland of Astros to starboard and along a brown, mountainous coastline that seemed unlikely to support life. Beside such barrenness, the sea was a profound, light-swallowing cobalt. "Wine-dark" Homer had called it – a sweet intoxication.

The blonde girl appeared from round the port side and stood at the railing before us, leaning her elbows on rust blooms, looking inland. She seemed as oblivious to our presence as to the offshore breeze that tossed her hair and rippled her clothes.

Bastounis nudged me and gestured towards her with his head.

'What?' I said.

'You could have her, you know. You're of an appropriate age and commensurable appearance. You're travellers in common and speak the same language.'

'*Have* her?'

'Sleep with her. Do whatever you want with her.'

There was no comedic leer – no winking lechery. He was serious.

'That's not a very... feministic attitude.'

'Ah, feminism. It's feminism that has made modern men eunuchs. Equality? Yes, by all means! But give a woman everything she asks for? Absolutely no. She doesn't want that. She'll take it if you offer it – of course she will – but then she'll consider it too easily won: devalued in her estimation. Have you not read Chaucer? Or Byron. She doesn't respect what she doesn't have to fight for. A woman is a contrary being, even to herself and her own kind. Like Narcissus, she spends her life chasing a reflection, not realising that the silvered self is a reversal, an opposite, a chimera. A man battles external monsters, but a woman fights only herself.'

'I think maybe your view of women is out-dated.'

'Is it? Is it? Let's observe this girl, this young woman, you covet. Yes. Let's make his your next challenge. Observation. A man must learn to observe – not merely to see. Tell me – what do you read in her?'

'Right, okay. She's travelling alone, so she's independent and confident... but not so confident that she wasn't unnerved by those guys at the port. She's fit – perhaps she does some kind of sport. Running maybe. Her hair looks to be naturally blonde rather than dyed, so I guess that makes her genuine and happy with the way she is.'

Bastounis wrinkled his nose. 'A child could see such things. Is she currently ovulating?'

'*What?*'

'A fair question.'

'Am I dog to sense that? Am I supposed to, I don't know, *smell* it?'

'Just observe. Brief white shorts and periods do not mix – and note how she bends over the rail thus, offering the secrets of her pelvis to the world. Her skin is clear. See how she enjoys the wind on her body. Her hair is shining – not tied back, but blowing freely. She's mid-cycle. Ripe. A voluptuary. Her ovaries are grapes bursting with fructose. Of course, she doesn't know she gives off such signs. In her own mind – that opaque Narcissean realm – she's merely enjoying the sea air. But she would capitulate in a heart-beat. Her body craves it even if her mind can't crystallise the thought. Those Greek boys on the quay knew it, even if they couldn't articulate it. Consider: why is she here now, of all places on the ferry? Not because of you, to be sure, but because *I* was her saviour on the quay. Now she offers herself to me in gratitude and in recognition of the mastery she seeks: the deliverer of her submission.'

'*You?*'

'Not consciously. Not at any level she would understand or accept. It's an animal response, as when a cat raises its posterior on being stroked. An offering beyond volition or understanding.'

'*You?*'

'Or you. If *I* tried, she would be flattered and no doubt aroused in some confusing way that would return to her in a dream or a counter-intuitive fever fantasy where consumma-tion might occur – but she'd reject me in reality. Rationality would triumph. But you? *You* might succeed if you could be the thing she's instinctively looking for.'

'What thing?'

'*Your* thing.'

'You're saying, basically, that she ... craves cock?'

'Exactly that. And all that comes with it.'

'Unbelievable.'

'Not at all. It's only your indoctrination in the liberal arts that causes you – and indeed she – to think otherwise. Of course, I'm talking not only about the literal phallus, but also what it represents: potency, passion, possession ... Also worship. In the man's erection a woman sees the infallible indicator of her own allure. It's an affirmation, a celebration of her desirability. The man's interest in her is the interest she so struggles to realise or conceptualise in herself. He confirms it in his satyric urgency – in his thirst to have her.'

'Satyric urgency ... Jesus!'

'Have it your way. Woo her with Greer, Wollstonecraft and Winfrey and see where it gets you. Do you want my advice? Ask her to meet you for a drink tonight in Monemvasia. Tell her you'll meet her in the little square in front of the Christos Elkomenos church. That's a nice spot for a rendezvous. And for God's sake, don't say too much. Play it cool, as they used to say.'

'Christos Elkomenos?'

'That's it.' He tipped the cap over his eyes and folded his arms.

I watched the girl and tried to see the things he'd seen. The feral harlot he'd described seemed like a girl my own age: free, happy, unconcerned by the saline wind that would thicken her hair and stiffen her clothes.

But what did I know? Bastounis was allegedly a great connoisseur of women, with his five wives and his gypsy fling and his Venezuelan beauty queen who called him mid-coitus. On the cargo vessels, he'd tasted every variety of female flesh from San Francisco to Tanjung Priok. At one point, he'd spent six months working as a bus boy at Madame Chen's in Macao, where he'd been the darling of all the working girls. By the time he was my age, he'd had the experience of a Don Juan, of a Casanova. So much wanton desire, indeed – so much moaning expenditure – that he'd supposedly retired to Mount Athos for a year and pursued holy orders. Or so he'd written in *Dionysus in Rehab*. Naturally, the celibacy couldn't last. No monastery could circumscribe his glands. From there, he went to Hollywood.

I looked at him: the pale stubble, the boxer's nose, the powerful jaw. What a life he'd had. All that, and an artist as well. Or rather, all that and an artist *because* of it. Konstantinopoulos had surely been correct.

When I looked up, the girl was facing us. She smiled. Bastounis' elbow hit my side. He missed nothing. I stood and went to her, swaying to counteract the yawing deck.

'I wanted to say thanks again to your grandfather,' she said. 'Those guys at the port were really horrible.'

'Oh, he's not… not awake at the moment.'

Her eyes were pale blue. She had freckles. She drew the hair away from her face with slim fingers. I realised with a lurch that she was too beautiful for me. There was the vaguest of accents. Swedish, perhaps, or Norwegian.

'I don't know what he said to them, but they looked terrified.'

'He's quite a man, it's true. Are you planning to stay in Monemvasia…?'

'For a day or two, yes. I've heard it's beautiful.'

'It really is. Listen… do you fancy meeting in the old town tonight for a coffee or something? We could meet in the little square in front of the Christos Elkomenos church. Say, nine o'clock?'

'Okay!'

'That's great. I'm sure it'll be on the map if you have a guidebook—'

Bastounis gave an exaggerated cough-gargle and knocked his walking stick to the floor as if in some soporific spasm.

'See you there then!' I said with rolling eyes (the responsibilities of the carer!) and returned to his side, restoring the walking stick to its perch.

'Too much talking,' he said under his hat brim. 'Jerk the line once the bait is taken. Hook quick and reel at leisure.'

'Now it's *The Old Man and the Sea* is it?'

'A good book. Perhaps his best. He rated it highly.'

Of course. Bastounis had known Hemingway in the later years.

The girl waved and walked back around the deck. I'd forgotten to ask her name or give mine.

SIX

We left the Peugeot in the new town near the port and took a bus out along the causeway to the island itself: a barren geometric rock rising almost vertically one-hundred metres into the sky. No buildings were visible from the mainland. Even the shore road gave no indication of a town there. It was just rocks to the left and sea to the right – a journey into elemental space.

The bus stopped at a blank arch set in fortified masonry. No cars could pass through this single entrance to the old town. A dingy tunnel within looked like somewhere you might find litter and discarded toilet paper, but Bastounis limped confidently inside as I followed with the bags.

The tunnel was a portal. We emerged into a narrow and twisting cobbled street shaded by coloured awnings, plants and vines on trellises. The medieval stone was a patchwork of dressed blocks, rough mortar, arches and foot-polished steps. It might almost have been a historical theme park, but the age was palpable in its fabric and function: a classic walled town built against siege.

Bastounis walked assuredly, taking a right down some steps and under an arch where bougainvillea flourished. He seemed to have no trouble with the shining cobbles as we went further into the labyrinth. Finally, he ascended seven weighty steps and rapped on the door with the hook of his stick.

An old man opened up and peered at the visitor, his expression changing from polite inquiry through vague confusion to delighted recognition. The two embraced in laughter, stepping apart to look at each other before joining again. I stood at the foot of the stairs, a bag in each hand. The lackey.

We were invited into the dark and musty home. Would Bastounis and I mind sharing a room? Of course not! No problem. The old novelist would have the bed and I would have the folding steel-mesh cot that resembled something an interrogator might combine with electricity. The wallpaper was shiny with a century or more of exhalations and the floor was curling linoleum laid on newspaper. It was a room in which elderly relatives had probably died.

The homeowner stood observing me. He clearly had questions. Who's the pale guy? Is he English? American? I sensed my presence was extraneous.

'Leave us,' said Bastounis. 'Go and explore Monemvasia. I recommend the castle and the ruined monastery. Very atmospheric. Come back in an hour or three.'

I was his Sancho Panza. Not even worthy of a proper introduction. What would Bastounis have said to his friend anyway? *Here's a young man of no consequence I've been condescending to for the last couple of days since he ruined my coffee in the village. He's my temporary prosthesis. He can't even tell the temperature of a woman's cervix by the colour of her earrings!*

I went back into the streets beneath a nimbus of preoccupation, amid collapsed vaults, sinuous passages and fig-shaded alleys, ascending and descending bowed stone steps, until I joined a path that led above the rooftops. It was the track up to the castle, zig-zagging ever steeper up the cliff side until the town was a miniature walled garden below. It was hot and the air was still. Light reflected white from the stones. The sea was a glassy blue vastness beneath. I paused to sit on a wall and take in the view, wiping my forehead with a sleeve. Up ahead, the fortifications reared massively around the crown of the hill – a place of last refuge when the enemy descended with siege-enraged bloodlust. How many had died here of starvation and plague and butchery? So benign now in the sunshine, but once a place of pestilence and putrescence. History hides its crimes in the roots of trees.

I walked the remaining distance to a colossal gate with a staggered tunnel, presumably designed for more efficient slaughter. Thence up to the battlements where the wind buffeted hair and whipped at clothes. Only a handful of people had come this far. The coach-tour invaders pooled below in the cafés and restaurants, on sun terraces and in curio shops selling antique coins or aquebuses. There was nothing up here but the view.

I ventured further on a path of cracked and scattered rock, up onto the top of the island and towards the large ruined church ahead. Its dome seemed whole, but the windows around it had long been blasted by wind and time. Jagged brickwork showed where chapels or colonnades or apses had fallen, their stones no doubt recycled into homes or defences. Up close, the masonry was a crude agglomeration of different sized fragments: tiles, blocks, rubble and rock held together with quartz-sparkling mortar.

The church interior was empty – just a few rickety wooden chairs scattered over stone flags. Wind whistled through the voided windows and a bird twittered unseen somewhere above. The dome was illuminated with apertures like the numbers on a clock face, and the crutch of each supporting arch revealed the flaking remains of icons in blue and red and gold – a human vestige of the scouring centuries. Faith had left the building. The elements had moved back in.

I sat on a chair and listened to the gossiping wind. The whole edifice might have been rushing through space with me its sole passenger. But rushing where? To the future? The future: that narrowing cone, that temporal funnel, leading ineluctably to a claustrophobic pipe whose terminal aperture was death. *Now* was the time of greatest choice and freedom. Only now.

Clara had called me a dreamer as if it were a bad thing. She'd wanted to rush headlong into the confines of the pipe as if any prior possibility or alternative – life itself! – was a hindrance. Why wait to start a career, get married, get a mortgage, have kids, grow old and die? All of those things were necessary. Everyone else did them, so they must be normal and desirable – right? Only a madman like me (like Bastounis?) would scrabble for purchase on the slippery sides of the funnel, trying to halt his descent just long enough to peer through its opaque sides at what might exist beyond. That was the job of the artist, the visionary, the iconoclast – to cling momentarily against the fall, dodging the downpour of souls.

Clara had no time for the funnel. She wanted someone sensible, responsible. I don't think either of us really believed her ultimatum. Come October, she'd said, she was moving north to do her masters and I was either accompanying her with firm plans of my own to start a career ... or agreeing that we had no common future and I could go off to pursue my silly dream of travelling and "finding myself" (always the scare quotes). Either/or – that was her demand.

Well, I acquiesced. I chose "or". Cue anger and recrimination, tears and insomnia. The last time I saw her was puffy eyed and bereft in our bed, pleading with me not to leave for the airport. I hadn't wanted to go. I hadn't wanted to hurt her. I was terrified of making the wrong decision and of being alone when it had taken so long to find someone. Walking out of that flat in the brittle dawn felt like walking down a passage to a ledge above a precipice whose void demanded me. Not death, necessarily, but an escape that might prove worse.

She hadn't written since. The chasm was too deep, too wide and too permanent. It was easier to avoid contact. Still, the connection wasn't entirely broken. I still dreamed of her almost nightly. A few times, I'd woken holding a pillow to my chest. The idea of meeting this Scandinavian girl later was tinged with guilt and illegality. If Clara found out, she'd think I'd forgotten her so quickly. Moved on. I still haven't.

A path around the back of the church led to the lip of the cliff: a sheer drop into nothingness, where seagulls wheeled above silently breaking surf. The monks had built their sanctuary on the very edge, teetering between earth and air. An eternal scale: on this side, sanctity and order; on that side, chaos and oblivion. Which side would Bastounis occupy? Or would he be the fulcrum, tipping the balance between worlds? William Golding (another Nobel laureate) had said that the author's art was to be both: insensate creativity married to a level-headed editor.

Bastounis. Believers *and* atheists liked his work. His heroes were heroes of humanism: self-determining, independent, flawed – but he also dealt in a kind of amorphous spirituality beyond the realm and understanding of his characters. Not a directing power, or even a force of good, but rather a limitless dimension that echoed with the entomological rustlings of man. That was it: Bastounis's characters were ants on the edge of this precipice – ignorant of the void, occasionally twitching their antennae uncomprehendingly at its immensity. I was one of them.

I walked slowly back into the town and found the little house. Its owner let me in and showed me to a tiny kitchen that smelled of fish oil and bore the signatures of male solitude: the overflowing bin, the canned food, the unwashed pans. Not a mess – a *system.* He poured ouzo into a smeary shot glass and took sugar-dusted biscuits from a branded cardboard box using fingers he then licked. All the while, he muttered incomprehensibly in tones I interpreted as gratefulness from his constant patting of my back and squeezing of my shoulder. *Thanks for looking after Irakles. He's an old man and infirm, but a great artist. Yes, he's cantankerous and a curmudgeon and, yes, a bit of an arrogant shit, but, well, he's an artist and they can be like that, can't they? They're different to us. Better. So we allow them their eccentricities, eh?*

The man himself was asleep on his back in our sepulchral bedroom, cap over his eyes and hands folded across his chest: Agamemnon disinterred, but with white stubble instead of a golden mask. He was snoring with a low, glutinous bubbling and didn't stir as I settled myself on the squeaking fold-out. The ouzo and the stale heat weighed heavy and soon enough I, too, slipped into sleep, jolted only briefly by a depth-charge fart from the eminent author.

It was dark when I awoke. Bastounis was sitting in front of a dusty oval mirror, examining his jawline in a stripe of glass he'd cleaned with his cap. He was wearing a fresh shirt and there was a woody perfume that must have been cologne. I observed him for a while, not yet having seen any vanity in him. In those early Hollywood days, he'd been as pretty as a young Gore Vidal, albeit with the bluff masculinity of an Errol Flynn. He pinched the loose skin under his chin and turned to the side experimentally, watching it tighten. His eyes caught me watching.

'Go ahead – laugh.'

'No ... I ...'

'Wait until age takes *you*. It comes like a raptor when you're sleeping. Everything is fine and taut, then one morning you wake and there's a sag, a dip, a bag, a hollow. Your ears keep on growing to mock your head. The nose becomes a tuber. Your face slides irrevocably into a scrotal chin – Judas to the ageless man inside.'

'I didn't say anything.'

'Your gaze did. Don't pity me. Envy what this face has seen and done. Consider it a relic.'

'I do. I *do* envy it.'

'Don't call it ageing – call it patina. You know that the Parthenon marbles were once coloured, yes? Gaudy pigments like a child's painting. Then the centuries wiped their faces clean and millennia knocked them loose. Chipped by war, stained by industry, caressed by classicists, their blank eyes have seen more than any breathing man ... their ... their ... '

His expression fell. Confusion slackened his mouth. He appeared to pale and leaned heavily against the dressing table.

'Mister Bastounis? Are you okay? Should I ...?'

He blinked and shook his head. 'It's nothing. Forget it. What was I saying?'

'"Caressed by classicists ..."'

'Right. Right. Don't pity me. Age comes like a raptor when you're sleeping.'

'I should probably get ready.'

'Ah yes. Your date. Remember – you must observe. Read her like a piece of art. Better still, consider her a symphony, from piccolo to double bass.'

'Are *you* going out?'

'I'll be talking to my old friend.'

'The man who lives here?'

He pretended not to hear.

'It's just that… Well, you told me to observe. Does a man wear cologne and a fresh shirt to meet another man?'

Bastounis narrowed his eyes at me. Perhaps he smiled.

'Good luck tonight,' he said.

The tiny, rough-paved square in front of Christos Elkomenos was indeed charming: one of the few relatively open spaces in the old town. The ornamental door to the church gave little sense of its true size, and was outclassed by the beautiful stone campanile occupying the square's northern side. A few small trees exhaled their verdure into the shadows. Towards the south, over the rooftops, the sea glittered. The streets beyond sounded with the convivial hubbub of voices and tinkling cutlery.

She appeared exactly on time, emerging from an alley in white linen trousers and a blue sleeveless top. I tried rapidly to observe: newly washed hair, perhaps a hint of eye make-up, trousers not too tight – perhaps an unconscious indication of…

'Hi!' she said. 'What a wonderful place! Did you go up to the castle and the little church there on the cliff?'

'I did.'

'I've read there's a place near Sparta called Mystra – a ruined town where nobody lives – but Monemvasia is supposed better and bigger. And people actually live here. It's kind of like Nafplio, but concentrated – you know?'

'I know exactly what you mean, yeah. Yeah, that's a good way to put it.'

She smiled. I smiled.

Lime polish on her toenails. Floral perfume. No bra.

'Would you like to eat?' she said.

'Yes. I'm starving.'

We walked necessarily close in the narrow street, the cool skin of her arm occasionally touching mine. When it did, she smiled as if to say that it was no problem – that we northern Europeans needn't fear human contact. We were free and young and alive.

The choice of where to eat seemed tacitly mine, so I chose a *taverna* behind the campanile. It had red tablecloths and the thigh-torturing wooden chairs with straw seats that seemed to indicate tradition. It was only after we sat that I wondered whether I should have pulled out her chair like a gentleman.

'Do you know much about Greek food?' she said.

'Not really ... I mean, I've had *mousaka* and Greek salad a lot.'

'I'm a vegetarian.'

'Well ... I'm sure they'll have something. Do you eat fish?'

She shook her head charmingly and took a mobile phone out of her bag. It had been pinging and buzzing from the moment she'd arrived. Now she set it on the table and zipped through messages with a finger.

The waiter brought menus with a little wicker basket of bread and a carafe of water with sliced lemon. I watched her over the top my menu, biting her lip, considering the dishes. Selecting and rejecting. She caught me gazing and twitched a quizzical eyebrow.

'Sorry ... It's just that ... I like your ... make-up. I mean, you're pretty.'

I guess that's when I lost her. My utter lack of fluency aside, she already knew she was pretty. She knew she was much more than a face and a body. She needed some subtler form of veneration – with my hands or my eyes or my brain – but not mere stuttered compliments. Romance was a language of codes and allusions – not crass statements. Her gratitude was politely unspoken, but there was disappointment in her eyes.

Her phone pinged and she checked it, smiling at whatever she'd been sent. Tapping a reply, she absently tossed a question without looking up from the screen.

'Where is your grandfather tonight?'

'He … he's not my grandfather. He's not even, you know, a relative.'

'Oh?' She looked up from the phone.

'No. He's a famous Greek author. Irakles Bastounis? He won the Nobel Prize. In the early eighties. A novelist. I'm just driving him as a favour.'

She showed no recognition of his name. Why would she? How many people would recognise the names of Wislawa Szymborska, Jaroslav Seifert or Miguel Angel Asturias. I wondered if she'd Google it there and then.

The waiter returned and we ordered. I'd quite wanted to order the *souvlaki* but went for an omelette to suit her sensibilities.

'Yes, he's actually a great, great artist,' I said. 'One of my literary heroes. I went to his ancestral village in the vague hope of just glimpsing him, I suppose, and he asked me to drive him around. His leg, you see …'

'What kind of novels does he write?'

'I guess you'd call them studies in the frailties and contradictions of man. He's primarily a humanist. His protagonist is usually someone whose fall or failure, paradoxically, is ultimately their salvation.'

She was nodding politely. It was small talk, killing time until the brush-off. We should have enjoyed the meal as fellow

travellers sharing friendship in an exotic place, but that hadn't
been either of our intentions when we'd made the date. There's
always that subtext. This was consolation. Besides, her phone
was a third presence at the table – her conduit to another,
more interesting, unsleeping world. Bastounis's words in
Dimitsana came back to me: the electronic umbilical.

We were eating when I noticed Bastounis arrive at a *taverna* further down the street. He chose a table out on the
pavement and sat with his back to me. Some minutes later,
a woman arrived and he stood to face her. She must have
been about his age but was tall and slim. Her long, silver
hair was tied into a loose ponytail and her eyes were heavily
made up. She looked like an artist: a sculptor or a painter,
perhaps. I'd seen many Greek women of her age dressed
in the black or grey of widowhood, but she wore her black
trousers and T-shirt in defiance of age and convention. She
carried herself as if famous.

They didn't speak or embrace. They just stood looking
at each other: assessing, measuring, adjusting. Though his
face was hidden, I could see his fingers working urgently
in the hook of his stick. He said something and she smiled.
He gestured towards the seat and she hesitated. He sat and
finally she capitulated, sitting opposite him in a manner
that said her presence was provisional.

'What is it?' said the girl, turning to see what had captured my attention.

'Bastounis and a lady. Just under the lamp there.'

'The beautiful one? I like her T-shirt. Is she his wife?'

'I don't think so. I don't know. He doesn't tell me
anything.'

'Do you think it's a date? Wait a minute…'

She pulled her chair round closer to me and moved her
plate.

We watched them order wine but no food, the woman looking at Bastounis all the while with intent, inexpressible feeling. Meanwhile, he talked. The monologue went on and on, without urgency, without gesticulation – but its effect seemed clear in the way her expression softened: her defences weakening, her eyes darkening wetly, her gradual leaning closer until she reached across the table to take his hand in both of hers.

'Maybe he's asking her to marry him,' said the girl, checking her phone.

'He's been married five times already. I'm not sure it works for him.'

Now the woman started to talk: questions perhaps, as she held Bastounis's hand and listened. The waiter brought them menus but was waved away.

Was *this* why I'd driven him south to Monemvasia? He'd told me not to talk too much to women, yet there he was reeling off his characteristic soliloquys – no doubt beguiling her with startling imagery and metaphorical unity. Shouldn't he be silently observing her and making assured gynaecological assessments based on her mascara?

I found myself saying, 'Bastounis says that all women, at some elemental subliminal level, want to be sexually possessed.'

The girl paused, a forkful of Greek salad before her lips.

'I mean... He'd say that your lack of a bra tonight, and your fresh nail polish, and your washed hair and eye make-up, and the way we inadvertently touched arms are all unconscious displays of urgent sexual ardour aimed at me.'

The words gushed as a terrifyingly thrilling logorrhoea. To say what one actually thought – what a revelation! What a horror.

She returned the fork to the bowl.

'I *am* wearing a bra, actually. And if I made myself look pretty, it's for myself. Not for you.'

'See, that's exactly what *I* told *him*! But he said that's something women only tell themselves because they're unaware of their animal urges. He claims to know the stage of a woman's ovulation just by looking at them. For instance … Well, he's obviously wrong. It's his generation, I suppose. Pre-feminist.'

'For instance what? You started to say something.'

'Did I? It's nothing. I suppose I'm just angry with him.'

'Have you discussed *my* menstrual cycle with him?'

'Me? No! *He* did. I'm sorry. He's an old man. He said you're probably mid-cycle, but …'

Her mouth opened slightly. She appeared to blush.

'Sorry,' I said. 'Sorry. It's really not my … It's nobody's business.' I was glad not to have mentioned Bastounis's claim that she'd have erotic dreams about him. I put food automatically into my mouth and wished I'd ordered meat.

Without further words, and as a form of necessary distraction, we returned to our preoccupations. She attended to her screen with somewhat aggressive swipes and taps; I watched the author down the street. He was still talking with the sculptor lady but now they had food on the table. She was smiling, even laughing, and his gestures had become more expansive. I wondered vaguely whether he'd organised this *tableau vivant* as an exemplary lesson for me: a demonstration both of how it should and shouldn't be done.

'She's a very attractive older woman,' I said. 'I mean, I'm sure you'll age beautifully, too … Wait, that didn't really come out right …'

She looked sidelong at me. 'What's my name?'

'Your …? You haven't told me your name.'

'You haven't *asked*. But you noticed I'm not wearing a bra.'

'You said you *are* wearing a bra.'

'I *am*.'

She took a fabric wallet from her trouser pocket and put notes on the table. She pushed her chair back, stood and held out her hand for a shake.

'No hard feelings? Enjoy your relationship with the great author.'

I shook her hand (she had a good grip) and watched her walk without turning down the street towards Bastounis. Would she stop, bend to greet him and say something about her fallopians, about my ineptitude and about the feckless race of men in general? Perhaps he'd turn and point me out to sculptor lady and the three of them would laugh. But the girl kept on walking and Bastounis didn't seem to notice her.

I got the waiter's attention and ordered a plate of *souvlaki*.

I was asleep when he returned to the room. His dragging footsteps and clumsy pinballing among the furniture suggested he was drunk, as did the extravagant vomiting that echoed from the tiny, airless toilet next door. Then I had to listen to a prolonged and complicated bowel movement – all visceral gurgling, wet vibration, spelaean splashes and moans. His rhythmic snoring was soothing in comparison.

But I couldn't get back to sleep for a long time after. The air was as blood-hot and a mosquito whined intermittently at my ears. I thought of the girl and tried to rationalise why I hadn't asked her name. Had she asked *mine*? Were such things even important? Should I have also asked her age and nationality? They were irrelevancies – just data for official forms or a CV. A name given to a person was no more meaningful or true than a Linnaean tag pinned to a butterfly, or a collar on a dog – just an imposed classification one has to acknowledge and live under.

Such thoughts had exasperated Clara. She'd said I was aberrant and wilfully perverse. Maybe I'd got it from Bastounis and other favourite writers, who'd made it seem like there was another way to live. Independently. Consciously. Wilfully. It was only in that wilderness of aporia after university that I realised I'd spent my life previously as an unthinking passenger on a prescribed journey: kindergarten, school, college, university, job, retirement, death. No choice in the matter. No question at each transition whether I wanted the next stage, or whether there was any alternative. Leaving Clara was the first real decision I'd made. Was it Melville who'd said that he dated his life from his early twenties – that he'd developed not at all prior to that?

There was a sense of urgency. So much time had already been wasted and I'd only just begun. Bastounis had been fifteen – fifteen! – when he'd run off with those gypsies. Twenty when he'd gone to sea. Almost my age now when he'd jumped ship in California. And what had *I* done? Read some books. Got a certificate for it. Failed to ask a girl her name and fatally misread the outline of her underwear. Such thoughts would keep anyone awake.

SEVEN

Next morning found us on the road again, Bastounis pale and sombre in the passenger seat. He'd spoken rarely and only with telegraphic brevity since we'd picked up the car and headed over to the small fishing village of Gytheio. Hungover? Or perhaps nursing the secret of whatever had happened with the glamorous woman. There was no likelihood of him telling me, or of my asking.

The road was virtually empty – a narrow asphalt ribbon through low-level villages, scrubby orange groves and cuttings through hills whose fractured, ferric rock looked prehistoric. Above us, the featureless blue vault of that Indian summer. It was a minor road to and from nowhere in particular, tracing the lazy arch at the top of the Laconic Gulf.

Laconic gulf – a perfect synopsis of the situation in the car: the author seemingly unwilling to reveal anything about himself and the young nobody with little to reveal. It was absurd. Imagine being married to the man. He'd be alone, writing, and unreachable in his canyon of introspection – visible, but out of range. He'd return only when ready, whereupon the charisma would gush and all wounds would be healed. Until they weren't. Until the build-up of scar tissue rendered his victim finally unfeeling and impervious. Had the woman in Monemvasia been one of those?

We drove. I was getting used to the Peugeot now, learning its foibles and responses. It was my servant as I was Bastounis's and I was growing to appreciate its stolid obedience. There were no tricks, no betrayals in its assured steering and undramatic braking. I wondered what Bastounis thought about me, if he thought about me at all. About half an hour into the trip, he said:

'Why don't you just spit it out?'

'What?'

'You've been clearing your throat and taking breaths for the last five minutes as if you were going to say something. Then you swallow it. Speak! Unspoken words are like restrained farts – they'll bloat you and rot your insides.'

'Well, it seems kind of absurd that we don't talk, doesn't it?'

'We're talking now.'

'Yes, but I started it.'

'No. I started it. You were gulping and panting like child at the teat. I'm listening. Go on.'

'There's so much … Okay. Let me ask you. You never went to university right? You just read for your own interest on the cargo ships, at the … in Macao and when you got to California. Did you miss, I don't know, the structure of a standard education?'

'I seem to have done all right without it.'

'No, I didn't mean—'

'I know want you meant – you just phrased it execrably. I didn't go to university because, first, I didn't have the option and, later, because it wasn't necessary. The books exist without the course. Why should I spend three years patiently waiting for someone to give me a list of books and then talk about them with a load of young people as ignorant as I am? University now is about getting wrecked and reading half a book on the night you write a synoptic essay. Then someone who's too busy and underpaid to care gives you a grade. What does this grade mean? That you're *qualified*? Qualified to do what? Does it mean you've perceived the depths of Shakespeare or Beckett or Melville? Young people know nothing. University is futile – a hothouse for delicate flowers who need a label to prove their provenance. Nobody understands a book after reading it once and writing an essay about it. You have to live with a book, read it over and over – and read it at different stages of your life. You think any sixteen-year-old grasps the black, haunted nihilism of *Macbeth*? You think anyone at all fathoms *Moby Dick* at a single reading? I've *lived* with books. On the cargo ships, there'd be nothing to do for weeks and months. It was just you and your bunk and the engines and whatever book you had to hand. A novel is a world – do you see that? A world must be inhabited, not merely viewed from the glancing orbit of a satellite. University? I pity you your university. It's not your fault. Education now is just another product to be packaged and advertised and bought. We learn nothing worthwhile unless we learn it alone. I include writing in that. Creative Writing courses... ha!'

'But didn't you teach the course at Iowa for—?'

'For the money! Sure, you get one really promising writer in every hundred that turn up in your class. It's probably the same percentage out in the world. But that's where the real writers are. They're sitting at a desk in an office somewhere, despising everything about their lives. They're shovelling shit or digging graves or driving buses – adrift in life's incoordinate futility with only the lifebelt of writing to keep them from drowning. That's when you really write: when it's your very breath. Not for grades. Not for discussion in a fucking workshop. And not as some form of masturbatory delusion. Writing is about not drowning.'

'Are you…Are you researching a book now? On this trip, I mean?'

His head turned slowly. 'Why do you ask?'

I kept my eyes on the road. 'Well, you know…I mean, where are we going? And why to these places? Is it such a big secret that you don't tell me where I'm driving from day to day? Why Gytheio, for example?'

I gripped the wheel and waited for the explosion that must surely result from such impertinence. Instead, there was just the buzz of the road for interminable seconds.

'Did Kostas say anything in Nafplio?' said Bastounis.

'Only something about an unpublished manuscript or plans for a book.'

'Hmm. People can't let go, can they? They want another Led Zeppelin album, or a previously unpublished Kafka story. What's wrong with what they have?'

'But you must understand it. You haven't published for twenty or more years and…'

'And what? People *deserve* another book? Am I some galley slave to fawn and pander to the market? I write for *myself.* Yes, and also for money, but…'

He held up his palms and shrugged. The magnitude of his "but" was a solar system of unexpressed complications: the ex-wives, the gambling, the legal fees. Perhaps his refusal to write another book was his retaliation against all of that. His only power. Why share it?

'Has anyone asked you about this?' said Bastounis. 'About a book?'

'Who would ask me? I've been with you the whole time, pretty much.'

He nodded slowly and stroked his stubble.

'I mean, there was a strange situation in Nafplio. In the square.'

He turned to me. 'What situation?'

'Just some guy in a café. He started talking to me about Dimitsana and asked if I knew a writer lived there. I didn't answer him. Oh, and he asked how I'd travelled to Nafplio from the village. It was bit weird, but I don't think he mentioned your name at all.'

'Is that it?'

'That's it. I think saw him again at the dock when we were leaving. He was making a phone call.'

'What did he look like?'

'Pretty nondescript. Hair, shirt, shaved. I'm not sure if he was Greek. The accent was a strange mixture of something.'

'Have you seen him since? In Monemvasia?'

'No ... but I wasn't really looking.'

'Hmm. A Greek American, perhaps. Being overfriendly. They can be like that: exaggerating their ancestry into a pantomime of Greekness.'

We joined a larger road heading south to Gytheio. There were more cars, this being the main road north to Sparta and looping south to Kalamata. The landscape seemed lusher than at Monemvasia. There were olive groves and what looked like pastureland for sheep or goats. Many of the vehicles were vans or trucks carrying agricultural produce. A pair of sheep watched us indifferently from the back of a Toyota pick-up as I overtook.

Bastounis seemed to be brooding. Had I lost him again to his meditative crevasse? Maybe I could keep his attention a little longer.

'My date didn't go too well last night. With the blonde girl.'

'Oh?'

'No. It was a bit of a mismatch. And she couldn't keep her eyes of her phone.'

'What did I tell you about that?'

'Right. And besides, I think she was looking for something different.'

'Of course she was. And so were you. That's the problem with your generation. Not only yours, but especially yours. Call it the curse of postmodernism. You all think you're living inside a movie or a sitcom – as if cameras are watching you at every moment. I've observed it. The exaggerated gestures and expressions. The catchphrases. You've absorbed so much TV and cinema that it's warped your sense of reality inside out. Your notions of romance or heroism or lust or enlightenment are not your own – not real. But you live by them as if they're ideals, sensing vaguely that there's something wrong with you because you don't feel what you expected, or what you were supposed to feel. The ideal you've unthinkingly embraced is an empty, fictional myth.'

'I thought you were a big fan of mythology.'

'That's different.'

'But the Homeric heroes—'

'No. The heroes of Troy didn't get their warrior cult and cosmogony from fiction – though it's become that. Their ideals were woven into their lives and culture. They communed directly with their gods. Theirs was an ideal of action, not of the camera's passive gaze.'

'I...I don't feel there's a camera on me all the time.'

'Maybe not consciously. But you're a prisoner of the unseen script. When you met this girl last night, you both came to the rendezvous with expectations of how it would go. Not *plans*, you see, but *expectations*. The scene would unfold to its own logic and pattern, taking you with it as passengers. A script. You'd say this; she'd say that. Stage directions. Close-up. But there *is no script*! Only in your indoctrinated minds is there a pattern or a narrative destiny. And what actually happens? The words don't come – or at least not as expected. The two would-be lovers flounder in the gap between reality and fiction, waiting and hoping for a plot to take over. There is no plot! There's no existential author. We, alone, are responsible.'

I drove, gripping the wheel. His words were loosening the conceptual bedrock under me, hinting at a void yawning beneath.

'In fact…Yes – let's make this your third challenge: understand that life is not a movie, not a plot. There is no inevitability. You are not at the centre of any lens. There's no performance. It's all real. Awesomely, terrifyingly real. Accept that, and you start to live. Or, at least, you case to be a cipher.'

'So I've failed the observation challenge…'

'You've failed nothing yet. These challenges are not singular or temporally unique. They stand for an entire lifespan. Learn them and apply them. Try again. Nothing worthwhile is easy. It's a fight. You know ancient Greek tragedy right?'

'A little… Euripides, Sophocles—'

'Right. So you'll know that the core of the play is the *agon*: the conflict between two characters – each representing some elemental force or reason. It's where we get the word "agony". That's fiction – fine – but it drew its fundamental truth from the struggle I'm talking about: the fight for control and to live life honestly, righteously, fully…As a man.'

I saw the final turn towards Gytheio and flicked the indicator. Its rhythmic clicking was a metronome. I waited for more from Bastounis but he'd gone again into whatever abyss his thoughts had sent him.

'And how was *your* evening?' I ventured. 'Did you spend time with your friend?'

'My friend?' His eyes were on the road.

'The old man we stayed with.'

'I had a very pleasant evening. Thank-you.'

I waited. I sensed there was something more. I thought he was on the edge of telling me about the woman. But no.

'You asked me earlier why Gytheio,' he said. 'It's not our destination. We have no particular destination. It's about the journey. As for Gytheio, we're here for one reason only: to eat. Now pay attention – the traffic along the front can be hell.'

We left the car up a side street and I walked with Bastounis along the seafront. The promenade was lined with rows of sun umbrellas shading ranks of tables and chairs, mostly empty in the dregs of the season. Even the sea looked apathetic: a vitreous plate stretching off into heat haze. Lacklustre waiters lounged at their respective tavernas over the road, ready to dance through the traffic with a menu and a glib professional patter at the prospect of a diner.

Bastounis nullified any such offers with a raised hand and a curt word. Most seemed to sense he was no idle customer. In his Ray Bans and his cap, he might have been a fisherman going home to sleep. Though limping with his stick, he went eagerly ahead of me as the traffic curled around us. We stopped at a place called *Omorfi Tavernaki* and he tottered through a room of empty tables to a dim galley-style kitchen where a man stood smoking as he stirred a pan.

'*Oriste!*' said the cook without looking up.

Bastounis said something in reply and the man turned with a slow grin. It was just as it had been with Konstantinopoulos and with the old man in

Monemvasia – that recognitory illumination he evoked in people: the embracing, the kissing, the shaking hands and the laughter.

They talked and I stood on the threshold between street and interior: a shadow at the door. Presently, the cook nodded towards me as if to say, 'Is he with you?' and Bastounis responded with some terse encapsulation of my function. He turned to me.

'You want to eat inside or outside?'

'Outside is cooler... And there's a view.'

The cook shrugged magnanimously and said something to Bastounis.

'Choose a table,' said the author. 'I'll order.'

I crossed the road and took a seat facing the small islet just along the coast. The paper tablecloth was stained with the evidence of previous diners' meals: an irregular punctuation of oil parentheses, full-stop breadcrumbs, cedillas of rice. Tomato-sauce tildes. The sides of the wooden chair were sticky where I gripped it to move closer to the table.

Bastounis emerged carrying a basket of bread and a carafe of rose-coloured wine with two glasses sitting in its neck. His stick was looped over a forearm. I stood to help.

'Sit, sit! I'm fine. Try this wine. He makes it himself in his village and keeps a barrel in the bar there.'

He poured it into the two stubby toothglasses and held his up for a toast. 'To good food!'

We clinked glasses. The wine was cool, sweet and floral – a light taste. I felt I could probably drink a litre of it right away.

'Mm. It's tasty. What are we eating?'

'I've asked Michaelis to prepare a feast of *mezedes* – you know what that is, right? Like tapas? Some meat, some fish, some vegetables... a proper exposition of the Greek kitchen.'

'Is this one of the challenges?'

'You mean like one of those hotdog-eating competitions in America? Or like that scene in Tony Burgess's book about the spy who tries to out-eat the villain? No. No such thing. But wait... Maybe it can be a challenge: a challenge to appreciate the senses more fully. The senses are everything – all we truly know. Protagoras said that the soul was nothing but our senses. For that, they said all of his books should be destroyed.'

He drank off the glass and poured more. 'How many people truly learn to savour food, for example? I'm not talking about Greeks, of course, or any of the Latin peoples. But you Northern Europeans – yes, and the Americans – you starve your senses. You toss them a treat now and then as if they're a begging dog. Pleasure with you is something to be rationed, feared and repented. Do you think a Greek or an Italian ever asks how many calories are in the crust he uses to swab the oil from his finished plate? Ha! Eat with your mouth, your nose and your eyes – not with your goddamn logic! It's all there in Epicurus: pleasure is the first principle directing all action. And pleasure comes primarily through the senses. I'll show you. What have you been eating since you've been in Greece?'

'*Mousaka*, Greek salad, *souvlaki*...'

'Right: tourist food. You'll see. Ah, here he comes.'

Michaelis wove between cars to bring a tray of small dishes that he laid on the table with their names: '*Fava, melitsanasalata kai horta. Kali orexi!*' There was also a cruet with olive oil and balsamic vinegar.

'Did you hear that?' said Bastounis. '"Kali orexi" means good appetite. There's not even a term for that in English, is there? You're forced to use the French! You might as well use a phrase like "Go easy now" or "Not too much!" Okay– what we have here is fava bean puree topped with chopped raw onions and paprika, aubergine salad, and wild greens.'

He upended the bottle of olive oil over the fava and the *horta*, squeezing a half lemon over the latter before mixing the chopped onions into the fava. He ripped a hunk from the bread, scooped a trench through the *fava* with it and pushed it into his mouth.

'What are you waiting for?' he said, his mouth half full.

'Will we get serving plates or something?'

'Serving plates? Christ! Maybe you'd like someone to eat it for you and write a report! Get some bread and fucking eat like a human!'

I repeated what he'd done and steered it to my mouth.

'Now,' he said. 'Can you taste the sharpness of the onions in there? The richness of the oil, slightly piquant? It's from his own olives. Feel it all cloying your palate with flavour and nipping at your tongue? But the bread gives it body, no?'

I nodded. It was good.

Bastounis jabbed his fork into the *horta* and lofted it across the table, green tendrils dripping oil, into an ecstatic mouth. His stubble glistened like Neptune's.

I followed suit, surprised how sweet the greens tasted – not at all like the gagging, cupric altruism of kale. They were soft and silky in the mouth.

Michaelis arrived with more plates and shifted the salads aside for space. Here were small grilled sausages, meatballs in tomato sauce, slices of battered and deep-fried courgette, and a small pot of some rich-looking stew that smelled amazing.

'*Stifado*,' said Bastounis, stirring the stew to reveal whole baby onions conjured into oleaginous pearls. 'Rabbit stew. Now, listen – this is how we eat: a mouthful of this, a

mouthful of that – balance, contrast, juxtaposition. A bite
of sausage, then a fork of *horta*; a meatball, then a scoop
of fava, see? The bread works in-between for soaking sauce
and clearing the palate. Right?'

I nodded, cutting into a sausage even as Bastounis
squeezed lemon onto it. It tasted like no other sausage I'd
eaten: an eruption of meat and seasoning that rendered
every previous burger or sausage a pale imposter. It had texture. It was palpably and unashamedly animal. And there
was something else: a sweet surprise...'

'Orange zest!' said Bastounis through a mouthful. 'He
grinds it with the meat. His own recipe.'

I thought I might weep when I ate the *stifado*. The rabbit dissolved with no need for teeth. The sauce was rich
and gamey, each jewelled onion a small bomb of sweetness.
Bread absorbed the red-orange sauce hungrily. Emulating
Bastounis, I alternated a taste of meat with a taste of fava or
aubergine salad so that every mouthful was a different taste
and texture. The wine and bread were soon gone and we
ordered more.

'Eat! Eat!' said Bastounis. 'What do you like the most?'

'I couldn't say ... The *stifado*. The sausage? I love the
horta.'

'What about the meatballs? Describe the taste.'

'God...they're so well seasoned, so tender. Sweet,
almost. The mild acidity of the tomato somehow comple-
ments the meat.'

'Yes, that's it! Exactly.'

Next came the fish dishes: a mound of tiny deep-fried
things mere centimetres long, grilled octopus legs, and
octopus in a red-wine sauce that shone and undulated
darkly. The combinations were multiplying. Each new
mouthful was a game of possibilities. Even as I plucked a

tender tentacle from its viscous depths, I was thinking about the next mouthful and the next: a gustatory chess in which checkmate was a wasteland of crust-smeared plates and bulging waistlines.

Bastounis was slowing his pace, but still ate like a man faced with his last meal. At one point, we both went for the last piece of bread in the basket and he deferred to me with a wink that filled me with almost as much satisfaction as the octopus legs. I'd done something right. I was learning to gorge myself on food that was more than just bulk or sustenance. Somehow, this cornucopia – this calculus of flavour combinations – had awakened something in my primitive brain that told me I was eating for the first time: eating not only with my mouth and throat but with my eyes and whatever glands were secreting the pleasure chemicals that made this a form of multi-sensory music.

I thought Michaelis had finished when the plates stopped coming for around ten minutes, but his final tray contained a plate of water melon slices, a plate of deep-fried mini doughnuts soaked in syrup, and a couple of *baklava* triangles. There were also two balloon glasses of dark liquor.

'Metaxa, seven star,' said Bastounis, sniffing his glass.

'I don't think…I can eat any more,' I said leaning back in my chair and unbuttoning my shorts.

'Ha! Will you let an old man beat you?'

'You said it wasn't a competition.'

'I challenge you to eat only one of the *loukoumades*: the tiny doughnuts. Try it. Just one.'

I forked one of the balls from its syrup slick and dropped it into my mouth. Impossibly soft and light, yet with a gravitational fulsomeness of flavour, the tiny globe burst its sweetness against my tongue.

'Holy Jesus, that's good!'

'Now try to stop yourself eating another.'

I ate five more, jousting with Bastounis with clinking forks for the last one. The *baklava* filled my mouth as an organ recital fills a cathedral, or so it seemed as I sweated in the final throes. My arms were heavy and my breathing shallow. Had I eaten so much that my thorax was short of space?

'I think… I think I'm going to die.'

'*Kali orexi*! Drink your brandy. It's good for digestion.'

The spirit rolled over my tonsils like a tropical sunset.

Bastounis, too, leaned back in his chair. He dabbed his stubble with a napkin and belched. 'See the islet there? That's Marathonisi, anciently known as Cranae. It's where Paris and Helen spent their first night together after he abducted her. One night of passion for ten years of war at Ilium.'

'I guess she must have been worth it.'

Bastounis looked out at the island. 'Would *I* have brought war upon a nation for the most beautiful woman in the world? I think so. I would have done it then. I would do it now if Helen were willing. Is that the ultimate selfishness, or the ultimate expression of humanity?'

I had no answer to that. I wasn't even sure if that was his real question. Satiety had brought on some melancholy in him beyond my understanding.

He seemed about to say more when Michaelis arrived to collect the plates and spoke with Bastounis, handing him a key. The cook then turned to me:

'Good? You like my food?'

'You're a genius.'

He nodded in acknowledgement and went back across the road.

Bastounis pushed the key across the spattered table to me. 'Michaelis has a room in the street behind the kitchen.

Number 27. You take the keys and go. I need to talk to him for a while. Leave the door open for me, okay?'

His tone was emotionless. I was the unpaid driver again – just like that. His gaze was set on the islet. He took his sunglasses out of his breast pocket and put them on, blacking his eyes. Closing the curtain.

'Oh … right. I'll see you later.'

He unhooked his stick from the edge of the table and began working the crook in his hands. He didn't watch me leave. It was as if I'd already gone.

EIGHT

I waddled towards the room carrying my lunch like a delayed pregnancy. Number 27 was an inconspicuous door to an unremarkable one-bedroom flat that smelled of air freshener and cleaning solutions. The two single beds were neatly made up with their sheets folded back – a woman's touch.

I dropped to the nearest bed and lay on my back. My face shone with perspiration. It seemed that a cough or a sneeze might cause some membrane inside me to pop and rip agonisingly. If I could just lie still for three or four hours, I'd be safe.

As at Monemvasia, the thought occurred that nobody knew where I was. I'd not emailed or tweeted or Instagrammed anyone. I was back in the twentieth century. If I died here from a surfeit of *loukoumades* – my body found bloated but with a curious beatific smile – nobody would know what I'd been doing here, where I'd been, where I was going. It'd be a mystery. For sure, Bastounis wouldn't stick around to answer questions. I might as well have dreamed him.

For that matter, he seemed a ghost in his own life, renouncing his fame and haunting the places of his past glories. He was appearing now to people who hadn't seen him for years – people who might have imagined him long ago dead. He was my spirit guide in a realm new to both of us. Who had been Aeneas's guide in Hades? Had that been Heracles…?

In the fever of my overconsumption, I dreamed Homeric scenes: myself in armour on a ship of many oarsmen. I held a great leather shield. Odysseus was our captain, but he was also Bastounis. "Tie me to the mast," he commanded us, "that I might hear the Sirens sing without losing my mind." I was supposed to push beeswax into my ears for protection, but I couldn't seal the join and the choral cadences reached me from the shore. The madness of pleasure threatened…

I woke suddenly to the sound of shouting in the street: a man's enraged barking and a woman's shrieks. It didn't seem to be Greek. Romanian? Turkish? Armenian?

The woman's shoes clattered. The man's threats reverberated between houses. She was knocking at doors, screeching, apparently in fear for her life. I sat up on the bed. The door was unlocked. She was coming closer, rapping on doors, begging for access at each as the man's growling threats came closer. I fumbled for the key among tangled sheets.

Her hand hammered flat against the door, her tumbling pleas or prayers rising in pitch as he stalked her. I felt the key wrapped in cotton. The door handle rattled and I watched it turn.

She burst inside: a woman of perhaps thirty, her blonde-streaked hair wild around her face, her red lipstick a diagonal smear, her mascara a black massacre of ribbons down her cheeks. Her eyes were burning. She slammed the door behind her and looked for a latch or a key. She turned and saw me sitting futilely on the bed. She held a finger to her lips and whispered entreaties fast and foreign but compellingly clear. She frantically mimed a turning key.

His voice came closer to the door: a low, stalking promise of destruction. *I see you. There's no escape. You think a door will stop me? And if you have a man in there … Just you wait.*

I was rigid with terror. She mimed to me that I should toss her the key I now had in my slippery hand. I did so. She snatched it from its parabola and rattled it into the lock with a triumphant gesture just as the thunder of his fists and feet and execrations rained upon the door.

Now her demeanour changed. Hands on hips, she sneered, she jeered, she kicked the back of the door as his tirade thrashed against the other side. "Think you own me?" she might have said. "Where are your threats now? Go ahead – beat the door. Bloody your fists on something more intelligent than yourself!"

I wondered whether I might wet myself. At any moment, the door would burst inwards on a wind of splinters and the man, insane with goaded fury, would beat me sense-less before killing the woman and framing me for it. Why couldn't she have chosen the opposite side of the street!

Other voices joined the fracas outside. This was, after all, siesta time. The scene had probably woken everyone. His hammering stopped and his voice faded as he stamped away, muttering and occasionally shouting Tourette's-style. A humid silence returned.

The woman again acknowledged my existence, clasping her hands in heartfelt thanks and jerking her thumb outside in voluble condemnation of her boyfriend. Or so I inter-preted. I recognised nothing in her language. She might have been a migrant, judging from her hair, Anatolian eyes and dark skin. I noticed only now a gaudiness to her that I hadn't seen in Greek women: a fondness for gold, glitter and colour. Her high-heeled shoes had the red soles I knew signi-fied some hallmark of style (if genuine) and her tight jeans had leopard-print trim. The Lycra of her peach-coloured top was a sheath around her bounteous bust. She must have been wearing at least eight rings on her red-lacquered fingers, and a very thin one though her nostril. There was something feral in her stance, emphasised by the chaos of her make-up and general dishevelment. She could have been a bacchanal just returned from a sylvan rage through the forests with Pan – a frenzy of dismemberment.

She sat on the other bed and wiped the mascara from her face with the back of her hand, showing it to me with bitter mirth. I laughed politely, still shaking from the stress. What did she expect was going to happen now?

I looked to the tiny kitchen area in search of tea-making facilities. Tea would solve any short-term problem. Even Bastounis would have to admit that English contribution to the life worth living. I mimed drinking and she nodded, kissing her fingers at me in some gesture of gratitude.

I was looking for a kettle when the door handle rattled.

The woman screamed and pulled off a shoe to use for stabbing.

'What are you doing in there?' called Bastounis. 'Open the door.'

Signalling frantically to the woman that this was a friend, I unlocked the door and Bastounis entered. He removed his sunglasses and stood looking at the woman. He turned to me with a sly smile.

'I don't know what you're thinking,' I said. 'Her boy-friend was chasing her and she just came in while I was asleep. He was trying to batter the door down and she was screaming. I don't think she speaks English. I was about to make her a cup of tea …'

Bastounis observed her. She put her shoe back on. She raised her chin defiantly and swept hair from her face with a "So what?" gesture.

He spoke to her in her language – calmly but firmly – and she smiled with a mixture of relief, surprise and coquettishness. Her perilous situation was turning to advantage and the transformation in her was remarkable. She was forming a connection to Bastounis, her saviour, virtually as I watched – actually flirting with him, maelstrom make-up and Medusa hair no hindrance.

Bastounis opened the fridge and found some bottles of mineral water. He poured her a glass and drank one himself as she talked. Finally, he turned to me.

'She was trying to leave her boyfriend without his knowledge but he caught her. He threatened to cut her. She says "boyfriend", but she may mean pimp. Obviously, she can't go back to him. You have to go and collect her bag.'

'What?'

'*She* can't go. He'll beat and cut her. *I* can't go – I'm too unstable to be getting into a knife fight. My leg. My eyes. I can't do that anymore. But you … You'll be safe.'

'How do you figure that?'

He sighed. 'Really? I have to explain this? You'll be safe because you're no threat to him. He'll look at you and know immediately that you're not her lover or protector. You'll be an obvious messenger: some guy she's persuaded to help. Speak English – it'll confuse him and protect you. Use complicated vocabulary – it'll give you a psychological edge.'

He asked the woman something and she replied with one word.

'Okay, so the guy speaks a little English. He won't be fluent.'

'Are you serious? I'm not going. You didn't hear him shouting and knocking. He's angry. He won't be thinking logically. He might think she's run off with me.'

Bastounis translated this to the woman and they laughed.

'Look at her,' he said. 'Remember your second challenge about observing? You think this is a woman who'd run away with *you*?'

I looked at her in her skin-tight jeans, her jutting bust, her wild hair and her cosmetic disarray. Even in this condition, she was a voluptuary. Barely a decade older than me, she could conceivably have been my pre-teen-pregnancy mother.

'I'm not doing it. It's crazy. Get the police to intervene.'

'The police? The police don't care about this. Besides, they're all asleep at this time. Consider it your next challenge—'

'Enough of the challenges! I'm not getting beaten up just to prove something. There's no wisdom in that.'

The woman looked between us. She seemed to understand the stalemate. She shuffled off the bed and kneeled by the side of mine, holding my knees with her polished talons, cooing in supplication. "Please go and get my bag for me," she seemed to say. "I'm sure he won't hit you more than twenty or thirty times. You might even be unconscious after the first few blows. You'll feel almost nothing…"

Bastounis tapped his walking stick irritably against the marble tiles. 'So you'd make this woman go back to him on her own? Maybe he'd take her back, but you'd have her scars on your conscience. A man like that – he's not going to allow this kind of rebellion in his woman. She'll have to be punished. Something to remember the occasion by. A painful cut somewhere out of sight.'

'It's *their* life! *Their* problem! It has nothing to do with us.'

'It does now, doesn't it? She's here. We're already involved. This is the challenge we all face at some point. Do we recognise and face our fears? Or do we meekly accept our failures and live with them, accreting a carapace of inaction and apathy to protect ourselves from taking responsibility – to protect ourselves from *truly* living? We progress and evolve as humans only by facing and overcoming our fears. Or else we live as victims. Didn't you feel fear when you left your home to travel here? Didn't you wonder at all the things that might go wrong? Of course you did – that's human nature. But you did it anyway. The plane might have crashed. You might have been robbed in Athens. You might have been run over or stricken with some illness.'

'But I *wanted* to travel. I don't *want* to face this ... thug.'

'Right. But sometimes the options are not what we want or what we expect. They're beyond our control. They're the big decisions in life. Not choosing what toaster to buy, but choosing what kind of person you're going to be. These decisions have only two possible outcomes: growth or diminution. You become greater and stronger, or you accept your failure and gradually fade into nothingness. Which state is easier to live with?'

'It's all rhetoric ... It's just sophistry what you're saying.'

'Is it? Is it? Maybe if you were reading it in a self-help book, perhaps, or paying a few hundred dollars to hear it at a seminar. Look at my nose. You see that?'

'I know. It was broken in the ring.'

'Broken, yes. I was knocked out and humiliated in that fight. Out of my depth. It was the first time I'd genuinely felt fear at the strength of an opponent. But I fought. I had to – there was no choice right then. It's easier when you have no choice. The difficult part was going back later. Would I be the man who gave in after his first defeat? What kind of man would that be? Better to go back and be beaten again.'

'You said I *wouldn't* be beaten by this guy!'

'You won't be. If I know anything about men, you won't be.'

The woman was still on her knees, her hands stroking my lower legs as she plied those big brown eyes.

'Please,' she said, the foreign word thick with unfamiliarity in her mouth. 'Please help.'

I walked the street on legs of rubber. It was nearing the end of siesta and everything was still quiet. The sea glittered at me through gaps in the buildings.

I walked as an automaton, driven by no conscious compulsion or volition. This was something I comprehensively did not want to do. If there was a God, or any suprahuman force at work, I waited for it to intervene with some salvation. Better to be run over or hit by a meteorite than go wilfully into danger.

I walked slowly, invoking Zeno's paradox that a set distance can never be covered due to its infinitely subdivided increments. But relentless physics drew me ever closer to number three and certain violence.

My plan was to walk nonchalantly past the door in reconnaissance. The guy had no idea who I was or that I'd been behind the door of twenty-seven. If there were broken windows, flames or signs of armed ambush, I'd continue walking. I checked to see if there were any other people around to hear my screams, but the town was sleeping.

And then a golden ray of fortune. A suitcase sat on the top step outside number three. A lurid purple-patterned suitcase with a ribbon attached to its handle. The house itself – a whitewashed concrete box with closed shutters – seemed vacant.

I veered across the street and approached the steps on the same side. He wouldn't see me at this oblique angle. I'd just grab the case and keep walking at the same pace, looping around the block to glory and gratitude back at twenty-seven.

I gripped the handle and lifted. The case didn't budge. What did she have in it – a set of encyclopaedias? I hoisted. The door opened and he was standing there.

A squat man with colossal shoulders and a hairline starting just above his eyebrows. There was a tattoo creeping out of his collar onto his neck. He had a stiff-looking mullet. An Adidas T-shirt was stretched tight over untrained muscle. He looked at me like I was an insect in his coffee.

'Who are you?' (*Hu err yu?*)

'Er, hi! Hello. I'm just taking the suitcase if that's okay. I was sent here as…as an emissary to retrieve the lady's possessions.'

'*Emisar?*'

Trust me to choose a word that was the same in his language. He examined me as he might something unusual he'd expectorated. A smirk played at the corners of his mouth.

'So, anyway,' I said. 'I'll just be taking this and…'

He rested a huge hairy hand on top of the suitcase and leaned close to me, his breath sour with garlic and salami.

'You tell *kurva* bitch she dead, okay? I find her. I know. You tell.'

'I tell. Yes.'

His hand stayed on the suitcase. His eyes bored into me, looking for a reason to brutalise me. My smile was a piano wire.

He stood and stepped back into the house. 'Go, *emisar.* Tell.'

I strained to lift the case and dragged it on its rattling wheels back along the road, my ignominy magnified by its garish colour and by the fact that he watched me as I went. Would he wait until I was almost there and charge after me? The case weighed about 30 kilos and twisted reluctantly behind me.

I quickened my pace on rounding the corner. The baggage's trundling mass was impossibly loud in the narrow street. I visualised Bastounis waiting for me at the open door.

He wasn't. I ran the final steps and almost fell into the flat.

The woman gasped at my sudden arrival. Her eyes were wild. She was kneeling over the prostrate form of Bastounis on the marble floor.

I froze amid a blizzard of suppositions. She'd clubbed him. She was robbing him. It was all a set-up. Now the tattooed troglodyte would come and empty the flat. Perhaps he'd violate me: the over-polite *emisar*.

'What… What's going on? What are you doing?'

I saw now that she was slapping his face in an attempt to bring him round. The mascara was once again flowing and I understood. If Bastounis was dead, this animal-print Jezebel would almost certainly face jail. Imagine the headlines: *Gypsy Whore Kills Nobel Laureate*. Never mind an autopsy or investigation.

I stood there holding the absurd purple suitcase. I knew no first aid. I'd be as implicated as she would, but because of my utter ineffectuality. *Tourist Graduate Lets Nobel Winner Die. Impotently Holds Decorative Suitcase.*

I knelt beside her and looked at him. Very pale. Shallow breathing. Eyelids not entirely closed. No use asking her what had happened. Recovery position? I indicated to her that we should roll him and I wrestled his arms and legs into angles I vaguely remembered. That's when he came round

He jerked briefly and opened his eyes. He seemed shocked to be on the floor looking up.

'What happened?' I said. 'Did you faint? I found her trying to slap you awake.'

He levered himself onto an elbow, still worryingly pale. He looked around and found his cap, setting it back on his head. He was clearly angry and embarrassed at the attention.

'Nothing. It's nothing. Too much wine and food ... The heat, you know. Stand back. Give me some space.'

I stepped back and urged the woman to do the same.

'Did you get the case?' he said.

I pointed to it.

'Bravo. I wasn't sure you would. How do you feel?'

'I've had better days.'

He looked around for his stick. I offered my hand and pulled him up. He sat on the edge of a bed and said something to the woman, who clacked to the kitchen area to get him water.

'Better days?' he said, taking the glass. 'I don't think so. You'll remember this day for the rest of your life. The meal, the woman, the pimp. I said there'd be monsters, didn't I? Today you faced a monster and survived. You've captured the cattle of Geryon. Or perhaps the mare of Diomedes is a better one. You don't feel it yet. You almost never feel things when they happen. They need distance and reflection. Trust me – in twenty years the story of this day will be like one of those knives you see in village houses: honed to a new moon.'

'I'll take your word for it.'

The woman – cause of all my terror – was now joyfully reunited with her suitcase. She put an arm around my waist and laid an enthusiastic kiss on the corner of my mouth.

Bastounis winked. 'I think she likes you. You're her hero.'

'Great. Are you...Do you need to see a doctor or something?'

'For what – overeating? Too much brandy? Such things are the cure, not the disease. I'll drink some water. I'll be fine.'

'And what about our... our friend here? What's next?'

The woman knew we were talking about her. She smirked and sat on the end of the other bed, happy for us to fight her battles and take responsibility for her fate.

'She can't stay here in Gythio,' said Bastounis. 'He'll find her.'

'That's what he said. And that he'd kill her, or intentions roughly approximate.'

'Right. She'll have to come with us. I was planning to spend the night here, but that might give him an opportunity. We wouldn't sleep. Better to rest a little now and leave later.'

'What about the police. Couldn't you—?'

'What? Ask the police to stake out number three in case he thinks about committing a crime? The police here exist for traffic, tourist matters and arbitrating in family squabbles. What do you care if she comes along?'

'I don't... It's just that...'

'Fine. So it's settled.'

Bastounis told her the plan and she leapt to cover his face and hands in kisses half-heartedly resisted.

What was his game? Did the old goat have ambitions with this nose-ringed free spirit less than half his age? Or did he just like playing saviour to our damaged damsel?

'I'm going to rest a little,' he said, lying back on the bed. 'Wake me in a couple of hours.'

He was snoring within seconds, cap over his eyes, hands folded on his chest.

My choice: attempt two hours of frustrating mime dialogue with our new co-traveller, or join Bastounis in the arms of Morpheus. I took off my shoes and sat on the same bed as her, making the universal 'pillow' sign with my hands. She nodded and wheeled her suitcase to the bathroom, presumably to clean the day's traumas from her face.

I was falling into sleep when she joined me, spooning herself against my hips and thighs, her fragrant hair damp in my face on the pillow. The last thing I remember was her reaching to grab my arm and fold it round her torso, my limp palm becoming satellite to the heavy orbit of a breast. My reward? Or some childhood atavism of hers? Bastounis had said it: I was no threat. I was the soft-toy hero – the teddy bear Heracles.

NINE

He called her Calypso and she accepted the name readily enough – probably one of many she'd been given. He was a different person around her. He stood taller and seemed magnified in essence. It reminded me of the way he'd seen off the two youths on the quay in Nafplio – not the words he'd used, but the force of authority behind them. Women made him more of man: the stalwart protector. There seemed nothing overtly sexual in it. He had no designs on her. It was just a powerful manifestation of gender difference. She deferred to him as one might to a venerable patriarch, yet craved his gaze and attentions. She was constantly touching his arm or shoulder or knee as if there was some transmissible power in his body that drew and held her.

She touched me, too – she was a tactile woman – but in a different way. I was the dutiful puppy or the harmless friend – her partner in crime. Having no language in common with me, she quickly developed one of her own. Nudges, winks – exaggerated broad-stroke gestures and expressions. She didn't feel any self-conscious awkwardness. It was all a game to her. Like him, she had an accommodating gypsy soul.

The three of us drove west out of Gytheio. The daylight was mellowing into the more intense colours of incipient evening and the sun was a spotlight on us through the windscreen. Calypso had insisted on playing the ancient car radio, which had almost instantly locked into a station playing her kind of music: all plaintive *bouzouki* and clarinet, *santouri* and violin. She danced languorously on the back seat, arms out-stretched, shoulders waggling, eyes closed. With the copper sun gilding her and glinting off the nosering, she might have been a Salome, a Cleopatra – some timeless voluptuary snatched from the papyri of history and dropped into a Peugeot.

I watched her now and then in the mirror. Unselfconscious, uninhibited, she was an instrument herself, responding to whatever life played on her: harmony or discordance, melody or painful noise. At one point, she opened her dark eyes and caught me watching. No embarrassment in her. She kept dancing with me held in the web of her gaze until it was too much and I had to stare back at the asphalt as she laughed.

Bastounis sat sultanically in the passenger seat, cap down over his eyes and the sunglasses on. His window was all the way down and he smiled into the rushing air, his hand following the beat against the door panel. There'd been no further symptoms of whatever had caused his earlier faint. He was serene as we turned south.

There'd been no discussion of a specific destination. We were simply heading down into the deep Mani: that untamed region of stone towers and blood feuds, pirates and bandits. I hadn't asked why. Calypso had made no objection. The most important thing was to leave Gytheio and to keep moving. Bastounis had actually seemed happy about the sudden change of events and the necessity to go. It had given him new energy.

The day was now dying and the stony mountains along the coast road were glowing golden. To our left, the

Messinian Gulf revealed itself in azure-malachite bays and sapphire deeps. It was a barren, wasted landscape cooked dry by the sun and the African sirocco. Collapsed walls hatched the hills as evidence of failed farms. Even the olive trees were stunted and cowed. As far as I knew, this was a place of no notable myths or ancient history. A place to get lost and be forgotten.

We'd already passed a few tiny villages: cubist arrangements in pale stone that seemed to grow out of the landscape. Surely soon we'd reach the end of the peninsula and be at the southernmost limit of mainland Greece. Then what? Turn back?

'Where exactly are we going?' I said.

'Does it matter? If I tell you Kounos, or Kita, or Keria, would that help you?'

'I was thinking more about how much longer.'

'Why this obsession with time and destination? We don't know when we'll die, but we make plans all the same. We study, we invest, we save. And yet it could all end at any time – sometimes so quickly you don't even know it happened.'

'Yeah, but…You couldn't live if you thought like that. You'd always be waiting.'

'Exactly! Where's the purpose in a hesitant life? Tell me: where do you *think* we might be going? I'm certain you've thought about it. I can almost see your mind working on it: scanning the landscape, making deductions, searching for patterns in the journey so far. That's how your mind works. Not Calypso here. She doesn't care. She won't think about the place until the car stops and we tell her she's arrived. Forethought is no benefit to her because it's unreal. Only the here-and-now is real to our Calypso.'

He said something to her and she blew a kiss from her palm.

'I suppose we're going to one of these angular villages,' I said.

'That's hardly Sherlock Holmes, is it? Give me more. Don't you feel *any* sense of anticipation? Have I not taken you to pleasant places so far?'

'I'm sure it'll be nice – somewhere rustic and remote. An end-of-the-world feel to it, maybe. I guess I'm expecting something interesting. As for *why*, I haven't a clue.'

'Do you want to know why? Will that make it more fun? I'll tell you.'

'No. Don't tell me.'

'Ha! That's the spirit!' He folded his arms and turned, smiling, to look at the naked peaks.

I *did* want to know. Not knowing infuriated me. *He* infuriated me. If Calypso didn't care where we were going, maybe it's because she was essentially ... not dumb exactly, but unanalytical. A free spirit, yes. A willing kite of circumstance, sure. But who gets in a car with two strangers without asking where or why? It went against all sense. Anything could have happened to her.

'Will she be joining us for the rest of the trip?' I said.

'We'll see. I don't know. She may have her own plans. I'd be surprised if she didn't. Would you like her to travel with us?'

'I don't know her at all. She's ... entertaining in her way.'

'You think I want to sleep with her.'

'I didn't say that. I—'

'I won't deny I've thought about it. Look at her.'

She was now lying across the back seat and examining her nails, her bare feet against the window. Humming to herself.

'A woman like that ...' said Bastounis. 'Remember what I told you on the ferry? You can tell. She's not the kind you'd take home to mother. Any man would think about it. If you haven't thought about it yourself, you're not a man. You have, haven't you? I saw you with your arm round her in the room. Did you sleep a wink, I wonder? Or were you nursing a priapic tumescence? Ha!'

I'm sure I blushed.

'Nothing to be ashamed of. Quite natural. But I have other plans – other things to do. More important things. I've had my years of ecstasy and abandon. I wouldn't change them. But I don't need the distraction right now.'

I drove. I waited for more. There was no denying the fascination of his reputation as a ladies' man. The great beauties he'd supposedly been with were enough to make any man jealous. Not mere Hollywood airheads, but women of substance and achievement. He'd never written about them. He'd been discreet in his autobiographies, despite all of the public knowledge of his conquests. He'd even made that famous comment about he being the vanquished rather than they the conquered. How many men alive knew what he knew about women?

But he said nothing more. We drove into darkness, snaking off down a side road and arriving unexpectedly at a small bay encircled by buildings. The sea was right there beside us, shimmering with the village's lights. A great shadow blotted the sky beyond: the mountainous coastline south to a dead and uninhabited headland.

'Gerolimenas,' announced Bastounis. 'Park here. I'll ask about rooms.'

He took his stick and walked inside a tavern whose tables lined a small patio by the sea. Locals sitting there watched our arrival with interest. Calypso drew eyes and comments. I wondered vaguely how Bastounis could go so freely and completely unrecognised among his people.

Did nobody even question his name? Or was he – like Conrad, like Nabokov or Kosinski – one of those writers more famous in his adoptive country? A linguistic apostate?

He returned and spoke through the window. 'Two rooms available. Calypso takes one and we the other. Grab the bags. Then we eat.'

Again, the bag man.

Our room had a balcony that overlooked the road and the tables. It'd be noisy until after midnight with chatter and the inevitable youths racing mopeds up and down in fantasies of horsepower.

We ate together on the front: just light bites after the banquet of lunchtime. Bastounis drank brandy and I ouzo. Calypso asked for *tsipouro*, a kind of supercharged ouzo that she drank in frozen shots – a jerk of the elbow and down in one, her gold adornments glinting the candlelight.

'See how they look at her,' said Bastounis, swirling his Metaxa. 'Disgust and desire at the same time. In public they scorn and despise her, but in private … There you have the essence of morality. We make religions and philosophies of the higher faculties, but we're animals primarily. Look for the soul not in a man's heart or brain, but in his glands, in his secretions.'

Calypso seemed not to notice their disapproval or lust. She laughed, she drank, she picked daintily at the food in way that nevertheless betrayed her hunger. She flirted harmlessly with Bastounis and mocked my caution with the ouzo. She was a visiting queen in this village – she of Sheba, or Nefertiti among the slaves. There was more life in her than in the whole of this fractured austral wilderness, and it cringed in her presence. I began to see why Bastounis had brought her along. She was life.

❧   ❧   ❧

He woke me next morning from heavy-limbed, gum-lipped sleep.

'Come on – wake up. We have things to do today.'

'What time is it?'

'I don't know. Seven-ish. We need to get going.'

'Where? We've only just—'

'Fishing. That's why we're here. Bring swimming trunks if you have them.'

I dressed groggily as he rustled about with carrier bags. The view from the balcony was of a mirror-smooth sea.

'Is Calypso coming?'

'She's probably asleep. We needn't wake her. Let's go.'

We drove about five minutes along the coast and turned down a track to a notch-like inlet. Two ruined windmills stood by the rocky shore and the land around was littered with fallen walls, collapsed buildings and general evidence of ruin. A stone chapel crouched beside an empty concrete parking area. All was silent stillness.

I'd not seen any fishing rods hidden in the car, and I didn't see any now as I followed him behind the chapel and over the rocks to a coarse-sand beach the size of a table-cloth. Here, he began to take off his clothes.

'I thought you said we were going fishing.'

'We are. For octopus.'

He'd now stripped to a pair of faded swimming trunks that he must have last worn in the 1970s. His chest was furry with white hair and his gut hung over the waistband. I guessed that the scar on his right leg – his bad leg – was from surgery following a car accident he'd had in Argentina. Had it been a Porsche or a Jaguar he'd crashed into the side of a tunnel while participating in the playboys' race from

Buenos Aires down to Bahia? Another legacy of that adventure was the son he'd had with one of the pretty nurses attending him. How many children had he sired? Where were they now?

'Behold the ruins!' he said, arms outstretched. '*Et in Arcadia ego.*'

I changed into my trunks while he took masks, snorkels and flippers out of a carrier bag. When had be bought these? Or had he borrowed them from the rooms?

'Okay,' he said. 'Your next challenge.'

'I'm not fighting some massive octopus to the death.'

'Relax. This is about learning new skills. You think you already have skills because you went to university and you have a resumé, but can you butcher a carcase? Can you repair an engine? Can you cure a sick horse or cook a lamb *kleftiko*? Sure, you can parse a stanza or follow a thematic development in Joyce, but such things are useless beyond the writing desk and the lecture theatre. Read Ecclesiastes – all is vanity: "The sleep of a labouring man is sweet, whether he eat little or much: but the abundance of the rich will not suffer him to sleep." Today, you'll learn how to catch, prepare and cook an octopus.'

'Is it dangerous?'

'Less dangerous than taking a suitcase from a violent pimp. Now – put on this stuff and acclimatise yourself to the water. Have you snorkelled before? Good. Adjust the mask. Practise a little. No – don't try to walk in the flippers. Go backwards. That's it.'

'It's cold.'

'Don't be ridiculous. The water's warmer now than in July or August.'

Whereas I'd shuffled into the sea, balletically attempting to delay the scrotal dip, he strode splashing to his waist and put on the flippers with the water buoying him. His lameness was irrelevant here. He was vigorous.

'Okay. Listen carefully. There are three places we find octopus: between rocks, inside manmade rubbish like car tyres or tin cans, and in their gardens. We're looking for the gardens. A garden is just a hole in the sand. They dig down and gather stones around the hole so only their eyes peek out. They think they're invisible and safe, but they have nowhere to run and no purchase.'

'And then?'

'Just grab them.'

'That's it? They don't bite? Don't they have, you know, beaks or something?'

'They have a tiny mouth, but it can't bite a flat surface – only a fingertip or a knuckle. It's the grip you need to worry about – as strong a man's hand. At least, until it's dead. You should kill quickly, for both of your sakes.'

I looked at him through smeary Perspex. I was no killer.

'There are two ways,' he said. 'You can bite it between the eyes to crush its brain or you can turn the head inside out and rip its organs out. The head is basically a sock. Stick your thumb up the back and flip it. Pull out everything that looks like an organ. It'll stop writhing shortly after.'

'Right…'

'Just watch me, okay?'

He put the snorkel in his mouth, gave a thumbs-up and began kicking across the surface. I followed, entering a world of dancing turquoise light and the claustrophobic rhythm of my own breath through the tube. The water seemed to alternate between blood-warm and icy cold, sometimes oily against the mask and sometimes crystal clear. I understood that there was an underwater spring here somewhere. It had probably formed the inlet in some immemorial era.

The surface water got warmer as the sea-floor descended and I marvelled at Bastounis's easy athleticism. He kicked with slow, powerful strokes of his flippers, occasionally jack-knifing four or five metres down to the sandy bottom and swimming parallel to it with barely a bubble. Sometimes he'd be directly below me: a pale spirit fracturedly refracted in reticular sunlight – no longer flesh and hair and voice, but mere metaphysical form. This was young Bastounis: the Greek lad who'd later go out into the world and describe it, define it, conquer it and become jaded with it. For the mountain boy, this must have been paradise.

He paused and turned to look up at me against the rippling mercury of the surface. He pointed at some feature on the bottom and beckoned me down. I upended and kicked hard, repressurising by pinching my nostrils through the rubber and blowing.

A small circle of stones in the sand. Two reddish-brown eyes watching us through the aperture. The octopus's garden. Bastounis gestured with forked fingers between his mask and mine: watch this.

He grabbed straight for the eyes. The sand convulsed. Eight red-brown legs erupted from the hole and fastened on his hand, writhing and coiling madly. A black cloud billowed. Within it, Bastounis's free hand worked at the cephalic hood. A mess of membranes floated free: a dark bulb, jellied wisps, sundered strands.

The ink cleared and the thing still clung, tentacles questing up his forearm. But now the motion was sluggish: the death throes. Its ripped head swayed limp and ravaged. Bastounis pointed to the surface and we ascended.

He pulled out the snorkel. 'See? That's all there is to it. Quick. Decisive. But this is a small one. We need something bigger. Your turn. Let's go!'

And he was back into the deep, the limp octopus stuffed inside a pocket of his trunks. I hung back, hoping there'd be no more. Would it be unrealistic to suppose that this one had communicated its ecstatic agony to others in the seconds before its guts were torn? *Beware! Predators close!*

I followed him further and deeper. The sand was giving way to more rocks covered with growths of swaying kelpy stuff. Hadn't he said that we sought only octopus gardens? That rocks gave our prey greater purchase?

He paused and waved me down to the brow of a large boulder. Two rectangular pupils watched us from the aperture – larger eyes than our previous victim. Bastounis gave me the thumbs-up and waved me in for the kill.

We were deep. Maybe four metres. I could feel the pressure on my mask and on my lungs as I let a few bubbles out. Bastounis watched me; the octopus watched me. Could I plead humanity? It was no weakness to admit I didn't want to fight and kill. But I knew what he'd say. I could virtually write the monologue for him. *Hypocrite! You'll eat your* souvlaki *and your whitebait and your meatballs but you won't accept the death behind them – the murders committed in your name.*

But wasn't that just rhetoric? Nobody lives strictly by ethics and logic. We inhabit a penumbra of wilful blindness to absolutes. Philosophy demands rational rectitude, but philosophy is just ideas. Did any philosopher live and die by his own system? Socrates, maybe…

"Penumbra"? Yours is a life of get-out clauses, isn't it? Always an argument to explain the things you don't want to do, and to justify the things you do want. Call on psychology. Call on literature and books of quotations. Even religion if you really have to. Have them all lined up behind your decision (or lack thereof) – an all-star

eleven: Freud, Gandhi, Sartre, King Solomon. Nabokov in goal.
Anything but impulse. Anything but decisive action. Better to do
nothing than to do anything wrong.

He was watching me. I could see the scorn through his mask. Had he known all along that I'd choke at the last minute? The last of the air was leaving me.

I kicked hard with both flippers and thrust my hand into the garden. The tentacles whipped out – much longer, much thicker than the previous one – and grabbed my arm. The pressure was indeed that of strong man's hand. The cold suckers worked up my arm, past my elbow, and I realised that half of it was still anchored to some crevice within the hole. It was holding me. I tugged, but it was immovable in its panic. I was tethered to the sea floor.

I turned to Bastounis. He'd gone. He was up on the surface looking down.

I planted a flipper each side of the garden – now obliterated in a cloud of sand – and hoisted. The ink sac billowed. I was out of air. Just one option.

I hooked my thumb under its hood and tugged. The octopus thrashed, its naked organs exposed. Its grip was terrifying. My teeth clenched around the snorkel, I pinched at gelatinous horrors and ripped and ripped until nothing was left. Its grip slackened and the bulk of it tumbled thickly from the hole.

I paddled madly for the surface and ripped off the mask, heaving for breath.

'Bravo!' he said. 'Look at the size of it. Fantastic!'

'*I nearly died*! Didn't you see? Where were you?'

'Relax. You didn't die. It's a mollusc; you're man. What a beauty it is!'

The thing was still gripping my arm and hand, though with less power. Lines of circular marks pocked my skin where it had sucked with such fury. The head flopped obscenely pale. Eviscerated. I'd done that.

'Now we eat,' said Bastounis.

I followed him back into the inlet with the slimy weight of it still pulsing in my hand. I was shaking with the adrenaline, with anger and with exhilaration. I'd nearly died. I'd killed an animal with my bare hands. I was fearfully mortal. I was a god. I had triumphed against the monster, against myself and against Bastounis.

On the beach, he was like a boy. He sat in his cap and arranged his octopus as a glistening flower in the theatre of his out-stretched legs. It curled and twisted in post-mortem spasms.

'Watch carefully,' said Bastounis. 'Now we have to clean and tenderise the flesh. See this? This slime is its skin. We need to abrade if off until there's only white flesh. We do that by shampooing the animal against a rough rock.'

He poured some water from his mask onto the octopus and began rubbing it vigorously against a porous-looking white rock. The legs clenched repulsively into a viscous knot.

'Ignore this. It's a kind of rigor mortis. See? It's relaxing even now.'

As he rubbed, the skin appeared to foam into suds over his fingers. He added water and kept on rubbing until the skin began to slough off in sticky strands. In no time, he'd reduced the red-brown body to a ghost of itself. He held it up with a thumb hooked under the hood.

'There's only one part we can't eat: the mouth. Watch this.'

He'd opened the thing on the sand underside upwards. Rows of suckers led to the dark aperture in the centre. He pressed either side of it with his thumbnails and the entire mouthpiece popped out to leave a neat hole.

'Now you do yours. I'll go get firewood.'

He went off with his stick – the Sphinx's riddle made flesh – and I sat on the sand with my slowly roiling octopus. The sun was getting hotter. The sky, sea and rocks were timeless. There was still no sound but for the sigh of the inch-high waves. I might have been on the shores of some mythical shore: a castaway Crusoe or Jonah. The century was irrelevant.

I followed his instructions until my forearms were bespattered with dark adhesive strands and the octopus was cleaned. By then, the sun had dried my skin and I felt the saline tightness across my shoulders. My face was gritty with it, my hair stiff and my lips puckered. There was an inchoate sense – Joyce might have called it an epiphany – that I was somehow happier now than I'd ever been. Why? There was no sense or structure to it. It was pure focus. The moment was everything.

Bastounis returned with a bundle of tortured branches under his arm. He was grinning. He threw the wood to the sand and sat beside me.

'Good job. But we can't eat them in this condition – they'll be like rubber. We need to tenderise them. Watch.'

He searched for a fist-sized stone and laid one of the octopus legs along the larger stone we'd used to wash them. He began to work his way along the leg, beating it hard enough to spread the muscle fibres but not enough smash them. I took a stone for myself and together we diligently hammered away.

There was no conversation – no reference to my near-death experience, to Calypso, to the purpose or plan of this extemporary odyssey. He was entirely absorbed. In just his cap, his trunks and his sunglasses, he was any old man. A fisherman. An indigent. A widowed Adam on the riverbank in Eden, Eve long exhausted by multiple births.

'I've been thinking about the Nobel medal,' I said. 'Why you buried it.'

'And?' He didn't look up from his work.

'At first, I thought maybe you were hiding it from others. You might have thrown it in the pot of poker game and changed your mind later. Or perhaps lawyers saw it as an asset.'

He smiled to himself. He said nothing.

'But then I remembered what you said while we were there. I think you buried it in Tiryns to accrue some sort of primal energy: that strange power in the rocks. After a decade or more, it might become a talisman – or a transmitter. But why reclaim it now after years? And why leave it with Mister Konstantinopoulos to look after? Did you think somebody was looking for it?'

'I didn't leave it with him. I gave it to him.'

'You *gave* him your Nobel prize?'

'He's a better writer than I am. He's more of an artist. No committee would recognise him, so I conferred the prize myself. He deserves it more. Besides, what use is it to me? You write or you don't write; you're good or you're not – the prize changes nothing. Acclaim is a dangerous currency.'

He stood and formed a circular fire pit with sand and stones. I helped stack the wood and we let the wind-twisted branches burn down to embers before we skewered the octopus legs and dangled them over the heat. Their wispy tips shrivelled and burned, but the flesh cooked. It smelled fantastic.

'There's a place along the coast from Nafplio,' said Bastounis. 'Ancient Asine – a fortified promontory. Homer mentions it in the *Iliad*'s catalogue of ships: Asine of the broad bay. Its people painted octopus on their vases – beautiful naturalistic images and geometric abstracts. Parts of the defensive walls are still standing and there's a little stony beach beneath the masonry. Very much like this one. They would have sat on that beach, thirty centuries ago, preparing octopus in just this way. Salt on their skin. Hungry from their efforts. The immutable sun and sky. What a world was that? A world before the hollow equivocations of philosophy and theology. Before the hygienic certainties of science and logic. It was a world of heroes and bards. A world of mystery and magic and wonder. Earthquakes, storms, rainbows … they were glimpses of an infinitely unknowable realm. Where's that wonder now? There's no magic now. Only children perceive it. We know everything. We're dead.'

He plucked a leg from its twisted skewer and ate, indicating I should do the same. The meat was not entirely tenderised, but it tasted good. It was seasoned by the hunt, the kill, the sun and by the serried millennia evoked by Bastounis.

'I almost died down there,' I said.

'Ha! But now you're alive. Doesn't it feel great?'

TEN

We swam again after eating. He lay prostrate in the shallows, the waves lapping at his thighs, while I poked about the beach's perimeter. It was all cracked rock, tumbled walls and effaced foundations, flotsam, brittle fishing line and seashells. There was a memory of boyhood in the activity of exploring the little realm – the promise some quotidian discovery. An interesting stone. A coin. A message in a bottle. Funny how wonder can come out of nothing.

When the sun became too hot, we drove back to the rooms and ate a salad with bread and hummus. We also discovered some news about Calypso.

'She's gone,' said Bastounis.

'What?'

'She must have gone just after we left this morning.'

'What happened? Is she okay, do you think? Should we, you know, contact somebody?'

'She's not been abducted. She's taken the next step. You think she wanted to keep travelling with an old man and you? No – she's had a better offer. Weren't you observing her last night? That was advertising. We were just extras in that performance.'

'But what will she do now?'

'Don't worry about her. She'll find her own way. She knows what she's doing.'

'As a … prostitute?'

'What life would you wish on her? Dress her in a branded tabard and put her behind a till in a supermarket? Reclaim her for society? Marry her to some guy who's her anaemic shadow? Would that be more dignified? Send her to school?'

'I don't know…'

'There are no vegan tigers, okay? She's gone and she's thankful for our help, wherever she's gone. She'll remember us. We did a good thing.'

'I'll remember *her*.'

'I'm sure you will. I'm going for a sleep. You do whatever you like.'

I sat at the tables by the sea with an iced coffee.

There'd barely been time to think in the last day or two. Monemvasia, Nafplio and Gytheio seemed already distant memories. I'd not yet written about them in my journal, which meant they didn't fully exist. Was this how it felt when you were really living – not just repeating the same day for months and years on end? Dimitsana seemed weeks ago. I realised had no idea of the day or date. Losing my phone had been like cutting an anchor rope. I was drifting free in the current, in the tides of Bastounis.

And yet the future unknown hovered with Damoclean persistence. This journey had to end some time. Then what? Back to England and the life I didn't want to face? The thought settled black over me. The people he'd spoken about, those ancients on the shore – had they dreaded their future? Were they expected to follow specific life patterns? Or was every day simply a question whether the sun would rise and the fishes bite? I didn't want to go back. Going back was death.

What were they doing now, my uni friends, as I sat in the sun by a serene sea? Staring at screens in strip-lighted offices? Rushing out to buy a pre-packaged sandwich and a coloured drink so they could eat lunch at their keyboard? Emails blipping. Clock-watching. Each day just the same – only the clothes and the weather changing. Were they really happy with so little?

And me? How was I using my time? Was this just a glorified holiday? It *felt* like something more. It felt like someone had opened a door previously unnoticed: not one of the official options. *Was* this an option in any realistic universe?

The owner brought me a triangle of *spanakopita* and told me it was on the house. It looked homemade – perhaps a left-over from his own family's breakfast. It was delicious. Could I live here in Gerolimenas forever? Maybe rent a small room somewhere on the outskirts of town, do odd-jobs … learn the language, learn to fish. Never go back.

I went up to the room at siesta time and listened at the door. No snoring from Bastounis. Maybe I'd actually be able to get some sleep. I turned the knob as quietly as possible and entered.

He was lying on his back in just his underwear, slack mouth open and one arm hanging off the bed. His cap lay beside his head on the pillow. There was a hypodermic syringe on the floor close to his dangling hand. There was a small puncture in his forearm.

I stiffened and stared. Heroin?

He'd admitted using in his autobiography. Those dark years in Marseille, after Hollywood. He'd overdosed twice back then, once during a spat with that volatile actress, and again amid a bout of writer's block and his anger about the cultural sterility of his screenplay years.

I went closer, nudging the needle aside with my trainer. His face was a sheen of sweat. His breathing was shallow but regular. There was a trickle of drool down his white-stubbled chin. I pressed two fingers to his wrist – a slow but regular pulse. Alive. But for how long? Had he taken an overdose?

'Mister Bastounis?'

I waggled his arm. No response.

Call an ambulance? The idea of it seemed ludicrous. Where was the nearest hospital anyway? Sparta? Kalamata? Athens? I'd have to wake the landlord from his siesta. But if Bastounis was dying right now … What did a dying man look like? There were no blue lips. No unearthly pallor. If I had my phone …

'Mister Bastounis?' Louder this time.

Maybe it wasn't heroin. It could have been an anti-histamine or … What kind of drugs needed to be injected? Nothing over-the-counter, probably. Syphilis? Could it be penicillin? Multi-vitamins? There must be a packet or a bottle somewhere.

I opened the bedside drawer. Nothing. I looked among the bedclothes and through the dressing table where he'd left his watch and sunglasses. Nothing. His clothes on the back of the chair revealed nothing but a substantial roll of euros. Was I expecting to find a phial with "Heroin" typed on it? A label clearly marked "Harmless. May cause sleep"?

If it *was* heroin, was I somehow an accomplice? Was I his potential supplier? What was the penalty for that in Greece?

His bag was against the wall by the door.

'Mister Bastounis?'

Still nothing. It was no normal sleep. I went to the bag. Circumstance was forcing me to do this. I didn't want to open his bag. Doing so might be a life-saving act. What other choice did I have?

I kneeled and unzipped the leather holdall. Neatly rolled clothes. I palpated them for objects within but felt nothing. Glancing back at him on the bed, I began removing each rolled piece and placing it carefully on the floor. If I didn't find anything here – some hint of what medication he was on – I'd have to go in search of the landlord and tell him. Tell him that Nobel laureate Irakles Bastounis had overdosed in his rented room...

Papers rustled at the bottom of the bag. I paused. The same sheaf of papers he'd taken from the trunk in Dimitsana? Maybe there was a phone number written on them. Konstantinopoulos in Nafplio, maybe. He'd know. I could call him for advice.

The sheets were dog-eared and different colours, evidently gathered from different times and places. Notes and diagrams were written in pencil and pen, some Greek and some English. There was no obvious coherence, continuity or order. I looked quickly at each piece for a number or email address. No obvious contact details. Nothing official. Nothing that looked like a prescription.

How was it possible he was travelling with so little? No phone. No address book. Not even a novel or a magazine in his bag. Here was a man in his late seventies, famous according to the Internet and literary history, husband to five ex-wives, father to an unknown number of children... and all he had with him was the clothes he was wearing. The clothes, a walking stick and a handful of old paper.

The uppermost page looked like a rough shopping list appended with quotes. I scanned it:

Omorfi Tavernaki – Gytheio. Eat!!

Olympia Temple Zeus – absence and presence

Mani/Asine? Octopus vase (Athens?)

Ithaki

Delphi: γνῶθι σεαυτόν

Thess: *Narghilaiki*

"That life signifies nothing, everyone knows or suspects; let it at least be saved by a turn of phrase!"

Research notes for a book? A travel book, maybe. His notorious last book? I realised dizzily that I might be part of a process conceived long before I'd appeared. The meal at Gytheio had been his intention from the start. That stuff about the people on the beach at ancient Asine … I thought it had been spontaneous – a spark from the man's kaleidoscope mind. How long had he been working on the idea?

How much of everything he'd said and done so far was part of a bigger, preconceived project? All those eloquent speeches. Was he … Was he actually writing the book now as we travelled? Doing his research? The thought was astounding. I was part of an Irakles Bastounis book. I was *inside* its genesis! As driver and bag-carrier, I was making it possible. Would there be a dedication?

Olympia was to come. And Thessalonika? Or did the note refer to the larger region of Thessaly? Was Ithaki the island of Ithaca: home to Odysseus? I turned again to the papers, but Bastounis moaned in his sleep. His leg twitched.

I thrust the papers into the bottom of the holdall and replaced the rolled clothes as quickly as possible, trying to remember the order. It was only when zipping it closed that I thought about the order of the papers. Was there a correct sequence? It had looked random.

I stood over Bastounis. Still apparently unconscious. His gaping mouth closed and he jerked. His eyes opened as viscous slits.

'Mister Bastounis?'

'Eh? What?'

'There's a syringe by your arm … I thought you—'

'Yes. Medicine. It's to help me sleep.'

'An injection?'

'Yes, an injection. What did you think? That I was shooting heroin?'

'Well...'

'Where would I get heroin in provincial Greece? You think they process opium poppies in the Mani? Or in Gytheio? This isn't Afghanistan.'

'I was just worried that, you know, if you died...'

'I'm not going to die.'

He sat on the edge of the bed and picked up the syringe.

'What do you think'd happen if I died?' he said. 'State funeral? Newspapers' front pages blacked out in mourning? Bastounis has passed! The literary world convulses with grief.'

'I was just worried—'

'That's not what happens. It's a feeding frenzy. What happens is that the old books go into new editions and the publishers rub their hands. The out-of-print stuff comes back. Then come the parasites: the wives, the girlfriends, the bastards. The unauthorised biographies. Where's the money? Where's the advantage to this old man's death? And you – maybe you'd be one of them. "I drove Bastounis. I saw Bastounis shooting H in a rented room in Gerolimenas... This is my story."'

'I wouldn't do that. I'm... I'm honoured to be driving you around. I wouldn't sell a story.'

'Wouldn't you? I wonder. Not even if they came knocking? Not even if they offered you money? It's seductive. It appeals to your vanity. Why are you travelling with me anyway? Would you have agreed if I were just any old man? Be honest – it's the fame that lures you: the glamour of being close to it, no matter how peripherally. It's addictive, I know. I've felt it myself in earlier days, in Hollywood. Those people were gods to me, just a kid fresh off the boat. I would have done anything. What's the saying? "Whom the gods want to destroy, they first make mad". Renown is a kind of madness. You, you're ensorcelled. The fact that you've stayed with me this far is proof of it. You're cataloguing every minute of this for a future retelling.'

'That's not—'

'What if I told you I *was* just any old man? Not literary lion Irakles Bastounis, but just some old guy from a village. Can you be absolutely sure I'm Bastounis? Do you recognise me? Has anyone else recognised me or referred to me by name? Would Bastounis be driving that battered old Peugeot, living in that dusty old mausoleum in Dimitsana and travelling with just a holdall of clothes? What proof have you that I'm the writer?'

'The medal... The Nobel medal. Mr Konstantinopoulos...'

'Ah, yes. The great poet Konstantinopoulos. Read any of his work? Seen any in libraries or bookshops? Would you recognise him from a picture? Maybe I made him up as well. As for that medal, did you see my name on it? Have you seen a genuine Nobel medal for comparison? Indeed, did you see me pull it from under a rock in Tiryns – or was it just something else wrapped in material? It could have been a saucer or a piece of roof tile for all you know.'

'This is crazy...You keep referring to your past. In Hollywood. With the Venezuelan woman. You did it just now!'

'Maybe I've read the autobiographies just as you have. They're still available in libraries, even in Greece. What are they called? *Dionysus Goes to Rehab*? Something about Augeas? Imagine that! Imagine the futility of you travelling around Greece with just any old guy. Some delusional old madman. Are you still interested? Am I as interesting when I'm a nobody? Because let me tell you: I *am* just an old man. I *am* a nobody. And now I'm going outside for a brandy.'

He dressed quickly in the clothes from the back of the chair, not looking at me the whole time. I stood dumbfounded, the tumult of thoughts failing to emerge as speech. His cap and sunglasses on, he closed the door behind him and banged down the stars with his stick.

The silence of the room was oppressive.

He *was* Irakles Bastounis. I clung to that certainty even as his arguments washed at the foundations of my conviction. This was just some clever rhetoric to make me reassess my motivations. Wasn't it?

He'd been right, of course, about the glamour of travelling with him. But that hardly made me a parasite. It didn't make me a Judas. *He'd* come to *me* with the idea of driving him. I'd never pushed that agenda or expected anything like it.

And now? Was it all over? I felt like a child sent to his room to think about what he'd done. But I wasn't a child and I hadn't done anything. *He* was the child. If this was the end, I had nothing to lose by going downstairs and confronting him. I wouldn't win any argument, but I'd least I'd always remember that I'd not just crumbled to this outspoken curmudgeon.

He was sitting by the sea, a balloon glass of brandy in front of him and his stick hooked on the table. I pulled out a chair and sat opposite him.

'Look – if you think I'm driving you just because—'

'Tomorrow we go to Olympia. It's quite a long drive so we'll leave early. Or maybe we'll break the journey. Let's see. But for tonight, the landlord tells me he has some excellent *gemista* and some fresh squids caught today. We'll feast! Order an ouzo. Let's watch the town wake up.'

Was this the same man? Or were there identical twins engaging me in some bizarre game? I wanted to continue the argument, but I recognised it was better this way. I wanted to see Olympia. And Ithaca, and Thessaloniki. He was right. The glamour of it all ... It was irresistible. All that stuff he'd said about life not being a movie, not a script, and here we were in the middle of a book he was writing. Research scouts. First settlers. I caught the landlord's attention and called across the street for an ouzo, holding thumb and forefinger apart as an indication of dosage.

Out in the bay, a shoal of tiny fish burst from the surface: a coruscating second of silver fragments splintering the sun. The surface rippled and returned to calm. What was the word Bastounis had used? Ensorcelled.

ELEVEN

We took the same route back out of the Mani but it was a different road and a different world in the light of early morning. Our arrival had been triumphal: all gold and burnished bronze, copper and gleaming brass. Calypso the pagan goddess had been our mascot and protectrix. How long ago was that? Now, the landscape was lucid and profoundly simple. We might have been traversing the surface of some extra-galactic moon – apocalyptic child of colliding stars, now cooled and eternally still. I imagined the car seen from space: a tiny, moving dot across the barren wastes.

Bastounis wasn't good with mornings. He'd eaten his *tiropita* and drunk his Greek coffee in silence. He'd vomited in the night and woken with a headache he'd described as a dagger through his forehead. I assumed it was side-effect of whatever he'd injected the previous day. Or one too many brandies after we'd gorged ourselves. The food had been excellent – more so with his commentary and prompts for me to taste this, combine that, and report exactly the tastes or textures I was experiencing.

We drove without conversation or music, the windows open and the smell of the waking earth. His plan was to head north on the main road towards Sparta and branch off through the mountains towards Olympia. According to the map in my guidebook, that meant passing again through Arcadia in the centre of the Peloponnese. It would be an epic drive. The colossal Taygettus range soon began to crowd the sky to our left.

Sparta, however, was disappointing. It looked like any of the larger Greek towns I'd seen: concrete blocks with shaded balconies, plate-glass shop fronts and artless signs, awnings, kiosks, traffic. There was no sense of its illustrious history – no castle or temple standing sentinel over it. No glimpse of ancient walls. Perhaps it was all elsewhere. When we stopped outside a supermarket to buy water and snacks for lunch, I was keen to get moving again.

'Of course,' said Bastounis, when I mentioned the feeling. 'You're in love with the fantasy of Greece: a pastiche of literature and myth. The Greece you revere never existed – at least, not all at the same time. Most of what you venerate was just Athens. Socrates, Plato, Euripides – a dash of Homer for seasoning. You don't know your Cleisthenes from your Peisistratus, or when Alexander was in charge. People forget how many of the city-states were ruled by psychotic tyrants, or that philosophers like Diogenes were sold into slavery. It's just a blurry romanticism.'

'Don't you do the same with the age of Homer?'

'Absolutely not. No. That era exists beyond history. There can be no proof for or against it. It simply *is*.'

'Yeah, sure...but the Lernaean hydra? The Nemean lion? The assistance of gods?'

'Such things can't exist now. We won't let them. There are explanations for everything. A child can turn on his computer and see satellite images of the remotest and most inaccessible mountain passes. Delphi – once the omphalos of the ancient world and long journey on foot – now has a regular bus service. Our minds won't let the mythical exist. We've lost that ability forever. But when Heracles sought the lion, it existed. Gods aided him. Nobody questioned it.'

'But doesn't archaeology—?'

'Archaeology deals in bones and dust and the dull numbers of chronology. It says nothing about the minds of the immemorial dead. What does the fragment of pottery tell us about the man whose fingers left spirals within it, or the man who painted it? What does carbon dating say about his dreams, his prayers, his fears when the earth shook or the volcano spewed lava into the night? The truth of the Lernaean hydra is scattered to atoms – still with us in the wind and in our very breath, but … Archaeology digs in vain for the lost wonder of man. We can only excavate ourselves.'

'I guess …'

'Don't guess. Think. Observe. Be receptive. Learn some skills of living. Don't stumble blindly through your life. Drive. Don't be the passenger.'

I drove, and I wondered whether this was another pre-prepared element he'd been working on overnight. Or for years. Part of the book. Was he testing it now on me: seeing what objections I might raise? Did he believe any of it himself?

'Up ahead there,' he said. 'A hitchhiker.'

I looked. A tall skinny man standing by the side of the road with a small backpack at his feet. He was wearing a shapeless cloth hat, geek-chic glasses and had a ragged beard. He looked like fifties beatnik.

'What. You want to pick him up? Is it safe?'

'I trusted you to drive me, didn't I? I didn't know *you*.'

'I wasn't hitching.'

'Ten minutes later and you might have been. I might have picked *you* up.'

'He could be anyone. An illegal immigrant.'

'He's a fellow traveller as Calypso was, as you are. Slow down. Pull over just here.'

I steered into the gritty lay-by and the hitcher snatched his bag with a smile. He strode over to the passenger window and bent to face Bastounis.

'Where are you going?' said Bastounis.

'Hey, great! You speak English. Wherever, man. I'm just going with the flow. Arcadia? The coast? I'm just out of Sparta and heading north.'

He was American or Canadian. Mid-to late-twenties?

'Get in the back,' said Bastounis. 'Just push that stuff to the side.'

'Thanks, man. Where you headed?'

'North through Arcadia. You comfortable? Okay. Let's go.'

That was my cue. I, the chauffer. The tyres skidded as we swerved back onto the road.

His name was Buddy – named for Guy, not Holly – and he was from some obscure American town that probably had an alien water tower. He'd been travelling for weeks, apparently, without purpose or direction. Just "going with the flow" and "looking for inspiration". He called himself a writer. He talked about writing. I thought he might wet himself when he found out who was in the passenger seat.

'Irakles *Bastounis*? Shit, man – you're my hero! I was even thinking about getting a line from *Cassandra* inked on my side. That book, man … That book is what made me want to be a writer. I don't care what anyone says – you shit on Mailer and Roth. And DeLillo and Easton Ellis. Amis, Rushdie, all of them. They're just gimmick artists next to you. Man, you're a *stylist*. You're the *poet*-novelist. That's why people don't get you these days … Look – don't kill the messenger, you know? – but if your books aren't selling now, it's because readers are too dumb. They just want story. Your reign, the seventies and eighties – that was the last golden era of the superstar novelist, right? Now they're all hacks.

Crowd pleasers. Who now is writing for himself? Nobody –
that's who. Writing for yourself means not getting published. You gotta kiss corporate ass. You gotta run your first
drafts by a focus group get a product tie-in. It's like ... like
Led Zeppelin, right? You know what I mean? Where's the
rock 'n' roll? Where's the ten-minute drum solo?'

I looked at him in the rear view mirror as he spoke. He
was all gesticulation and earnestness. Was he even born
when Bastounis was at his peak? Or when Zeppelin had a
record out that wasn't a remaster? What did Buddy know
about the seventies and eighties? With his wispy beard
and his *Where's Wally?* glasses, he looked like Beat clone, a
Greenwich-Village Dylan wannabe.

'I think you're absolutely right, Buddy,' said Bastounis.

I almost veered into the middle of the road.

'What do you write, Buddy?' said Bastounis. 'Prose?
Poetry?'

'You know, I think if you're a writer you should be able
to write anything, right? I've written a screenplay. Some
poetry – free verse. But I'd say novels are my thing. I'm writing one now. It's kind of my take on Kerouac. No plot, no
story – just characters and situations and movement. Pure
narrative. Whatever happens, that's the story. I'm experi-
menting with a post-post-modernist style. Like, sometimes
I have no form of control in the prose. No punctuation or
paragraphs or capitals. Because there are no paragraphs in
lived experience, right?'

I may have snorted derisively.

'But I'm forgetting,' said Bastounis. "Our designated
driver here's a writer.'

'Hey!' said Buddy, slapping my shoulder. 'What d'you
write, man?'

'I never said I was a writer – just that maybe I had ambitions in the future.'

'Shit, that's no good man. There's no future – there's only now. If you're not writing, you're no writer. You know how many people I met who said they were writers and they never did anything?'

'He keeps a journal,' said Bastounis, turning to Buddy with a look I didn't catch.

'I've been neglecting it,' I said, empurpling. 'Circumstances recently...'

'Like a travel diary?' said Buddy, smirking. 'You ever read what Twain wrote about that? How you start off writing every little thing and then, you know, gradually...'

He started laughing. Bastounis joined him. I didn't know what bit from Twain they were talking about. I saw that we'd started to accelerate and eased off the pedal.

'But you've read Irakles, right?' said Buddy. 'What's your favourite book?'

First-name terms. He was leaning forward, a hand on each of the front seats, his face between us. There was a goatish smell about him.

'I like all of them. But... *Gods and Satyrs* if I had to choose just one.'

'Nah, *Cassandra* is the best. There's no question. What do you say, Irakles?'

'I suppose *Cassandra* nudges it,' said Bastounis. 'It won the prizes.'

'Yeah!' Buddy held up his hand for a high five and Bastounis reciprocated.

What was going on here? Where was the vitriol? Where were the withering monologues and put-downs? Could it be that Bastounis found some mollifying affinity with Buddy's accent? Maybe fond memories of the American years that had shaped his language and his early style?

'But where's your next book, man? You been keeping us waiting too long. Is that what you're doing now with your driver here? Research?'

I gripped the wheel. I glanced sidelong at Bastounis whose face under the cap and sunglasses was unreadable. The pause was satisfyingly long.

'Hey, I didn't mean to pry. But I'm a fan, you know? It's a real buzz just being here right now.'

'I never discuss work in progress,' said Bastounis.

Buddy whooped. 'I knew it! Man, if people knew I was in a car with Irakles Bastounis. It's like sitting in the corner while da Vinci sketches the helicopter, you know? Just knowing I was there and nobody else was. It's history. I'm part of history. Just tell me one thing: is it true you KO'd Kerouac with one punch? I have to know.'

A dry laugh from Bastounis. 'We were both so drunk. Probably he just fell while taking a swing and hit his head on a table. But Burroughs ... He was an interesting guy.'

And Bastounis started on an anecdote about a drive into the Mojave Desert and an experiment with peyote and how Burroughs wanted to be sacrificed on a monolith he believed to be sacred. Meanwhile, Buddy whistled and cooed and coaxed, his hand nudging my shoulder as he lunged back and forth between the seats. There seemed little chance of him disappearing at the next town as Calypso had. Maybe he'd become the driver and I the hitcher.

I drove on past the cooling towers, pylons and candy-cane smokestacks of Megalopoli's generating plant, on into the stony peaks of Arcadia. We passed a chasm between the peaks with no visible bottom, a fortified village on the other side of it clinging to a sheer cliff. The road kept ascending so that each vanishing corner promised an amazing view, but more peaks appeared, more corners and more unrelenting ascent. I was constantly changing gears. I'd expected the landscape to become ever more barren, yet the earth's undulations were growing thicker with trees and shrubs. This was the true realm of shaggy-legged Pan – a remote and verdant upland, where ancient shepherds would have feared the dark of caves and valleys.

It turned out that Buddy had done a classical mythology option at whatever mid-west college he'd attended. 'Imagine it,' he said. 'Up in these hills in the pagan moonlight. The trill of Pan's syrinx. The rustle of the undergrowth. The dryads gather in a clearing for some erotic rite. Maybe a virgin sacrifice – a girl from a nearby village trussed and offered to the god, right? A shepherd boy stumbles on the scene and watches, half terrified, half aroused by the bestial horror enacted. A twig snaps under him. Pan lets forth his cry: panic! The shepherd boy runs, but his legs are merely human. He's torn to pieces by the unholy host, his members scattered variously, glistening from the branches: poison fruit of mortal curiosity. Yeah!'

'You tell it well,' said Bastounis. 'You have a feel for the old ways, I think.'

'*Woo*! Can I quote you on that, man? Wait – I need to write this stuff down before I forget it. What was that last bit? "…poison fruit of mortal curiosity"? Yeah. Yeah. Good rhythm.'

He pulled a battered spiral-bound notebook from his bag and started scribbling with it rested on his knee. I glanced sidelong at Bastounis to see if he was mocking in his praise, but he gave nothing away. Hadn't I been thinking exactly the same thing about Pan? I could have said it just as well, though I didn't know the word "syrinx". I'd look it up as soon as I had the opportunity.

'Andritsaina,' said Bastounis as a large stone building appeared round the bend. 'We'll stop here tonight, I think. There's an ancient temple of Apollo on a peak near here. It's worth seeing. Buddy – you're welcome to stay with us if you like.'

'You think I'm gonna say no to Irakles Bastounis?'

'Just one thing – have you got a cell phone with you?'

'Nah, man. I'm travelling strictly twentieth century. Just me, the pen and the page. Good enough for Kerouac, good enough for me. You need to make a call?'

'No. I also like to keep it twentieth century.'

He turned to me. 'Drive on through the village. I recall there used to be some rooms overlooking the valley.'

The village was a mixture of new concrete buildings and original stone houses that were all multiple arches, massy lintels and balconies. Huge trees by the roadside cast shade over tiny squares. Cobbled streets led off from the road up the hill and down into the valley. We passed an ancient-looking double-arched drinking fountain with four spouts gushing water. The village seemed much grander than Dimitsana had, though it was further away from any large towns. It was a place beyond the world.

'This is it,' said Bastounis. 'Pull in here.'

It was the forecourt of an old petrol station: cracked concrete pocked with weeds and two obsolete pumps standing like tombstones, their dials frozen mid-measure through glaucous glass. A good place to not refuel for a journey with no destination. Bastounis went inside and we waited.

'Irakles Bastounis, man!' said Buddy. 'I can't believe it. Car comes round the bend and it's a Nobel Prize-winner. What are the odds? How'd you get this gig?'

'I was in his village, just visiting. He asked me to drive him.' No need to mention the insults, the belittling, the situation with my phone. The general weirdness.

'Shiiit! That's what I call a story. What's he like? Have you been doing wild stuff together? Has he hit anyone?'

'I think he's mellowed. He's not the same man. He's not what people expect.'

'Yeah, it's a privilege. Getting to know the man. Getting inside his head. Maybe I'll stick around – ride the Nobel train a little.'

Bastounis came out and leaned against the sill. 'I've organised a room. Bring in your bags. Also, the landlord tells me that the Temple of Bassae is undergoing some work. It's normally under a huge tent to protect it from the elements but they're replacing the material. It's open to the air for the first time in two generations. You boys should go and see it.'

'Aren't *you* coming?' said Buddy.

'I need to sleep. I'm an old fart like that. You go. It's only about six miles up the road. Something to write about, eh?'

I took the bags up to a rustic, wood-beamed room with a view over the wooded valley. It must have been a sheer fifty-metre drop from the balcony. Buddy dropped his bag by the door but then tossed it on to the second of the single beds, leaving me with the tiny fold-out.

Bastounis went straight into the bathroom and stayed there, frustrating my hopes to confer about Buddy. We didn't know anything about this guy, but here we were sharing a room with him. He could be a thief. Certainly, he was an irritating buffoon. Why humour him? Was I missing a bigger strategy? I began to suspect that Bastounis was impatient for us to leave for the temple, and eventually we had to if we wanted to catch the light.

'Floor it, man!' said Buddy from the passenger seat as we began the climb out of the valley.

'It's not really safe on the bends. They tend to have a lot of grit from—'

'Live a little! Use the horsepower. I'll drive if you want. I'm a good driver.'

'It's fine. We're nearly there.'

'You know anything about this temple? Is it worth seeing?'

'It was built about the same time as the Parthenon: about 450 BC. They had the same architect. Some say it was built as a due to Apollo, who saved a local village from plague. The frieze sculptures are in the British Museum.'

'D'you get all that from your guidebook?'

'Yes…?'

He smiled. He didn't need a guidebook. He'd know it was classical Greek from "gut instinct" alone, or from his innate receptivity to the ghostly voices of eternity.

We pulled into an empty car park and immediately the corner of the temple was visible against the sky: a grey, bleak-looking limestone angle whose presence here was jarring. It was like stumbling across a Notre Dame or Chartres cathedral in a boggy Scottish glen. But we were a thousand metres and more above sea level, peaks stretching out westwards to the horizon and a cool wind shivering the grasses. Was this what Delphi felt like – the far-distant pilgrimage site gained only after many days of faithful travel?

We walked up a track around the temple's southern end and the temple became fully visible. The white plastic of its habitual shroud lay curled all about it. Steel struts stood naked in anticipation for the new covering. But the stone itself was free: a sturdy, stepped base and intact rows of Doric columns defying twenty centuries of earthquake, wind and lightning. Not as pale or as majestic as the Parthenon's marble, it seemed yet more ancient. The weather-fissured pillars were crazed like the glaze on an aged oil painting.

'Pretty neat,' said Buddy.

'Bastounis talks about the power of place,' I said. 'How the land itself holds an energy. I'm not sure I feel it here. I mean, the site is fantastic, but it's like the energy's gone cold. It's a fossil. The resident deity has long since abandoned it.'

A satisfying pause from Buddy. I purposefully didn't look at him.

'I don't know, man ... I think I do feel something. A subsonic vibration, you know? A soundless note. There's some temulence, some thew, some puissance that attracts, you know? You sure you don't feel it?'

I looked hard at the temple – squat, stolid, monumental. The wind passed through its bones with a continuous sigh. A bird darted into the blue from its fluted ribs. What the fuck was temulence?

I heard the match rasp and turned to him. A blossom of smoke blew by me. Weed.

'Sorry, man. Selfish of me. You wanna hit?' He offered it between thumb and forefinger.

'No. Thanks.'

A shrug. 'Is Irakles still into it? I know he was on some pretty hard stuff. Back the eighties was it? The dark days. Man, he was a monster. H, coke, weed, amphetamines ... you seen any of that while you're driving?'

I knew what I should have said. The sentence was ready-formed. Discretion was my instinct. But he'd got to me, this goateed Pan, with his certainties and over-familiarity and his thesaurus glibness and his sub-Kerouac cool.

'Well, I did catch him shooting up.' Insouciant. Blasé. 'Just yesterday, in fact.'

'Yeah? Shooting what?'

'I don't know. He said it was to help him sleep.'

'Yeah, right! Did you notice his pupils? Like, were they pinned or dilated?'

'I don't know. I didn't notice. I thought he'd OD'd on me.'

'Sweaty? Blue lips?'

'Sweating, but it was a hot afternoon. We were down in the deep Mani hunting for octopus. Just me and him.'

'You seen him scratching and twitching?'

'I'm not sure I should be saying ... I mean, I don't know what it was in the syringe. He's a hard sleeper anyway. It could have been vitamins. It's really not our business.'

'Sure. Vitamins. This is Irakles Bastounis, man. They say he's got another book in him, right? The big one. The one everyone's been waiting for, right? You seen anything like that? Is he writing? Is this trip research?'

'He doesn't like to talk about it. You know ... the ex-wives and the lawyers and all that. It's a touchy subject with him.'

'Yeah, but just imagine.' He drew on his joint, eyes squinted. 'If he *was*. And if we were with him. That's history. That's a foot in the door. We might even feature in it somewhere, you know? Like, something we said and he remembered it subliminally. Maybe that riff I did on Pan and the dryads. He liked that. And I wrote it down, so I have corroboration.'

'Hmm.'

The temple was surrounded by a flimsy barrier of string looped on metal rods. It twitched and quivered in the wind. A joke, really. With the canopy removed, any animal could enter the sacred *naos*. Birds, goats, mice, foxes.

'It's a pity we can't go inside,' I said. 'It's not like we'd do any damage when it was open to the elements for two millennia.'

'Just do it, man. Nobody's watching.'

I looked around. The guy who'd sold us tickets had seemed uninterested in his little kiosk. There was no sign of him now. But the string... The string represented rules and order.

'Fuck it,' said Buddy.

He ground the last of his joint under a shoe and stepped over the loop. In a moment, he was up the fractured steps and inside the columns. He traced his hand along the exterior wall of the *naos* and followed it around to the entrance until he passed out of sight.

I looked around. I looked at the sagging bow of string that might as well have been an electrified cable. I moved closer so it touched my thigh, pretending to be entranced by some detail at the top of a pillar.

A whistle blew. I jerked back from the barrier. The site guardian – where had he come from? – gestured for me to move away from the string. He pointed to a sign clearly forbidding entry. At that moment, Buddy came strolling round the other side of the temple with a grin, nodding hello to the suspicious guardian.

'Man, it was cool,' he said, *sotto voce*. 'There was, like, an altar, and these buttresses fluted just like the columns. It was eerie in there. In the holy sanctuary of Apollo!'

'You could have been caught. The guardian appeared just after you went inside.'

'So what? I'm not gonna let a piece of string stop me. You should do it, man. What's he gonna do? Blow his whistle? Call the police? Just wait for him to walk off.'

The guardian was watching us, his arms folded. Maybe he'd smelled Buddy's joint.

'We'd better go,' I said. 'It's getting cold. I'm starting to get hungry.'

'Whatever, man. You want me to drive?'
'No.'

Bastounis had left a note in the room. He'd be waiting for us up the cobbled street off the main road. There was a *taverna* he'd heard was good.

I took a sweater against the mountain chill and waited at the door as Buddy went through his bag. He crouched with his back deliberately facing me. Maybe it was full of joints and Kerouac.

'What the shit?' he muttered.

'What is it?'

'You carried my bag up to the room, right?'

'Yes?'

'Did you, like, throw it down? Kick it?'

'No. Why?'

He held up a smartphone. The screen was starred with an impact crack.

'There's an old cast-iron shoetree here – probably a doorstop. You might have dropped the bag against it. By accident.'

'I didn't see any shoetree when I came in … Wait – you told him you didn't have a phone. You said you were strictly twentieth century.'

'D'you think *he* did it? Made it look like an accident with the doorstop?'

'Ask him. But then you'd have to admit to the phone.'

'I'm guessing that's his idea. A *fait accompli*. Smart old dog.'

'Or it could just be an accident.'

'Yeah, right.'

'Look – shall we go and meet him? I'm starving.'

He stuffed the phone into the bag. 'Don't mention this to him, right?'

'Okay.'

We crossed the road and went up the cobbled alleyway. There was a scent of wood smoke, pine resin and foliage: mountain smells. The rush and gurgle of multiple springs came from between the houses. Our breath actually steamed. Buddy walked head down, hands in his pockets, quiet for once.

I couldn't see any chairs or tables out. There was no sign. It was just single-story houses with stone-slab roofs. Had there been another alley?

'In here!' Bastounis's voice. 'The bead curtain. Yes, this one. Come in.'

We passed through the clacking beads into someone's home. The walls were whitewashed stone hung with sepia prints of ancestors. A tiny cot bed was made up with a hairy blanket and in the corner flames flickered at the window of an old pot-bellied stove. Bastounis sat at a 1950s-style yellow Formica table with a toothglass of brandy in front of him.

'This is a *taverna*?' said Buddy.

'It's an old widow's house,' said Bastounis. 'Sit. She's making us something to eat.'

The woman came from a back room carrying a tray. She was bent-backed and gummy with infirmity. Her black stockings were half-mast on pale legs knotty with veins. I pushed back my chair to intercept her and offer to carry the tray. Bastounis stopped me.

'Don't. It's not a man's job to serve. She'd be insulted. Just eat and show her you're grateful.'

The food was simple and delicious: stuffed peppers, fried potatoes and some kind of meat stew (goat?) in an ancient iron pot. None of the plates or cutlery matched. The handle of my fork was bandaged with blue electrical tape. We ate mostly in silence, the stove periodically cracking and popping. Bastounis seemed subdued. Buddy was apparently nursing a grievance. I was entranced by the authentic poverty of the house, by the gauzy filaments of smoke about the naked bulb above our table, and by the gazes of long-dead relatives watching from the walls. There was nothing like this in my guidebook. I'd literally gone behind the curtain, under the string, to the real Greece.

From the kitchen, we heard the old woman singing to herself – a thin, reedy song from her youth, perhaps. Something with the promise of romance and gaiety, played over and over on a once-new gramophone now obsolete and dusty, the stylus worn away, the fingers that set it no longer nimble but claw-warped with age and labour.

We were effusive in our praise when she brought coffee.

TWELVE

It was cold when I carried our bags the bags down to the disused forecourt next morning. The ground was wet, the car was beaded with dew and the valley below the village was submerged in vapour. A damp scent of earth and leaves and raw stone filled the air with a palpable sense of nature – as if these streets and their encircling hills had risen, Genesiacally new, overnight. The quiet was absolute.

The driver's door was already open. Buddy was in the seat.

I looked to Bastounis.

'Buddy's driving today,' he said.

Nothing more. No reason why. Had they discussed it earlier when I'd walked into the village to buy hot pastries from the bakery? Or had he just arrogated the role while I was away? Making a fuss would only seem petulant. Better to let him drive us off the road and into a precipice and then make some pithy condemnation with my dying breath. I took my place in the back seat with studious indifference – dignitary rather than passenger.

He drove recklessly and badly as we ascended from the village: too wide around the bends and unnecessarily fast. He waited too long before changing gear, revving until I thought Bastounis might say something. But Bastounis said nothing. No criticism, no pointers – not even any indication of fear when the tyres seemed to hang over a void or when Buddy overtook a battered 4X4 on a blind uphill corner. Had Bastounis shown any trepidation at all, I would have said something. Instead, I gripped the door, clenched my jaw and tried to think.

Olympia. Why Olympia? The note I'd glimpsed in his bag had said something about the Temple of Zeus: one of the original Seven Wonders thanks to its monumental chryselephantine statue of the resident god. It was an oddly touristic place to go considering his journey so far. A key part of his book? A thematic link with Tiryns? Civilisations lost? Maybe he had something buried there.

And why Buddy? He wasn't a deserving fugitive as Calypso had been. He wasn't especially interesting or entertaining. Perhaps Bastounis saw in him some vestige of his own formative adventures. He, too, had wandered as a vagrant through the Balkans after his opioid nadir in France – sleeping under hedges and in monasteries, hitching rides, earning money as a farmhand, and enjoying the promiscuous favours of the rustic girls he met. His book about that time – *Harvest of Chronos* – wasn't considered one of his best because it didn't deal with so-called big issues. It occurred to me only now that it was his *Old Man and the Sea* or his *Dubliners*. There wasn't necessarily more of him in it than the other books, but there was more of his vulnerability and joy. That's the book I should have named as my favourite when we'd been talking about his work. Plus, Buddy probably hadn't read it.

The road descended slowly through patchy agricultural settlements and I was glad that Buddy seemed unable to drive and talk simultaneously. Bastounis remained taciturn, giving only directions. After one terrifyingly aborted overtaking manoeuvre, I wondered what the press and our relatives would make of the wreckage and the human remains. What combination of factors had put these three people in this car on this road? My name might one day become a quiz question. *Name one of the two other people in the car when Irakles Bastounis…*

'Look. Do you see that?' said Bastounis.

The flat area down to our left looked like a poor-quality school football pitch or a rural runway. It was surrounded by mown grass.

'The ancient stadium,' said Bastounis. 'Imagine it surrounded by tens of thousands of ecstatic spectators – philosophers, tyrants, sculptors, poets, merchants, craftsmen. We're here!'

His excitement was infectious. Within seconds, we'd left the nondescript, narrow highway and entered an area of advanced development: smartly paved roadside, metal bollards and signs directing us on to the purpose-built town. The trip from Andritsaina had taken barely an hour. We left the Peugeot in a largely empty car park and walked the short distance back to the site entrance, Bastounis leading despite his limp.

'Why are we here?' muttered Buddy alongside me. 'I'm not a tourist; I'm a traveller. Is it for his book?'

'I don't know.'

'Have you read about it in your guidebook? One of the Seven Wonders… the big sculpture of Zeus *et cetera*?'

'No.'

We passed a sign forbidding smoking and I worked on a daydream of Buddy lighting up a joint before the Temple of Hera. Alarms would ring. A SWAT team would rappel from the trees and take him down with unnecessary force. Shock and awe. Collateral damage.

Bastounis strode ahead into the sanctuary, past the palaestra, past the Phillippeion and the Heraion. We were almost
alone at the site so early in the day and so late in the season.
The plane trees had started to change colour – yellow, gold
and scarlet flames flickering in their heads. There was a coolness to the air despite the pure blue sky. All around us lay
scattered stones, pitted columns, remnants and foundations
that hinted at a vanished presence. The air was conspicuously
empty where once gleaming marble had towered and thousands had attended from across the Greek-speaking city-states.

He walked around to the eastern entrance of the Temple
of Zeus, where a flight of stairs ascended past the inevitable
string. Just a single, parodic column remained standing at
the far end. The rest had fallen in earthquakes and lay scattered all about, some still in jagged rows of drums where
they'd tumbled. Barely a stone was above knee-height.
There wasn't the least sense of what it had once been.

I followed close behind; Buddy, with less enthusiasm. Had
Bastounis imagined this scene already? Was it part of a chapter, with an associated monologue like the octopus speech
in Gerolimenas? What was my role in the scene? I watched
him. Was he writing in his head at that very moment?

We paused at the string. A light wind was stirring the
plane trees, susurrating through the leaves as massed whis-
pers – ten thousand hushed spectators before the final race.
A collective inheld breath. Dust vortices rose around the
sanctuary and wisped across the ruins.

'Do you hear them?' said Bastounis. 'Do you sense
them?'

And I could. It was as if he'd called forth their populous
absence merely by his presence. As if they'd been waiting
eons for him to arrive as the vital conductor of their immortal static. Through him, the multitudes could coalesce from

the earth and trees and air they'd inhabited beyond the limits of their pagan world, beneath the weight of inundation as the river changed its course – victims of seismic shock, purging winds and history's indifference.

'Hear who?' muttered Buddy.

Bastounis ignored him. I sensed a monologue gathering in the gilded leaves and dust devils.

'Imagine no Parthenon. No Hagia Sophia. No Temple of Apollo at Bassae. Just the space they occupied. Just disrupted earth. Only human memory remains. When memory's elapsed, there are only images in out-dated formats: yellowed photos, etchings of fantastic overstatement. Then words. Frail, faded words. Like leaves from the trees. They also vanish. Languages metamorphose or become obsolete. Cultures evolve. Religions change. What remains?'

'Imagination?'

He turned to me. Not in anger that I'd interrupted his flow and answered his rhetorical question. Nor with any evident interest in what I'd said. More with a kind of mild surprise that I existed at all – that I might be one of the whispering multitudes he'd intuited, made briefly flesh through his incantation. It was almost as if he didn't see me at all. A sudden thought: if I expanded on my thought, perhaps it would lodge in his distracted mind and make it into the pages of his book.

'I mean, these places are greater in imagination than in any other form, aren't they? Bigger. More majestic. Seeing them now, in the present, with modern eyes, diminishes them. You have to see this temple through the imagined eyes of a classical visitor from Patmos or Crete or Nemea. That's where the wonder is. Once you've seen Manhattan, or travelled by air, you're spoiled for any ancient site. Even the pyramids…'

I realised I'd wandered into the Cretan labyrinth of a concept too large for me to handle. I'd got lost within its convolutions.

Bastounis hadn't seemed to hear, though he was standing right beside me. Buddy snorted mockingly. He mouthed a word – 'Guidebook' – and sauntered towards the stadium.

'A good idea,' said Bastounis, returned from his reverie. 'Let's go to the stadium.'

They walked towards the stone arch of its entrance: the old writer and the itinerant beatnik. Frustration burned. Like being back at school – other people making and knowing the codes. You said what you'd diligently discerned to be the cool thing … and discover it's become uncool in the meantime. People laugh.

A few tourists were gathered in the stadium. They posed for "starting blocks" pictures at the stone that was actually the finishing line. Perhaps 50,000 spectators would have surrounded this space during an Olympic race – an audience drawn from across the known world. The cacophony of it would have—

'How about a race?' said Buddy. 'Me and you.'

'I thought you weren't into the tourist stuff. Isn't racing here a little … obvious?'

'A bit of fun,' said Bastounis. 'Why not? Go down to the other end and watch for my signal.'

'What's the prize?' said Buddy.

'I'll think of something.'

I hesitated. I knew it was a trap of some kind. A test. Bastounis was watching me with the shadow of a grin – watching to see what I do. Would I have a tantrum? Would I rise to the challenge as I had with the Romanian pimp and the Maniot octopus?

'Fine. Fine. Let's go.'

'*Woo!*' said Buddy, causing others to stare.

We walked over the sun-baked earth towards the start. I hadn't run competitively since school. Even then, I was the one most likely to retire with a feigned asthma attack or impressive fall. School sports were a form of propaganda I'd refused to buy into.

'He's choosing a champion, man,' said Buddy. 'He doesn't need two drivers. I just gave him the means to make his decision. No hard feelings, right? You're not good for him. You know it. He knows it. Circumstance has thrown me in his path. We're alike, me and him. We're kindred souls – adventurers. I can see he's been thinking about how to do it. It's like a plot mechanism, right? Sometimes a character becomes redundant and you have to engineer an exit. This is it. Don't fight it man, you've had a good go. You've got a few anecdotes. I'll be picking it up from here.'

'Fuck you, Buddy.'

'*Heh!* So you *do* have some balls. But it's too late, man. I ran for my state back home.'

'How many joints have you smoked since?'

'I guess you'll see.'

We arrived at the end and Buddy scraped a line in the gravel with his toe. He bent and took a handful of dust as if communing with the spirits of Olympians past.

'Really?' I said.

'He's watching.'

Bastounis was a miniature figure at the other end, leaning on his stick. Seeing that we were both looking, he raised his other arm.

'Get set…' said Buddy, crouching.

It was ridiculous. I shouldn't even participate. That was the way to win: by showing my disdain. Let Buddy run it alone and look a fool. But that would seem like petulance from where Bastounis stood. He'd say I'd learned nothing from the challenges so far. I crouched wearily.

Bastounis dropped his arm.

We lurched. Gravel crunched. We sprinted. Buddy was soon a metre or so ahead, but our pace was the same. There was enough distance to pass him. I pumped hard, head down and started to close the gap.

He heard me coming. He saw me draw level. Our thumping feet reverberated across the track's pale expanse. We were both flat out with only a hundred metres to go.

I sensed I was going to win. I needed to push just a little harder. I imagined an ancient audience in the blur of the grassy banks – a sea of white robes, on their feet, arms in the air, cheering. Bastounis grew larger.

A gust of sand and gravel hit me in the face. It entered my mouth and stung my eyes. I stumbled to a halt and coughed, blinking, as I wiped my face with a sleeve. Blind, I heard Buddy's feet thunder on to the finish and his inevitable whoop. That handful of dust he'd gathered at the start…

Footsteps crunched towards me and a woman's voice said, 'Here, take this.' I felt a water bottle pressed into my hand. I sluiced my mouth and eyes, spitting to clear the taste of earth. My saviour was an elderly woman with a big straw hat.

'Your friend's a bad loser,' she said. American.

'He's not my friend.'

'I'd say not.'

'Thanks for the water. Enjoy Olympia.'

I walked towards where Bastounis and Buddy were talking.

'Bad luck, man!' said Buddy, still panting. 'To the victor go the spoils.'

'What do you mean "bad luck"? You threw dirt in my face. You cheated.'

'Don't be so dramatic. I was digging deep. I splayed my fingers and there must have been some dirt still on them.'

'You did it on purpose. You planned it.'

'Come on, man. A bad craftsman blames his tools. You lost.'

'A craftsman and his tools? Where'd you get that? *The Big Book of Cliché*? You're … you're a piece of shit. *You* lost because you cheated.'

'Hey, calm down, man. You'll have a stroke. We need an official judgement on this. Irakles?'

'Buddy won.' said Bastounis with a shrug. 'The dust was an accident. These things happen in the heat of competition.'

I glared, incredulous.

'What's my prize?' said Buddy.

'I'll think of something. In the meantime, let's enjoy the site while it's relatively empty. You two go off and explore. We'll meet back at the car in, what, an hour?'

Bastounis strolled back towards the temples. Buddy stood grinning.

'You can explore on your own,' I said.

An exaggerated *moue* of disappointment from Buddy.

I walked after Bastounis, too angry with him to attempt conversation. What would I say? He'd seen what he wanted to see. He'd already made his choice.

I walked over to the site of the old *palaestra* and *gymnasion*, where wrestlers and athletes would have exercised naked in the sun. It was now a square of parched grass surrounded by a colonnade. I sat on a lichen blossomed stone in the shade and watched tourists move between columns. How many of them had any sense of what used to happen here? How much, realistically, did *I* know? We were all visiting a vague pastiche of history and myth. The only true Olympia was the one each person fabricated from their brief impressions here.

I cursed Bastounis as a hypocrite and a manipulator. But I shouldn't have been surprised. Graham Greene had said every writer needed a splinter of ice in his heart – a gulf between artistic vision and frail human sensitivities. That explained why the five wives and none of the kids would talk to him. The books had been his priority. But Buddy? The guy was a prick. Bastounis must have seen it.

Better to be philosophical about the situation. I'd had some great and memorable experiences – more than I could have expected from travels on my own. Things like this never happened to me. There was plenty of time now to go my own way. Just get my bag from the car and start again. Bastounis would find out soon enough what a mistake he'd made and I'd be free of the whole situation. Maybe I'd read about it somewhere one day. I'd travelled with Irakles Bastounis and nobody could take that away.

I lay back on the stone and stared through the trees at a decoupage sky. Leaves rustled and occasionally fell in swaying, evasive descent. Bastounis had quoted Homer at the Temple of Zeus: "As generations of leaves, so is mankind." Just a brief season in the sun then pallor, fall, curling and compost. The most vibrant colours come just before the fall.

Olympia town was depressing. It was no worse aesthetically than Sparta or Tripoli or the newer parts of Nafplio, but its vulgar utility was utterly undisguised. The place existed solely to service the coach tours and the daily tourist influxes. Every business, it seemed, was a hotel, a restaurant or a souvenir shop selling vases, key rings, leather goods, postcards, replicas of Olympian statuary and the universe of dreck that filled such stores across the whole of Greece. It was easy enough to find a room.

Bastounis had said nothing about Buddy's "prize" or whether one of us wouldn't be travelling to the next place. My impression was that he was enjoying the uncertainty. Instead, he'd said he was tired after visiting the site and had retired for a siesta after we'd eaten a mediocre meal. Buddy and I had been sent out to entertain ourselves for an hour or two – something we opted to do separately.

I'd spent some of the time fending off a man determined to sell me a pair of badly-made sheepskin gloves, and about half an hour in a bookshop that had nothing by Bastounis. Evidently, he wasn't classed as tourist reading. The rest of the time, I sat in a café watching the tourists go by and working on daydreams. One featured Buddy being mangled by the multiple wheels of a coach – not killed, necessarily, but sufficiently maimed to prevent his driving ever again. I also dreamed of an attractive girl sitting next to me with a fat novel in her hand. She'd mention that she was a big fan of Irakles Bastounis and I'd casually drop the information that I was travelling with the great man. Would, perhaps, she like to meet him? Instead, a party of middle-aged Germans arrived and loudly drank beer. I decided to go back.

I sensed something was wrong before I even got to the rooms. A few people had gathered on the pavement and were looking up at our balcony. The noise became clearer as I approached – Bastounis bellowing.

I rushed through the marble reception and up the steps. Our door was open. Bastounis was in the doorway wearing only his underwear. He was pointing an accusatory arm at

Buddy, who had backed into a corner. Buddy was wearing his backpack. He had a syringe in his hand. I saw immediately that the fault was mine.

'What's going on?' I said, my voice fainter than I'd intended.

'He's crazy, man!' said Buddy. 'He threatened to kill me!'

Bastounis turned to me. '*You* – you told him about what happened in the Mani.'

'I ... I said it was just vitamins or medicine!'

'You said it was H,' said Buddy. 'And it virtually is.' He held up a small amber ampoule. 'Look at the label. It's *morphine*, man. You can't buy this shit over the counter. It's illegal.'

'Give it to me,' said Bastounis, 'or I swear you're going over the balcony headfirst. Just put it on the bed there and you can go. Nothing will happen. Do it now before the police come.'

'And catch you with morphine, right? Let 'em come. *I've* done nothing wrong.'

'You stole from me. While I was sleeping.'

'*He* said you were a hard sleeper.' Buddy's finger jabbed at me.

'Mister Bastounis ... I've got nothing to do with this. I ... I know it was a mistake to tell him anything. I should have kept my mouth shut.'

'Give me the ampoule and the syringe,' said Bastounis, his voice a blade.

'Let me keep it. And the money. My payment for all this. You're rich, man. I walk out of here and I don't tell anyone about your morphine habit or that you're writing another book.'

'You won't tell anybody anything. Give me the ampoule.'

'It was you, wasn't it? It was you who bust my phone?'

Bastounis smiled. 'What phone? You said you had no phone.'

'I'm keeping this, man. And I'm keeping the money. You owe me.'

'Over the balcony or through me. Your choice.'

'You're crazy, man! You could be my granddad.'

Bastounis glanced back at me. 'Stand here. Block the door.'

'What?'

'Stand in the doorway. He's not leaving with that ampoule.'

I moved reluctantly to take Bastounis's place as he advanced on Buddy.

'I'll go straight through you,' said Buddy. 'Don't try it, old man.'

'Last warning,' said Bastounis. 'Put the ampoule on the bed. You can keep the money.'

Buddy glanced frantically at Bastounis, at the balcony, at me. He dropped his head like a charging bull and ran at the door. At me. He didn't make it.

Bastounis stepped forward and crashed his knee into Buddy's forehead. Buddy jerked upwards, stunned, and wobbled on his feet. Bastounis pivoted, his fighting guard up, and drove a punch on to the point of Buddy's chin. The younger man crumpled to his knees and on to his face – a double thud that shook the room. Out cold.

'Jesus!'

I stood impotently in the doorway. Now Bastounis went down. He sank slowly to a knee, then on to all fours. He was deathly pale. Heart attack? Stroke? He was saying something faintly, raspingly.

'Mister Bastounis?'

'Hide … the ampoule …'

'What? What?'

There were footsteps on the stairs in the hall. I heard the garbled static of radios. Bastounis rolled over on his back, his eyes fluttering at the edge of consciousness.

'Hide. The. Morphine.'

He went limp and began to spasm, his entire body thrashing, arms and legs flailing at the floor. I recognised it from TV hospital shows: a *grand mal* seizure.

Somebody shouted in Greek from the hallway.

Buddy was still unconscious. I could see the ampoule in his slack palm. I didn't think. I took it and stuffed it into my pants. Were there more? Too late. I kicked the fallen syringe under a bed.

'Help!' I said. 'We need a doctor!'

The landlord was at the door, two policemen behind him. They took in the scene: two inert bodies on the floor – me between them, flustered. I raised my hands.

THIRTEEN

A female officer brought me a coffee in a plastic cup and looked reprovingly at me before returning to her desk. The morphine ampoule between my thigh and scrotum seemed to swell with every passing minute, threatening to burst from my shorts as a klaxon of incrimination.

The police station was a tiny, cluttered room above a lotto shop: computers, noticeboards, calendars, a photocopier. I had no idea what was happening. The two policemen had brought me here alone in a police car and immediately left, presumably to deal with Bastounis and Buddy. The woman had taken my name and my passport details, but hadn't interrogated me or accused me of anything. Instead, I waited with the ampoule burning guiltily in my crotch, imagining a CSI team going through the room and finding all the evidence. More ampoules. The discarded syringe. The roll of money Buddy had grabbed. Enough clues, surely, to suggest some kind of crime.

I sipped the coffee mechanically and wondered if my mother would be contacted. The ignominy of that was greater than any accusation or sentence. It would prove of all her points. Stop daydreaming and become responsible. Take your place in the hive with the rest. Look where your fantasies of travel and experience have landed you. And *drugs*? We're so disappointed! How's this going to look on your CV?

Worst case: Buddy and Bastounis die. Somebody would have to take the fall. The spectre of jail set my bowels quivering. The testosterone. The language barrier. I wouldn't survive jail. "Face your fears," Bastounis had challenged me, but not all fears were equal. Disease, death, and jail were worthy of fear. They were best avoided.

The policemen who'd attended the incident came laughing into the office on a gust of fresh cigarette smoke. Perhaps no one had died after all. The taller of the two came and sat opposite me, his expression changing immediately to professional indifference.

'So…Last man standing – what is the story? What happened?'

'I came back to the room and they were arguing. Mister Bastounis was shouting and—'

'Mister Irakles Bastounis.'

'You know who he is?'

'We checked his ID.'

'I mean, that he's a Nobel prize-winner. A famous writer.'

The policeman's face was blank. He jotted a note and waved his hand for me to continue.

'So Mister Bastounis accused him – accused Buddy – of stealing—'

'Mister Buddy Tannenbaum.'

'His name's Tannenbaum? Okay, yes – so Buddy had a roll of notes in his hand and Mister Bastounis told him to give it back or he'd…throw him over the balcony. He told me to block the door but Buddy made a run for it and Mister Bastounis hit him. With his knee and then with his fist.'

'He knocked out Mister Tannenbaum.'

'Yes.'

'And why you three stay in a room together?'

'We're travelling ... Oh, I see ... No. It's nothing immoral. Mister Bastounis can't drive because of his leg and I was visiting his village in Arcadia and he asked me to drive for him and then we saw Buddy hitching and Mister Bastounis said we should stop even though I said it was a bad idea because, you know, hitchhikers ... Can I ask if Mister Bastounis is okay? Where is he now?'

'You don't ask me about Mister Tannenbaum.'

'No ... Look – I don't really like him. I didn't trust him from the start. But Mister Bastounis said—'

'Why you don't trust him?'

'Well, he likes Kerouac for a start ... I mean, there's just something about him. I think he's a liar and a manipulator. He'll say anything, do anything ... Have you talked to him? Did you find the money?'

'Not only money.'

The ampoule throbbed in my shorts. I wondered if I'd start actually crying with fear.

The policeman opened his breast pocket and fanned a number of credit cards on the desk.

'Buddy had those?'

A slow nod. A long stare.

'Wait. You think ...? I don't know anything about those! I've only known him for two days. We picked him up by the side of the road somewhere north of Sparta – I don't know where exactly but ...'

The policeman held up a hand for silence.

'This Buddy. He said there was morphine.'

'Morphine? What, like opium?'

The ampoule throbbed like Poe's tell-tale heart from my pants. The policeman looked into my eyes and read the evasion. The tautening silence was excruciating. I had to say *something.*

167

'I think Mister Bastounis has some kind of medicine…Maybe that's what Buddy meant. He has bad headaches sometimes. I've heard him vomiting. He hasn't really spoken to me about it. Maybe his leg…'

'He is sick?'

'Yes. He's very ill. Can you tell me how he is now? Where is he?'

'And Buddy, he took this medicine, yes?'

'I don't know. Like I said: I only heard part of the argument. Mister Bastounis said Buddy had stolen from him while he was sleeping.'

'Where is this medicine now?'

'I don't know. Maybe Buddy dropped it when he fell.'

'Your friend Tannenbaum is in big trouble.'

'He's not my friend. He really isn't. Put him in prison. I don't care.'

A flicker of a smile.

'You can visit Mister Bastounis. He is at the medical centre here.'

'He's conscious? He's awake?'

'You can see him. I can take you. But we keep your passport and bag for now, eh?'

'Why?'

A shrug. 'Return here after you see Mister Bastounis.'

'And Buddy?'

'I think you will not see Buddy again. Come – we go to the health centre.'

The health centre was maybe five minutes away in the police car. It was a tiny building meant for minor tourist injuries and children who'd swallowed keys. At reception, the policeman chatted to an attractive girl who listened with occasional glances at me before making a brief phone call. I was then shown through to an office.

A woman doctor of about fifty came from behind her desk to shake my hand and introduce herself as Doctor Phillipou. She had an abundance of curly black hair and intense brown eyes. She indicated the seat in front of the desk and I sat. There was a plaster model of a hip joint to her left and a coloured poster of the circulatory system on the wall behind.

'You must be very worried,' she said.

'I saw him on the floor having a seizure. It looked serious, like epilepsy.'

'It's not epilepsy, though the symptoms can be similar.'

'Is he alright? Nobody's told me anything.'

'You aren't related to Irakles, are you?'

'No. I'm just…Just his driver.'

'He has refused to give me any next-of-kin details, but with his notorious family history…'

'You know who he is?'

'Of course. Irakles Bastounis is one of our greatest novelists, even if he wrote in English. He said I should consider you his next of kin.'

'Me?'

She nodded. 'He is stable. He will have some bad bruising from the seizure and from hitting the young man. For now, he is awake and lucid.'

'For now…?'

'Yes. I suppose he has told you nothing about his condition?'

'His condition? He's told me nothing…'

'Have you noticed perhaps the scar he has on his head – about here?'

'I haven't seen anything. He wears his cap all the time.'

'I'm sure he does. It's from a biopsy he had last year in Athens. Irakles has a brain tumour. It is large and surgery is not possible for a number of reasons. There are treatments, but they are difficult at his age and the side effects may be as bad as the symptoms themselves. Anyway, he has declined all treatment. He will not recover.'

'He's going to die?'

'We are all going to die. The difference is that he has an actual deadline. The doctors in Athens gave him around six months. I've spoken to his physician there.'

'But… didn't you say Athens was last year?'

'Around six months ago, yes.'

The preceding days crashed suddenly into focus. The meeting with Konstantinopoulos and the business with the medal. The glamorous woman in Monemvasia. The *taverna* guy in Gytheio … Was this Bastounis's farewell tour?

And my role? Was I merely the fantastic coincidence that made it possible? The pliable blank slate. The guileless young Englishman. If I hadn't arrived in Dimitsana on that day and agreed to drive him …

'I realise this must be difficult for you. I don't know what kind of relationship you have with Irakles …'

'There's no real relationship. He mocks me and makes me carry his bag.'

'He named you as his next of kin.'

'I … I don't really know what to say. It's … absurd. He has morphine – is that part of his treatment?'

'No. His condition is one of gradual physical deterioration rather than pain. His leg may be connected to the tumour, or it could be arthritis. In either case, morphine is too powerful a drug for such pain. I believe he may have got it from someone else. Not from his doctor. It's not for alleviating his symptoms. It's for later.'

'Later?'

A nod. 'What are your plans now that you know the truth? Will you continue travelling with him?'

'I don't know. I hadn't made plans. This wasn't a plan. You mean he wants to continue?'

'He's a stubborn man. You may know something about it.'

'Yes.'

'You should know that his symptoms will become worse. Right now, it's headaches, nausea, drowsiness and weakness on the side of his bad leg. There may be periods of blurred vision. He is losing his sense of taste and smell. You saw his seizure – perhaps you've noticed tics or twitches. There may be instances of memory loss and personality change: mood swings, melancholy, irritability, aggression. These are typical symptoms for this kind of tumour. Towards the end, he may become totally blind. When it comes, it will come quickly. If you are with him then, call me. I will give you my details. It will make things easier for you.'

'And the morphine? Do I need to know about that?'

She smiled. She rested her palms on the desk. 'Do you want to see him?'

'I suppose I should.'

'He knows he had a seizure but he doesn't remember it. That's normal. He's a little dehydrated. He's also embarrassed because he urinated during the fit.'

'I won't mention it.'

She took me through to a tiny ward with just four beds in it. Bastounis was the only person there, looking pale and impatient. Seeing me, he was caught between sheepishness and chin-out defiance. He reached for his cap and set it low over his eyes.

'I'll leave you,' she said.

The distance between the door and the bed was the furthest I'd ever covered. I didn't know what to say. He didn't want to talk to me. I'd seen him weak and piss-stained. Now

I was seeing him mortal. I was the placebo for his abandon-ment. The surrogate relative.

There was a clear tube going into his arm from a suspended bag. A half-drunk coffee was on the table by his bed.

'Buddy?' he said.

'No, it's me.'

'No, I meant, "What happened to Buddy?"'

'Oh. Turns out he's a serial thief. He had a load of stolen credit cards.'

'Hmm. Did you hide the morphine?'

'It's in my pants. But the police know about it. Buddy must have told them. I played ignorant. I said it was prob-ably medicine.'

I looked at the tube and the IV drip.

'I suppose you've spoken with Eleni,' he said. 'With Doctor Phillipou.'

'Yes.'

He took off his cap and dropped it on his legs.

'I'm sorry,' I said.

'Sorry why? It's death. You might as well say you're sorry for life, which lasts longer and has more suffering. We're all going to the same place. Forget religion, philosophy, science... Death is the single undeniable certainty. It's in everything we've ever thought and produced. I've been liv-ing with the news for months.'

'You could have mentioned it. The illness, I mean.'

'Call it what it is: the tumour. The invader. The Damoclean switch in my head. Why would I mention it? Are you happier now you know? Would you have accepted the proposal back in Dimitsana if you'd known I could have been a corpse at any moment? I didn't need a nurse; I needed a driver.'

He was right of course. Besides, who was I to share his fading life with? What right had I to know anything about those people he'd been visiting or what he might have said to them? Still, it stung – the utter arbitrariness of my role in the drama. The fact I hadn't been worthy of knowing the bigger story.

'Why me?'

'Don't be disingenuous. You know why. There was nobody else.'

He took up the cap and started working the brim with thumb and forefinger. I intuited what was coming.

'I'm not going to die in a hospital,' said Bastounis. 'These are the last drops. There are things I want to do, people I need to see. I'm not... I refuse to... I'm going to keep going until I can't. Then the morphine. All of it.'

'In Gerolimenas, when you... with the needle.'

'No, no. That was something different.' He smiled. 'I just wanted to try it. I couldn't help myself. Just a little taste for old times. I got it from Konstantinopoulos if you were wondering. His daughter, Chrysa – she's a cancer doctor in Thessaloniki.'

'I see.'

'The question is: will you keep driving me? Now that you know. I'm not asking for a decision right now – calm yourself. There are things you need to know. Doctor Eleni will write a letter detailing my condition and my decision to travel. She'll outline the probable causes of my death. There'll be contact details for her and my Athens doctor. When it happens, you – or whoever's with me – will give the letter to the authorities. It answers any difficult questions. I'll leave money in my bag for onwards travel or whatever. Maybe I'll write a letter, too – explaining it from my perspective. You – or whoever – can keep the car. Or abandon it. Whatever.'

I couldn't think of a single thing to say. Amid the chaos of my thoughts floated the absurdity of whether abandoning a car in Greece carried some penalty.

'You see now why I didn't tell you before,' he said. 'Sometimes, it's better to be ignorant, eh? Now you know. Now it's your decision. Remember what we've talked about so far. The challenges. Be spontaneous – take the risk. Face your fears. At the same time, recognise that life isn't a movie with a happy ending and a script you'd choose to write. This is the ragged dissatisfaction of real life. Can you face that? You don't have to, of course. You can run from it as so many millions do and anaesthetise yourself with the usual things: routine, family, pension plans. It's a kind of life, but barely sapient. It's self-induced coma. Peaceful, yes, and unchallenging. Easy. But time's so very short. You get it only once, and by the time you realise what it's worth – the colossal potential of that time – well, it's usually too late. It's gone – sand through your fingers. You have to live it. It's up to you. Look – let's make it easy. Don't say anything now. If you accept, I'll see you at the room tomorrow morning. I've told Eleni I'm leaving then and she knows she can't stop me. If you decide not to, just take your bag and I wish you *kalo taxidi*. Leave the car keys beside the bed. Here ...'

He put out his hand for a shake. I approached and we clasped hands: a firm, dry grip from the fingers that had written *Cassandra*, punched Mailer, pleasured starlets, driven racing cars, injected heroin, swung from a trapeze, lived life to the very last drop. He stared hard into my eyes with that titanium intensity – a brief burst that stopped as abruptly as it had begun. He looked away

'Leave the morphine here with me.'

His manner had changed in an instant. I was a stranger again. I extracted the ampoule and put it beside his half-drunk coffee. It was if I'd already left the room. Was this one of the mood swings caused by his tumour?

I went to the door, looking back just once. He wasn't watching me. He was examining the ampoule.

The policeman who'd brought me had left so I walked back to the police office. The streets were just as they'd been before – souvenir shops, tourists, tour buses, cafes and tavernas – but my situation was different. These people in their sun hats, with their guidebooks and their attitudes of awed reverence for the past were seeing a different reality – the same reality I'd experienced just that morning.

Now I was a person walking between health centre and police office. There was an old man with a terminal brain tumour and a young American called Tannenbaum arrested for theft. There'd been a fight. I'd smuggled morphine in my pants. My presence here in Olympia was now a cosmological joke, an aleatory accident. I hadn't planned any of it – had been powerless to influence any of it. I was caught in the current of what Bastounis would probably call the chaos of existence. I could only respond.

And yet there was glamour in it. Beneath the gravity of circumstance was a thrill of powerlessness. Things happened. Of course, things happened all the time to everyone. This was different. This wasn't a missed train or a new job or slipping on ice. The moment I'd first got in the car with Bastounis, I'd stepped out of control. Anything might have happened. Calypso might have happened. Octopus fishing and Buddy might have happened. Now Bastounis was dying.

Nobody else around me was part of this. They shopped, drank coffee and compared digital photos of the ancient site. Perhaps they'd seen the police car earlier and wondered vaguely at its purpose. Maybe they'd heard a rumour of an altercation at some nearby rooms. I was at the centre of that drama. This was *my* life veering off the rails of expectation and continuing, somehow unharmed, towards an unknown destination.

Except now there *was* a destination: Bastounis's death. That's how it would end if I chose to continue. Death. It was supposed to be an abstract – a vague and distant knowledge. Hazy acquaintances or old schoolmates died in freak accidents. Parents would notionally, eventually, die. My own death wouldn't need considering for another sixty years or more. I was insulated from it by youth and statistics. But Bastounis was at the door, waiting for it to open. Did I really want to be with him when it did? Could I be that close voluntarily and face the consequences? Wasn't the whole point of death that you were supposed to stay away from it as much and as far as possible?

Four things stopped me from running. The first was that word he'd used to needle me. He'd used it twice to make sure I got it. *Whoever.* Whoever else was driving. Whoever else would carry the letter from Doctor Phillipou. *Whoever* was my substitute as driver and bag-carrier. My replacement. As if I were interchangeable with any dupe he could pick off the street – ideally someone young and impressed by a Nobel Prize. Anyone would do – even a dickhead like Buddy. He'd used the word to belittle me. He was angry that the fact of his tumour had come out and that it might jeopardise his mobility. He was pre-emptively angry with me for withdrawing my service. But he also knew it would sting and potentially persuade. He'd seen the competitiveness with Buddy. He'd actively stoked it. Manipulative, yes, but perhaps he had cause.

Then there was that handshake – another piece of shameless theatre from Bastounis. The "farewell" shake loaded with pathos and recrimination. It might as well have been a kiss, Judas style. We'd not shaken on anything until that point. I hadn't been worthy of it as any kind of equal. There'd been no gratitude from him, no acknowledgement. He'd kept a measured, clinical distance. The handshake – with its piercing, fathomless stare – had been a grudging sacrifice. It had had its intended effect. He'd got to me.

He'd also been careful to repeat the challenges so far issued. He wanted me to know what I'd be missing if I left him. What other life lessons might here have been? What other essential drops of wisdom from the man? He knew that was bait I'd find hard to resist. The challenges were a narrative I had to pursue until the end. How could I not? This was Irakles Bastounis.

Finally: the glamour. That was the most powerful intoxicant. I'd come to Greece with fantasies of adventure and discovery, but pragmatically expecting the tawdry mediocrities of travel: the smelly hostel dorms, the crowded sites, the waiting, the rip-offs, the disappointments, the eventual realisation that you're no better or different to the thousands of other travellers having a supposedly unique experience. Dimitsana had sparked a radical trajectory away from all of that. It was better than an adventure. It was what happened in books. For all Bastounis's disdain for the scripted life and for camera-angle reality, that's exactly what he was encouraging. He'd made Greece itself a location and we were living according to his screenplay.

All highly persuasive. Apart from having to experience his death.

It all came back to that. The ultimate reality. Could I face it?

I arrived at the police office and walked up the steps on heavy legs. Again, the only one present was the female officer. I nodded a greeting and gestured a question as to whether I should sit and wait.

She tutted and shook her head. She clacked across the marble floor and opened a drawer in a desk. My passport and the key to the rented room dropped on to the desktop. She waved me to the door.

'I can go?'

'Go. Yes.' A professional smile. '*Kalo taxidi.*'

I walked numbly to the door, half expecting a burst of laughter and the news that actually I was under arrest. But I went down the stairs and into the street without challenge. Had they spoken to Bastounis and cleared it all up? Or was the paperwork just too much of a drag?

Back at the room, I saw that Buddy's bag was gone. Mine and Bastounis's remained, but in different places. I looked quickly through mine – nothing missing. I knelt and looked under the bed. The syringe was gone. An entirely separate drama had played out in the room after we'd been taken from it. I'd probably never know what.

I lay back on the bed and stared at the mute witness of the ceiling. I was hungry. I'd probably go out and see if any of the tavernas had *stifado* or *loukanika*. Maybe some *horta* and *fava* with a nice jug of homemade wine from a barrel. Plenty of bread with it, and then some *baklava* or *loukoumades*. I shouldn't decide anything on an empty stomach.

FOURTEEN

The rattling doorknob woke me. Then hammering knocks. It was still dark outside.

'Who is it?'

'Open the fucking door.' Bastounis. His voice weary.

I unlocked it, rubbing my eyes, sluggish with interrupted sleep. 'What time is it? It's still night.'

'It's morning. Early. Get your stuff together. We have a ferry to catch.'

He flicked on the light and I flinched. My arms and legs were heavy as I dressed. I felt as if I'd been clubbed over the head. We attended unspeakingly to our bags and he put money on the bedside table. I felt like a fugitive.

'Ready?'

'Yes.'

The car was wet with dew and the air was moist with the exhalation of trees and earth. A bar of pale rose light was appearing in the east. No birds yet sang.

'Wait a moment,' said Bastounis. 'Wait.'

I paused, breath steaming, the bags in my hands. I waited.

'Olympian dawn,' he said. 'Unchanged across millennia. You feel it? Precursor to victory and defeat. Wars rage, rivers inundate, religions change – the earth slowly erodes ... and still the immutable sky brightens. Is there not hope in that?'

'I guess so.'

'Get in the car.'

I tossed the bags on the back seat. I used a rag to wipe the back window and I started the engine. The steering wheel was cold but there was familiarity in the feel of it and in the proximity of the gear lever, the indicator, the window winder. The seat had been adjusted to Buddy's shorter legs so I set it back. Minutes later, we were on the empty road.

Mist hung over the fields and the olive groves. Autumn colours showed in taller trees. Bastounis had rolled his window down despite the cool and leaned his arm on the sill. I waited, expecting he might say something about the tumour. Things had changed. I'd seen him with a tube in his arm. I'd seen him thrashing in a seizure. It would be natural or rational to acknowledge the situation – to talk more about this sentence he'd been living with for six months. We were in it together now.

That's what I thought for the first few miles. But then I realised. What could I possibly say that would have any meaning? "Don't worry – it'll all be alright"? "Would you like to talk about the end of your life?" "How does it feel to know that this time next week you might be blind and insensible?" And I understood his silence. There was one thing, however, I needed to know.

'Did you actually like Buddy?'

A blank look from Bastounis. 'What do you mean?'

'Well, you were complimentary about his riff on Pan and the dryads. You seemed to like all that shit about being "twentieth century" even though he had a secret phone. You let him drive. And you *know* he cheated in our race.'

'He was a free spirit.'

'He liked Kerouac! He was a common thief. He robbed *you*.'

'You were threatened by him.'

'*What?*'

'Come on...Let's not play that game. You saw him immediately as a rival. You feared he was the genuine article whereas you were only playing at it. So what if he was a thief and a liar? That's the way of the drifter. I'd have been surprised if he didn't try to rob me. He was out hitching on the road, just going wherever. There's integrity in that. He believed in what he was doing.'

'And I don't?'

'You don't know what you're doing.'

'I don't believe this. I don't believe you liked him. It's almost as if...'

Bastounis tried to cover a smile with his hand.

'Seriously? I don't...Is that right? You picked him up purely to antagonise me?'

'Antagonise? Not only that. To challenge you. I was right to do it. His presence rocked your foundations, didn't it? He was a more original thinker, a more intrepid adventurer, a freer spirit – less afraid.'

'He was a dickhead.'

'And yet you compared yourself to him constantly, didn't you.'

'All of it...all just a challenge.'

'Don't think of it as frivolity. It's an important lesson. Look at this man you made your rival and competitor – a man you had no respect for. Why compare yourself to him? Because *I* seemed to value him? Who dictates your self-worth and the truth of your ideas? Only you. When you look for affirmation everywhere but in yourself, you're scattered to the winds. You're lost. You'll never be satisfied. D'you think I rushed out to read the reviews of my books? Reviews by people who could never have dreamed of writing what

I'd written, or of living the life I'd lived. Those people are dung beetles crawling among the turds of culture. I never wrote for insects. I wrote for myself. *I'm* my greatest critic. Look at the knots you twisted yourself into over Buddy. Was it worth it? Do you thirst so ardently for my approval that you'd humiliate yourself with Buddy?'

'I respect you.'

'Respect is fine. I'm not saying you can't learn from others, but you do it from a position of equal standing – as humans. Life's not about taking your prescribed position in some established hierarchy, though that's what they'd have you believe. It's about rejecting the hierarchy, and any other system that doesn't suit you. Don't measure yourself against what you despise.'

I drove. The sun had burned away the mist. We were passing through rural pastureland and the smell of goats came into the car. Their bells clanked and tinkled in fields either side of the road.

'Did you know his name was Tannenbaum?' I said.

'Of course. I went through his bag while you were visiting the temple.'

'It was you who broke his phone.'

'Yes?'

'The shoe-tree door stopper...'

'A plausible narrative mechanism.'

I shook my head slowly. The deception. The duplicity. Everything around Bastounis was drawn into his narrative mechanism. He flung stories centrifugally from his epicentre, characters and situations flying off into the margins. Calypso. Buddy. Konstantinopoulos. The closer to the core, the safer you were, provided you didn't mind being encompassed by a hurricane.

'Turn right here,' he said, as if nothing had happened, as if nothing was going to happen. 'We're going to Patras.'

I knew Patras was a big town – the main ferry port of the Peloponnese and the biggest town for me since Athens. It announced itself initially as factories, warehouses and car dealerships that increased in density until we turned right on to the coast road. This was Greece's industrial sea. It reminded me of the shipyards and refineries I'd seen coming out of the capital by bus. Half-constructed concrete skeletons glared in the sun. The traffic multiplied. There was a smell of diesel fumes, bilge and marine fuel coming off the water. I could see the cranes and massive hulls of the port.

Bastounis directed me to the ferry terminals and sent me into an office to buy two tickets for Sami in Kefalonia. But that wasn't our destination. We were going to Ithaca. Ithaca, where Odysseus had lived and returned after his odyssey from the ruined battlements of Troy. We were returning to Homer's realm.

I slept on the ferry, lulled by the engines' subterranean thunder as I stretched out across faux-leather seats. There was no sense of movement, so huge was the vessel and so stolid its belly ballast of serried cars and trucks. I dreamed a vaguely Ulyssean scene of sailing past a rocky shore on which my mother, Clara, a favoured university lecturer and friends were calling to me across the breaking waves. I couldn't hear their words, and couldn't discern whether their urging was entreaty or warning, sanctuary or peril. There seemed no safe place to land, or even to sail closer for clarity. As the wind bore me out of range – reducing their expressions to frenzied mime – I thought I saw Calypso among them: standing calmly, waving in happy recognition.

'We're here.'

Bastounis shook my arm. 'We're here. Come on – come to look at the view.'

I sat up and looked through a salt-crusted window. Hills, sea and sky. I followed him from the air-conditioned chamber into the humid breath of these Ionian islands. Tourists were on deck taking photos. The buzz of landfall. Sami was laid out at the foot of a mountain – a decent size town fed by ferries from Brindisi.

'All destroyed in the earthquake of '53,' said Bastounis. 'Just levelled. And those mountains over there – that's Ithaca.'

It looked like an extension of Kefalonia, but rockier and more barren. There wasn't a single house visible.

'And there where I'm pointing. D'you see the lazy M in the hills there? That's Pisaetos where our harbour is. The name refers to the shape of the hills. In Greek, *piso aetos* means roughly "back of the eagle." You see? The profile of the bird as it takes flight.'

'Yes … yes, I see it.'

'Ancient knowledge. How long has it been known? Before maps, all toponymy had such origins. The words expressed the shapes and temperament of the land. Ithaca's capital, also a port, is Vathy: "deep". It's the same root you find in "bathysphere." There's a village high in the mountains called Exogi: "out of the world". Timeless place names. People forget. They just hear the name and miss associations that go back beyond memory and history into myth. Perhaps Odysseus himself knew that piece of horizon as Pisaetos. Perhaps he was the one, as king, who named it.

Now we use the same word and understand his thinking. We're inside his mind. It's transcendent.'

When Bastounis said it, I believed it. I imagined the flotilla of dark ships – tiny against the peaks and the silver thread of surf – setting forth for Aulis, thence to Troy and eternal glory.

The engines throbbed. The propellers reverse-churned for docking.

'We'd better get in the car,' he said.

I managed to drive the car onto the dock without humiliating myself, and there we waited for the smaller Astakos ferry that would drop us at Pisaetos. Bastounis claimed his leg was hurting, so I walked to a nearby café and returned with iced coffees that we drank in the car. He was subdued. Had his seizure in Olympia been the strongest indication yet of his impending end? For six months he'd had a schedule. Now his deadline had passed. He'd lived the given term of life and was now journeying in limbo.

He'd spent half a year thinking about the void. All this stuff about Homer and the heroes – that was his vision of death. It echoed beyond time into ramifying depths of profundity I'd never guess at. My trying to talk to him about it would be like a monkey trying to discuss relativity with a man. To him, I was one those birds that picks the crocodile's teeth. He was happy for the volunteered service. I had to be grateful for the nugatory nourishment and the grace of not being smashed between his jaws.

The Ithaca ferry was even smaller than the one we'd taken from Nafplio, but by now I was able to reverse on to it with aplomb, earning an ironic 'Bravo!' from Bastounis. He stayed in the car when I walked up a deck to watch, though I could see no harbour at Pisaetos even by the halfway point. The Ithaca straight was a cobalt chasm beneath us,

absorbing light, sucking at the rusting hull. The hills opposite us were worn naked by wind, sun and rain. Only in the
last few minutes of the crossing did I see the tiny concrete
jetty and the track leading from it over the saddle of the
eagle's back. We were the sole passengers disembarking.

Bastounis had got darker still during the crossing, the
peak of his cap descending lower over his eyes. He seemed
to have slumped lower in his seat. His directions from the
deserted harbour were monosyllabic and he worked the
crook of his stick as we ascended the pot-holed hairpins.
At the top of the hill, he had me veer off the road along an
unsurfaced track that followed the ridge of the eagle's left
wing.

It led to a beautiful stone house perched just below the
crest of the ridge. Built from the surrounding stone, and
with a stone-paved roof, it blended almost invisibly into the
landscape. A car with foreign plates was parked in front of it.

'Here?' I said.

'Yes. Listen – you should drive back down to the road
and follow it round to the right. Go to Vathy and have a coffee or something. It's about ten minutes away. Come back in
two hours. Okay?'

His eyes were embers that discouraged questions or
negotiation.

'If you're sure…'

He got out, using his stick and the sill to lever himself
standing.

'Go. Go on.'

I reversed and turned the car. The last I saw of him in
the rearview, he was still in front of the house, facing it,
leaning on his stick with heavy shoulders. I thought perhaps
he was waiting for me to disappear down the track before
he entered.

The road went round to the right as he'd said, revealing Vathy spread around the head of its deep bay. I drove into town and parked the Peugeot up a side street, where I paused with the realisation that I'd temporarily abandoned the man and his car. I was adrift. I missed his gravity. I was a tiny, blank satellite to his Jupiter. Not even one of the cool moons, but a distant grey one with a boring name. Or just a number.

Every café, restaurant, souvenir shop and hotel seemed to be cashing in on the Odyssean legacy. I saw a Mentor hostel, a Penelope taverna, a Calypso diving emporium, a Telemachus ticket office and a Polyphemus gift shop. How did this crass appropriation of the story fit with Bastounis's riff on timeless toponymic knowledge? Should I perceive the immortal will of King Odysseus also in the Ulysses *souvlaki* stand across the road?

The Circe café at the head of the bay looked charming enough. I took a front-row seat under a beer-branded umbrella and ordered my usual iced coffee. It had become a default ritual since I'd been in Greece: the perspiring drink, the marble-topped table, the view of arid peaks and ocean – the uneventful drama of the town unfolding to a chronology of straw-sips. Vans unloaded, mopeds whined, pretty girls passed, be-capped old men walked arm-linked in quiet conspiracy. This was happiness. Observing, but not belonging. Out of time and beyond consequence. There had never been moments like this at home – of meditative lassitude, of idle contentment. Only now was I managing to get outside the test tube that was home.

Home. It seemed as distant as the Heroic Age. My dream on the ferry had been a postcard from the subconscious. Without my phone, I'd not been in touch since Nafplio. The drinks menu said Circe Café & Internet. Had I chosen the place for that reason – a subliminal prompt? I turned in my chair and looked back into the interior, where the ghosts of old monitors were visible in the gloom. Should I?

I took my coffee and organised a grubby computer for thirty minutes. There were thirty emails waiting, twenty-two of them spam. Among the legitimate messages were rushed epistles enquiring about my trip, dutiful questions from extended family, and a series of numbing bulletins from mother designed variously as ill-disguised rebukes, warnings and concerns. Nothing from Clara.

It was a world I barely recognised and didn't miss. My story of Buddy, the police and the morphine was more vivid than anything any of them had ever experienced. The trip with Bastounis... well, I didn't want to share it. They wouldn't appreciate or understand it. They didn't deserve it.

The thought of Buddy sent me back to the search page. I typed in his full name, feeling superior that I knew it, and set the parameters to the last two weeks. What had happened to young Mr Tannenbaum since the police had got him? Perhaps he'd discovered the love that dare not speak its name with a burly new bunkmate at some correctional facility in the far north.

He had a blog. Of course he had. *Dharma Karma*, he called it. I clicked and felt my viscera clench at the most recent post, dated late the previous evening.

"Bastounis Lives! New Book Coming...

Hold the front page! I bet most of you thought novelistic Titan Irakles Bastounis was dead, right? Wrong! The man was just dormant like Vesuvius, living in his ancestral village and trying to escape the alimony lawyers. But now he's moving – off the grid and incognito. He's got one final book in him and

he's researching it right now as you read this. How do
I know? Shit – I've been travelling with him, man!"

I read on with growing nausea. Buddy described it all:
being picked up in the Peugeot, the trip to Andritsaina, the
Temple of Apollo, Olympia. There wasn't a single mention
of me. The way he told it, Bastounis had been driving the car
near Sparta. Buddy had visited the temple with Bastounis
and they'd entered it together. They'd shared a transcen-
dental moment in the sanctuary at Olympia. Not only that,
but Buddy had written about Nafplio, Monemvasia, Gytheio
and the Mani as if he'd been there. There's no way he could
have known these things unless…

My journal. He'd read my journal. At Olympia? At
Andritsaina? He would have read about the overdose scare
in Gytheio. Details. Corroboration.

Coffee bile bubbled hotly in my throat. I imagined him
holding my journal, sniggering at my style, leafing through
it in a febrile state. Who knows what he was thinking? If he
hadn't been caught, maybe he would have pinned the theft
of the morphine on me. I'd have made a good scapegoat.

Now the story was out: Irakles Bastounis was researching a
new book. It was something about the heroic legacy of Greece.
It would be his last and greatest work. The great man was riff-
ing, popping – on a roll. And Buddy was there at the white-
hot core of the book's gestation. There was nothing about his
arrest – no mention of being discarded by Bastounis. Nor had
he written anything about the seizure and the tumour. He
didn't know about those. Both had occurred while Buddy was
unconscious. He promised a revelation in his next post. What
revelation? Something more from my journal?

Dizzy. Not the caffeine. Konstantinopoulos. Tiryns. The
Nobel medal. Had Buddy read those pages? *That* was a story

to rank with Muhammad Ali throwing his Olympic medal into the Ohio River after they'd refused him service in a diner. It was a story the press might pick up. Human interest.

Or – even worse – might it be the story of the seeming overdose in Gytheio? An even better headline-grabber. Bastounis back on the opiates. Polish the obituary, guys!

This was all on me. That's how Bastounis would see it. Me and my amateurish, try-hard journal that he, too, had read and ridiculed. When he found out about this… The wrath was unimaginable.

How had Buddy done it? Did Greek prisons have wifi? Was he free already? Maybe there'd been a simple fine. Maybe a powerful daddy pulling strings. What an absolute shit!

I looked at my watch. I'd soon have to collect him. I started to rationalise. Whatever he was doing at the stone house had preoccupied him and was probably demanding all of his attention. He had no phone and didn't appear to use the Internet. He wouldn't know about any of this. There was little chance he'd find out if we kept moving from town to town. He didn't need to know. He had bigger problems.

Still, the drive back towards Pisaetos seemed longer. I went more slowly, rehearsing things to say if he found out, if he blamed me. I knew it wasn't my fault. It was Buddy's. In fact, it was Bastounis's. That whole charade – the challenge about comparison and not looking for affirmation… all *his* doing.

He was standing just where I'd left him but now he was facing the track. He looked smaller. Hadn't there been a story of Heracles in which he'd offered to bear the weight of the world for Atlas? That was Bastounis now: bowed by an invisible planetary mass.

'Let's go,' he said, reaching for the door.

'Are you okay?'

'Just drive.'

The cap was down low over his eyes. He had his sunglasses on.

I put the car into reverse was about to release the clutch when a young woman came out of the house. She didn't look Greek. Her hair was home-dyed blonde and she wore the sloppy branded casuals of some alternative sub-culture. Maybe a little older than me. She was striding to my side of the car.

'Go,' said Bastounis, his jaw tight. 'Quickly.'

She arrived at my open window. 'Who are you?'

'I'm… I'm driving Mister Bastounis.'

'He's nobody,' said Bastounis. 'Leave it, Dora. We're going now.'

She stared at him then back at me. Her eyes were almost the same colour as his. 'You're English.'

'Yes.'

Her own accent sounded American. 'Has he told you who *I* am or why he's here?'

'Leave it, Dora. We're leaving. That's what you want.'

'I'd like to talk to you,' she said to me. 'Will you come in for a drink?'

'Dora, please…'

I looked to Bastounis. He was staring straight ahead, his hands working at the walking stick between his legs. He gave no guidance.

'What – you need his permission?' she said. 'I can see he's chosen well. He has you trained.'

'It's not really my… I don't want to get involved in…'

'Go,' said Bastounis. 'Go if she wants you to. I'll wait here.'

'His highness has spoken!' She opened my door. 'Come on.'

She walked back to the house without turning to see whether I was following.

'It's fine,' said Bastounis. 'I'll wait. If you get the chance, tell her ... tell her I'm sorry. She'll do most of the talking.'

'I'm not really comfortable—'

'Forget comfort. Remember your challenges. If you want comfort, you become a monk or a madman. This is real life.'

The challenges, the challenges. Always the challenges. I got out of the car and walked to the house's open door. There was a smell of baking and freshly brewed coffee. A hallway led to a kitchen, which led to a terrace overlooking the sea to the north. She was sitting at a table there.

'Coffee?' she said. 'I don't drink that frappe shit or the Greek stuff that leaves you with a mouthful of grounds. This is filter. There's milk if you want it.'

'That's fine.'

She poured. 'I'm Theodora. I'm his granddaughter. I see from your face he hadn't told you.'

'He tells me nothing.'

'Of course he doesn't. This used to be his house – his pride and joy. His Odyssean eyrie. He virtually built it himself. Now it's my grandmother's. She had the better lawyers. Anyway – how did you end up as his chauffer?'

'Accidentally, I suppose. I was in Dimitsana and he kind of press-ganged me into it.'

'Nothing's accidental with him. He probably knew you were coming before you arrived. You never know you're in the web. You might live your whole life in it and not know. Until you're sucked dry in the cocoon he's woven around you. Then you blame yourself – as if you should have seen it earlier. No. You see what he wants you to see. Will you eat *tiropita*? I made it this morning. The cheese here is excellent.'

'I suppose he can be challenging.'

'Challenging? Did you know that he walked out on my grandmother?'

'Yes, he wrote about it in—'

'No, he's never told the full truth about that. About anything. Those autobiographies – they're as fictional as his novels. When I say he walked out, I mean it literally. No warning. There wasn't even any kind of argument between them. He left a note saying he had to go somewhere and that was it. He left almost everything behind. Next she knew, he was with Hemingway in Idaho. The *Art* – the Art came before anything and anyone else. Can you believe that? That a man would leave his wife and young daughter – his family – to go and see Hemingway?'

'I'm sorry…'

'Don't apologise. That's what grandma did. Had she done something wrong? Could she have been better? Had she listened enough and paid him enough attention? It was nothing to do with her. No mere human can hold his interest. And now he turns up here after all this time. He wants to use me to get to her. He knows she'd never speak to him again. Not even through a ouija board.'

'Hmm. The *tiropita* is really—'

'Is it true? The tumour? The prognosis? He showed me the scar on his head and a letter from a doctor in Athens, but… I know it sounds crazy, but the scar could be from a drunken fall. He could have written the letter himself. He'd do it more convincingly than any doctor. Do you see where I'm coming from?'

'I was with him when he had a seizure in Olympia. I spoke to a doctor there. He was given six months six months ago. I've seen symptoms – memory loss, twitches.'

'That's what he said.'

She sipped coffee and looked at the view. A tiny motorboat silently scythed a pale wake across the ocean. All human activity below was entomological from this height and distance. Was that how he saw the world?

'Why are you driving him? Especially now, after his seizure. Is he paying you?'

'He's not paying me. I don't know... He's a great artist. It's kind of a privilege. He has this... hypnotic charisma. I mean, I'm afraid of him dying – how I'll handle that. But he keeps challenging me. He's like a professor who demands more and more because he knows you're capable of it, even if you don't see it yourself. He sees something in me that I want to be in only the most inchoate sense. I've done things I'd never have chosen to do.'

She shook her head. 'You're caught in the web.'

'It doesn't feel like that.'

'Of course it doesn't. He's a seducer. You should hear the stories of Irakles and women. Bastard that he always was, he made them feel like queens, like empresses. You know some of it if you've read his books, but you should see the letters he wrote for her... Any woman would melt. At least until they realised they'd seen the best of him. That's all he is: words. Take them away and what do you have? Lies. Fantasy. Abstractions.'

'I don't know him that well. I only know the words. Have you considered...? Have you thought that maybe he feels the same about himself? He's dying now. It's years since he wrote. What else is there?'

'You're defending him now?'

'No. No. I don't want to get in between ... I guess I'm just playing Devil's Advocate. It's not my place to—'

'Did he arrange this? Tell me the truth. That was the plan wasn't it? He comes here first and tries to wheedle his way back to grandma for pity or absolution or whatever. He knows he'll probably fail. He fails. But he has you: the guileless Englishman with the open face. The empty apologist who'll speak for him. Tell me the truth. Is that how it is?'

'It really isn't…'

'But you're not sure, right? Now that I've said it. Because he wouldn't discuss it with you in advance, would he. He wouldn't trust you. He'd need you to be genuinely artless and naïve. You're his tool even if you don't realise it. Everybody is. But do you know: he didn't mention you at all. He didn't even say he had a young Englishman driving him. I wonder if he's thanked you at any stage for your help. I wonder if he's even acknowledged your existence at any point. Or perhaps he's done it only when he saw you wavering – a crumb of gratitude from the great Nobel laureate to keep you on-side. But do you know what's worse? You're just like him. You see all of this as some big adventure, don't you? Travelling with the artist in an artificial world. Catching the honeyed drops of wisdom from his lips. Waiting to be the one who can say "I was there when he died" – just as *he* did with Hemingway. The two of you are in a dream he's made. I don't know how or why he's using you, but you're letting him. Maybe you're a proxy or some vicarious effigy he's fashioned for his purposes. But the reality is right here: divorce, abandonment, lies, betrayal. This is what he leaves behind him. Wake up!'

Her eyes were lasers. I looked away. I looked into the eagle's-eye view he'd chosen all those years ago. Distant from everything. Higher. Had it been for a writer's peace and quiet, or for oneiric hygiene – to separate himself from reality's stain? I didn't know if she meant me to leave.

'He said I should tell you he's sorry.'

'And that makes everything okay? Really? Have you listened to a word I've…? You should go.'

'I'm sorry.'

'No you're not. You'll be writing about this one day in a journal or a diary or a book. It'll be a "scene" and I'll be a character and there'll be a theme and … You're just another version of him. Please just go.'

I stood. I wanted to tell her that she was more like him than she thought. She had the same eyes. She had the same propensity for devastating monologue. She was living in the same eyrie, nursing a narrative of bitter condemnation. But I figured she wouldn't be receptive to that point of view. I left.

He was sitting in the car just as before. I sat and slammed the door.

'She got to you,' said Bastounis.

'Was it your plan all along to send me in there as your apologist?'

'You were my back-up.'

'Well, thanks. I really enjoyed it.'

'Is she okay?'

'She's very like you.'

A pause. 'Thank you. I think so, too.'

I started the engine.

FIFTEEN

There was a ferry back to the mainland that evening, but Bastounis wanted to see Ithaca first. I'd drive him to the northern lobe of the island, where most of the villages were and where, I assumed, he had memories to revisit.

We said nothing about Theodora. He stared out of the window, facing away from me in his mask of hat and sunglasses. I watched the road, which rose in hairpins to a terrifying stretch above the Molou Gulf before following a ridgeline with abyssal sapphire either side.

Her accusations swayed with the bends and braking and in the dust of our wake. Me: the unwitting tool and stooge. Me, the co-fantasist enabling the delusions of a dying artist. True, he *had* used me. He'd sent me in there knowing she'd probably see through it – not caring if I was humiliated or embarrassed. Maybe it was another challenge. Maybe it was just a continuation of the challenges already issued. But for what ultimate purpose? Did he find it entertaining?

Madness might ensue from trying to discern his method. It didn't seem likely that he'd initially intended me to talk to her, especially knowing her opinions. Unless … unless he meant it as some kind of inoculation. One takes an inert form of the illness to build resistance to its lethal strain. Immunity increases. But immunity to what exactly? The reality or the fantasy – or the ability to differentiate?

I was glad not to talk. Buddy's blog was a conversation I'd pushed into a memory pocket. It might never occur. I might be able to build a stone house above it, beyond it, so it became just a camouflaged fleck on the opposite peaks.

We rose ever higher through tenacious scrub, tracing buttresses and cornering ridges to a blasted, blinding landscape atop the island. The views across the Ionian to the mainland were aeronautic and Bastounis pointed out the islands with laconic reverence.

'Astokos. Arkoudi. Kastos, Praso. Fillipos.'

I took him at his word. It was irrelevant what their real names were, or whether they were islands. Their existence was purely in his naming, as Eden under Adam. He pronounced them with their Greek inflections, and in Homer's tongue they could have been demi-gods, or city-states, or moons of planets yet unmapped.

'Anogi,' he said as we passed through a scattering of houses at Ithaca's crown. 'It means "above the world".'

I drove without instruction or purpose. More important was movement and the murmur of the engine. Ethereal air washed through the car via the four open windows, flapping clothes and stroking skin. Occasionally, the asphalt would be written with the thick, black bodies of snakes crushed while basking, some of them still twisting in slow agony. I felt them thud under the wheels.

We stopped for coffee at a roadside café in the village of Stavros. Bastounis kept his cap low and his sunglasses on. If he knew anyone there, or if anyone recognised him, there seemed no interest in re-acquaintance. He was like one of the heroes who'd entered a forbidden realm with divine protection. Was this Olympus, or his Hades?

I waited for some further mention of Theodora. We'd both met her, both discussed the same subject, both been ejected. Yet I was sure only I'd been made to feel so awkward amid another family's issues. I believed what she'd said. I understood her anger and frustration. Bastounis didn't care. I was a pebble he tossed into the water to see how deep it was, or just to watch the ripples. Now he sipped his coffee as if nothing had happened – not serene exactly, but outwardly indifferent.

'Theodora said you walked out on her grandmother,' said my voice.

No response.

'She said there wasn't even an argument. You just left as if the marriage had never existed.'

No reaction. I saw myself in the black reflection of his lenses.

'Is it true? Did you really do that your family? In *The Stables of*—'

'I did it. Just as Dora said.'

'But…why? Didn't you love her anymore? What about your daughter?'

'You wouldn't understand.'

Of course, because emotions were radically different among artists. The motivations of the mighty were inconceivable and unfathomable to the common man. How could I, a mere human, understand why he'd done anything? Even if I'd been drawn within his influence.

'Or maybe you would,' he said.

'What?'

'Have you been in touch with your family since Dimitsana?'

'I've had emails, yes.'

'A politician's answer. Have you written or spoken to them? Have you addressed their concerns? Do they know where you are right now?'

'It's kind of difficult after someone's thrown your phone from a moving car.'

'You're just proving my point.'

'What *is* your point?'

'You came here looking for something – something you knew you were never going to find at home. I think you've found it. You're in the right place – let's agree that much. There are different kinds of people. Some never question or seek anything more than compatibility with the norms of their society, their education, their family. Such people are generally happy, whether or not they realise it. They don't need to think. Thinking, for them, is futile. They have patterns and processes instead. But other people find those patterns suffocating and claustrophobic, even if they bring happiness. Happiness is anaesthesia. It's pre-emptive death. We humans possess potential that most of us can barely imagine. If we push, if we seek, we can reach heights of perception and feeling that make us divine. We can transcend this slowly rotting carcase. We become immortal. But it means sacrifice. You have to choose. You can't have both. When I saw you walking into Dimitsana, I knew you'd chosen. You're only just starting on the path, but you know which one you want. You're willing to make the sacrifices. You've made them, I know. I read about Clara in your journal. Don't ask me "why?" Don't ask me if I regret anything. Ask yourself the same questions. Excuse me for a moment – I drank a lot at Dora's.'

He used his stick and the seat to lever himself upright and walked inside the café.

I wasn't like him. It was a different situation. He was wrong. Theodora was wrong. I'd not made any decisions – not yet. I was just travelling, just trying new things. There was still time before I reached any fork in the road. Or had I already passed it?

Talking to him had been a bad idea. There were no rules. He'd say anything and make it seem the only way of seeing. Happiness was anaesthesia! That was one for the quotation books. Know thyself. Nothing in excess. Happiness is anaesthesia. And what he'd said about Clara...

'Let's go,' he said. 'Or are you sulking? Do you need some time?'

'It's about my journal.'

'Really? You're still harping on that? You've read both volumes of my autobiography – the divorces, the drugs, the breakdowns, the religious indecision – and you're sore about Clara? She wasn't right for you and you know it. Let's dispense with the soap-opera emotions. It's the past. There's only now.'

He limped to the car, his shadow a jagged black pool at his feet. I envisioned a fully-laden truck – something heavy: logs or anvils – swinging round the corner and annihilating him. But there was only a satellite silence, the cloudless vault, and the wind whispering at the island's skull.

I drove north, skirting the villages of Frikes and Platrithias – ever north onto the defiant clenched-fist salute of the empty cape, beyond which ferry wakes criss-crossed *en route* to Ancona, Brindisi, Igoumenitsa. The sea thrashed mutely at the foot of white cliffs to our left, washing sandy tongues far out into the blue.

'Stop here,' said Bastounis. 'There's a track.'

I pulled into a tiny lay-by and turned off the engine. The car ticked in the heat. Our dust tail carried on along the road without us.

'I need to stretch my legs,' he said. 'Stay here if you want.'

'I will.'

I watched him picking his way along the stony track until he descended out of sight, his cap bobbing between stiff and silvery leaves. Let him stumble and fall. I'd go after him if he wasn't back within half an hour. It might be easier if he *did* fall. Some loose earth, a wobbling rock, a jutting root … the walking stick jabs ineffectually at air. A body falls silently unseen beside the precipice, dark limbs flailing against the white. The cap flies free, caught briefly on the wind and carried out to settle on the swell. The mortal flesh impacts the surf, or lands with single bounce on hard-packed sand. A sea bird dives to investigate the soaking cap but aborts its vector for some reason beyond reason – something not quite right about that piece of flotsam: some aura of the doomed … or was it jetsam? I was never quite sure of the difference.

The daydream entertained me for a moment. It was hot in the Peugeot. I got out and leaned on the bonnet, letting the wind dry the sweat from my shirt. The thump and hiss of waves was audible, but warped hollow and asynchronous by vagaries of wind and coast. Multiple thumps. A boom. Foam tittering in retreat. Was it Byron who'd sat on the shore and noted that every seventh wave was larger?

I looked at my watch. Bastounis could have stretched his legs more easily up here on the level road surface. Maybe he was digging. Had he won any other medals of note? I walked to the start of the track.

'Mister Bastounis?'

Stupid, really. He'd hear nothing down there in that scrubby echo chamber. I followed where he'd gone and saw immediately how uneven the ground was – more of a goat track than anything. It seemed unlikely he'd passed this way without falling. I had to use my hands for balance.

'Mister Bastounis?'

Shrubs had grown across the way at chest height, their leaves dusty and cobwebbed. Broken stems and fresh earth showed where he'd blundered through.

'Mister Bastounis? Are you okay down here?'

I rounded a cluster of boulders that looked like they'd fallen just the previous winter. The rock was fresh and clean where they'd sheared off the mountain. Beyond them lay a field of fractured rubble, incandescent in the sun. I squinted at a darker shape silhouetted against the sea: Bastounis perched at the edge.

'Mister Bastounis?'

No response. He seemed to be leaning out into the wind, held by its updraft, arms slightly extended in embrace. I couldn't see his stick. It wasn't clear how hazardous his position might be.

I began making my way across the rubble. There was no way he could hear me, but I trod carefully in case I startled him from his equilibrium between air and earth. I veered around to his right so that he'd see me coming and I began to perceive that he was on a beetling ledge above a vertical drop to the sea – nothing between feet and waves but his fragile rock perch. A change in wind, a tremor off balance and he'd topple into nothingness.

He'd seen me, I was sure, but gave no sign of it as I came haltingly closer over crevices, cracks and through bushes. Only when I was standing a few feet from him did I attempt to speak.

'Mister Bastounis? What's happening?'

He'd definitely heard me.

'Miste—'

'Why do you call me that? You've heard others call me Irakles but you persist in the formality, as if I'm a school-master and you have your hand raised, straining to be the one who answers.'

He spoke not to me but to the Ionian's bisected blue, his words winnowed on the wind. I had to strain to catch them.

I didn't answer. I didn't want to agitate him. I sensed this was another scene.

'It was quite common for the ancients to commit suicide. The stoics in particular. There was no sin or shame in it. It was the ultimate expression of rationality. Why linger and decline? Why be a burden on your family and on society if you'd reached the limit of productive life? The work is done. Why struggle with your weakness and fight nature's will? Our power – our greatest power – is that *we* control the limit of our lives. Not God. Not fate. Not time. The choice is ours at any moment. Volition – *that's* the essence of freedom. No need to open a vein or leap into the bubbling caldera. Nothing so dramatic. Those old stoics – they'd simply stop eating. They barely ate anyway…'

I tested sentiments to offer him. *Don't do it. You have so much to live for. Think of your family. The prognosis might be wrong. This is your tumour talking – a flood of melancholy. It'll pass. It could be worse…* But I said nothing. I couldn't even call him by his name.

I realised that my greatest fear wasn't that he would die. It was that he would fall. The terrible sight of it would shock me and stay with me – the visceral clench, the withheld breath, the telescoping stare as time slowed and his body fell. The hectic crash of gravity. I couldn't bear to see it.

A snatch of something flashed from memory. Something I'd studied. My role in the school's production of *Hamlet*. Not for me the starring role of ink-cloaked Dane, but rather Horatio: typecast even then as the boring voice of reason. The one who lives. The lines were apt and fully formed by youthful repetition. I tried to project so he'd hear me:

"The very place puts toys of desperation / Without more motive, into every brain / That looks so many fathoms to the sea / And hears it roar beneath." '

Bastounis turned to me, apparently surprised. He smiled and opened his arms, declaiming to the sea:

" 'My fate cries out / And makes each petty artery in this body / As hardy as the Nemean lion's nerve." '

Hamlet's response to Horatio in that same scene. I struggled to remember what came next, but it was gone. I leaned back on a wind-chiselled rock and Bastounis's perch disappeared behind some heather-like undergrowth. The perspective made it seem that he was levitating out there, caught in weightless levitation.

A glance at my watch.

'We should probably start making our way back to Vathy. If you want to get the ferry, I mean ...'

He turned unsteadily on his tiny pedestal. There was barely enough room for his feet. Was he looking for his walking stick? I stood and scanned the tumbled scrub. The stick was higher up the hill, caught in a crack and snapped about halfway – a messy eruption of splinters. Had he fallen?

'Broken,' he said. 'Bastounis is broken, ha!'

It took forty minutes to get back to the car, Bastounis leaning on my shoulder or gripping my hand to clamber over rocks. We were sweaty, dusty and reeking by the time we made it to the road, but he seemed in good cheer. He started talking once we were heading south.

'You didn't really think I'd jump, did you?'

'I had no idea what you'd do.'

'I've never been able to do it. My attempts were all half-hearted. Self-pity – nothing more. But there's exhilaration in the opportunity, in the promise of relief. Do you see?'

'I suppose so.'

'Ah, you've yet to feel it. You will. The climactic darkness. The despair. You shouldn't flee such things. They're what make us human. Look at the tragedies. Look at Oedipus's predicament. Look at Macbeth. My God – the darkness is what truly shines. What comedian was ever truly great?'

'Twain?'

'A great entertainer. Not great.'

'Wilde?'

'A cocky pederast. Though I'll admit there's darkness in *De Profundis*.'

'Rabelais?'

'Have you read him? The holy man who bathed in sewers of sin. He's crying as he laughs, caught between heaven and damnation.'

'Is it true you were with Hemingway at the end?'

Bastounis tipped back his hat and stroked his stubble. 'Did you know that in '61 he was asked to write a sentence for Kennedy's inauguration? Some kind of presentation thing. He couldn't do it. Just a single sentence. He was *that* blocked. He wept like a child. A few months later, he put his shotgun against his forehead.'

'Is that what happened to you?'

He turned.

'I mean, the block. It happens with a lot of Nobel winners, doesn't it? The pressure of expectation after the prize.'

'Not me.'

He maintained the look for a second before turning back to the road.

'What was he like? Hemingway, I mean.'

'He was finished. You could see it in his eyes. He was already dead.'

'Did he tell you anything? Did he pass on some wisdom? Did you get what you went for?'

'No. Or at least I thought not. It's becoming clearer now. Especially now.'

'What is? What's clearer?'

He tipped the cap back over his eyes and reclined his seat. 'I need to get a new walking stick in Patras. Maybe aluminium. You can help me.'

'I will, of course … Aluminium would be good.'

The light was beginning to fade and the ferry was already in dock when we came over the hill into Vathy. I joined the line of cars and trucks crawling into its belly and the crew found a stick in lost property so Bastounis could climb the stairs.

He was asleep before the chains rattled and the engines changed pitch. The peaks soon circled around us and we passed out of Ithaca's arms into the open sea. I went up on deck amid the funnel fumes and salt and noted that night's descent seemed faster out there. Isolated lights blinked from the islands he'd named, or from the darkening mainland mass – it wasn't clear which was which.

That scene at the cliff edge … What had that really been about? He'd wanted me to think he was going to jump. Maybe he'd wanted to shock me. Maybe it was another challenge and I'd be informed in a few days. There was an abstract sense that he couldn't possibly die. It was nothing to do with his health – which was clearly failing – but more to do with his relation to reality. If someone told me he was dead, I wouldn't believe it. I'd have to see evidence. There'd have to be a certificate.

Could I take the drama when it happened for real? For the first time – absurdly, incredibly – I was questioning whether this adventure was a path I may have followed too far and for too long. And yet, like Macbeth, I was stepped in sufficiently far that, should I wade no more, returning would be as difficult as continuing. This was a book I had to finish, if only to find my own role in it.

Next hurdle: the deferred threat from Buddy's blog. That stone in my shoe. If we could blast through Patras and on to wherever (north?), Bastounis need never know. He might be gone before he ever heard about it. And anyway, he didn't care about the real world any longer. He wasn't part of it.

SIXTEEN

Patras was a burst of ugly light as we joined the snaking outflow into concrete spaces forested with streetlights, cranes and pylons. The idea of spending the night here was unappealing, but there were chores and shopping to be done next day: a hypodermic syringe to replace the one he'd lost at Olympia, a new walking stick, some urgent laundry.

Bastounis sat uncommunicative in the passenger seat. He was always grumpy after waking. He'd come to life later when we found a room and when he ordered his first brandy. In the meantime, we crawled in first gear towards the gates of the ferry terminal.

There was a knot of people there – the usual immigrant hawkers of tissues, bottled water, windscreen cleaning and Chinese-made mobile accessories – waiting to harass drivers as they turned on to the coast road. As we approached, a man approached Bastounis's side of the car. The man I'd seen in Napflio. The one who'd been in the square and at the quay when we'd left for Monemvasia. He held a dicta-phone through the open window.

I didn't understand his tumbling Greek, but I thought I heard the name "Konstantinopoulos". I definitely heard "Nobel". I heard "Tiryntha" and "Dimitsana" and "Ithaki".

Bastounis stiffened. His face was stone. He said nothing.

'And you,' said the man, addressing me. 'Can *you* confirm that Irakles Bastounis is working on a new book? It must be a great privilege to travel with him on his trip around Greece. Did you know that he'd given away his Nobel medal to a poet? Perhaps you were there when it happened. Many people would love to know these things. If you could give me just ten minutes...'

'Say nothing,' growled Bastounis.

There was no escape. We were trapped front and rear by vehicles. The dictaphone pointed.

'Mister Bastounis – are you writing under pressure from your publisher? I understand that legal action has... *ela malaka!*'

Bastounis had jerked the door open, hitting the man's knee. The dictaphone clattered off the interior sill and fell beside the passenger seat. Bastounis rolled up the window and gestured for me to do the same.

'He's the man I saw in Nafplio,' I said. 'Do you know him?'

'They're all the same. Turn left out of the gate as soon as you can.'

I watched in the rearview as the man limped to a moped.

'How did he know where we were?' I said.

Bastounis was silent.

I had to pre-empt an eruption.

'Look, there's something you should know. I should probably have told you before but I thought... It's Buddy. This is all Buddy. He has a blog. I saw it in Vathy. I don't how he's managed it with the police situation and everything, but he says you're writing a new book and he makes out that he's still travelling with you. He doesn't mention me at all. He says you and he visited the Temple at Andritsaina...'

He raised his hand for silence.

We passed cinemas and cafés, shops and restaurants. Music thumped, horns blared, mopeds whined weaving through the traffic. Neon slithered up the bonnet.

'Mister … It wasn't me. I didn't tell …'

The hand became a slowly wagging finger. 'Turn right just there.'

I pulled into the unlit sidestreet. An extractor from the adjacent *taverna* was noisily venting *souvlaki* smoke. There was a reek of urine. Puddles of water or cooking oil quivered.

'Buddy didn't know about the medal,' he said, staring straight ahead.

'No, no – that's right. He must have looked at my journal … when you were asleep in Olympia. Or even before then. My bag was available. He must have read all about it. But he doesn't mention the tumour anywhere. He doesn't know because the seizure hadn't happened. He only knows what he read. That's the proof – do you see? He's only written what he read. He's a total narcissist. He's made it all about him. I knew we shouldn't have—'

'You wrote all about it in your journal.'

'Well, yes. But it's a private journal. I don't show it to anyone.'

'I thought I could trust you.'

'You can! You *can* trust me. *He's* the one you couldn't trust. He went behind my back to read my journal.'

'You've given him all the material he needs.'

'No! I've given him nothing. He *stole* it! Besides … it's not true that you're writing a new book, is it? He's just assumed that part. He saw what he wanted to see. And, anyway – does it matter what people think? You don't care about that? Who cares what they say or think? I mean, sure, it must be embarrassing for Mister Konstantinopulos, but … This isn't me. I didn't do this. Do you think I did it on purpose? I'm not like Buddy.'

'Everybody wants a story.' His voice weary. 'It never ends.'

'Not me. *I* don't. I just wanted the experience. It's a privilege for me to—'

'You're complicit.'

'What? How can you…? How am I complicit? He read it without my permission – just like you did in Dimitsana, remember? Are you saying that it's okay for you to steal it but not for Buddy? How am I the guilty one?'

'I had good cause.'

'Buddy thought *he* had good cause!'

'You should go. Take your bag.'

'What?'

'This is the end of the journey for you.'

'Are you serious?'

'It's a matter of trust.'

'I can't believe this! I was helping you up a cliff today after you seemed ready to jump off it.'

'My decision is made.' He crossed his arms.

'But… Who's going to drive you? Who's going to help? You shouldn't be alone.'

'It's not your problem.'

'At least let me drive you to a room somewhere. Tomorrow—'

'There's no tomorrow for us. Get out of the car. Don't make me angrier.'

'Will you punch me, too?'

He turned with the titanium glare.

'Okay, but this is… I can't believe you're doing this.'

I got out and took my bag from the back seat. I stood by the side of the car waiting for him to say this was all a joke or a misunderstanding – that this was another challenge I'd failed.

'Keep going down the main street,' he said. 'There are cheap hotels down there. Maybe a hostel.'

'You don't need to do this. I know the meeting with Theodora must have been hard, but…You don't have to do this. I won't tell anybody anything. That was never my plan. You can trust me.'

He leaned over and rolled up the window.

I stood. It couldn't end here in a filthy alley in charmless Patras. I couldn't go back to the superficiality of the back-packer's hostel and the souvenir stands and the guidebook itineraries and the tourist queues. I couldn't go back from *this*. But he just sat there, arms folded, staring ahead. He wasn't going to change his mind. Fine.

'Fine. I'm going. Good luck.'

I walked slowly to the alley entrance, waiting for the sound of the Peugeot's door clunking open and his laughter. It had all been a test! A prank. Come back, you gullible fool and drive us to a great little taverna that only the locals know.

But there was only the extractor's exhalation and the noise of the main street. I paused at the corner and looked back. His head was a dark silhouette, unmoving. Was he watching me through the mirror? Okay – let him watch me go.

I stepped on to the street and looked at the time. Five minutes – then I'd go back if he hadn't come limping after me. He couldn't go anywhere on his own. He needed me. He'd realise that in a few minutes.

Locals passed, staring at me with my backpack. Some young people sniggered. I was clearly lost. After ten minutes, I walked the few steps back to the alley entrance. The car was gone. I went quickly to where it'd been parked and continued on to an intersection with another grimy alley.

The ground was greasy. Refuse sacks were stacked among vegetable detritus. No Peugeot.

So he'd been able to drive all this time? Or had he already found someone new to drive him?

I walked back to the main street and stood on the corner. I waited for perhaps twenty minutes, scanning traffic for the dark Peugeot and seeing it constantly, mistakenly. I was about to walk in the direction of the hotels when a moped rattled up to kerb in front of me. It was the same guy who'd tried to question us at the port.

'Fuck off,' I said.

'I'd really like to talk you and Irakles.'

'He's gone. He left me because I couldn't be trusted. Because of you.'

'I've done nothing except ask questions.'

'He doesn't like questions. Just leave me alone. He might come back. If he sees me talking to you ...'

'You met him in Dimitsana, right?'

'Go away.'

'Did you know that he's being sued by his publisher? He took a huge advance from them and never wrote the book.'

'It's none of my business. I'm not interested. I've got nothing to tell you. I wouldn't tell you if I had.'

'Has he been writing? Making notes maybe?'

'Didn't you hear me?'

'Confirm one thing for me. One thing, and I'll go.'

I started walking. He dismounted and followed.

'In Olympia. He stayed overnight in the medical centre. There was an arrest – a young American. What happened? Was Bastounis hurt? Is he ill? I know he visited a hospital in Athens last year.'

'Why do you care about any of this?'

'He's Irakles Bastounis – one of only three Greeks who won the Nobel. He's a great artist. You must know this. People are interested.'

'People aren't interested. They have no idea who he is. He's not been recognised once since I've been with him. You mean that people are interested in scandal and ephemera. They're interested in death and drama. Plane crashes, earthquakes. Until the next day, at least. Then there has to be something new.'

'Is he dying?'

'What? I didn't say that.'

'You said people are interested in death.'

'You know what I meant.'

'Just one more thing. Can you tell me if the facts in the *Dharma Karma* blog are true? Did Buddy Tannenbaum travel with you?'

I stopped. 'You want to know the truth about Buddy?'

'Look – there's a café over the road. Let me get you something. You don't have to tell me anything you don't want to. Just about Buddy if you want.'

'Nothing about Bastounis. Only Buddy.'

'It's a deal.'

We crossed the road, me looking for a dark Peugeot in the traffic. He bought two frappes to the table.

'Do you mind if I take notes? I'd normally record you but…'

'Yes, I do mind. It's all off the record. None of this is from me.'

'Right. So, Buddy…'

'We picked him up somewhere outside Sparta. He was hitching. He doesn't mention that in his blog. He implies he's been travelling with Bastounis since Dimitsana.'

'But that was you.'

'Yes. Just me. Buddy took my experiences and wrote himself into them. He wrote me out.'

'How did he know what had happened before Sparta? Did you tell him?'

'I didn't tell him anything. He looked at my journal while I was out or asleep…I don't know when exactly. He also stole from Mister Bastounis. That's what caused the fight.'

'Stole what?'

'Money. I didn't see the whole thing because I arrived back at the room while they were mid-argument. Buddy said he was due payment and he tried to run. Mister Bastounis hit him.'

'Hit him where?'

'On the chin, I guess. He knocked him out with a single punch. It was amazing.'

'*Heh!* It seems the old goat still has a haymaker. Did Buddy try to steal anything else? Apart from money, I mean.'

'Like what?'

'I don't know. Did Irakles have anything else valuable? Anything potentially incriminating?'

'What are you thinking of?'

'I think we both know he has a history with narcotics…'

'Absolutely not. I've not seen anything like that.'

'I'm sorry. You know it's what some people might think. An old man like Irakles, he might have had some prescription drugs that someone like Buddy might want to steal.'

'I've told you – I don't know anything about his health. He wouldn't tell me anyway. I'm a nobody to him.'

'Okay, fine. So, the journey Buddy describes – Nafplio, Monemvasia, Gytheio *et cetera* – it all happened? But to you rather than him. The Nobel medal and Tiryns…'

'I'm not talking about that. Only about Buddy.

'Look – the story is already out. It can be checked. The only question is whether you were there, or whether it was Buddy.'

'It was me. He was with us only in Andritsaina and Olympia. That story about the Temple of Apollo? It was just me and him. He went inside the temple on his own. Illegally.'

'Is there anything else?'

'What do you mean?'

'Is there anything else from the journal that Buddy hasn't revealed but which he might know? He knows how to drip a story. He might be saving the juicier bits for when his audience has grown. He's already got my attention.'

'He doesn't know anything more.'

'Is there more to know? In your journal, I mean.'

'I'm not showing you the journal.'

'I'm not trying to trick you. I'm just trying to confirm if what Buddy said is true. For example, that Irakles is writing a book. Have you seen him writing anything? Making notes? Buddy says he's working on a book about—'

'I've been with him since Dimitsana and I've not seen him write anything. He eats, he sleeps, he visits places. It's like he's on holiday.'

'He hasn't told you why he's going to these places?'

'He doesn't tell me anything.'

'In Monemvasia, Buddy describes him talking to an older woman—'

'It's *my* description. He stole it.'

'Right. Do you know who she is?'

'We were never introduced. Mister Bastounis didn't want me to know anything about it.'

'Her name is Danäe Tegou. She's a painter. It's said that they were lovers a long time ago but they've never spoken about it. She was the one woman who wouldn't marry him. She's painted portraits of him. Some critics believe she's a character in his novel *Cassandra*. You didn't know this?'

'No. He doesn't tell me anything.'

'I understand. It's just that... I'll be checking all of the facts. I'll be contacting the health centre in Olympia, and the rooms you stayed at. I'll talk to the landlord there. If there's more to find, I'll find it.'

'That sounds like a threat.'

'I'm just asking questions. You have nothing to hide, do you?'

'Who are you working for?'

'I'm a freelancer.'

'A freelance what? You sound like a journalist, but... How did you know we were in Ithaca? And how did you know about the health centre? Buddy didn't write about that. Are you following us? First Nafplio and now you're here.'

'Relax, okay? It's nothing sinister. Theodora tweeted about her father visiting. She doesn't have a lot of followers, but I'm one of them. The car is very distinctive – easy to spot.'

'And the health centre?'

He raised his hands in surrender and smiled. 'That was a guess. I'm afraid you've confirmed it.'

'Right. Another liar. Well, *I'm* afraid you've hit a dead-end with me. I have no idea where he is or where he's gone. If you have any professional integrity, you'll report that Buddy's a liar.'

I stood but he remained sitting. I sensed he was waiting for me to leave so he could hastily jot whatever I'd revealed. He took a card from the breast pocket of his shirt.

'If you remember anything else...'

No name. Just a mobile number.

I tossed it back on to the table.

He smiled, leaned forward and slipped it into the side pocket of my bag. 'Sometimes people change their minds.'

I walked towards the hotels, resenting every curious or derisive look from the locals. Just another backpacker off the late ferry. Marginal. Anonymous.

I checked into the Agamemnon Hostel via a surly Dutch receptionist wearing a haircut and a "Blow Thyself" t-shirt. It was a dank place with institutional two-tone green hallways and traffic noise moaning through the windows. A radio somewhere was playing too-loud rap. Metallic clangs echoed from a doorway with a blue exterminator light above it.

Three men, caught mid-drinking game, looked up when I entered the dorm room. I nodded a greeting and lay back on my allotted bed to watch the ceiling fan gyre amid listless flies. The drinkers – Manchester? – got rowdier and more inane until their beer was gone and they'd reached the requisite level of offensiveness to go out and advertise their national shortcomings.

'Comin' out, mate?' said one. 'We're gonna get wankered at this club round the corner. It's full of Romanian girls.'

'No. Thanks. Have a good one.'

They'd wake me up at three or four next morning with much inebriated whispering, giggling and a minor scuffle over who'd lost a treasured lighter. Then two of them would snore like hogs drowning in gelatine. Hostel dorms – as predictable as lunar orbits. Elsewhere in these rooms, there'd be couples in the thrilling and the terminal stages of romance; there'd be people high on the adrenaline of travel, and others wondering at their incongruous ambivalence; there'd be a lonely Japanese boy who barely spoke a word of English, and a Scandinavian girl weary of the leering. And always, I supposed, at least one alone among the empty beds convinced that he was different.

I disgorged the contents of my bag on to the bed: dirty clothes, guidebook, travel towel, sun cream, toiletries, the journal. The journal. I'd not written in it for a couple of days. I wanted to destroy it but I wanted to preserve it forever. I'd initially planned to keep on writing it until every page was full, but nothing hereafter would have any colour or depth or meaning. There was Bastounis and then banality. I turned to the page where he'd jotted the name of the extemporised Romanian nihilist who was really a cobbler. Or a barber. Which had he said? Whatever – it was vital evidence – proof that I'd travelled with the man.

'Keeping a journal? Good idea.'

A new arrival in the dorm: a skinny guy with a deep tan and a battered straw hat. His clothes and his pack were sun-faded and streaked with salt. One big toe poked through the end of a canvas sneaker. He fell onto his bed with a sigh.

'God, I'm tired.'

'Have you come far?'

'From Corfu. Ferry was three hours late. Typical.'

There was a trace of accent – probably Scandinavian. Maybe Danish. He turned to me on his elbow. 'What about you? Are you travelling?'

'A little.'

'Where've you been so far?'

'Oh, Athens, Nafplio, Monemvasia…some Arcadian villages.'

'Yeah? Did you go Epidaurus and Mycenae? They're in that general area. Or Mystra? Mystra's amazing. Or the castles at Methoni and Koroni? The Kalyvrita railway? That's just a short bus ride from here. Olympia – Olympia is amazing. Or Corinth. I spent a week at Corinth. I know it's a cliché, but it's the Peloponnesian trail, right? I'm not even talking about the north – Meteora, Dodona, Delphi, the Zagorohori, Ioannina…'

'Right. I guess I've just been bumbling around without a plan. I don't like to follow the guidebook.'

'Yeah, me neither.' He'd surely seen it tented on my bed. 'Although, what's the point of coming to Greece if you're not going to see Epidaurus and Corinth, you know what I mean?'

Every fibre of me wanted to tell him: I've hunted octopus with my bare hands; I've watched a sunset over drinks with Greece's greatest living poet; I've eaten *stifado* and *kleftiko* and *soutzoukaikia* with sauces glistening down my chin; I've communed with the illustrious dead at the pedestal of Zeus's temple in Olympia; I've freed an exotic courtesan named Calypso from her pimp slave-master; I've witnessed a fight between a Nobel laureate and a delusional narcissist over an illegal morphine supply. I was held by the police and had my passport confiscated, unofficially.

But they were *my* stories. They wouldn't mean much to this guy. He'd have his own. Maybe his were better. He might have spent a week on Spielberg's yacht anchored off Hydra or Kythera. Hanks and Clooney serving drinks. People had heard of Spielberg. Bastounis was a literary fossil.

'Anyway… he said. 'Excuse me. I really need to sleep.'

'No problem.'

Good luck with that when the Three Wankerteers return and the kitchen becomes the weed smoking capital of Patras, a Bob Marley track playing with the tired inevitability of Manchester rain.

I flicked through the journal. More empty pages than full. Where was Bastounis now? In the passenger seat on an

ill-lit road somewhere? In a cheap room nursing his griev-
ances? Blind and convulsing in the final throes of his time-
bomb tumour? Would there be a single thought or memory
of me?

I noticed the journal was falling open towards the back
as if there was a postcard or folded page. I couldn't see any
insert or triangled corner. I inverted the spine, expecting a
piece of lint or tiny stone drop out. Instead, I saw Bastounis's
arachnid writing. He'd written very small and vertically
along the spine as if to hide the text.

THE CHALLENGES: 1. Be spontaneous – say
"why not?" 2. Observe – don't just see 3. Life isn't
a movie. 4. Appreciate the pleasures of your senses
5. Recognize and face your fears. 6. Acquire skills
and use them 7. Avoid comparisons and slavery to
affirmation. 8. Don't hope or wish – do! 9. Discover
the irrational spiritual…

He must have written it when I was asleep on the ferry
over to Ithaca, or when I was up on deck during the return
journey… or anytime, really. But eight and nine… Those
challenges hadn't been issued. Bastounis had been working
to a plan all along – at least, as far as number nine. They
would have been the next ones if Buddy hadn't fucked it
all. What would they have looked like? What had I missed?
Again, I wished a martyr's death on Buddy.

I ate a bad *gyros* from a place across the street and a
so-so coffee from a nearby café. I scanned the traffic for
a dark blue Peugeot and worked on the eloquent apology
I'd give if he came back. I was woken at 2.00 by echoing
laughter and reggae from the kitchen, and at about 4.00 by
the Mancunians having an argument with my Danish (?)

neighbour. Then came the snoring and a fitful sleep during which I dreamed of the moped guy reading my journal and copying from it as I lay inexplicably paralysed.

At 6.00, I woke with the sudden clarity of oneiric eureka. What if numbers eight and nine weren't cancelled challenges at all, but challenges intended for future action? Action right now – just as the whole Buddy thing had turned out to be a challenge in retrospect. "Don't hope or wish – do!" Don't lie here pining for what could have been. Chase Bastounis. He couldn't complain if that was his explicit challenge. But how to act on it? And where to follow him?

I tried to recall the list of places I'd glimpsed on the papers at the bottom of his bag – places we'd been and places we'd probably be going. Thessalonika had been one. Delphi? There'd been some kind of Greek phrase jotted alongside it. I got my travel guide and went to the Delphi section. Γνῶθι σεαυτόν: know thyself. It had been inscribed on the pediment of the Temple of Apollo, seat of the Delphic oracle. A clue? A prompt? The "irrational spiritual" mentioned in number nine could conceivably apply to Delphi …

Number eight was the key. Don't hope or wish – do!

I needed to get to the bus station immediately.

SEVENTEEN

Patras passed tired and grubby through the window. I leaned my head against the juddering glass and knew I wouldn't sleep. We thundered beyond dwindling suburbs towards the Gulf of Corinth and the avenue of repeating cathedrals that was the Rio-Antirio bridge across the void.

The irony was palpable. Bastounis had told me, 'Drive. Don't be a passenger.' And here I was, again a passenger – just as I'd been when I'd first arrived in Dimitsana. Just as I'd been my whole tedious, inconsequential, hoop-jumping life thus far. I missed being in the driving seat.

Though, when I thought about it, Bastounis had always been the driver. Only he'd known where we were going. He'd given the directions and I followed them. He was directing me still. I remembered what Theodora had said and I wondered just how much I was his puppet. It didn't matter. I'd rather he was dictating my fate than some other force I didn't know or understand. His books were his manifesto. He stood for life. He stood for experience.

At least now there was a purpose to my journey. I had a mission. A quest. There'd be no more covert glances at the guidebook, which I'd left on my dorm bed at the hostel. Bastounis had acknowledged me – albeit in his oblique and unsentimental manner. He *wanted* me behind the wheel. He trusted me, perhaps. If nothing else, he needed my help.

He had nobody else. His two extra challenges in my journal proved it.

The road traced the coast eastwards through shoreline villages and scattered agricultural buildings, rising high above the sea and descending in adherence to geography. Near Itea, we passed the bauxite strip mine with its terraced red-brown wounds, dust rising from the workings and its abattoir smears along the asphalt. It was here that I experienced a flash of panic.

Whenever Bastounis had written those challenges in my journal, it had been *before* the incident at Patras ferry port. He hadn't known about Buddy's – my – betrayal. Perhaps he really *didn't* want to see me. He *didn't* trust me. I was about to make a colossal fool of myself.

Deep breaths. Rational thought. The evidence in defence. His challenges so far suggested I try anyway, whatever the circumstances. Don't wish or hope – do! There was nothing to lose. Bastounis himself had quoted Twain to me: you regret the things you didn't do rather than the things you did. If I'd learned anything from him, it was surely this.

The road started to climb north, away from the sea. It was the approach to Delphi: the *omphalos* – centre of the ancient world. Zeus released two eagles in opposite directions round the globe and they met here at the seat of Pythia, where the fates might be read in Apollo's oracular fumes. Such was the guidebook story. The actuality was more compelling. This place had been the focus of religious rites for a thousand years – a centre of double-tongued truth whose interpretation was as much in the hands of the supplicant as in the infallibility of the god. A good place to find Bastounis.

I'd expected a remote mountain settlement on the majestic flanks of Parnassus, but life is not a movie. The bus instead passed through a gauntlet of jewellery shops, souvenir shops, ceramic shops, cafés, moped rentals and kiosks. It was another Olympia: a gummy rag tied round a tree trunk to snare the teeming insects as they rose. There were fewer tourists now, but most of the places were still open – many with proprietors loitering on thresholds, their light-switch smiles ready.

An old blue Peugeot. A 504.

I jerked my head round to confirm. It was parked aslant between a moped and a delivery van. Nobody inside. *His* car. I was sure of it.

The bus kept going, past the emporia, past the cafés and jewellers and restaurants and hotels to a terrace the other side of the village. Air brakes sighed. The automatic doors yawned lazily open. The view into the valley may have been amazing, but I was jostling for my bag and striding back towards the car. If I'd missed him in the few minutes it'd taken…

The car was there. I looked around as if he'd be standing nearby waiting for me. Shop owners emerged. They'd felt vibrations in their web of commerce.

'Looking for a room?' said one. 'Good price for singles.'

'Have you seen the driver of this car? An old man with a white beard? He'll be wearing a cap. White shirt, dark trousers. His name's Irakles. He probably arrived last night.'

A shrug. A 25-watt smile. 'You want to see the room?'

'Maybe later. Thanks.'

I unshouldered the bag and ripped a blank page from the back of the journal. I scribbled a note on the Peugeot's dusty front wing and tucked it behind a wiper:

"Mister Bastounis – I'm here for challenges number eight and nine. I'll come back to the car every couple of hours on the hour, starting now at 10.00am."

With a nod to the would-be landlord I walked back the way the bus had come. If Bastounis was in town, he might be having his breakfast at one of these places. I checked every café and every bakery, wanting desperately to ask at each place if they'd served a man meeting his description, but not doing so. What help would it be? I already knew he had to be here somewhere. They could tell me only where he'd been. I walked back and forth for two hours, haunted by the idea that each moment would be the one I was furthest away from him, or that I'd not be looking the moment he passed through my shadow. The note remained under the car's wiper.

At 12.00, it had gone.

Would-be landlord was on duty at his shop-front. He'd been bemusedly observing my rhythmic vigil.

'Excuse me,' I said. 'Did you see who took the note from the car? An old man?'

The shrug. The Greek shrug that spoke the depths of Homer, but saw with his supposed blindness. Seers see what no one else sees... on the sea shore.

Bastounis was playing with me. My feet were tired and I was hungry.

'Can I see the single room?'

'No more singles. Only a twin. You want to see a twin?'

'Yes.'

He asked a fellow shop owner to watch his door and escorted me two floors up a narrow staircase to a room that was no better or worse than most I'd stayed in with Bastounis. It was expensive, but at least there'd be no snoring or flatulence. We settled for cash there in the hallway.

On the way downstairs, a door opened on the first floor and Bastounis faced me. I stopped, momentarily confused, and turned to the landlord.

'Is this the man you haven't seen? The old man with the white shirt, cap and beard? The one called Irakles? The one I've been trying to find for two hours, whose car is parked in front of your place?'

A sphinx-like smile and a mock salute. He walked down to the shop alone.

'What are you doing here?' said Bastounis.

He looked bad. His torso seemed twisted, clenched, and he hunched a little. He rested on an ugly aluminium crutch with a grey-plastic forearm brace and a pale rubber foot. One eye squinted.

'Mister Bastounis – are you okay?'

'What are you doing here? Didn't I tell you to leave me?'

'You wrote in my journal. Two more challenges.'

'That was before. And I said nothing about Delphi. Look – I'm going out for a drink.'

'Let me help you.'

He locked his door and went slowly down the steps, leaving heavily against the wall-mounted bannister.

'If you'd just let me explain ...'

He seemed not to hear. I followed him along the road to the nearest café, where he sat. I stood by his table and waited. I'd wait all day if I had to.

'All right, then,' he said. 'Christ. Don't just stand there like the ugly debutante nobody wants to dance with. Sit. Sit. Give me the speech you've been working on for your entire journey here. Let's hear it if I must.'

I sat. 'You wrote that I shouldn't wish or hope – I should act. That's what I've done. I'm here. I didn't want it to end like that and for you to continue without me. I didn't do anything wrong. That's all.'

'Do you want me to applaud? Do you think you've conquered that particular challenge? Trust me – it's one of the most difficult. We all wish. We all hope. It's the simplest solution to everything. "One day I'll write a book... One day I'll get fit... One day I'll meet the person of my dreams". There's no "one day". There's now, or there's nothing. Entire lives are lost that way. It's the most potent prophylactic against progress and talent and happiness.'

'That's why I came.'

'Hmm. How did you know it would be Delphi?'

'Number nine: the irrational spiritual. After Tiryns and Olympia, Delphi seemed like a good bet. A part of the pattern.'

'What about the papers in my bag – the list of destinations? The one you looked at when you thought I was over-dosing in Gerolimenas?'

'I... You saw that? Well... I don't see that you can complain, the amount of times you've been in my bag reading my journal. Didn't you *want* me to come here? Wasn't it another test? Like Buddy?'

I thought I saw him smile. The waiter came and we ordered frappes. Bastounis considered a toasted sandwich and decided against it.

'I can't taste anything,' he said, scanning the menu. 'I can barely smell. It's just texture now. My left eye – it's getting dark. As in the cinema when they first start to turn down the house lights and there's that moment you're not sure – before your brain can fully processes the change. Exactly like that, but constantly. The lights going down constantly.'

He spoke offhandedly to the menu, his tone flat as if discussing a mechanical issue with the Peugeot.

'Did you drive here on your own?'

'What does it matter how? I'm here now.' He put down the menu. 'This thing about not hoping and dreaming – it's important. You need to understand. It's not that you shouldn't dream or wish – it's that these things are not substitutes for action. They're placebos. You don't know it yet – you can't possibly conceive it – but life is unutterably short. We prevaricate. We procrastinate. We delay our pleasures and fulfilments in expectation of a time to come – but there's no such time. The only time is now!'

He slapped the marble table-top.

'You think you already know this,' he said, 'because you know all those moronic platitudes: "There's no time like the present" and "Procrastination is the thief of time" *et cetera*. That's fossilised wisdom. It's so embedded in the strata of experience that it's petrified. We "know" it so we don't have to act on it. Our lives dribble out through various glands and orifices, we jerk and spasm with the futility of love and work, and we cling on to these idiotic sayings as we'd cling to a wine cork for safety in the shark-finned mid-Pacific vastness. The bite-ravaged body sinks but the cork bobs happily along.'

'I see what you're saying but... look at your life. How full. The women, the books, the travel, the triumphs. You've lived. You're a part of literary history.'

'History? What good is that? Shakespeare would laugh if he knew what he'd become. All that legacy didn't help him during life – when his son died, when his dick rotted with syphilis. If my life were a minute, I've lived maybe seven seconds of it. The rest... wasted. Yeah, sure, I wrote *Cassandra* blah blah blah. But only *one Cassandra*, right? How many more could I have written if I'd tried harder? Apathy. Laziness. I wished. I hoped. I didn't act. These afflictions have blighted my life. I allowed them to because it was easier that way. It's like ... you're sitting at a banqueting table loaded with the finest food and drink – the most exquisite delicacies – and your host says, "Eat! Fill yourself. Gorge on all that's offered" and you take a dainty bite. You risk a teaspoon of caviar for the luxury of it. You covet the whole roast turkey and take just a wing. No! My God – take me back to that table and let me eat until I puke through my nose. Until my stomach haemorrhages. Listen – we're going to eat this evening. Nothing until then – I don't care how hungry you are right now. This is your Ramadan. Your purification. We're going to eat later and you're going to tell me how everything tastes.'

'Is that the "irrational spiritual"?'

'That comes later.'

'So you *did* intend me to follow you here. How did you know I'd come?'

'I didn't. How could I know?'

'But you wanted me to, right?'

'Challenge seven: avoid a slavish need for affirmation. Right? If you came at all, you should have come for your own benefit.'

'And to help you. To drive and …'

'See me safely to my grave? Keep your altruism. Eternity awaits me with or without your help. But … Well, you're here. You can be of service.'

'And the business with Buddy? His stuff about you writing a book? Doesn't that cause you problems?'

'Problems? My problems are on a sliding scale, wouldn't you say? Is there anything they can do to me that's worse than this grenade in my head? Ha! You think that *malakas* Buddy got to me with his blog? Have you read some of my early reviews? Any one of my wives has tormented and betrayed me more than Buddy. There's no trust or loyalty in the world except your trust in yourself.'

'I feel I should be writing these *bon mots* for posterity.'

'Ha! Write them. Add them to the strata of fossilised dung we call wisdom. There's greater meaning in the greasy thumb stain you leave on the corner of the page. That's the real proof of life.'

'Who was the guy who tried to interview you at Patras? Do you know him?'

'Who knows? A journalist? An investigator working for one of my ex-wives' lawyers? Maybe even someone from my publisher. A nobody. A parasite.'

'He found me on the street after you left. He said you were being sued by your publisher for taking a large advance and not delivering the book. He asked about Buddy and Olympia.'

'What did you tell him?'

'Nothing about your illness or the morphine. I said Buddy was a thief. Those other things … well, I have no idea. I couldn't tell him anything. Is it true? About being sued?'

'It's nothing. They'll never see that money again. What do they care? They'll be creaming profits off my books long after we're all dead. They and my agent and my ex-wives. You didn't show him your journal, did you?'

'Of course not.'

'Good. But listen – keep your journal safe. I'm serious. It may be all callow solecisms, purple prose and naivety enough to nauseate a donkey, but it's true. It's a net in which you've caught some fragments of time and thought and youth. In ten years, in twenty, you'll look back on it and weep that you ever had the innocence or enthusiasm to write a page on how to drink a coffee.'

'You saw that?'

'I read it and it shamed me. You can't write – let's be clear on that point – but you're seeking. You're trying, and no amount of derivative pastiche can obstruct your expression of it. To that, I say "bravo" – but remember challenge number three. Life is not a movie or a script. If you must write about it, write its truth. Without lenses, without filters and stage direction and lighting. Write the starlet with her cellulite and greasy hair and her right breast larger than her left. Get her from her bad side and you'll see her truth.'

I sipped my coffee and wondered at his volubility. Could it be that he was actually pleased to see me? Relieved I'd risen to his challenge?

'How are you feeling?' I said.

'Eh, what does it matter? My head feels clear – that's the main thing. It must be the altitude here. Something to do with reduced pressure, maybe. Whatever – I'm seeing clearly through the pane.'

'Is that a pun?'

A grimace from Bastounis. One shouldn't draw attention to puns.

'Did you say we're going to the ancient sanctuary later?'

'Yes. You should rest now. It'll be a late night. Go to your room. You'll sleep better there away from the street. I have some things to arrange.'

It was twilight when he knocked on the door. Bats were flickering against a darkening sky outside my window. The timpani of tour buses that had lulled me to sleep had given way to the immense quiet of Parnassus.

'Ready?' he said. 'We're taking the car. And bring something warm.'

It was only a short drive, out of the village towards Itea and up the side of the hill until we'd left most buildings below us. I could have walked the distance in twenty minutes, but Bastounis couldn't. He looked pale and was sweating despite the coolness of the evening.

'Do you know this place?' I said.

'I asked around. It's where the locals go to escape the tourists. Good food.'

The road stopped abruptly and became a gravel track that led to an old single-storey stone house. There was no sign, but a couple of dusty pick-ups were parked outside.

'Are you sure this is the place? It looks like somebody's home.'

'It is somebody's home. Come on.'

A black-clad widow answered the door and took us through an unlit and low-ceilinged hallway to a rear court-yard that had been hewn out of the mountainside. A vine-choked trellis hung over half a dozen tables beside the house and a grill was being stoked by a huge mountain man in muddy jeans. The freshly flayed carcass of some rumi-nant (sheep or goat) hung from a steel hook: a haematite sculpture veined with quartz and true to every tendon.

'*Oriste!*' said the woman, attending our table with a note-pad and a candle in a jar.

Bastounis first ordered a symphony of *mezedes* from a smeary blackboard menu: battered courgette slices, meat-balls in sauce, *tzatziki*, *horta*, local sausage, deep-fried cheese, goat stew, rabbit *stifado*, creamed mushrooms and fried potatoes. The family had a barrel of home-made wine, so naturally we'd have a carafe.

'Mountain food,' he said, rubbing his hands. 'They have fish, but I don't trust the Gulf of Corinth. All that crap from Itea and the pollution from the ships.'

'You really can't taste anything?'

'It depends. It comes and goes. A lot of it is neurologi-cal. If I bit into an onion or a clove of garlic, I'd taste it because I have that memory. But I couldn't taste them in a dish. Combined tastes are faded. But the textures – oil, crisp batter, a tender onion, a good coarse sausage – they still work.'

The food arrived as it was prepared and we ate it as if the world would end: jabbing bread, forking morsels, slurping, dribbling, crunching. Each sip of icy wine was a cleanser for the next taste. Each new addition to the table multiplied the combinations. Bastounis called for pork chops and they flashed fire from the charcoal. He asked if they might prepare some chicken-thigh kebabs interleaved with sweet peppers, baby onions and aubergine.

'This fried cheese...' I said, squeezing lemon on it.

'*Saganaki tiri*,' he said. 'My favourite as a boy. The way it bubbles and melts without becoming entirely liquid. The crisp shell. The saltiness and the lemon cutting the oil. Can you taste it?'

'Yes, exactly that. And it squeaks on my teeth.'

'The squeak! Yes. That's right. Ah, here come the chops. No – not with fucking *cutlery*. Use your napkin if it's hot. Pick it up by the bone and gnaw on it. Look at that crispy fat.'

Meat juices ran over his beard and down his shirt, on which tomato sauce and olive oil had already Pollocked a design. He pointed the parenthetical bone at me.

'What would you do if I died right now? If I just dropped into my food.'

'I... I don't know.' I put down my chop. 'I'd be shocked.'

'Then you're ill prepared. You have to be ready for it. You know it's coming. Have you not thought about it?'

'I have... but only in an abstract way.'

'Abstract is useless. I may have a terminal seizure. I may soil myself luxuriantly. I may lose my mind temporarily and

235

run amok with tempestuous wrath. I don't know how it's going to end.'

'Are you afraid?'

'I'm not afraid. I'm angry. I've been cheated by this sorry carrion my body. The mind and the flesh become ever more at odds. The meat deteriorates with age but our minds achieve greater subtlety and sophistication. It's a cosmic joke. An insult. The fittest and most able bodies go to the emptiest vessels – the young. Those careless years fly by, unappreciated, unexploited. Only later do you realise what they were truly worth. Too late. Give me your hand.'

'What?'

'Give me your hand! You think I'm going to propose?'

I tentatively extended my hand. He gripped it with greasy fingers and stared.

'Promise you won't waste your youth. Promise me you'll use your time to live. I don't care how you do it, but do it. The sand is running right now. It's been running since you were born and one day you'll realise you're slipping down the funnel and that's it. It's over. Promise you won't waste these years.'

'I promise…'

He dropped my hand. 'We'll see. You'll see. In another fifty or sixty years, you'll see. Then you'll remember. You'll feel the anger, too.'

'Aren't you proud of your achievements? If I'd done what you've done—'

'I'd give it back. I'd give it all back to have my sense of taste and a working leg. I'd be a nameless nobody to have this swelling death excised. What use is it to have my name on a list or a web page somewhere? In ten years, I'll be the quiz question nobody can answer or the subject of a tedious thesis: another of those obscure Nobel Prize-winners.'

'Not to me.'

A brief burning flicker from Bastounis. 'Have we finished here?'

'I think so.'

The table was littered with plates, bowls, stains and breadcrumbs. The candle cast jittering shadows. Bastounis paid and we went out to the car.

It was now fully dark and stars were out with stunning clarity. A pale limen at the peak proclaimed the moon's arrival. Away from the sheltered courtyard, the air was crisp and cold. Our breath steamed. The windscreen was damp.

He said nothing as we drove back into the village, along the tourist road and out past the bus stop where I'd arrived. Vast melanic blots against the sky hinted at louring cliffs and outcrops.

'Park here,' he said.

'But the site's closed. There are no lights on.'

'The site is open for me. I am Irakles Bastounis.'

I followed him up a stone-paved path to the closed gates of the ticket booth, where a red tip zig-zagged amid blossoms of white. The site guard, smoking, shook Bastounis's hand and pushed open the gate.

'We have an hour only,' said Bastounis. 'It's enough. Come on.'

I didn't question this unorthodox access. I assumed a bribe had changed hands. The undergrowth exhaled a scent of earth and herbs as we began to ascend the sacred way. Above Parnassus's peak, the swollen moon had risen and cast its frosty light on all the stones of Delphi. We walked amid silver blocks and platinum facades, between bisected circles and among the frozen beams of solitary columns. Cypress trees stood in dark exclamations against the sky, or huddled as darker shadows in the hollows of the hill. Our crunching footsteps seemed magnified by the sanctuary's silence.

Bastounis limped and grunted, his crutch clinking as he went. His face was glistening. He stopped at the first bend and leaned against a pitted wall.

'This is the Athenian treasury,' he said, breathing heavily. 'The richest. Always show-offs, the Athenians.'

'Are you okay? Do you want to rest?'

'No time for that. Keep going. You go ahead.'

I went ahead into the phantom landscape of scattered pillar drums and empty pedestals, etched inscriptions and epic vacancy. This had been a Lourdes, a Vatican, a Jerusalem to the ancients. Kings and emperors came in pilgrimage here. Alexander walked this very path. Midas, Pythagoras, Croesus, and Nero passed by these same stones before English was a language and Christ a concept. Now only two ascended: an old man at the end of life and a young man at its start. Night's quiet erased time. All were one here at Delphi.

'Do you see it?' called Bastounis behind me. 'The platform. The pillars.'

The temple of Apollo above and to our left. It sat on a mighty stone base, its remaining pillars like five rotten teeth in an exhumed jawbone. Centre of wisdom, where the words "Know thyself" were carved into the stone. Direct line to destiny.

I paused at the ramp to the platform, further access barred by the limp arc of string. The sanctuary below us was a field of pale, tumbled dice divided by the path's meandering. My breath billowed iridescent in the moonlight.

'We're going inside,' said Bastounis, wiping his face with a sleeve. 'Help me – the base is very uneven.'

We stepped over the string and up the stone ramp to the levelled base of the temple – a chaotic chequerboard of

blocks and gaps and grassy nooks that would have been hazardous for Bastounis even in daylight. I held his free arm
as we negotiated our way to the place where the smoking
tripod would have been: seat of the Pythia, the oracle who
called upon the swirls of fate.

'This is close enough,' he said. 'We'll lie here on these
blocks. Go on – lie.'

I lay with my back on the cold stone and he settled beside
me, the crutch clattering. Our breathing steamed towards
the stars and I felt the thrill of it rushing upon me. We were
lying at the core, in the very womb, of western civilisation,
beneath the timeless moon and infinite constellations – flat
against the mute slabs of history but at a portal to something beyond it. I waited for him to recover from his exer-
tions. Had he prepared a speech for this? I hoped for some
of his magic.

'There are places,' said Bastounis, 'that transcend.
Tiryns was one. Athos is another. But this – this is beyond
religion. Did the oracle really receive messages from the
ether? Or was she high on ethylene or weed? It doesn't
matter. What matters is that people for a millennium
and more have believed it. Here, on this spot, the divine
passed through a wild-haired woman. When Theodosius
outlawed all religions but Christianity and decreed that
Delphi should be razed, he wasn't denying the existence
of this power – he was fearful of it. Why destroy a temple
to eradicate something that doesn't exist? No – it existed
as surely as Christianity did, but as a rival truth. The walls
are gone and the columns fallen and the civilisation that
made them scoured to foundations by millennia, but here
we are: at the same place where Alexander waited, where
vapour ascended, where wars were decided and where king-
doms rose or fell. Right here. Do you feel it? That hope, that

expectation. The wonder – it connects us all. That desire for something more is what makes us more than animal. It's the irrational spiritual. Science and progress tell us that it doesn't exist, but the whole of human experience has sought it in different places and with different names. It's a root going back to our origins and a skein stretching into infinity. It's a continuum. Do you feel it?'

'I feel heavy. Like I'm being drawn to the earth.'

'That's it! Give in to it. Don't try to name it or rationalise it or verbalise it. Just feel.'

The stone was cold against my back and calves. I pressed my palms flat and stared at the moon: witness to ceaseless cycles of triumph and glory, defeat and decay. My life was an insect's solitary wing beat beneath it.

Bastounis raised his hand as if to clasp it.

'Helios's sister Selene,' he said 'Witchcraft's pale Hecate. For the Canaananites, that face was Yarikh, the bringer of the dew. For Hittites, winged Kaskuh. For Hindoos, Chandra. In ancient Egypt, she was Khonsu, called Mah by Persians, and Nanna in Sumeria. Different names, different myths but the same thing, do you see? Unchanged by naming, culture and perception.'

The world of CVs and job applications and rental agreements and travel passes and wifi connections and annual leave was a distant as ancient Sumeria. *This* was the stationary omphalos beyond which everything circled.

'You were at Athos, weren't you,' I said. 'When you were a young man.'

'For a year only. I was so young. I was actually tonsured by the abbot. I thought I might talk to God, but that was the level of my vanity. I wasn't really interested in anything he might have to say. I wanted him to listen. That's the hallmark of a novelist. Why? Are you thinking about it?'

'I don't know what I'm thinking. I don't know where I'm going.'

'A hermit's life seems attractive when you're young, but it doesn't work. Not then. There's nothing to fill the time and silence. You can go insane. Hormones bubble and seep into every thought. Monasticism is an old man's indulgence. The young man must sail or walk. You know why Homer's *Odyssey* is so beloved, or the adventures of Heracles? Because they represent the pattern of a perfect life: a journey with challenges and passions, monsters and discoveries and the supernatural. It's all there.'

'I can't go back. That life they want for me at home ... I don't want it. This is where I want to be.'

'You don't have to go back. As for this place, it's no more the container of its significance than a church is of Christ. Its energy goes beyond time and life. It's integral to us as humans. If we're receptive to it. If we seek it and nurture it. Call it creativity or imagination or wonder or dreaming – anything that projects or seeks. If my books succeeded in anything, it was in that evangelism.'

I wanted to tell him then that his evangelism was what had brought me to Dimitsana and persuaded me to follow him to the end. I wanted to tell him that his novels repre-sented another Delphi, another Tiryns to me – places where an elemental truth was always present. But he already knew that. Instead, I said:

'Alexander must have stood on this very stone.'

'Ha! Do you know what happened when he approached the oracle? He asked if he'd conquer the world and she couldn't give him an answer. A rare occurrence. So he dragged her by the hair into the light until she proclaimed him invincible. That happened where we're lying. Right here. We're part of it now.'

A distant whistle blew.

'That's our cue,' said Bastounis. 'Time to leave.'

Neither of us moved. We were pinned by a telluric gravity. The frosted constellations watched.

'Where's next?' I said. 'Where are we going tomorrow?'

'Higher, further. Closer to the source. Come on, help me up.'

Eighteen

I was parking outside the rooms when he spoke again.

'How tired are you?'

'I'm fine. Energised. Did you want to go for a brandy?'

'No. I'm thinking that we keep going. Don't sleep here – just keep driving north. Keep going.'

'Really? It's almost eleven. Where would we go?'

'Wherever. I don't want to sleep. There's no reason to stay here. Forget the money. We'll drive until we're tired or until we get somewhere.'

'You want me to go and get the bags?'

'Here's my key. Just leave it in the door.'

I cleared the two rooms. Bastounis had left nothing in the bathroom or beside the bed. He hadn't unpacked at all. His world was the old leather holdall and the clothes he stood in.

Back in the street, I opened the rear door and threw the bags on the seat. There was something silver in the footwell: the dictaphone that had clattered inside when Bastounis had assaulted the guy. Its LCD screen was blank. Broken? I tossed it on the seat with the luggage.

'So,' I said, getting behind the wheel. 'North?'

'We'll follow the signs towards Lamia and see where we get.'

I drove out of Delphi the way we'd come, then north towards Amfissa. A starry panorama filled the windscreen and I toyed with the idea of the road as our launch strip direct to Polaris, the Pleiades, Orion's belt. Dark-horizon peaks were swelling nebulae. Silvered olive groves shot peripherally as astral dust. I checked the instruments and prepared for the jump to light speed.

Bastounis sat according to his habit: hands folded in his lap, eyes watching the road but lost in some other vision. Movement was the thing. Progress and direction. He was a comet orbiting but ever burning in an upper atmosphere that must eventually deplete him in a single fiery scar across the sky. Sometimes he mumbled, his lips moving and his fingers twitching. I took these as conversations remembered or rehearsed – projections in the planetarium of his skull.

We were north of Amfissa, ascending a set of hairpins in lulling low gears, when he fell asleep. The road was empty and relentlessly upwards. His head lolled against the window and his shoulder twitched mildly. A few miles further on, he started muttering in his sleep – at first unintelligibly and then in recognisable Greek. There was a rhythm to it, like a song or a poem.

I reached behind me and searched for the dictaphone. The record button was a red dot, but nothing happened when I pressed it. Only a brief appearance of the time on screen. I slid a knobbly button on the side and the screen filled with icons. Ready to go. It beeped and a red LED showed it was recording his hypnogogic monologue.

The incline evened out after the sleeping town of Gravia and we were on some higher plateau of the Pindus foothills. The olive trees had been replaced by evergreens and fading oaks. I still felt fine – like I could drive all night. If I didn't have to eat or sleep, I could keep going forever. Never stop.

Bastounis was now snoring and occasionally jerking an arm or leg. I'd stopped recording him and now tried the dictaphone to see if I had anything. The tinny speaker close to my ear played background road noise and his voice faint but clearly audible. With more volume, the words would be clearer. Maybe I'd ask him later to translate.

The screen said that this was file number six. Less than two minutes' duration. The other five were longer. What else had the guy been recording? I reached behind me again and tugged the earbuds from the side pocket of my bag, pulling socks out in the tangled cable. I inserted the jack and selected file five. I put one bud in the ear facing away from Bastounis and pressed play.

Something rustled against the microphone. A man cleared his throat. A dial tone. Keys pressed. The dictaphone must have been pressed close to the speaker on a phone.

'Hello?' [A woman's voice]

'Yes, hello. Is this Theodora Bastounis?'

'I don't use that surname. Who is this?'

'I'm a researcher for *Kathimerini*. I saw your tweet earlier today about a visit from your grandfather Irakles Bastounis and I was wondering if you have any comment about his health or the rumour that he may be working on a book.'

'How did you get this number? Did he give it you?'

'Naturally, your grandfather is a highly respected artist here in Greece and there's a lot of interest in another novel.'

'Is there?'

'Of course. And I'd be very grateful if you could—'

'Why don't you leave his family alone? Don't you think he's brought us enough trouble? We're not celebrities. We're just normal people. Chase him, not us.'

'Could you tell me if there's an issue with his health? Did he discuss it with you?'

[Pause]

'What did you say your name was? I'm going to contact *Kathimerini* to confirm.'

'I understand he's travelling with a young Englishman – a driver. You might—'

'I said nothing about that in my tweet. Who are you? Are you recording this? I'm not giving permission for you to use any of this in any way. Do you understand? Tell me your name right now—'

[Beep]

Pity the reporter who tried to interview Theodora. But he was good. He had the interrogator's rat-like cunning and total lack of scruple. I clicked the next file. It was another phone conversation.

'Yes?' [An English voice]

'Professor Macgregor?'

'Yes?'

'Oh, good. I'm hoping you can help me, professor. It's my understanding that many British newspapers prepare obituaries in advance for older artists and celebrities, and that you're responsible for writing certain literary obituaries for the *Times* of London. Is that right?'

'Excuse me, but who am I talking to?'

'Oh, sorry, sorry. Yes. I'm a researcher calling from *Ta Nea*, the Greek daily.'

'"The New".'

'Excuse me?'

'"Ta Nea" – it means "The New" in Greek, doesn't it?'

'Yes! Yes, very good, professor. You know Greek?'

'Just a little New Testament. It's a hobby of mine. We have a group ... but you didn't call about that. To answer your question: yes, I've written some obituaries. It's a little macabre, I know, but the research can take time and they like to print as quickly as possible ... but you already know how it works, I'm sure.'

'Yes. My question concerns Irakles Bastounis. I'm not sure if you've heard, but there are rumours of ill health. Am I correct in thinking you've produced an obituary for him? I know that you've written on him before.'

'I'm sorry to hear that about Bastounis, but, yes, I have something on file. He was one of the easier ones, of course, because he's been inactive for the last two decades or so. His work is done. He's in his late seventies isn't he?"

'That's right. I wonder if you might summarise for me what your obituary says about him.'

'Well, I'm not sure exactly where ... It would be in the *Times* for everyone to read if the worst happens. I'm not sure I'm allowed to email it to you. I expect it's subject to copyright.'

'I understand, professor. I don't need the actual text. If you could just speak about his literary reputation and his contribution, I'm sure our Greek readers would be interested to hear what Southampton University has to say about their native son. I'm afraid he's not especially well known here. He's probably considered more of an American author.'

'Well, that's an important question, of course. His subjects owe so much to Greek mythology and history, but he wrote only in English. And American English at that. His interest is in a Greece that ceased to exist before the birth of Christ. That's not to say his subjects are out-dated – his themes are as universal as the themes of the great tragedians and oral storytellers.'

'How would you characterise those themes ... for the common reader, I mean.'

'Oh, the importance of narrative as a cultural and existential cohesive; the protean, interchangeable nature of reality and fantasy; myth and legend brought into the realm of the modern day... There are more, but you should tell your readers it's his style that really marked him out. I suppose you'd call it a variety of late-Modernism: formal experimentation in search of a truer reality. Some believe he was an early progenitor of so-called Magic Realism but he didn't follow that path. He was too interested in the real. A one-off, really – like Nabokov. An autodidact. And, of course, he won the Nobel if you consider that a sign of anything. It's my opinion that the last decade or so has seen... but no, I shouldn't get into that.'

'You're putting this is the past tense.'

'Yes, yes... Well, as I say, he's not published for almost two decades. It's easy to see his work in a historical frame even if he's alive. It's not too popular now. I suspect he's one of those – like Henry Miller – who became larger than their books. When the face and name fade or become old-fashioned, so does the work. His was a very masculine, egocentric literary period. It's a pity – he was a very good writer. Inspirational. He belonged to the party who believed there was more to prose than being a mere a carrier of story. They've been dying out. It's a different market. I think, in ten years or so, we'll be seeing more work inspired by him.'

'Would you be surprised by a new book?'

'A new book from Bastounis? That would be... Do you know something about a new book?'

'There's a rumour.'

'Do you mean a new book, or an old book to be published for the first time?'

'New. It's said he's working on it as we speak.'

'Well, that would be commercially very valuable – even more so if it proved to be posthumous. It sounds callous, I know, but you appreciate how these things are.'

'You think it would sell.'

'I don't work in publishing, naturally, but I'm pretty sure it would. Look at the posthumous stuff from Nabokov. And that was just notes, really, for unfinished work. A Nobel winner tends to get publicity.'

Could you predict – based on his previous work, I mean – what kind of subject he might write on?'

'Well, who knows? But his own death might be his grandest subject yet. It would… It could tie together most of his long-running themes and it might explain why – and why now – he might be working on something new. In fact, the idea is quite exciting. Bastounis on death and eternity would be quite a read. Do you know more?'

'I'm trying to gather information. The man himself doesn't like interviews. I'm going to try and catch him today.'

'Would you let me know if you discover anything else? It might be useful information for the obituary.'

'Of course, professor.'

'Many thanks. It was good to talk to you… I'm sorry, what was your name again? Hello?'

[Beep]

Bastounis in the past tense – obituaries pre-written. He'd already entered Hades in his funereal Peugeot. The vultures were circling. He'd predicted it all. I clicked on the previous file.

'Oriste!'

'Er, hi? It's Buddy. Buddy Tannenbaum? You emailed me your number and—'

'Of course! Many thanks for calling, Buddy. I've been following your blog.'

'Yeah, man, the hit rate is off the chart, but don't expect me to give you any exclusives. I made agreements with some people, so, you know...'

'I understand. My research is not in competition with your blog. I'm really interested in only a couple of things that you might be able to confirm.'

'Shoot, man.'

'You suggest in your blog that Bastounis may be researching a book. What evidence did you see for that?'

'It's smoke and mirrors. Why else would he be going to all these places? He didn't seem to do anything there. At Olympia, it was like he wanted to soak up the atmosphere, you know? I saw a load of papers in his bag but it didn't look like a manuscript – more like notes. Place names. Like, spider diagrams. Some of it was in Greek.'

'Do you remember any detail? Which place names?'

'Shit, it was a just glance. I think I saw Delphi. Maybe Thessalonika? I should have taken it all, but...Anyway, I didn't see him write a thing the whole time. Maybe he's got, like, a photographic memory or total recall or whatever and he'll write it all later.'

'Maybe. My other question is about his health. Did he seem in good health? Did he show any unusual symptoms?'

'He didn't seem sick. Knocked me out pretty good.'

'You didn't see any prescription drugs around?'

'Hey, listen man. I don't know what you know, but I don't wanna start getting into too much detail here. I'm in a lot of trouble already. My dad's coming over and he says he's gonna fix this, but there are some things I can't talk about, right?'

'It's okay, Buddy. I don't need any details. All I need to know is if Bastounis might be ill. If he might be dying.'

'Dying?'

'Prescription or serious drugs might be an indication of that. You don't have to tell me anything about your case, Buddy. Buddy? Are you still there?'

'All I'm gonna say is that the man's not clean. That's all.'

'That's all you need to say, Buddy. And listen – this can be our secret but I know there was someone else: an English guy. He drove Bastounis from Dimitsana. They were together at Nafplio and Monemvasia and the Mani. They're in Ithaca now.'

'You know about him, huh?'

'What's the story there?'

'Story? There's no story. The old man needed a driver and he chose this guy, this cipher. Typical stiff-ass Brit. Easy to control. He was never gonna tell any tales – you know what I mean? He'd take it with him to the grave. Me, I say life's too short and I think Bastounis's with me on that. But someone has to be the driver, right? Carry the bags. He must be pretty pissed with my blog, but he won't do shit about it. That's the beauty of him.'

'Okay, Buddy. Thanks for calling. If you remember anything else about those papers, you can call me. Right?'

'Sure, man. Hey, you're not recording any of this are you?'

'No. It's all strictly confidential.'

'Cool. Well, see you, man.'

[Beep]

Fucking Buddy. Was there no escape from his drawling inanities and parasitism? I began to understand why Bastounis had hidden out in Dimitsana all that time. Once you've shared your mind with the world, you become its property. You've made an involuntary non-privacy pact that extends to everyone you know or love.

I listened to the remaining two files, but both were in Greek and very short. One of the voices seemed to be Konstantinopoulos. The other was a woman. Maybe Danäe Tegou – the painter from Monemvasia? There was a question containing Bastounis's name and then a very long pause. She clearly didn't trust the caller.

Bastounis was still asleep – oblivious to these cross currents and riptides running parallel to his end. What maelstrom would his death provoke?

I had no idea where we were. The road had been climbing again but all was lunar chiaroscuro. Dark peaks had risen to the right and a level patchwork of monochrome plain had rolled out far below. An illuminated layby up ahead offered the chance to stop and stretch my legs.

The wheels crunched over gravel and I saw it was a monument in pale marble and ruddy sandstone: a stone frieze with a battle scene and an enormous bronze warrior illuminated against the stars. I opened the door and stepped out. It was cold and silent. A road sign we'd passed recently prompted my memory... This was Thermopylae – site of Leonidas's stand against the Persians. The 300 Spartans. Thousands had died here in the fury of battle, and not only against the Persians. Civilisations had crashed here like continents. This had been a corridor of history, pinched between sea and mountain, between empire and empire. I wondered if I should wake Bastounis, but he was already watching me.

'You see the inscription?' he said. '"Molon lave".'

'What is it?'

'The Persians sent a message to Leonidas: surrender your weapons. The inscription was his reply: "Come and get them".'

'A bit macho.'

'He and his men were annihilated right here. If we'd been standing on this spot in 480BC, we'd have been on the beach watching it. Their blood is in this earth. Their glory is a scarlet ribbon woven through a hundred and twenty-five generations. What record will there be of *your* death? An official document? A name scratched on a stone? Grave markers don't last, unless they're pyramids. You'll be another of the anonymous millions – insignificant as dust.'

'And you?'

'Me, too. Me, too.'

'But your books...'

'The books aren't me. They're commercial products. The really great works – Homer, Aeschylus, Solomon, Shakespeare, Milton... they were conceived as *living* texts. Enacted, sung, memorised – adhered to as systems of behaviour and ethics. They were participatory. They created and nurtured a life of their own – beyond the page and beyond their time. Nobody owns them. Prose is a solitary, too-cerebral activity. There's no life in it. It's a game. It's a distraction.'

'Is... Is that why you stopped writing?'

Bastounis was staring at the colossal Leonidas. He must have heard me.

'Once the fulcrum of a culture's destiny,' he said. 'Now a car park by a highway.'

'Hmm.'

'There's a hot spring near here – a waterfall. It's what gives the place its name. Leonidas's men would have bathed in it. Back then, of course, all volcanic phenomena were considered portals to the underworld. They knew where they were headed. Shall we go? Shall we enter Hades?'

'Now? It's two in the morning or something.'

'I see you've learned nothing from your challenges. "I can't steal the apples of the Hesperides right now," whined Heracles – "My mom's expecting me home for supper". There's nothing to fear. It's just hot water.'

'Fine. Let's go.'

'Bravo. It's back along the road there. About five minutes, I guess.'

I drove deeper into this surreal night – someone else's dream. Different voices from different times. The dictaphone was in my pocket. Should I?

'You were talking in your sleep.'

'Was I?'

'In Greek. It sounded like verse. I recorded it on this.'

'You recorded me?'

'Here – listen. It's not very good quality but... Just press play.'

He inserted the earbud unfamiliarly and sat listening without movement or expression, pressing at his ear occasionally when the quality faltered.

'What is it?' I said.

'It's from *The Odyssey*. Book eleven: the hero's descent into hell. I learned it years ago at school ... I was just a child. It's the part at the end where he meets Heracles and the big man bemoans his fate.'

'They taught you that at school?'

'Eh, it's Homer. You know – I never thought about it then: the hypocrisy of it. The priests would tell us that Heaven was all glory – a golden life after life. Existence itself was just a burden to bear, our bodies mere corrupted carriers. But there was no heaven for the ancients – only hell. Everyone ended up in the same place, good and bad. Life was everything. There was no promise of an afterlife. Hades was loss of form and memory. You were just a shadow there.

Nobody venerated death. But nor did they fear it. An end was as necessary as a beginning ... I haven't thought about those verses for sixty years or more.'

'I found other files on the machine. Interviews. Buddy, Theodora ... Some of them are in Greek. I don't know if you want to ...'

'Show me.'

'You press this to go back a file. Then play.'

He listened as I arrived at a small parking area for the hot springs. The smell of sulphur was strong even there and I could see steam rising high into the chill air. Which Hadean river was this? Acheron the sorrowful? Phlegethon of fire? Forgetful Lethe? The Styx, hate-black?

Bastounis was silent. He clicked through the files without utterance or evident emotion, though towards the end I thought I saw his jaw reacting. Clenched teeth. Tight lips. I think he listened to the last one twice before removing the earbud and turning to me. He looked haunted.

'It's my fault,' he said. 'I should've known someone would come after me. I led him straight to them.'

'Was one Mister Konstantinopulos?'

A nod. 'The interviewer told them I was already dead. To get a reaction. To make them talk.'

'Did they believe him?'

'I don't know.'

We both knew the call would soon come again and be true. Now he'd heard the reaction to it from the other side. He'd heard his friends experience it. He was the man standing at his own funeral, impotently watching the mourners.

'You could call them,' I said. 'Reassure them. I saw signs for Lamia. It's close.'

'I've already said goodbye. How many times more?'

'But you're still alive.'

'Am I? Can't you smell the sulphur? We're at the gates of Erebus.'

'What are you going to do? About the journalist, I mean.'

'Are you familiar with the Erinyes? The Furies?'

'I've heard of them.'

'They lived in hell – subterranean spirits even older than Olympians. Spirits of divine vengeance. They favoured the cause of the elderly. Come on – let's offer supplication at the gates of Hades.'

'Really?'

'You think because new religions came that the old ones went away? Remember the many names of Luna? The Bible threatens lakes of fire; the Furies delivered it to order. Same fire, different name. Embrace the irrational spiritual. Let's go.'

We walked down a gravel incline to where the spring gushed steaming from an ugly concrete spout and exploded over flat, mossy rocks. The sulphur stench was powerful. Vapour swirled.

'Are you sure you want to do this?' I said. 'The ground's very uneven. You could slip.'

'And what? Hurt my arm or leg? Sustain a nasty graze? We're going in. Hold this.'

I held the crutch as he began to take off his clothes. The air temperature must have been about seven degrees. Naked and pale, he went to the gingerly to the edge and eased himself from a sitting position into the spectral pool. His hoary head drifted to its centre.

'Ah!'

'Is it hot?'

'Hotter than blood, colder than coffee. Come on – I promise I won't stare at your weiner.'

I looked around. Two in the morning off a highway in northern Greece and an English graduate was bathing *al fresco* in Leonidas's volcanic spring with a dying novelist. The Furies were about to be summoned from abyssal Tartarus. Elsewhere, in a fantasy world, alarms were set and ironed clothes laid out for work. A hundred-million sleepers were enslaved to screens and sandwiches and public-transport schedules.

I began to strip. The night air was cold on my skin and the gritty earth painful underfoot. Sulphurous wraiths writhed about me, absorbing and concealing the pool with Bastounis's disembodied head.

'Are you coming or not?' he said.

'I'm here. Wait a minute … I can't see you.'

The water was a hot bath. I eased myself from toe to ankle, ankle to knee, knee to groin. Halfway in, the heat was more appealing than the cold and I descended, buoyant, to discover it was barely waist deep. I crouched on the stony bottom. Spray from the waterfall speckled my face from within its cloaking shroud.

'Where are you?' I said.

'Here, by the rocks.'

He was grinning – a different man without his cap and sunglasses. He was a milky daguerreotype negative, overexposed, water rilling down his face from the mossy overhang.

'We need an offering,' he said. 'It should be flesh.'

'I'm not giving you any flesh.'

'Maybe this?' He drew the dictaphone dripping from the pool.

'You know, you have a very bad track record with electronic devices.'

'Ha! Come closer. Take it seriously. Hold your hands in the running water to purify them – that's the rule. Right. Now take the other end of the machine. We both hold it. But listen – you have to mean this. You can't think about other things during the supplication or they'll know. They're not forgiving women. This isn't a joke. The heat, the smell – we're at the very lip of black eternity. Unnumbered souls may hear our voices. Are you ready?'

'No. Okay … do it.'

He closed his eyes and held up the ruined dictaphone.

'Vengeful Erinyes – hear me!

Alekto, Megaera, Tisiphone!

I call on you to make wrong right

And, with screaming eagles' might,

Feast terrible upon the tender parts

Of this man's lies and petty art.

Inside this box his voice resides

Know it, seek it, though it hides.

And leave his organs scattered, strewn

And down to Hades drag his doom.

He jerked the dictaphone into the water. It belonged to the Furies now. The waterfall crashed without cease. Steam billowed.

'How do you know if they've heard?' I said.

'You never do. They might object to my awful verse. It's always good to have a back-up plan. Did the guy give you any contact details?'

'No … wait … Yes. A card with phone number. He put it in my bag. I must still have it.'

'Good. Good. This hellish water is good for me. I can feel it. It gives me energy.'

'It stinks. These bubbles …'

'That was me. Sorry. Pork chops always do it.'

'Right, that's enough Hades for one night. I'm getting out.'

NINETEEN

The bedside phone trilled electronically into my sleep. Where was I? Delphi? Patras? Home?

'Stop the fucking phone,' muttered Bastounis from the other bed.

The Hotel Amerika in Lamia. He'd insisted on this one because it was spelled the same way as Kafka's first novel. It had been about half three in the morning, both of us damp and sulphurous.

'The phone!' groaned Bastounis.

I picked it up. 'Hello?'

A click. A hollow echo. A different skein of fate and time. A woman's voice: 'Oh, thank God! I've been worried sick!'

'Mum?'

'Where have you been? You haven't called or written. I've been worried sick. They told me you're in Lamia. Why are you in Lamia? That's not a tourist town. Are you safe? Are you hurt? Can you hear me?'

'How did you find me—?'

'I called the Greek police, of course. They said they'd be able to find you from your passport details if you'd checked into a hotel, but most of the hotels are too small to have a computer system and anyway most don't even enter the details when they should because of tax evasion, but if you stayed in a place where they did—'

'You called the police?'

'I was worried sick! A man called and left a message you were at the Hotel Amerika. Why did you stop texting? I've been imagining you dead in a ditch. You know what it's like with all those people traffickers—'

'My phone got broken. I sent you an email about it.'

'Did somebody rob you?'

'Nobody robbed me. It was an accident.'

'Well, don't they have more internet cafes there?'

Bastounis was awake and leaning on an elbow, watching me.

'What's going on with you?' she said. 'What are you doing over there? I'm worried sick.'

'You've said that three times now.'

'Well, I am! You know Clara is heartbroken. She feels so betrayed.'

'You've been in touch with Clara?'

'Of course I have. Did you expect me to just abandon her like you did? She's doing very well on her course but—'

'Don't tell me about her.'

'Why not? What's *wrong* with you? All of your friends have started paying off their loans and making a life for themselves, but you're swanning around on holiday in Lamia. What's in Lamia anyway? I looked it up and there's nothing even there.'

'*I'm* here.'

'I'm so worried about you!'

Bastounis was intent, feasting on the scene.

'Look – mother… I'm perfectly fine. I'm safe. You can't go calling the police every time you don't hear from me for a week—'

'A week? It's more like—'

'It doesn't matter how long. This is… This is my *life*. I've finished school. I've finished university. I've jumped through all the hoops. I'm not jumping through any more. I don't want to sit in an office while my life and my spirit leaks slowly away. I don't want to just *work*. Its slavery. It's mindless. It's the existence of a dumb animal shuffling towards the abattoir—'

'Everyone has to work.'

'No. I'm not working. I'm in Greece. I'm seeing what it's like to actually be a person and make choices. What was the point of studying all those years? Shakespeare, Socrates … All that focus on art and human experience and the purpose of existence … and then what? What? Put on a suit and run round the hamster wheel until I'm dead, anaesthetising myself at weekends with alcohol and looking forward to a brief blink of holiday sunshine once a year. That's not life. That's not being a person. It's *hell!* Can't you see that?'

'Being a person isn't just about going to Lamia in Greece.'

'For fuck's sake, mother! You should be pleased for me. For the first time in my life … Look – I'm not coming home until I'm ready. Maybe not at all, I don't know. I'm not ready yet. And if I decide not to write or call, then there'll be no calls and texts. Don't call the police again. I'm serious. If anything happens to me … well, someone'll inform you. But if something does happen, you should know that it happened when I was actually living. You should be glad.'

'That's the first time you've ever sworn at me.'

'I'm hanging up now. I'm safe. I'm happy. You have no reason to worry. Goodbye. Take care. Bye.'

My hands were shaking. I lay back and stared at the mosquito-spotted ceiling. He was still watching me.

'Go on, then,' I said.

'Challenge ten: choose who you're living for. It's difficult. Families, relationships – they're difficult. They don't add people together; they subdivide. You become half or a quarter of a unit: functional only within the unit – fractured and incomplete outside of it. It makes sense. Weaknesses are dissipated in the unit. They're absorbed. Any amount of pathologies find home in a relationship. Families are fucked up. You only know it when you try to break away and realise you've been crippled by dependency. You've abrogated your identity to some significant degree. You've lost yourself. Sure, you'll be fine if you never leave and never question. You'll never even notice. But look at how widows flourish a year or so after their bereavement. Look how life and youth return as they start to be themselves for the first time in decades. Colour suffuses them. They stand taller. No longer wives or mothers, but women. Some go mad, it's true, but many start to live again.'

'Do I pass this challenge?'

'It's too early to say. But… it took balls to say what you said. You did good.'

I stared at the ceiling. Mosquito spots blurred aqueous.

'Anyway…' He rolled out of bed and clinked naked to the bathroom with his crutch.

'Is that right?' I called to the open door. 'That the police can find you in a hotel that easily? Someone knows where we are all the time?'

'Eh, it's all electronic now,' his voice flat off the ceramics. 'If you want to be free, you have to pay cash, show no documents, carry no phone. Use a false name if necessary. Only two kinds of people are free: the grossly rich and the destitute ruined. You have to get lost.'

I thought of Marseille and his drug oblivion there. Off the grid: an opioid zombie. Crashing in squats and under bridges. Invisible for years. An obituary appeared even then – an overeager Italian tabloid. What was the headline?

Basta Bastounis? Had that whole period been about getting lost? I bet his mother never called *him*.

His guts gurgled in the bathroom. A cloacal splash.

'Do you want to shut that door?'

The crutch rattled. Its rubber foot pushed the door closed.

My mother's call had been such an occasion. She'd caught me at a time of intense privacy and focus. She'd just burst into my existence as if she had some right of possession over me. Clara had been the same. *What are you thinking?* she'd ask whenever I found silence in a sliver of reflection. *You must share your thoughts. You can't have your own thoughts.* Turned out she didn't like them much.

It was 10.00am. Not enough sleep. Earlier that morning, driving into deserted Lamia, Bastounis had asked for the card the journalist guy had slipped in my bag. He'd made me stop at the first payphone we saw and got out of the car to call him. It must have been about 3.00am. I heard the whole call.

'Hello. Did I wake you? This is Irakles Bastounis. Yes. That's right. You've been contacting people about me, trying to write a story. You want a story? I'll be in Plateia Parkou, Lamia, at 5.00pm today. Come and get it.'

The Furies were Plan A. This was the back-up. Bastounis said nothing thereafter about his intentions for the meeting, or whether there'd actually be one. It might just be a gambit or retaliation – drag the guy up to Lamia from wherever he was and distract him from causing more trouble. Or maybe Bastounis had something a little more Leonidas in mind. Whatever the deal, I needed to witness it.

The toilet flushed – an acoustic mask for his vomiting. In a moment, I'd hear the tap running into a toothglass as he took something for the headache. Not the morphine, though. We were still far from that. I hadn't seen the ampoule since Olympia, but I was sure he had it hidden somewhere. Maybe more than one. Had he purchased a new syringe at the same time he'd got the crutch? A dry raspberry honked as he blew his nose. The bathroom door opened.

'I can't get the smell of the sulphur out of my nose. How's that for irony? I can't smell brandy or apples, but the spice of brimstone piques my primitive brain. What's up with you? Why do you look away like a blushing maiden? Does my nakedness discomfort you? Must I wrap a shroud around my loins? No. You should look – look upon the ravages of time and destiny: these brittle tent poles, this saggy canvas – this sloshing wineskin of assembled organs. Phallus, the withered traitor, with tired balls his Rocinante saddle. This is you at the end. This is all of us. Listen – we need to talk about some things.'

'Really?'

'Yes, really.'

He went to his bag. I heard him rustling among that sheaf of haphazard notes.

'This is the letter from Doctor Eleni in Olympia. Keep it safe.'

'Do we have to do this now?'

'Yes.'

'Is it getting worse?'

'It's not getting better. The tank is empty. You know that, don't you? My time was up two weeks ago. Take the letter. It's in Greek but it says everything. Her details are on there, and the consultant in Athens. When it happens, see that you give this to the police or whoever. Maybe we can make some copies today.'

'Okay.'

'I'll write a letter explaining who you are and what you're doing. Corroboration is good when dealing with authorities. They like the paperwork.'

'Okay.'

'You know this is going to happen, right? There's no last-minute reprieve. You've got to be ready.'

'I know.'

'I can't tell you how it's going to end. They've talked about gradual deterioration rather than some dramatic rupture. I'll keep on going as long as I can – as long as it's worth it. Then the morphine. I'll say in the letter that I injected myself and that you were unaware of it. But you may have to help. If I can't move or if I'm otherwise incapacitated. We need to agree the circumstances when that might happen. I'll show you where to put the needle.'

'I have to kill you.'

'Idiot. This thing in my head is killing me. I've been dying since my forties. We all do. You think death is hard? Wait until you've lived seventy, eighty, years and tell me death doesn't look like rest. It's a sigh. Everything bad – all the pain, all the anxiety, all the errors and regrets – they're all gone. This isn't murder. It's compassion. Wait – let me get a towel.'

He went into the bathroom and returned with a large white towel sarong-like around his hips. He sat on the edge of my bed and bared a forearm.

'Here, in the crook of my arm – see? That vein there. Touch it. Go on. That's it. Right there. I'm guessing you've never injected anything? Right. So it's not like you see in films when they stab adrenaline into the heart like Van Helsing with Dracula. Just a prick through the vein wall and a slow depression of the syringe. Give me the whole lot. The ampoule and needle are in my bag, in a little side pocket near the label. Maybe we'll practice a little. But later. Go on – you have a question.'

'The timing of this… Is it connected to meeting the journalist tonight? Are you planning something violent?'

'He might not even turn up. And I'm not planning anything. We'll see what happens.'

'I want to be there.'

'You'll be there. But for now, are you hungry?'

'Starving.'

'Then let's go. Today, you'll experience *bougatsa*.'

Bougatsa turned out to be an open filo-pastry pillow full
of semi-liquid custard, dusted liberally within from shak-
ers of cinnamon and icing sugar. I ate three with a frappe
and described the sensations to an ecstatic Bastounis. It
reminded me of when I'd had my TB jab and mother had
taken me for fish and chips straight afterwards.

He said he didn't feel like walking round the town. He
went back to the room to sleep and write the absolution
letter. I found Park Square and strolled retail streets that
looked little different to Patras. Only the air was different:
colder, fresher. Winter was coming faster to this hyper-
borean realm. I thought I saw snow forecasted on a *souvlaki*
shop's muted television.

In a square, I sat encircled by mopeds, cars and buses at
a grubby open-air café. The locals wore coats and hats, their
collars drawn up and hands in pockets. Cigarette smoke
drifted. I must have been the only foreigner in town. Was
I lost? Lost in the sense Bastounis spoke about – escaping,
evading expectation, reformulating identity? Or just lost –
stumbling clueless and off the track. Was there a difference?

I knew what Bastounis would say. He'd say you belong
wherever you are. Your location is the sum of your choices,
or your indecision. If I was sitting with a gritty coffee in a
traffic-choked square, rejecting family and accompanying

an old man to his morphine suicide, that's just where I should be. It wasn't an accident or coincidence. Just as it was no coincidence that Clara was probably now sitting at a desk reading a book, or Dave chained to a screen writing an email, or mother calling all the relatives to rant about my swearing. All choices – made or evaded.

Bastounis. Days ago, he'd been a name on a book cover – a figure almost as mythical and ethereal as one of his characters. The celestial artist. A Nobel laureate. Now, he was an old man with recalcitrant bowels who snored and who dribbled as he ate. Now, he was a soft blue vein in a forearm's hollow.

I rationalised. It was possible I wouldn't have to do it. Some infinitesimal pressure or imbalance in his head might shut him down. A cerebral nerve pinched, a vein impinged upon. A membrane delicate as wet tissue rupturing to spill instant darkness on his eyes. Fast, painless – nothing to do with me.

One thing was certain: he was in no hurry. He'd had his chance at the precipice in Ithaca. He didn't want to go that way. It was too easy, despite what he'd said about the stoic philosophers. Would Diomedes or Telemon have taken that option? Would Achilles – petulant as he was? The great Homeric heroes died amid a battle's fury, by divine betrayal or as victims of the Furies' rage. Only Odysseus, of all the Trojan crew, slipped slowly into dotage and dementia.

Or so I thought. I'd later learn that Heracles had sacrificed himself upon a pyre of his own construction, assembled even as his flesh bubbled and peeled with Nessusian toxins. His mortal parts were burned away, but his divinity remained unscorched by fire or poison. Someone else had had to light the flames – an inadvertent passer-by. A stumbler into myth. It had happened on the summit of Mount

Oiti, just ten miles from where I sat. But for the concrete balconies and plate glass and hoardings and my ignorance of its existence, I might have seen it darkening the horizon.

Also out there, on the road somewhere, the journalist was approaching for the showdown. What was Bastounis's game? Confrontation? Placation? Dissimulation? Annihilation? Or perhaps the Erinyes would intercept him on the way – a collision with a truck, a slippery corner, a lapse of concentration and a silent screaming arc across the sky.

I looked at my watch. Lunchtime. The *bougatses* hadn't filled me. I'd go for *gyros*, stroll the shops and let him sleep.

Five o'clock. Drizzle glistened on the trees and paving of Plateia Parkou, dripping from umbrellas and plashing under tyres. The waiter asked us if we'd rather be inside, but Bastounis declined with steaming breath. He'd bought a down-filled jacket from a mountaineering store and a black wool scarf that he folded high around his chin. In the room, he'd shown how his left hand was failing – sometimes shivering, sometimes slackly numb. He kept it inside the coat pocket.

'He might not come,' I said.

'He'll come. Are you sure you're warm enough?'

'I really don't need a coat. My fleece is fine. You're not actually going to give him a story, are you?'

'What do you care?'

'Well, that's what he wants.'

'Hmm. The fish wants the maggot, never knowing the hook exists.'

'Is that a Buddhist *koan* or something?'

'I doubt it.'

'You could just let it go. Whatever harm he's done is done. Why be angry about it? What's there to gain? He's irrelevant to you. Besides, you've said it yourself – these parasites never go away. They've always plagued you. They'll always plague someone. You just rise above it. You're better than them.'

'How far have you risen above Buddy, eh? Or is that different? Maybe I've got a thicker skin, but that doesn't mean I don't have to submit to constant harpooning. It's true I have nothing to gain, but I also have nothing to lose. That's a powerful freedom. A rare freedom.'

I watched people moving round the square's perimeter. My coffee was cold.

'Over there', said Bastounis. 'Is it him on the corner? I can't see clearly. Put your hand down! Let him search. Let him find us.'

I watched the guy looking through windows and peering between leaves. Bastounis hadn't said exactly where we'd be. What would happen if he didn't see us? If he just walked away? It might have been better for everyone.

But that wasn't going to happen. He was on to a story and he'd hound Bastounis to the death to get it.

'He's seen us,' I said.

'Good.' He sat straighter in his chair. He rolled his shoulders. 'Don't say anything, okay? This is all me.'

The guy came over and stood by our table. '*Kalo kairo, eh?*'

'In English,' said Bastounis, jerking his head my way.

'Sorry. I was just saying it's nice weather. Can I join you?' He sat. He held out a hand. 'Call me Theo.'

Bastounis kept his hands in his pockets. 'I listened to the interviews on your machine.'

A shrug from Theo. Truth was an occupational hazard.

'You told them I was dead,' said Bastounis.

'And they weren't surprised. Why would that be? You're ill, Irakles. I think you're dying. Why the big secret? Why the evasion?'

'What's *your* interest? Who cares about my health one way or the other? My career's been over for twenty years. It's not at all about my health, is it? That's not your real interest.'

'You're working on a book.'

'Am I?'

'Come on, Irakles. You leave Dimitsana; you travel all over the place; you get this English guy to drive you. You want me to believe you're on *holiday* here?'

He waved a hand, taking in the rain-stained city, the relentless traffic, the sodden cigarette butts and neon-calligraphy puddles.

'Should I think it's a coincidence,' he continued, 'that Lamia is so close to Thermopylae and to Mount Oiti, or that you've visited the birthplace of Odysseus and the realm of King Eurystheus? You're writing a book about your own death. Your last great work.'

'Who says so? I didn't hear any evidence of that on your machine. Has anyone seen me writing?'

'Really, Irakles? I may not be an author, but I know how it works. You don't need pen and paper to research a novel, or even to write one. You're amassing facts and impressions. You're building the content. When you're ready, you'll write. It'll flood out.'

'Is that how it's done?'

'I'm quoting your own work: *Dionysus in Rehab.*'

'Who are you working for?'

'I'm freelance.'

'Freelance what? Journalist. Investigator? Tax inspector? Even if you discover a story, what use is it to you? A single feature in a magazine: "Bastounis might be writing another book"? There's no story until a book is finished and sold. There's no profit for you in just learning there's a work in progress. Tell me – who are you working for?'

'You tell me, Irakles. You seem to know something more than I'm saying.'

Bastounis smiled. 'Okay. There *is* a book.'

We both looked at him.

'But there's a condition if you want me to tell you more: no more calls and interviews. No more pestering people. I'll tell you want you want to know, then you'll drop it.'

'Can I make notes?'

Bastounis nodded, magnanimous, and waited for the notebook and pen.

'Ready? Right. It's a novel. The theme is eternity, which of course takes in life and death. It draws on Homer's line about generations of men and leaves.'

'Which line?'

'Look it up. Death is not the end. It's a continuum: in thought, in history, in literature, in myth. Is Odysseus dead? Is Agamemnon, Socrates or Christ? Did they ever genuinely live? Does a place retain the memory or spirit of what happened there?'

'Themes. Got it. What's the story?'

'An old man, a writer, is living in his ancestral village. He's bored and disillusioned. He wants to go on one last tour of the pleasures of his youth, so he press-gangs a young tourist into driving him. They drive around Greece, visiting some places and following the theme. Maybe a journalist is pursuing them for a story.'

Theo put down his pen and leaned back in his chair. He smiled stiffly, looking between me and Bastounis. 'How does the story end?'

'I've not worked it out yet. The book is still in flux. Endings are always difficult.'

'Why's the journalist pursuing them?'

'Oh, I don't know… Maybe the writer has had multiple marriages and some expensive divorces. His publishers and agent turned on him a long time ago but he's still worth some money to them. Royalties will amass long after he's died. He's been bled dry by parasitic lawyers and the press. When these bottom-feeders suspect that there's a sniff of something new, they send some greasy little lackey in pursuit – someone who won't mind debasing himself utterly in the quest for cash. Someone who'll lie about being a journalist and cheat and harass whoever he has to. A real piece of 24-carat human garbage. A great character to write. Or maybe there's no journalist. As I say, nothing's written yet. You've stopped making notes… Didn't you want to know all about the book? I'd hate to think you've wasted your time and your journey.'

Theo put the pad and pen into a pocket. He seemed amused. 'I should tell you that Buddy Tannenbaum is planning to sue you.'

Bastounis mock-yawned. 'Really.'

'Your young driver here told me that you hit Buddy. Knocked him out cold. Bravo. I've spoken to him since. I advised him to see a doctor and a dentist. There may have been a concussion. If not that, then probably some psychological trauma. He may need counselling.'

'Naturally.'

'His father's a lawyer. I believe he's in Greece right now. You may be receiving a visit from a process server sometime soon. Let's see what you have to say in court.'

'Thanks for the heads-up.'

'My pleasure. I understand you're going to Thessaloniki next.'

'Are we?'

'If I had to guess, I'd say Athos from there.'

'You can't just go to Mount Athos, Theo. You need permissions and permits. And I couldn't take my car there. Pilgrims travel only on foot.'

'Come on, Irakles – we both know you have contacts.'

'I think we're finished here. You have your story.'

'It turns out I have friends in Thessaloniki. Maybe I'll visit since I'm here.'

A shrug from Bastounis. '*Kalo taxidi.*'

Theo stood and looked at us. He nodded at some ambiguous certainty and walked towards the corner we'd first see him.

'Follow him,' said Bastounis.

'What?'

'Follow him. I want to know where he's staying. Quick, so he doesn't lose you.'

'Are you serious?'

'Yes I'm fucking serious. Go! I'll wait here.'

I stood and saw Theo take the corner. I wove through exhaust fumes and drizzle to the opposite pavement and ran self-consciously to the place. He was ahead of me, jabbing his phone with a thumb as he walked. If he looked back, he'd catch me just standing there like an idiot. I pretended to look at a window display of plumbing supplies.

He didn't look back. He took another corner and I trotted towards it feeling ever more conspicuous. It was a long, narrow street lined with shops. Again, I stood close by a window looking sideways at his progress until I saw him take a left into a doorway. A large two-storey sign announced the building as the Hotel Athina. I checked the street name on a blue plaque and hurried back towards the square.

'Hotel Athina,' I said. 'I saw him go in.'

'Did you wait to see if he came out? He might've known you were following. It could've been a ruse.'

'I've not done this before.'

'Right. Okay. Are you hungry?'

'Of course.'

He took me to a place that served *kokoretsi*: normally an Easter dish of offal cooked inside a sausage skin of wound intestines and grilled over charcoal. We ate it with *tzatziki*, *fava* and chips and it was fantastic – a greasy, carnal feast that warmed us. An open fire flickered and flared in the *taverna*.

'Do you think Buddy is really suing you?' I said.

'Let him. Greek lawyers will bleed him dry or drive him mad. The case could go for years after I'm gone. It's not about that anyway. There's some ulterior motive here. Publicity. Leverage. We may never know.'

'I thought you might hit him. *I* wanted to.'

'You can't stop these people. They're like cockroaches or dung beetles. They live among the trash. They feed on it. Kill one and another takes its place. I'm used to it – other people aren't. You, Konstantinopoulos…It's a different world. Reality doesn't exist, nor ethics, nor conscience – only the story.'

'Was he right about Thessaloniki? Are we going there?'

'And to Athos…if we make it.'

'You think he'll follow?'

'We'll see. Look – I have some things to do in town. Go back to the room or whatever you want to do. Consider getting that coat – it's going to be much colder in the north. I'll give you the money.'

'Don't you need my help?'

'I'll be fine.'

It was dark when I went back to the room, glad of the warmth and the comfort. I looked through my purchases from earlier in the day, turned on the TV and watched a hyperactive game show for a few minutes before muting it. The swerving camera angles, flashing lights and orthodontic glory were even more surreal without sound. I became briefly hypnotised.

Surrealism was apt. I might as well have been living inside a Bastounis novel. And next was Athos – a place not quite of this world. I'd read about it in my discarded travel guide, never expecting to go. Tourists didn't go there. As Bastounis had said, you had to apply in advance for permits to visit the monastic republic. Women had been forbidden access for almost a thousand years. Even female goats or sheep were banned. Instead, the thin peninsula existed as it had since the late Roman Empire – a protected bastion of Orthodoxy governed by bell and book and prayer. They still used the Julian calendar. They were on Byzantine time.

How could I, an unapologetic atheist, be permitted access? I'd be Odysseus or Aeneas entering an unnatural realm – not Hades, but the other one. Bastounis had called it transcendent. Would it be his Mount Oiti? His ultimate immolation?

I fell into a shallow sleep, waking occasionally to the twitching TV glare or a moped's flatus. The city's canyons echoed noise and neon upwards past my window to haze against the sky in veils of rain. Horns, shouts, reversing signals. Wet tyres on asphalt.

A thud woke me. A rattling door handle and futzing round the lock. He must have been at the brandy. It was sometime after midnight.

'Hold on. I'm coming.'

Bastounis leaned heavily against the jamb. His upper lip was split. Fresh blood filmed his teeth and stained his beard. There was a graze on his temple.

'Jesus! What happened?'

'I fell.'

'Come on. Come in. Where's your crutch?'

'Lost it.'

'Here – lean on my shoulder. Over to the bed. Should I go to reception? Get a doctor?'

'I just passed reception, didn't I?'

'Right.'

He didn't seem drunk. At least, no drunker than I'd seen him previously. He fell on the bed with a groan, leaving bloodstains on the sheets. His knuckles were split and raw.

'Was it a blackout or something? A fit?'

'An accident – that's all. I tripped. There was a pothole.'

'Do you want me to go and find your crutch?'

'No. Leave it. I think a bus went over it. I just need to rest. My head is killing me.'

'Do you want a pill? We've got Ibuprofen.'

'Give me three.'

'Are you going to be alright?'

'Stop fussing! Christ – you're like a little girl. I've not been in a car wreck. I'll just rest. I'll be fine in the morning. Leave me alone.'

'Fine.'

I daren't sleep at first. I watched a muted documentary about olive cultivation until he started to snore. Then I checked intermittently for signs of imminent *grand mal*. In the screen-light, he was white and blue – a sarcophagus sculpture in a cold English cathedral, hands crossed loosely on his chest. A Crusader knight who'd slaughtered his way to salvation. So still.

It was dawn when I felt him tugging at my duvet. He was sitting on the edge of his bed, elbows on his knees, looking down.

'What is it? Are you okay?'

'I can't see,' he said. 'Nothing. It's finally gone.'

TWENTY

Morning saw us on the road north to Larissa. Bastounis sat silent in the passenger seat, his cap and sunglasses fixed, his jaw and cheekbone a rotten aubergine of bruising. His right hand worked the forked top of his new walking stick.

I'd bought the stick. He'd sent me out as soon as the shops were open in Lamia, saying he had to make some calls. The guy on reception had Googled a place for me and written the address of what turned out to be a disability emporium of wheelchairs, crutches, supports, walkers and mobility vehicles. Greys and whites predominated. Everything was wipe-clean and coldly ergonomic. The smells of rubber, PVC and moulded plastic caught in my throat. *Eau de senescence.*

How do you buy a stick for a man struck blind? The assistant, with much grave interpretation of my dumbshow, took me to a display of sticks designed for visual impairment. Here were articulated and extendable wands in aluminium, painted white or striped with warning red. Some had balls on the end or wrist straps at the top. Bastounis would hate them. The regular sticks were not much better: safe, utilitarian – EU-certified badges of infirmity.

Reluctant to return without a stick, I recalled passing an agricultural and hunting shop on the way. There, I found a bin full of country-style sticks: shepherd's crooks and heather-beaters, staffs and whittled alpenstocks. I found among them a gnarled and knotty rod of varnished blonde that may have been oak. It was heavy and impractical. The top had been carved roughly forked to accommodate a thumb and facilitate an authoritative grasp. Here was the club of Heracles. Here was Tiresias's staff.

Bastounis had handled it wordlessly, running his hands along the length, hefting it, levering himself upright from the hotel bed. He'd hooked his thumb into the notch and driven the tip hard into the floor. He'd nodded, smiling. He was ready to go.

Now we ranged the vast horizons of Thessaly's plain – Greece's largest flat expanse. Titans and Olympians had battled here between Olympus and Mount Oiti, but our view was more prosaic: stubble fields to the sky, two-minute towns and faded petrol stations.

Not *our* view. *My* view. Bastounis travelled in darkness – just the sound of the car on the road and his crowding thoughts. He must have prepared for this. He'd known for months that it might happen. But still...

I recalled the *Iliad* and Homer, himself a blind man according to legend. Whenever a hero fell in battle – his soul sobbed out in purple spray, his head hacked free with smoking bronze – night descended on his eyes. His spirit passed into Hades, there to wander unseen, unseeing – his earthly body carrion thereafter for the birds and dogs. All shadows. Bastounis was walking there.

I reached back into my bag and struggled with the zip. Bastounis cocked an ear but said nothing. I was looking for something I'd bought on a whim from a junk shop in Lamia: an old cassette of Richard Burton reading Pope's version of the *Odyssey*. I'd heard somewhere it was the nearest thing to

Greek in terms of musicality. It wasn't fully rewound, but if
ever there was a time for voices other than our own – voices
from beyond recorded history – now had to be that time.

I slotted the cassette – white plastic with a celluloid window – and pressed play on the Peugeot's twentieth-century
console. Bastounis heard the hiss and crackle, his head
attentive. And out it came, that honeyed tenor, pitched for
ancient verse:

"The man for wisdom's various arts renown'd
Long exercised in woes, O Muse! resound;
Who, when his arms had wrought the destined fall
Of sacred Troy, and razed her heaven-built wall,
Wandering from clime to clime, observant stray'd,
Their manners noted, and their states surveyed
On stormy seas unnumber'd toils he bore
Safe with his friends to gain the natal shore."

I looked sidelong at Bastounis. His hands stopped
wringing at the staff. Some tension seemed to drain from
his shoulders. He reached waveringly for the controls and
found the volume knob, increasing Burton's *basso*.

"An exile from his dear paternal coast,
Deplored his absent queen and empire lost.
Calypso in her caves constrained his stay,
With sweet, reluctant, amorous delay."

I drove on through the endless eastern suburbs of
Larissa; on, ascending, through familiar hills; on, beside
the blue Thermaikos Gulf, and always northwards, the early
snows of Mount Olympus distant to our right.

Things would be harder in Thessaloniki. I'd have to be
with him almost all the time. He wouldn't be able to walk
anywhere without me. He'd be Oedipus at Colonus. He
needed me now more than ever and I felt the memory of
that soft blue vein in the hollow of his forearm. If we could

just make it to Athos. There'd be monks at Athos who'd help. Monks would know the rituals of death.

The city announced itself in the usual way: corporate blocks and stacked containers, proliferating lanes, industrial lots and petrol stations. Buildings increased in size and height and density. Before long, we were first-gear stop-and-go in traffic.

'We're here,' said Bastounis.

'Yes.'

'Turn off the Homer. You need to concentrate. Shout out if you see what street we're on. It might be Nikis or Tsimiski if you've taken a straight line off the highway. Can you see the sea through the buildings to our right?'

'I think I … wait. We're on Tsimiski. There's a sign.'

'Okay. Make a left whenever you can and turn right on to the next main street you see. It's called Egnatia. Keep going in that direction until you see an ancient arch.'

Egnatia seemed to be the city's central artery – a four-lane boulevard of shabby multi-storeys, stacked balconies, shop fronts and graffiti. The trees along its length had started to turn and were partially bald, their yellow leaves speckling pavement and gutter.

'The arch – up ahead on our left,' I said.

'Good. Take the next right after it. There's a church on the corner.'

'I see it.'

'There's long-stay car park somewhere on the road. Pull in to it.'

A guy smoking in a plastic picnic chair waved us through into the car park and I descended in right-angle loops, tyres squeaking on the polished concrete. I centred the Peugeot in a vacant bay and turned the engine off. Muffled quiet. The engine ticked.

'Listen,' said Bastounis. 'We're not using the car from now on. It's too conspicuous. We'll use buses or taxis. You keep the keys. When everything's over, you can have it. It's yours. Make a note of the street name so you can find it again.'

'What do you mean "too conspicuous"?'

'And no more hotels. We'll stay in a friend's apartment on this street. Just one night. We're going to Athos tomorrow.'

He still wore his cap and sunglasses, not knowing we'd passed from day to subterranean fluorescence. The artificial light emphasised his bruising and decay – his cut lip black, the jawline jaundice-mottled. But for the beard, his face might have been an autumn windfall exposed by winter's thaw. He turned, somehow cognizant of my gaze.

'What?'

'Nothing.'

'Getting cold feet? Thinking about that vein?'

'No … No.'

'I need you strong. You're committed now. I'm not dying in a hospital hooked up to tubes as the vultures gather. I'm not dying with drool on my lips and my body wasted. Do you hear me? *I* choose when and how – not them. Not anybody. The monks wouldn't give me the *coup de grace* if I needed it. They'd let me fester as they do with their own. God's will. You're my insurance.'

'Got it. Third-party, fire and theft.'

'Ha! It's only the fire I have to fear. Besides, you have two more challenges before then. Should I tell you what they are?'

'No.'

'Good. Then let's go.'

We were now Tiresias and his acolyte. Bastounis shuffled with one hand on my shoulder and the other holding his rustic staff. I called out the hazards of up-thrust paving and kerbstones, but people gave us space. They parted before him, veered around him. His sensations transmitted through my shoulder in telegraphic grips.

The foyer of the residential building was sepulchral in grey marble. The lift smelled of teenage perfume and reflected us in tinted mirrors. In a dark corridor, I pressed the bell of number seven.

A monk answered the door. His hair and beard were black and he wore the black silk robe over a white t-shirt. Bastounis did the talking and I guessed they didn't know each other. The monk – soft spoken and showing no surprise at the blindness – handed me a key and showed me where to flick the fuse for hot water. The décor had an ecclesiastical flavour, with Byzantine-style icons on the walls and a prominent crucifix in the bedroom. He asked Bastounis something about me on the way out and responded with an air-drawn cross in my direction.

'What was that about?' I said once the door was closed.

'He asked what religion you were. I said none. He said you should convert to Orthodoxy forthwith or spend eternity in Hell.'

'Nice.'

'They take it very seriously. You'll have to curb your irony on the Holy Mountain. It's their world, their rules. If the bells ring at 3.00am for service, you get up at three with the rest.'

'Even if you don't believe?'

'Especially so.'

'You did it?'

'Of course I did. You'll see. Athos affects you. It's not like visiting a church as a tourist. You're stepping back into the roots of Christianity. Miracles occur there. Fragments of the Holy Cross are held. Yes, scoff if you like – but remember your reverence at pagan Pythia's seat or the walls of Tiryns. Each fragment of the cross is saturated in two millennia of pious awe, no matter what its truth. But that's tomorrow. Today – we experience the Saloniki fleshpots. Here's the plan…'

The first part of the plan was a form of advanced vicarious voyeurism. Bastounis took me to a café along the seafront avenue and chose a table outside, despite the chill and blanket cloud. He sat with his back to the traffic, coat zipped up around his chin, and ordered coffees.

'I'd sit here as a young man,' he said, 'and watch the girls. The girls of Thessaloniki were known – *are* known – as the most beautiful, the most exciting in Greece. They'd walk the street as if it were a catwalk, parading themselves. There was far less traffic then. It was more civilised. Why don't you describe them for me?'

'What?'

'Describe the girls as they pass. And remember what I told you: observe – don't just see. Tell me what they don't see in themselves.'

'Really?'

'Yes really. You need to learn how to express yourself. It's all inside with you – all thoughts. You write things in your journal that you'd never dream of saying. There's a hinterland in there somewhere. But the face you show the world… It's a blank. An effigy. You might as well be mute. It's why people don't notice you.'

'Say what you really think.'

'I'm telling you what's true. Who else would?'

'Is this one of the challenges?'

'No. Just humour me. I'm old and blind and dying. Ha!'

Was it a desperate laugh? A madman's laugh? A laugh from the edge? His smile seemed real enough. A lifetime's span had brought him back to this place of careless youth. His time was all but over.

'What's it like?' I heard my voice say. 'You know… coming to the end.'

'What's it like? That's your question?' He adjusted his cap. 'You know, I've read *the Iliad* all my life and I've always wondered: what's it like to enter battle knowing that men will die? Bodies will cover the ground. It's inevitable. You've seen it yourself as a soldier. How do you go voluntarily towards that? How do you race towards your foe's shining panoply again and again, knowing each time that the probabilities will claim you in the end? The answer is obvious: you never think it'll be you. Death's beyond imagination. We can't conceive it, though we know it as an abstract. When the limb is severed by the Trojan sword, when the Black Death darkens at your groin, when the cancer bites… even then, you don't think of death. Even as its signs are marked on your body. There's something fundamentally human that denies it. I *know* I'm going, but I don't *believe* it. It's what we believe that matters. If I believed it, I'd go right now. We all would. You'll see. It's the same with ageing. I'm twenty-five in my mind – sitting here, ogling girls. I never got older. Birthdays after that were numbers of increasing irrelevance. Fiction. The blindness, the infirmity – sure, they're irritants. They're ironies. But don't worry – none of this makes sense to you yet. Retrospect is a distorting mirror. It rewrites every story. Whatever you're experiencing now, it'll change and grow in memory. By the time you're my age, these last few days'll be almost mythical. This coffee, this table, my words: a past inseparable from dream. You won't need to separate. Now – enough of this gibbering. Tell me about women.'

I looked to the street. The lunchtime flux had started and it was coffee hour for the young professionals, the idle wealthy, the peacocks – a catwalk, just as Bastounis had said. I saw a target.

'Okay – here's one coming. She's wearing mirrored blue aviators even though it's dull today. They've been in fashion all through summer and this might be her last chance to show them off. Her hair is loose and flowing – dyed blonde, but done well. She's wearing scarlet lipstick. It's really all about the sunglasses. The whole look radiates from them. She's got a biker jacket that says she's badass, but she'd never ride a bike in those heeled boots, even if they do have studs in them. I was going to say she looks confident from the way she's walking – all hips – but now I'm thinking it looks like armour. The whole look is … it's a carapace. Do you want me to guess if she's ovulating?'

'Ha! Good. Do another.'

'Wait a minute. Right. This one looks like a foreigner. She hasn't got the local style. She's strictly utilitarian: well-worn trainers, jeans, a down-filled jacket in silvery grey. She probably could have bought it in green or orange but that would have been too conspicuous. She's pretty without any adornment but I think she knows she's being watched. It's like she won't give in to the feeling of it. And anyway, it looks like she's on her way somewhere. She's not just strolling. Not a tourist. Maybe she's a language teacher come here from England or America. She's new to it. Another five years here and she'd be scarlet-lipped and mirrored …'

'Hmm. Not bad. But I thought you might say more about their tits.'

'You're a dirty old man.'

'Ha!

The game went on, but I watched him slowly drift and fade into other thoughts. My voice was background to wherever else he'd gone, and justification for his silence. He kept his hands deep in his pockets. I was mid-flow, describing a couple of likely students, when he interrupted me.

'Listen – we should go to a bookshop. I'll ask the waitress if she knows a big one.'

'What do you want to get?'

'I like the Richard Burton Homer. Maybe there'll be some more recorded books. I could get a CD player – one of those portable ones. If they haven't got CDs ... You can read to me. We'll get something you can read.'

'I'm not a very good reader ... Out loud, I mean.'

'You're a better reader than I am right now. Besides, good writing directs you how to read it. Yes. Let's do that. There'll be more choice that way. Come on – my legs are getting stiff.'

There was a multi-storey bookshop on Tsimiski. It had its own café and Bastounis said he'd wait for me there. His requirements were specific.

'Get the good stuff. The best. This is the last literature I'm ever going to hear so it needs to be sublime. The ancient tragedians. Shakespeare is good – *Lear* or *Macbeth* if you can get them. A Bible – King James Version or nothing at all. Milton I don't mind. But no short stories. No novels ... not unless you can find Sterne or Cervantes. Pope's Homer would be a bonus. Nothing by women.'

He wasn't interested in long narratives, he said. There wasn't time for anything unread. He wanted what he knew and he wanted to dip into it at random – cool draughts from the well of memory. Re-reading, he said, was the only worthwhile reading. Nabokov had said the same.

I browsed, finding some of what he'd asked for. I also found his own books bunched alphabetically with Baldwin, Barthes and Beard. I took out *Harvest of Chronos* and started reading. Here was the young Bastounis: full of life and hope after his drugs purgatory, enjoying his freedom, eschewing the more challenging literary style of his famous books in favour of a stark simplicity. When he'd written these words, he'd still had half of his life before him. There'd been no tumour. There'd been only two wives. The gambling had yet to ruin him. The Nobel was yet to come. Ageing was something that happened to others. In another week, another fortnight, the author of these pages would be dead. The books would probably be reprinted with different covers. Obituaries would drive a spike in sales. The young man who'd written these words – already yellowed, already faded – would join the fallen leaves of Homer's generations.

How would he feel to hear his own words read to him? It would be like me hearing my journal as I lay decaying. A reminder of naivety, perhaps. A reminder of innocence lost and knowledge since developed. He'd probably hate it. But I decided to buy the book for myself. Perhaps I'd be brave enough to ask him for an autograph or dedication. He owed me that, at least.

'Hungry?' he said when I returned to him. 'What do you say to seafood? I've been talking to the waiter. He says there's a place that does *kalamari gemista* – stuffed squid.'

'Great. I'm starving.'

Midnight found us getting out of a taxi in a dirty light-industrial district between the railway lines north of the port. The streets were dark and puddled. There were no residential blocks – only graffiti, broken windows and litter. We were looking for a club called *Narghilaiki*.

Bastounis had made me sleep in the afternoon. He'd told me – with a smile that made me nervous – that we'd be having a late night and that I'd need my stamina. Then he'd taunted me for being afraid, reminding me of challenges issued.

We heard the place before we found it: *bouzouki* music coming from an alley. People were arriving on foot and by car – young and old but mostly men. The women seemed older: wives and mothers attending for the music rather than to dance or preen. No tourists were among them. The doorman looked askance at me, overtly Anglo-Saxon as I was, and allowed me in (I supposed) because I had a blind Greek trailing from my shoulder.

People like me weren't supposed to visit places like this. Bastounis had made me buy a new shirt and had told me to be cool. He might as well have told me to be Abyssinian. *He* looked cool. He was the essence of cool with his cap and his Ray Bans and his longshoreman beard and his facial bruising. He wore a black knitted-silk tie bought especially for the evening.

The murky space looked like it had been recently vacated by a 1980s wedding reception. Stackable event chairs were set around tables, swags of material had been draped inexpertly over windows and a disco ball hung dusty at the centre of the room. The industrial carpet was threadbare and there was a powerful reek of stale smoke. The dais at the front was empty for the moment, though the chairs and instruments were waiting. The music we'd heard was being played through speakers.

I led Bastounis to a table at the rear and leaned his staff against the wall. A man came with a tray and unloaded it between us: a bottle of whisky, a carafe of water and two glasses. Bastounis handed over money and said something I didn't catch.

'A whole bottle of whisky?' I said.

'That's how it works. They charge triple or quadruple for the whisky and it pays for the performance. Now listen – this is *rebetika*. It's lowlife music. Smyrna style. It's music of intoxication and nostalgia, forgetting and remembering. We'll drink. I've ordered us a hash pipe.'

'Hash?'

'Listen. Remember your challenges. Be spontaneous, face your fears, observe, appreciate your senses…These are lessons on how to live. This is challenge number eleven. You're a prisoner of control. You've misinterpreted the ancient wisdom of the Golden Mean and "Moderation in all things". The rule applies to moderation, too, don't forget. Apollo makes his shrine on the peaks, but Dionysus lurks in the forests' shadows – two sides of one spirit. Restraint and impetuosity. You might think you're well balanced, but you're a ball weighted only on one side – the side of cautious rationality. Rolled, you'll move only in circles for a lifetime. Challenge eleven is to lose yourself. Let go sometimes. Not everything must be a sculpted thought. Creativity lies in chaos. That's how it works. First the frenzy – the insensate rush. Get the words on paper as if you're haemorrhaging. Only when we truly risk insanity do we move higher and beyond. Later, you review it with a cooler mind. Later, when the rush has passed. Now – open that bottle and pour us a couple of excessive slugs. No water for me.'

I poured. I worried. Hash? I'd barely even smoked a cigarette. Would psychosis descend immediately, leaving me a drooling wreck, my irises blown to wells of oblivion? I recalled reading somewhere – Thomas de Quincey? – that different drugs offset each other. Might the whisky protect me from the weed? I drank as the place filled to capacity and others came to sit at our table. Maybe I'd not have to smoke anything – it wasn't as if he'd see.

A roar went up as the musicians came on stage and settled with their instruments: *bouzouki, oud, baglama,* violin and guitar. A woman in a long vermilion dress sat to the side with a *toubeleki* hand drum. The house lights went down. A hush fell. Cigarette smoke drifted in the stage lights. Whisky burned in my chest.

The central *bouzouki* player – an old man in a fedora and with hands that looked like they could crush his instrument – began a complex fret-roaming solo that spoke to my inexpert ear of Anatolia and minarets, of harems and pashas and the alleys of the spice market. He began to sing, his voice a raucous thing cured by whisky, hash and arguments with passionate women. The words were just sounds to me, but the tone was universal: pain, regret – knowledge arduously won through choice or imposition. A dozen lifetimes were written in it.

The rest of the band kicked in. Music expanded to fill the room – guitar and *toubeleki* laying the stumbling beat, tiny *baglamas* plucking high notes, violin tracing the melody. The woman began to harmonise alongside the man, her voice the plaintive wail of the feminine heart in every *rebetika* tale. Audience members clapped in time or beat the irregular pulse on table tops. Some mouthed along to lyrics they all seemed to know.

Discomfort gnawed at me. I should have felt the glamour and the privilege of the outsider welcomed in. But I felt conspicuous. I felt like an imposter. I didn't know the words or the culture. I had little stake in this ritual, and less understanding of it. And yet the music's rhythmic rawness was affecting. The emphases in their broken voices. The folk memory in the notes. Despite myself, despite my *froideur* exoskeleton, I was being compelled to feel. I was being lured to relinquishment. I felt exposed.

It was exactly as Bastounis had said. I feared what I couldn't control. I didn't know how to handle a feeling if it passed beyond the scope of words and concept. There was a terror of not knowing, of risking an emotion I couldn't name or measure.

He nudged me and held his empty glass. I filled it and topped up my own. We chinked an unspoken toast. The stage was becoming hazy through smoke and whisky.

The song ended to applause and the next began with a cheer of recognition. Some in the audience sang along, clapping or waving arms. By the dais, a man stood and began to dance alone to shouts of '*Opa!*' from his friends.

'Someone's dancing?' said Bastounis, his breath spiritous at my ear.

'Yes. Down at the front. He looks drunk.'

'That's the dance. The *zeibekiko*. It's just for men. Watch him. See how it works. If the urge takes you, do it.'

I watched. It didn't look much like a dance to me. It looked like a man prolonging a fall, toppling this way and that but always catching his balance with arms outstretched round absent friends. I began to understand. It was intoxication choreographed – a heavy staggering borne aloft with stumbling drum and stuttered strings. Tables were scraped back to our left and another started dancing. Friends knelt to form a circle, clapping in time.

The guy who'd brought our whisky now came with a hookah pipe and placed it on the table between us. Perhaps a dozen other people were receiving them, while still more were lighting joints insouciantly. The music throbbed with its aberrant double pulse. The *bouzouki* player sang rustily of waste and want, of lust and longing.

Bastounis had smelled the hash. He hand quested over the table for the hookah and he was hot at my ear again.

'The *narghile* – it's not like smoking tobacco. See the ice-water in the bowl? It cools the smoke. Take it in. Hold it. Exhale. Like this.'

He took the mouthpiece daintily and I watched the bubbles. A hiatus. Then smoke streams tusking from his nose. He passed it to me, waiting for me to take it.

I held it like an asp. Should I wipe it? I felt eyes upon me, though nobody was looking. Apollo to Dionysus was just a breath. I inhaled vapour no more disagreeable than autumnal fog. I held it, fearful. My exhalation joined the collective veil and I passed it back to Bastounis' waiting hand.

No cataclysm came. Sanity remained. Perhaps the whisky was my prophylactic. I drank and repoured.

'Capnomancy,' said Bastounis, holding the mouthpiece. 'The art of divination through the dance of smoke. Tiresias practised it, blind as he was.'

The woman in the red dress was singing, her voice torturing the notes, stretching and warping them over the lurching beat and string fills. She beat a tambourine against her hip, its jangles glinting like a belly dancer's silvered finger zills. Here was Scheherazade narrating. Here was Pythia oracular, or a sultan's concubine lamenting at the drumhead's stroke. I was at the court of Xerxes, incense burning – victory or defeat predicted by the seers for dawn. Chronology suspended. History inverted.

I saw my hand beating the *zeibekiko* atop the table. I saw the *narghile*'s mouthpiece passing back and forth. I saw men swaying and swooping in the billows of the music. Arms waved aloft.

'I'm going to dance,' said Bastounis. 'Help me.'

'What? There's not enough … You'll fall.'

'So help me! Take my hand. Find some space.'

He stood, holding on to the table and worked his way round to the front of it. His hand was damply hot in mine. I led him to a relatively clear area between tables and people shifted back to make space for the old *manga* in the dark glasses. I knew he'd try to coax me into dancing.

'Keep hold of my hand,' he said. 'Lift your arms like this.'

'I really don't want—'

'This is my last time, *Christe mou!* Help me do it.'

I raised my arms like him and he began to step around the bass line – a slow crossing of his feet, a toe tap to the rear, a bending of the knee. He swayed. He turned. He raised a foot and slapped his instep. All was slow and massy – a dance within a dream. I supported him best I could, connected by our bridge of plaited fingers. Neighbouring tables shouted '*Opa!*'

He shook free of my hand and I stepped back, glad to escape his gravity. Alone now, he danced the only dance that blindness and infirmity enhanced – the queasy equilibrium, the gyroscopic wobble, the pendulate rhythm and the raptor's dive. Arms outstretched, his back shaped the ridgeline profile of lost Pisaetos. He was a swimmer amid hash cirrostratus.

Some knelt and began to clap him on. I joined them as spectator of this old man circumscribing darkness. None knew that he was Irakles Bastounis. None knew about the Nobel or the death inside his skull. He was the underworld *rebetis*: outcast, wanderer, artist.

He swung back his bad leg and went to touch the floor. He over-balanced and fell. His ribs struck the edge of a table and his groping hands knocked glasses smashing. A cheer went up. He lay on his back, his sunglasses askew, his cap knocked off. The music never stopped. I rushed to him.

'Jesus! Are you okay?' I was laughing for some reason.

'I'm good. I'm good. Ha! Give me whisky. Help me up.'

We shuffled back to our seats amid slaps on the back and calls of 'Bravo!' for Bastounis. I poured. We drank.

The band drove into an up-tempo piece and the crowd thrilled to it. Up at the front, I saw people throwing handfuls of petals at the dais. They caught the lights as bloodied snowflakes falling. I felt I could smell them even through the resinous haze. I could smell the people, too – fresh perspiration, perfume and cologne. A stew of pheromones secreted. The music was distinct in every complementary note and harmony.

Bastounis's laboured breathing interposed at my ear. He face was glistening.

'Are you alright?' I said. 'You're very pale.'

'I need to … Let's go outside a minute.'

We levitated through the swirling noise with staff and shoulder, pushing through a fire door into a vault of frigid city air. Bastounis bent, both hands on his staff, and vomited extensively where he stood. He wiped his mouth with a sleeve.

'I think I broke a rib. Hurts when I breathe.'

'We should go to a hosp—'

'No hospitals. There's nothing they can do about a rib … I had them in the ring … Just have to bind and rest.'

He vomited again as I watched from a disassociated plane – narrator, not participant.

'Should we go back to the flat?'

'Eh, I think so. I can't party like I used to.'

'Your *zeibekika* was pretty impressive … while it lasted.'

'Fuck you.' A crooked smile. 'It was impressive, though. I've still got it.'

TWENTY-ONE

My brain felt bruised. Bruised and swollen. Cerebrospinal fluid had apparently leaked through my nose in the night, dampening my pillow. Now every tiny movement sloshed the organ against my inner skull. My eyes hurt. My tongue and throat were smoke-dried jerky. Bastounis moved through my pain-blurred vision. He was sitting on his bed and binding a bed sheet round his torso.

'Come on – get up,' he said. 'You have to shower. You puked in the night – probably all over yourself.'

Now I smelled it. Bile and whisky. I showered, leaning against the tiles as waves of nausea descended. If this was "losing myself" I preferred co-ordinates, GPS and compass. I drank water straight from the showerhead, hot and chlorinated as it was.

Too soon, we were at the Halkidiki bus station amid diesel fumes and groaning engines. Serious men – Athos pilgrims – observed us and shook their heads in disapproval. Bastounis sent me to buy *spanakopites* and coffee. We'd eat, he said, and sleep properly on the bus.

I wouldn't sleep. Buoyed by breakfast but heavy-limbed, I instead thought of Athos as we left the suburbs for an agricultural plain. Our destination was Ouranopolis – city of the sky. From there, we'd take the ferry to the Holy Mountain and leave the modern world. Bastounis wouldn't return.

What happened to its moons when mighty Jupiter vanished from the cosmos? Did they continue obliviously in their orbits, or did they spin on hectic trajectories to infinitude? Athos was the staging point for all that would come after.

With Bastounis snoring, I took Pope's *Odyssey* from my bag and flicked to book eleven where Odysseus converses with Heracles in Hades. It was the part he'd mumbled in his Homeric somniloquy on the road to Thermopylae. I found it on the same page as Tantalus and Sisyphus enduring endless tortures.

"Now I the strength of Hercules behold,
A towering spectre of gigantic mould,
A shadowy form! For high in heaven's abodes
Himself resides, a god among the gods:
There, in the bright assemblies of the skies,
He nectar quaffs, and Hebe crowns his joys.
Here hovering ghosts, like fowl, his shade surround,
And clang their pinions with terrific sound;
Gloomy as night he stands, in act to throw
The aerial arrow from the twanging bow."

Heracles the demi-god was a unique anomaly in hell. His body sat immortal at Olympus, but his soul was held below with mass humanity. It was Bastounis himself – his body worn and failing, his term about to end, but his works on shelves, on lists, in minds. He couldn't die.

"The mighty ghost advanced with awful look,
And, turning his grim visage, sternly spoke:
"O exercised in grief! By arts refined:
O taught to bear the wrongs of base mankind!
Such, such was I! still toss'd from care to care,
While in your world I drew the vital air!
E'en I, who from the Lord of Thunders rose,
Bore toils and dangers, and a weight of woes:

To a base monarch still a slave confined,
(The hardest bondage to a generous mind!)
Down to these worlds I trod the dismal way,
And dragg'd the three-mouth'd dog to upper day;
E'en hell I conquered, through the friendly aid
Of Maia's offspring, and the martial maid"

I thought of him at school in Dimitsana learning it. The words would have meant almost nothing to a child. Just a rote exercise to please the teachers. But every passing decade made it truer and more real. He'd become a hero amid the mythology of his epic lifetime.

Not that you'd know it as a passenger on this bus. He was a ragged blind man who'd slept in his clothes and who was now snoring glutinously with an open mouth. His face shone with a hangover fever. He smelled of weed and whisky. He gasped whenever a pot-hole jarred his rib. Behold: the fallen hero.

Ouranopolis appeared as a tiny tourist town now shuttered and cloaked for winter. Like Olympia and Delphi, it was a pretty parasite with its Athos café, Athos hotel, Athos jewellery shops and souvenir stands. Holiness had always been good business. I watched the sea revealed through buildings and remembered that wilderness cove at Gerolimenas – me and Bastounis glistening with salt and triumph. It seemed a distant dream.

Then I saw Theo.

His face was swollen and empurpled, one eye closed. He walked with a crutch – the missing crutch from Lamia? – and was accompanied by a policeman. I nudged Bastounis urgently.

'Christ! My rib.'

'I've just see Theo.'

'What?'

'Just now. He's in Ouranopoli. His face is all smashed up. He's walking with a crutch. He has the police with him.'

'Really?'

'You don't seem surprised.'

'He said he might follow us to Athos. Maybe he had a car accident or got mugged.'

I looked at Bastounis in his cap and sunglasses. The writer incognito. I thought I saw a smirk within his beard and suddenly I realised.

'It was you, wasn't it? You beat him up in Lamia. Perhaps Theo's come here with the police to press charges. He knows we need to collect permits and—'

'Keep your voice down.'

'Did you do that to him?'

'He bothered my friends. He told them I was dead.'

'Jesus! How are you going to get on the boat now? He'll be waiting there or at the permit office. What if the police—?'

'Quiet. You're like a woman with your fretting. Let me think. They'll be looking for the Peugeot. We should be quick getting off the bus. Okay... I've got it. Listen. Here's what we'll do.'

The ferry was waiting at the dock, its engines burbling. Pilgrims were boarding. Theo was waiting outside the permit office with his police escort. He knew this was the only boat today and that we couldn't get on it without the permit.

I was watching from a payphone a block away. Bastounis was leaning on his staff next to me, out of sight around the corner.

'Okay – do it,' he said.

I dialled the number he'd given me: the Ouranopolis
police office. It rang. It rang. I remembered the empty
police office at Olympia. If nobody was sitting there…

'*Oriste!*'

'Er, yes. Hello. Do you speak English?

'*Perimene leptaiki…*'

'What?'

Rustling. A different voice: 'Yes?'

'Ah, hello. I'm at the bus stop here in Ouranopolis. I'm
travelling with an old Greek man. Actually he's famous:
Irakles Bastounis? He won the Nobel Prize. He's fallen. I
think he might be dying. Can you help? Irakles Bastounis.
He's shaking He's having a fit.'

I heard muffled Greek involving Bastounis's name.
Then: 'You wait there. Somebody comes now.'

'Thank you!'

I replaced the receiver. I watched Theo and his
policeman.

'Anything?' said Bastounis.

'No. They're just talking…Wait. The policeman's
answering his radio. He's leaving. But Theo's still standing
there.'

'Shit.'

'No. Hold on. He's calling after the policeman…He's
going with him.'

'Right. Give me your shoulder. We need to do this fast.'

We went five-legged to the office and pushed to the
front of the queue, Bastounis muttering something about
his infirmity and blindness. Our permits were waiting,
sanctioned by some higher power judging from the reactions of the clerks. They eyed me dubiously: the patent
infidel.

'To the boat,' said Bastounis. 'Pick up the pace.'

The ferry horn sounded. He gripped my shoulder. He was panting. He still had the whisky sweats. I looked behind us for pursuing police or Theo. If only Bastounis had controlled his temper in Lamia... If only the sun didn't shine. If only water wasn't wet.

We were on the quay. Smoke rose from the ferry's stack. A crewmember helped Bastounis along the rattling gangplank as I glanced nervously back to the town

'Get below,' said Bastounis as I boarded. 'They mustn't see us.'

His right arm was spasming. He could barely hold the staff.

'Your arm...'

'It's nothing. Conceal yourself.'

We went inside and took seats among pilgrims and returning monks. The horn sounded again. I became aware of Bastounis muttering beside me. A fugitive's prayer? A prayer to whom?

I kept my head down and waited for the gangplank's bang, the reversing props, the slow swing away from land. I imagined the scene at the bus stop. The brief confusion... the realisation... the radio's crackle and the rush back to the permit office. Confirmation: Bastounis and the other one have taken their papers. Stop the ferry!

One last horn blast. The exhausts coughed. I saw the mountainous horizon move and we were free of the jetty. The ferry turned to face the morning breeze. A burst of power. Bastounis's hand reached tremblingly for my thigh and gripped.

'Do you see them on the shore?'

'No. They're not there.'

'Fifteen, twenty minutes and we're safe. We're getting off at the first harbour. They can't touch us after that. Stay inside in case they have binoculars.'

I stayed inside with the beards and black silk. Theo would guess it was me who'd made the call. Now I was implicated. I was an accomplice.

I knew that the Holy Mountain had a long history of fugitives among its Orthodox population. Romanians, Bulgarians and Russians had found sanctuary here from their crimes of blood and money. Diaspora Greeks from Australia and America had lost themselves in Athos. In older times, shipwrecks had brought pariahs, pirates, pagans and the ostracised. Europe's Tibet had swallowed men through history. I'd be the next inside a hermit's silent cell.

A voice over the PA system: '*Arsanas Anastasiou!*'

'That's us,' said Bastounis.

It was a tiny bay beneath an immensity of wooded crags whose leaves were yellowing. The handkerchief of pebble beach held a pale finger against the hills: a fortified stone tower with crenellations and iron-barred arrow slots. In the middle ages, it would have sounded the alarm when raiders came from the sea. The jetty was a mere concrete stub as at Pisaetos.

Water churned. The gangplank lowered. Bastounis felt his way across the void to solid ground and I followed with my hand on his shoulder. Nobody else was disembarking here. No one was waiting at the jetty. I couldn't see a monastery anywhere.

The ferry reversed and I watched it pass around the headland, its engine dwindling to silence. The wake plashed minimally along the shore. There was a powerful smell of earth and undergrowth. We'd just stepped a millennium into the past.

'What now?' I said.

'Now I'm safe. I'm ready. This is journey's end.'

He put out his hand.

I didn't take it. 'So... what? That's it? I just get the ferry back tomorrow? You don't need my help anymore?'

'I have friends here. They'll take care of me. You needn't worry about that soft blue vein any more.'

'It's not about that...'

'What *is* it about? What did you expect? Didn't I tell you life isn't a movie script? There's no big denouement, no climax. Or maybe you want to be there when it happens – to hear the death rattle and watch the spirit take flight. You want a proper ending – is that it?'

'I thought... I thought I'd spend some time here. With you.'

'Do what you like. You have four days on your permit. You could visit some of the other monasteries – make a visit of it. Whenever you decide to go back, just get to Thessaloniki. Pick up the car. Carry on. The monks will look after me now. They'll deal with the formalities.'

'You make it sound so easy.'

'Isn't it?'

'I'm going to stay. With you – not at the other monasteries.'

'I can't stop you.'

'You really don't care? I mean ... what have I been all this time? Just a driver? A butler? A literal shoulder to lean on?'

'What do you want me to tell you? That we're *friends*? Konstantinopoulos is a friend. Michaelis in Monemvasia is a friend. I've known you for barely two weeks. You're a child, for god's sake.'

'Right, right... and you're not good with children, are you? Not your own. Not Theodora. You know what? Maybe I *am* your friend. A friend to you is anyone who tolerates your endless shit and still stays loyal.'

'You're really so desperate for my gratitude? What did we say about affirmation?'

'*Are* you grateful? Is it so painful to admit? To need somebody else?'

'Here comes the pop psychology...'

'Fuck you, Irakles!'

My shout was insignificant in that natural amphitheatre. We were two Lilliputian men loitering at world's edge. If a temper snaps in the middle of a forest, does it make a sound?

'Bravo,' he said. 'Finally, you call me by my name. I hoped you'd show some balls before the end.'

'What? Is this another...?'

'It's what it is. Stay here at the monastery if that's what you want. Stay to the end. It makes sense. It has symmetry. I'm glad.'

'Listen... I'm sorry what I said about—'

'Don't apologise. You were angry. Good. Get angry when you should. Don't be anybody's whipping boy.'

A diesel engine sounded through the trees. A crunch of tyres on unsurfaced road. An old Toyota pick-up emerged and stopped where the beach touched the woods. A young monk got out and waved to me.

'That'll be our ride,' said Bastounis.

He sat in the front and I struggled to find comfort in the corrugated steel of the flatbed as the Toyota dipped and veered on a route riven by rain and landslip. As we rose higher into the trees, the sylvan smell intensified: a thick perfume of soil and composted leaves, wet bark, moss and lichened stone. The forest was primeval: untouched as long Europe had been populated.

The monastery of Anastasiou rose sheer out of the foliage: a fortress built on rocky outcrops, its towers, turrets and buttresses like extrusions of the landscape. Trees crowded close about it, clamouring to reclaim their rightful space. It wasn't one of the rich monasteries with prestigious endowments and real estate portfolios. It wasn't on the visitor map because it wasn't as pretty or famous or as well situated as the swallows-nest redoubts of Simonos Petras or Esfigmenou. It also lacked the crucial relics – no splinters of the True Cross or elbows of St Anthony. Its only draw was quiet piety.

We stopped at a colossal gate tower whose iron doors were studded with lion's-head bosses. An older monk was waiting there, his white beard wispy and his sulphur-steel hair drawn up behind his hat. He was smiling.

Bastounis emerged awkwardly with his staff and stood. He seemed to be expecting a welcome and waiting for a voice. Perhaps they were the same age. But while the writer was bowed and blind and trembling, the monk stood straight and vigorous. His eyes were white and sharp. He spoke Greek in tones that suggested mild rebuke and sorrow. Something like, 'Look at the state of you. What's become of Irakles the hero?'

'*Eh, etsi einai i zoi,*' said Bastounis. Such is life.

They embraced, Bastounis gasping as his broken rib was hugged. He turned to where he guessed I was standing.

'My brother. His monastic name is Philotheos, but he's always been Sofoklis to me. He speaks English.'

'Oh, hi. Nice to meet you.'

'You're surprised,' said Sofoklis. 'He never wrote about his brother. A shameful secret to have a monk in the family. Not very rock and roll. Not very Venezuelan beauty queen.'

'Stop it,' said Bastounis. '*You're* the black sheep of the family.'

A benign smile from Sofoklis. He addressed me: 'Thank-you for bringing him to me. You don't know it, but you've saved him. This was his final destination from the start. He just needed a shepherd to guide his wanderings. Will you stay?'

'I'd like to. I mean, the permit is for only four—'

'Don't worry about that. It's my decision who stays and for how long. Tell me – do you have faith?'

'Faith? I...'

'He's an atheist,' said Bastounis. 'Don't waste your time.'

'So were you, Irakles. But here you stand on holy ground. Don't speak of time until it's ending. He's young. He has more of it than you.'

My face was burning. I silently cursed Bastounis.

'Let me show you the monastery,' said Sofoklis. 'You've missed lunch, but a little hunger is good for the soul, eh Irakles? It focuses the thoughts on God.'

The place was colossal, but mostly closed to me. Much of it was monastic cells, but there were also workshops and kitchens, storerooms and studies. A small library held precious Byzantine manuscripts. My freedom extended only to the open areas: the cobbled central courtyard with its crouching terracotta-coloured church, the refectory and the vaulted corridors down which a fleeting chant might echo. Perhaps half of the monastery was vacant, as evidenced by the many empty cells I found – detritus scattered, birds disturbed, black mould creeping down the whitewash. Leaves and limbs had breached some windows in slow reclamation of the land.

My own cell was a place for contemplation: a single wood-framed bed with folded woollen blanket, a table and a chair. A carved crucifix hung above the bed and a painted icon watched above the door. There was a broom for me to sweep the floor. The window's aspect was of Athos's wooded gills, now softening in a haze. How many men had lived a life of silence in this room? Wrestling with profundity. Bowed by their mortality. Waking open-eyed in blackness as their doubts assailed.

The silence of the land was palpable – a weight, a texture. No cars. No voices. No air-conditioned hum or urban moan. One's hearing reached out into it in search of something, anything, and returned with nothing. Magnifying solitude. A few times on that first day, I found myself not breathing. The sound was too intrusive. I missed Bastounis' presence. He was further down the corridor with Sofoklis: the unknown alter-Bastounis. One brother Lucifer; the other, Gabriel.

The bell rang in its campanile – our signal to attend the evening meal. I met a sombre Bastounis in the corridor and with Sofoklis we descended to the refectory amid a swishing train of monks.

Two long tables occupied the central space of a vaulted hall whose walls were darkly frescoed with the righteous. In blues and reds beneath *trompe l' œil* arches, saints with gilded haloes held their talismanic keys and sceptres, scrolls and instruments of martyrdom. An intricately carved pulpit hung above the diners. Food was already laid out in metal bowls: salad leaves, *fasolada,* salted olives, cut bread in baskets and water in carafes. We sat in silence and I watched Sofoklis acquainting Bastounis with which dishes lay where.

A monk ascended to the pulpit. The others were so many bats twitching their wings at the promise of twilight's feast. Sofoklis leaned close to me.

'The reader rings his hand bell. From that moment, we have ten minutes to eat. He rings his bell again to stop us. He reads scripture through the meal. This way, we don't become slaves to the pleasures of our senses. We keep our thoughts at all times with God.'

'It's crazy,' muttered Bastounis.

Sofoklis nodded to the pulpit. The hand bell rang.

Hands darted. Water spilled. Spoons rattled. I grabbed bread and tipped olives on to my *fasolada*. Flavours burst: the earthy beans, the olives' piquant saltiness, the cloying bite of olive oil dashed over greens. I dipped my bread and swiped at sauce. Concentration burned in every face. My eyes darted to where the next spoonful might be found. I calculated which monks were eating faster or slower and targeted their bread. All the while, the pulpit-riding brother read from the giant bible of deserts or plagues, commandments or condemnations.

The bell rang.

Cutlery went down. Monks leaned back. Hands were withdrawn. The reading stopped. Calm settled on the tables… almost.

One diner was still clinking. Bastounis. His spoon worked at the beans. His bread swirled in the oil. Amid the silence of the space, all heads turned to watch him eat. He didn't stop. His hand sought the basket with its rough-hewn crusts. An olive stone pinged into a side bowl. He slurped at water.

'Irakles?' said his brother. 'The bell has sounded.'

'And still my appetite persists, brother.'

'Then we'll watch you eat. Your gluttony is a lesson to us all.'

Bastounis ate. Monks watched placidly, curiously, as the sinner gorged. Some smiled to themselves. Sitting right beside him, I watched first with embarrassment, then anger, then pity. Time elongated. There was a point when he seemed ready to stop – a sigh, a heaviness – but too many unseen eyes were on him. His bad arm was shaking. His face shone. He ate slower and slower still, his defiance a weakening tenuity. If Sofoklis had spoken now, he would have stopped. But his brother waited with the patience of a monk – waited for complete humiliation.

I put a hand on Bastounis's forearm. He paused. He sagged. He let his cutlery clatter to the table.

The monks rose at some hidden signal and filed out, flowing shadows. Only we and Sofoklis remained.

'I'll now hear my brother's confession,' he said. 'It may take some time. Feel free to walk or read or talk to any of the brothers. The lion doors close at midnight without fail.'

Bastounis sat like an admonished child, his sunglasses reflecting candle flames and gilded haloes. He said nothing.

I went back to my cell and lay on the bed. There was a vague smell of mould. The walls were prayer sodden. I opened the compilation of collected English poetry I'd bought in Thessalonika. Keats, Donne, Shakespeare, Byron, Shelley and the rest. But I couldn't read. The combination of their words and of the crushing quietude and the knowledge that Bastounis was fading down the corridor, haemorrhaging sin to cleanse his soul – it was a gravity I couldn't bear. I slipped the book into my trouser pocket and decided to walk down to the shore. The sky had cleared and the sun would soon be going down. It was cool and turning cold.

The rutted track was dark between the trees. Other monks had passed this way after supper and were returning now with nods of greeting. Some wore knitted scarves and gloves. Was their existence here an idyll of timeless rituals and calm? Or was it wilful avoidance of life's divagations and experience? Where was happiness to be found – in certain knowledge, or in ceaseless seeking? I could have asked, but they'd defend their path as Bastounis defended his. Once chosen, one's route becomes the truth.

I was alone at the jetty. I sat on its edge, dangling my legs above a glassy sea. It was that time, as at Nafplio on Konstantinopoulos's roof, when colours began to saturate, but this was the north and the edge of winter. The light was paler. I watched as the slender watchtower took on a honeyed hue and again opened the book of poetry. I'd seen a title that might appeal to Bastounis: *Ulysses* by Tennyson. The lines seemed written for him.

"I cannot rest from travel; I will drink
Life to the lees. All times I have enjoyed
Greatly, have suffered greatly, both with those
That loved me, and alone; on shore, and when
Through scudding drifts the rainy Hyades
Vext the dim sea. I am become a name;
For always roaming with a hungry heart
Much have I seen and known—cities of men
And manners, climates, councils, governments,
Myself not least, but honored of them all,—
And drunk delight of battle with my peers,
Far on the ringing plains of windy Troy."

"I am become a name." Bastounis was that. Novelist. Nobel laureate. Adventurer. Lover. Fighter. He'd earned his name. He deserved it. He'd won it from the world through hard experience and effort. It would remain when he departed. Already, it was bigger and more vivid than the man himself. It would live without his breath.

The sea had turned to milk, its trembling hollows violet. The sun sat low over Sithonia's peninsula and cast a beaten copper path across the surface to my seat. Beside me, the tower was a pinnacle of gold. Somewhere on the road between Dimitsana and Tripoli, my shattered phone was glinting. On that rooftop in Nafplio, an old man was likely drinking coffee. Waves were lapping in their trillion repetitions at the Mani's stony shore. Plane-tree shadows were lengthening across Olympus's stones. Mists were descending from Parnassus on to Delphi. The old widow of Andritsaina was standing at her beaded curtain web. Somewhere out there, Calypso was dancing with a *tsipuro*.

My breath was vapour. The walk back to the monastery was a couple of miles. Perhaps Bastounis had finished with his sins.

'Irakles would like to see you,' said Sofoklis as I returned through the lion gates. 'He's tired. You should see him now, then let him sleep.'

'Was it a long confession?'

A smile from the abbot. 'We all are sinners.'

I went first to collect the pile of the books, thinking he might want a little Shakespeare or Homer after his shriving. Despite his earlier words, I tried not to think about the soft blue vein. He might have changed his mind.

His door was open. He was lying clothed on his bed, hands folded across his chest. The cap was off. The sunglasses were on the floor. His head twitched at my entrance.

'It's me,' I said. 'Your brother said—'

'Close the door. Take a seat.'

'How are you feeling?'

'That's a pretty stupid question.'

'Right. How was your confession?'

'I confessed to nothing. I regret nothing. I told him a few things to make him happy. He wants to believe I'm going to heaven and, you know ... he's my brother in the end.'

'You don't believe in heaven?'

'Have you not been listening to anything I've said?'

'I guess not.'

'It's not a place or a time. It's got nothing to do with religion or the divine. It's human, but beyond human. You've felt it at Tiryns, at Olympia, at Delphi and Thermopylae. That's where I'm going.'

'I was reading the bit in the Odyssey, book eleven, where he meets Heracles in Hades…'

'I know it. The soul below, the body above. The demigod bipartite. It's ironic. Did you know that Heracles's final challenge was his descent into hell to capture Cerberus? He conquered death itself in that one, only to stay there for eternity as a phantom. I wonder if you also know that his challenges were imposed as a penance for killing his own wife and child? It's true. He did it in a fit of madness brought on by jealous gods, but he killed them all the same… It was the Pythia at Delphi who directed him to Tiryns and King Eurystheus.'

'I didn't know that…'

'Don't get maudlin on me now. I'm the one who's dying. There's no twist ending here.'

'I know. Sorry. I've got a lot to think about… afterwards.'

'You have. Indeed you have. And you *should* think. You have your whole life ahead of you. Don't piss it away. Use it well. Listen – these few days since Dimitsana have been a gift. They've been a pleasure.'

'Are you thanking me?'

'You should be thanking *me*. You will. Later. Anyway, it's been a ride.'

'Yes. It's funny. Everyone thought you were writing your last big book. I did. Buddy did. Theo did… if that was his real name. There was never a book, was there. You just kept everyone guessing.'

'Is that what you think?'

'I know Milton wrote *Paradise Lost* while blind, but your timing could be better.'

'Ha! I owe you one last challenge, don't I?'

'Number twelve.'

'The last one is most difficult, remember. Like Cerberus. It means venturing beyond.'

'Yes. I'm ready.'

'Maybe you are. Okay – here it is: reject your heroes. Surpass them, or you'll live in shadow all your life. You came to Dimitsana looking for a hero. Irakles Bastounis – the big man! The Nobel hero. The great artist. You've enjoyed the glamour of it all – admit it. You've kneeled at my feet for scraps of wisdom and copied my words into a journal. But have you paused at all to wonder why I've spent these final days with *you* – a stranger? Don't you wonder at me lying here alone? Where are the women I loved? Where are the children I had? Where are the supposed friends? I've poisoned everyone I ever loved because I had to write. I had to gamble. I've been chasing highs all my life, but when I clambered up the highest peak, I found I was alone. Nobody else wanted to be up there. Why would they? There's nothing there – no air. Only ethereal ego and the poisoned ozone of success. I stayed aloft because I was too proud to descend. *That's* why I didn't write since the '80s. I didn't want to fail. What kind of hero is that? What good is wisdom when it deifies the mad? I've failed. Don't you see? Is this how you want to end your life? Is this your idea of a hero – old and blind and twitching? Hated by his family. Chased by creditors. Of greatest value only when deceased. Even Sofoklis... even he is interested only in my soul. Souls are his business. But mine... mine is rotten.'

Athonite silence compressed the room. He lay just as he had, sepulchral on his bed. Unmoving.

'Irakles, you're just… This is just… You've *lived*. You've used your time. People revere your work.'

'Do they? Where are those people now? What do you know about life or death?'

'I… I don't know anything. It's true. Only what I've learned from you.'

'You've learned nothing from me. Forget it all. Forget me. Make your own decisions.'

He turned to face the wall, his back to me.

'Do you want me to go?' I said.

'Did you bring the books?'

'Yes. I can read if you like. I saw a good one by—'

'Start with *Macbeth*. The "tomorrow" soliloquy. Then we'll have some *Ecclesiastes*. Just read until I fall asleep.'

'Really? Isn't that a little…? Okay, fine. Whatever you want.'

I found the passage, but read it absent-mindedly, his words reverberating in my head.

"Tomorrow, and tomorrow, and tomorrow,
Creeps in this petty pace from day to day,
To the last syllable of recorded time;
And all our yesterdays have lighted fools
The way to dusty death. Out, out, brief candle!
Life's but a walking shadow, a poor player,
That struts and frets his hour upon the stage,
And then is heard no more. It is a tale
Told by an idiot, full of sound and fury,
Signifying nothing."

TWENTY-TWO

B ells woke me at 4.00am. A knock at my door followed. I'd been told by Sofoklis that I was obliged to attend the morning service regardless of my state of faith. Miracles happened in the churches of the Holy Mountain, he'd said – I might see the light in its pre-dawn darkness.

I joined a line of straggling monks descending. The cobbles shone with dew. The forest breathed its heavy compost. Massed chanting and candlelight spilled from the church, shimmering about the square. A monk showed me to a standing pew carved in dark wood and I stepped into its recess, resting elbows on its arms. My eyes became accustomed to the gloom.

It was another world – another level beyond the monastery itself. The male voices were a palpable vibration at my temples and my viscera. Drifting incense filaments blurred candle haloes. Gold glinted dully from fresco, chandelier, goblet and icon. Here was animated night: the crow-silk glisten of assembled monks, the creaking pews, the smoky *pantokrator* in the dome above us watching all. It was a ritual repeated across Athos at this hour, readying the world for its apocalypse.

The chanting stopped. Monks sat in their pews and I groped blindly for the hinged seat. Sofoklis was leading the liturgy but I didn't understand a word. It could have been the rites of Mithras, the Eleusinian mysteries or a form of pagan capnomancy. All were equally valid or invalid. Bastounis wasn't present. I pictured the inevitable argument: the knock on the door, the petulant response, the old fraternal tensions stirred.

I'd barely slept. Back in my room, after reading to him, I'd written off his final challenge. He didn't really feel that way. He was just reacting. Perhaps the confession to his brother had triggered something melancholic in him.

But then I'd woken wondering. What if it was true he saw his life as wasted and his adventures folly? What if he'd genuinely derived no satisfaction from his art and his achievements? Did that mean *all* of the challenges were false except the last? Did it mean that the sum of his novels was all a lie? I'd come this far with him only to arrive at another precipice of doubt.

The empewed monks stood again and the chanting resumed. I leaned against prayer-polished wood and thought amid the weaving melody. Iraklis or Sofoklis – who had chosen right? Who had peace? Who had truly lived? Might *I* choose this life of midnight robes and ritual? Might I relinquish pride of self to Orthodoxy?

A monk swished past me through the door and walked straight to Sofoklis. A whispered message. A brief reply. The abbot found my eyes among the shadows and nodded slowly, his eyes wells of darkness. I understood. I suppose I'd known the night before. He'd been ready. He'd known it was the end and shown me in his way.

I hung weightless on the wooden arm rests. I dissolved into the chanting. A tether had been cut, a bond broken. I was drifting free but couldn't move – immobile as the altarpiece's ebony-carved saints. Exposed. Abandoned.

The chanting stopped. The monks sat again. I was numb in my wooden frame. I wanted to see him. I didn't want to see him. I didn't want to leave the church or for the sun to rise. As long as it was dark, as long as they sang, time would stay suspended.

Had it been the tumour's final seismic rupture? Or the morphine in the soft blue vein? When had it happened? Was mine the final voice he'd heard, ineptly reading to him from the King James bible that all was vanity? Did he even know he'd died, or was he like one of those Achaeans of the Trojan plain who'd woken stunned in Hades, his headless body battlefield carrion?

The service took two hours. Two hours as he lay there in his cell. Two hours as I sat and stood according to an unknown ritual. Two hours of hiatus. Two hours of falling into an abyss without bottom. I stayed standing as the brothers finally ebbed.

'Do you want to see him?' said Sofoklis.

'I don't know.'

'You should meet death. There's nothing to fear. Come – see him before we make the arrangements.'

He was lying on his back with his hands folded. Capless and without his sunglasses – stripped of his hero's armour. His eyes were closed. His mouth was slightly open. Had one of the monks composed him like this? He could have been sleeping. I waited for him to wake and scowl and say something like, 'What are you two staring at?' He wasn't dead. He couldn't be. It was like he'd said – the mind can't imagine it. That sudden absolute.

I looked for a needle or an ampoule but there was nothing. Perhaps that, too, had been arranged. The books were stacked on the floor where I'd left them.

'Do you want to say anything for him?' said Sofoklis.

'You mean, like a prayer?'

'Anything you like.'

'I … Could you leave me alone with him for a minute?'

'I'll be outside.'

He pulled the door closed. Still, I waited for Bastounis to move. I quietly opened the book of poetry. The idea of reading aloud to myself in such a silence was absurd and embarrassing. He would have laughed at that. He would have mocked me for it. I began in a whisper but the words came easier as I read.

"Death closes all; but something ere the end,
Some work of noble note, may yet be done,
Not unbecoming men that strove with gods.
The lights begin to twinkle from the rocks;
The long day wanes; the slow moon climbs; the deep
Moans round with many voices. Come, my friends,
'Tis not too late to seek a newer world.
Push off, and sitting well in order smite
The sounding furrows; for my purpose holds
To sail beyond the sunset, and the baths
Of all the western stars, until I die.
It may be that the gulfs will wash us down;
It may be we shall touch the Happy Isles…"

I didn't realise then how prescient my choice of excerpt was. I hadn't realised so many things.

The door opened.

'You're welcome to stay as long as you like,' said Sofoklis. 'His soul is gone. You should attend to your own.'

'Thanks. Thanks. I don't know what I'm going to do. I have no idea. I think … I'll just go to my cell for now.'

I took the books. I sat on my bed. The sky was lightening. Perhaps I'd walk the many tracks of Athos, criss-crossing its hills and visiting the other monasteries. I'd have a base here at Anastasiou. I was invisible here. I could be lost for a while.

I realised I was angry with Bastounis. He'd left me before I was ready. He'd left me with the yawning ambiguity of his final challenge – the only one that didn't match the spirit of his published works.

I reached for my journal. I'd write these thoughts while fresh and make sense of them later. The pages parted naturally towards the end, as if someone had forced the spine. I looked at a blind man's scrawl, diagonal and oversized. It filled one blank page.

"Idiot! YOU were the book!"

Had he felt his way along the corridor to steal it one last time, rooting through my bag and knocking against furniture while I'd been down at the jetty? Had Sofoklis helped? I was the book? *I* was the book?

A knock at the door. Sofoklis.

'He wanted you to have these. He said you'd understand.'

It was the dog-eared sheaf of papers from the bottom of his holdall. The one from Dimitsana: different colours, different sizes, pen and pencil – a motley collage of notes and diagrams.

I lay back on the bed. I started to look through the previously forbidden sheets. It wasn't a coherent whole. There was no narrative order, but I recognised some elements. The more I read, the more I recognised and understood. The words of Tennyson's poem came back to me: "...something ere the end / Some work of noble note, may yet be done."

His papers were notes for a novel – just as I'd thought when I'd first glimpsed them. Perhaps, once, it was one he'd meant to write, but he never had. It was a novel destined to be lived rather than written. It was an idea that would ensnare a living individual as its protagonist. The story would grow around a person as the pearl grows round a speck of sand. I was that speck. I was the cipher, the *tabula rasa* on which the story would be written.

Our whole journey was there in the notes. Tiryns, Nafplio, Monemvasia, Olympia, Delphi... even Lamia and Thermopylae, where I'd driven seemingly at random. He must have known the roads would take us by it. So many of his monologues were pre-prepared in note-form: the ode to observing women on the ferry, the octopus speech at Gerolimenas, the whispering absences of Olympia, his monody at Delphi and the Furies supplication of the hot springs. With all his talk of life not being a movie, he'd written a script for himself and a screenplay for me. I thought I'd just been listening to him, but he'd been my narrator all along.

The notes went further still. I'd later ask a monk to translate the Greek, discovering that Bastounis had also sketched the structure in a kind of spider diagram. The twelve challenges had been part of it from the start – a classic mythological narrative technique. He hadn't planned all of them, it's true, but nine were listed in the notes. He'd delivered them as and when they'd seemed most fitting. The remaining three (I assumed) he'd conjured from whatever circumstance suggested them.

He'd even assembled a list of desirable character types. A *femme fatale* (Calypso?), a love interest (the girl from Nafplio?), a monster (the pimp?), a villain (Theo?), a seer (Konstantinopoulos?), a helper (Dr Phillipou?), a truth-teller (Theodora?) and a rival or a foil. That had to be Buddy. Buddy was the rival. It all made perfect sense. He'd openly admitted favouring and encouraging him just to rile me. He'd let him drive. Characters – we'd all been characters. Bastounis had sought and gathered us opportunistically, never knowing how they'd work out. He couldn't have known

Calypso would leave or that Buddy would steal ... could he? Characters had a habit of doing their own thing.

If the events weren't always predictable, their required effects were sketched. He'd collated a number of necessary engagement tools to make the story work. It was all there in the notes, pencilled inside little bubbles as part of a curious genetic diagram. There was the state of jeopardy (his faux-suicide attempt at Ithaca?), the revelation (my discovery of his illness?), the reversal (his leaving me in Patra?), the contemplative pause (my choosing to pursue him to Delphi?), the ascension (Athos?) and the twist ending he'd said didn't exist. There was also a cryptic note about transition and foundation work. Had that been the moment when he'd tossed my phone from the car and tied my fate to his?

Other things weren't written, but the scale of his manipulation set my mind in free fall. Everything had been a part of it, either by design or by the vortex of momentum. That letter from Nabokov in Dimitsana – had he left it there specifically to pique my interest, knowing of my reverence for the Russian? When he'd mumbled the Homer in his sleep, had it been on purpose? In the Mani, had he *allowed* me to see the page with the list of destinations? In Monemvasia, had he *intended* me to see him talking to the painter as a form of wilful intrigue? The scene had been so perfectly stage-managed. Was it possible he could have driven himself all along if he'd wanted? He'd managed to get to Delphi without me well enough.

Most disturbing of all: he'd seen my journal a few times and he'd seen the list of numbers or addresses in the back... Was it *he* who'd called my mother and told her I was in the Hotel Amerika in Lamia? Just to watch what happened? Just to add a narrative layer? She hadn't explicitly said the police had called – just 'a man.'

The ramifications gave me vertigo. The whole thing became a chasm. Did Theo even exist as an independent person? Did Buddy? Or had they been co-conspirators? Had Bastounis paid Calypso to come knocking at the door? The fight in Olympia… had that been staged? When the bus was "cancelled" in Dimitsana, obliging me to drive Bastounis… Had that been him? Did he even have a brain tumour? Was he even dead? Would he come through my door arm-in-arm with Sofoklis and laughingly reveal it all in person?

Theodora had perceived it all. She knew him. She was the true seer of the story. What had she said? That we were travelling in a dream of our making. That Bastounis was using me somehow. That I was a proxy or an effigy.

I had to put the notes aside. I had to think. I needed to reconstruct how it might have happened. Somehow, I had to reclaim authority as the teller of the tale. How had I become the book so blindly? How might I tell it as my own narrator?

Nobel laureate Irakles Bastounis has gone to ground in his ancestral village. He owes money to everyone. He's pursued by agents, lawyers and ex-wives. He's not written for two decades and now he's been given six months to live. He's bitter and angry. He fights people who come to meet him. Time slips ever faster. He thinks about a final journey around Greece but doesn't act on it, cursing his own apathy and procrastination. Meanwhile, in one of his trunks lies an outline for a novel never written and barely remembered. Something typically Bastounis – a piece that plays with narrative perceptions and eternal themes.

His time is up. Six months are over. This is borrowed time. Then a callow Englishman walks into the café:

A COLLAR FOR CERBERUS

another vacuous reader come to pay homage. But this one's different – so young and dumb. Irakles Bastounis thinks. He sneaks into the rented room and reads the journal, discovering how pliable, how impressionable, how unassertive this youth is. He could drive the Peugeot. He could be the Sancho Panza on a final Quixotic tour. The never-written novel drifts back into his mind and the idea forms that evening.

'Drive me to Nafplio,' says Bastounis. The Englishman squawks a bit when his phone is broken, but he doesn't get another. He's been hooked by the magic of Tiryns and the Heraclean tasks and the mystery of the excavated medal. Konstantinopoulos helps with that, allowing the kid to touch it as a talisman and dream. At the quay in Nafplio, there's the girl – there's always one. A perfect opportunity to drive the plot. No need to mention the tumour at this stage. See if the Englishman figures it out for himself. If not, the reveal can come later. The story pivots on it.

Thereafter, the living novel unfolds according to the pleasures and opportunities of fate. An immigrant girl is fleeing her pimp – send the kid to get her bag and fix it to a challenge. The kid walks in the room at the end of a morphine high – let him look through the bag a little to pique his curiosity. A hitchhiker is waiting by the road. He looks like a Kerouac-wannabe. Pick him up and see how it affects the dynamic. Needle the kid and give him a challenge. The fight at Olympia? A seizure and the police involved? Unexpected, but it comes at a good time. It falls in the right place. Now the kid has a decision to make. Now the pattern has switched. When in doubt, issue a challenge.

Should he be introduced to Dora? Why not? She'll warn him against everything and that'll increase his curiosity still further. Whenever possible, look in his journal to monitor his reactions and modify accordingly. Stick to the plot, but let him breathe and develop to his own rhythms. That's how characters work. Keep him on track and steer him through the locations.

Of course, there are some big unknowns. The gap between Patras and Delphi is a gamble. Will the kid have balls enough to follow? Are the clues and prompts compelling enough? Will he stay on the right road north and take us towards Lamia? If not, there's Plan B. There's always a Plan B. You've got all of his contact details. The tricky part is keeping the kid onside – not pushing him too hard, but hard enough to keep him interested. He's a good kid in the end. He'll be alright if only he can toughen up and take responsibility. If he can make it as far as Athos, I'll tell him about the book. Maybe I'll tell him.

Was that how it had happened?

I thought a long time about *why*. Why not just write the book in that terminal six months? Then I recalled all he'd said about the parasites and how they'd descend once he was dead. So many people had wanted that last book. He'd wanted to write it, but it would have been for them. He hated for them to win. Instead, he'd written it in me – as my experience. He'd chosen the locations and provided the themes. He'd selected the characters and structured the flow. I was the book that nobody could profit from. Nobody except me. My time with Irakles Bastounis was something he knew I'd never forget – something nobody else could take from me or sell. Book and reader were a single, perfect entity. The novel as experience. The life written. If one day in the far-flung future I chose to write it myself, it would be mine alone. No ex-wife, no publisher or lawyer would have prior claim on it. It was his gift to me.

He'd won.

And still I wondered. Had the challenges been genuine, or just necessary elements of story? Were they really lessons to be learned, or had the final one negated all the others?

So much of what he'd said seemed true. He'd lived his own life by them. They'd directed his books. Like Heracles's final challenge, perhaps the twelfth one was last for good reason. Only by completing all the others could you learn enough, become individual enough, to reject your heroes and surpass them. Only by living to his age could you know if what you'd done was right or wrong. Only by following a path to its end could you know if it had been the right one. No short cuts. No returns. Leaves last only one season before they curl and fall.

I went to the window. The sky was light now. Silent Athos breathed. The beeches, wild oak and chestnut trees were turning copper, russet, gold.

Time to start living.

Printed in Great Britain
by Amazon